Of Gryphons And Other Monsters

Shannon McGee

This book is for anyone whose story is just beginning.
(This book is for everyone.)

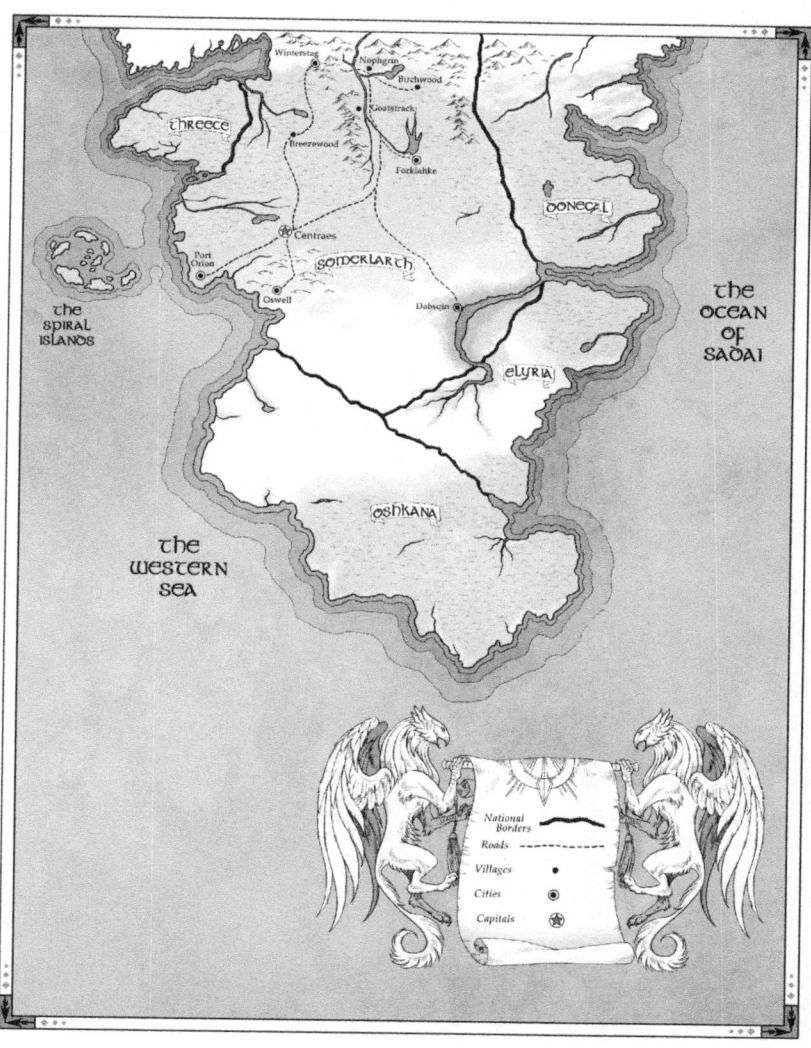

THREECE

Winterstag
Nephgrin
Birchwood
Goatstrack
Breezewood
Forklahke

DONEGEL

Centraes
Port Orion
SOMERLARTH
Oswell
Dabscin
ELYRIA

THE
SPIRAL
ISLANDS

THE
OCEAN
OF
SADAI

OSHKANA

THE
WESTERN
SEA

National Borders
Roads
Villages
Cities
Capitals

Of
Gryphons
And
Other Monsters

1

The wind outside was howling. Though the sun had only just sunk below the horizon, I could already tell it was going to be a cold night. We had been expecting the late summer heat to break for days now, and it seemed it had finally done so in earnest.

In even lines beside me were the product of my evening's work: three and a half pairs of boots. They gleamed dark and wet in the dim firelight. The beeswax and suet concoction didn't smell the best when it was heated, but now I was pleased I'd gotten it done. If it rained tonight my family would not have to worry about soaked feet or rotten boots.

I was scrubbing the last inch of the final boot with the weatherproofing mixture when a particularly ferocious gust struck the side of the house. I glanced up as the panes of glass behind me rattled, and was startled to find how dark the room had become while I focused on my task. Shadows gathered in the corners of the room, and the kitchen off to my left was entirely black.

To my right my mother's knitting needles continued to clack steadily, as she worked. The sound was soothing, and the garment she was working on was a skirt for me—one that was the creamy color of undyed wool. Like me, she'd been so engrossed in her work she hadn't noticed the fire dying.

Setting the finished boot next to its mate with a sigh, I rose to put more wood on the fire. Behind me the needles slowed. Mother shifted in her rocking chair, causing it to creak.

"When did it get so dark?" Her gentle voice held amusement at her own forgetfulness.

I grinned, scanning the stack for a piece of wood that would do. Some of them were still a little damp—the result of being left outside when the morning fog rolled in. "While you were working on my skirt. It looks nice, by the way."

"No, it isn't half bad, is it?"

"Not at all. The boots are all done."

"That's wonderful dear," she said absently. "You know Thomas was at the baker's when I went into town today."

I froze, my hand midway to a log. Her tone seemed casual, but I knew better. My bare toes flexed and dug anxiously into the warm stone surrounding the fireplace. I crouched to thrust the rough piece of wood onto the fire before responding.

"Was he?" I asked absently. If it seemed as though I couldn't have cared less perhaps she would take the hint.

She hummed a yes, that was almost drowned out as the fire flared higher. Fueled by the rush of air that shifting pieces of wood had caused, it began to greedily gutter and flick around the dry log. The wood crackled, and blackened quickly and I added one more piece as I waited for Mother's next reply. There was no way that would be all there was to it.

"He asked after you."

I didn't look at her. "That was kind of him."

"He's a nice boy. Handsome too."

"He is." I agreed.

"His mother invited us out for one last summer picnic, before it gets too chilly for them."

I pushed myself into a standing position. "I think I'm going to go open my hearth."

"You could wear your new skirt!" She called after me as I fled down the hallway, towards my bedroom. "We could all go!"

I waved backward at her, but I could only manage a noncommittal noise of agreement for a reply. It was a blessing she couldn't see the disgruntled expression on my face.

There were three doors at the end of the hallway. Instead of opening mine to the right side, I pushed into the one straight ahead. Instantly my eyes were drawn to a quick movement at the end of the room. My brother Michael stood there, appearing almost guilty with his shoulder high, and his movements crisp. He had just shut his small window, and when he turned to face me there was a startled quality to his features that so closely resembled my own.

Michael was my twin and we shared many characteristics: from our round freckled noses and gray-green eyes to our braided blonde hair. Our biggest difference came in our builds. I was strong enough to do any chore that needed done on the farm, but he had a head on me in height and was a tad bulkier. His frame nearly blocked the window behind him. His eyes were wide as he stared at me.

"Did you have that open long?" I asked, rubbing my arms. "It's freezing in here."

"No. Not too long."

"Then why's it so cold?"

"I know I've asked you to knock before you barge in. So, you must have a good reason for doing it anyway," Michael said mildly. "What's the matter?"

"Mother," I said by way of explanation.

His expression relaxed, and he smoothed a few errant strands of hair that stuck up at odd angles on his head. "Who has she suggested now?"

"*Thomas*," I said, crossing my eyes as I spoke. "She wants us to go on a picnic."

Michael grunted. Crossing his arms over his chest, he leaned against the wall behind him. "Nai thinks you should take up with him too, right?"

Nai was the best friend I had, besides my brother. She had been hinting that Thomas liked me, though she hadn't said it outright yet. All of which Michael knew because I had already told him. Instead of answering him, I settled on a more articulate scowl.

Unimpressed, Michael turned back to the window, locking it and speaking as he did so. "Well, you don't fancy him, right? Like the others they've suggested? Just tell them so."

It was what he would have done. Michael had no problem telling Mother and Father what he thought of their matchmaking. Or even me, when I made my own rare attempts. I hated to disappoint our parents though. Perhaps because Michael was so obstinate, I wanted them to feel as though their efforts weren't going unappreciated. There was nothing wrong with them wanting us to be happily settled, and I wanted to please them. It wasn't their fault Michael and I couldn't find anyone in town who pleased *us*.

Using my foot, I carefully nudging aside a few pieces of clothing with a toe. Somewhere under the mess that was his floor there was a loose board. Michael usually kept some sort of treat in there—a maple candy would cheer me up. He cleared his throat, causing me to pause.

"I don't have anything in there right now."

I crouched to find it anyway. "Are you sure?"

In a few long strides, he had come to stand on top of the proper board before I could lift it. He was so close that his shadow covered me entirely. "I'm sure. And I'd like it if you asked from now on, if you want to get into it."

"Why? You never cared before."

"Well, I do now."

"Don't come in my room without knocking," I groused mockingly. "Don't take from my candy stores without asking." With the lamp squarely behind him he was just a dark silhouette. I flopped back on my bottom, to better see his face. He wasn't laughing.

"I mean it, Taryn."

"Fine," I said, knowing I didn't truly have a leg to stand on. "I suppose it *is* yours. I'd want you to ask if you wanted to go into any of my drawers."

A smile twitched his lips. "Thanks ever so for being so understanding. Listen, I'd love to provide a safe haven for you, but I have sheep watch in the morning. I was hoping to turn in early."

I gazed up at him, my expression exaggeratedly forlorn. "Where is the familial sympathy?"

"In the family room."

I threw my hands in the air. "As you like! I'll go to my *own* room and hide *there,* and I definitely won't pray to the gods that mother has found a new prospect for you, or that she gives you the same treatment I've just gotten."

Michael grabbed me by my upraised hands, and pulled me to my feet. He was grinning widely now. "I'm sure it wasn't so bad, and you needn't bother the gods with it. It would happen even if you wished against it. That's why I do my mending in my own room, when I can."

"I don't mind spending time with her," I said. "I just wish she'd stop suggesting boys who are so..." I blew a raspberry with my tongue.

A sympathetic hand patted my shoulder. "She'll figure that out sooner than later."

"So *you* say," I muttered.

"So I do," he agreed, ushering me out the door.

"Well I—"

I had barely crossed the threshold when the door shut behind me with a firm *click.* I stumbled forward, and rubbed my hip which the doorknob had pushed into. It seemed he had been serious about wanting to go to bed. I'd have thought he'd want to keep the door open long enough for the heat from the rest of the house to warm his room. At the very least, he could have waited until I moved away before shutting it.

Unlike Michael, I didn't exactly want to be alone, but I wasn't about to return to the family room. Mother would be out there for another hour or so. Father would be in from the barn soon too, and then it would be two against one. With a last sulky bang of my fist on the door behind me, I retired to my own room.

The floor was icy, but at least I wouldn't have to start a fire from scratch. My fire was the same one that lit the room where I had worked on the boots. Both sides of the hearth were equipped with heavy iron doors. When one side was unoccupied, that door could be shut to direct the heat of the flames to the other room. I opened it now, before hurriedly hopping into bed.

I really didn't mind Mother's matchmaking. At least, not in the way Michael did. *He* took personal offense to any attempt at ferreting out a match for him. I would have been grateful if Mother could put her finger on what mine was. Sure as the gods knew all, I certainly couldn't figure out what it was. It wasn't tall boys, or short boys. It wasn't blond haired boys or brunets. I'd gone on outings with boys who liked hunting and ones who like cooking. They had all felt like something was missing.

Truth be told, I'd have been happier spending the rest of my life with Nai and not having to worry about boys at all. I'd mentioned that to her before and she had thought it was good for a laugh. It didn't seem so silly to me. What was the point of raising boys and girls so differently and then expecting them to find a partner who could relate to them? It seemed cruel. It would be far easier to find a girl who understood me than a boy. However, I hadn't mentioned it to her again after that. The last thing my parents needed were rumors that I wasn't interested in any of the young men in town at all. It was better to let them hope.

It would have been nice to have discussed these thoughts with Michael. He had heard them from me before, but bouncing ideas off my twin until an issue was resolved was as natural to me as breathing. It was as though we shared a burden, once I told it to him. But it seemed he wasn't in the mood to commiserate with me tonight.

At least Mother wasn't one to set aside time to harp on the matches she had in mind. She preferred finding convenient moments in conversation to mention them. All I had to do was avoid spending too much time with her until she came up with a new one, and hope that one suited me better. That would be simple enough.

I hadn't intended to turn in early, but wood chopping had been amongst the day's activities, so I *was* a little tired. I wiggled deeper into my mattress, trying to get more comfortable. Sleep was what I needed. Things were almost always better after a night's rest.

Outside crickets sang a harmony to the wind, and inside the heat from the fire had had time to seep across the room, and cocoon me pleasantly. Despite my disquiet, it wasn't long before I had slipped off to the court of sleep where Slarrow, the god of dreams and prophets, reigned.

I must have been more exhausted than I had thought. It wasn't until late the next morning that I teetered on the edge of wakefulness. I only knew I wasn't entirely asleep because I had already woken twice.

The first time had been due to noises outside. It had sounded as though a flock of wild geese had landed in the yard. They had quieted quickly though, and I had soon returned to sleep with little trouble.

The second time I had woken had been when Mother attempted to rouse me before she left for town. The good daughter in me could still hear and wished to heed her exasperated cries of "Taryn! Up! I'll not tell you again!" But only dimly, and that had not stopped me from doing my best to dive back into my dream as soon as I heard the door shut behind her.

It had been almost an hour since then, and I had finally drifted back into a sort of twilight state, grasping at the tendrils of the dream which I was bobbing in and out of. Naturally, it was then that a watery beam of sunlight chose to pierce my eyelids. I screwed my eyes shut tighter, trying to block it out, but it seemed no other clouds had lined up to take the errant one's place. The battle for sleep had been lost. The dream had been amazing, but it came back to me only foggily now, in the way most dreams did when I fully woke.

There had been a vast darkness, so rich and deep that I couldn't see my own hand in front of my face. I had sat in it as a small prick of light began to shine in the distance. The form at the center of the light had called out to me, its voice sounding like the eerie moan of a loon, echoing across the empty darkness. I could still feel the warmth from the light on my face. It and the heat rolling off it had grown more intense and I had known without clearly seeing it, in the way I always knew things in dreams, that it was a phoenix in the midst of a molt. A great fire had been spreading around it, eating up the darkness.

Bird wings beat noisily outside, and I scowled as the dream

slipped further away. I knew it was past time to rise and ready myself for the day, but the air outside my bed was cold. My coverlet, on the other hand, was thick, and cozy. I took a deep breath and tried to slip back into my dream once more. Had I actually seen the phoenix amidst the flames? Did phoenixes sound like loons, or had that been a real one, calling to its mate outside my window?

The next sound that came from the yard outside cut sharply through the morning calm, making me jump. It was a yowl, very unlike that of loons, dream phoenixes, or even geese. The strangled noise sounded somewhere between the harsh cry of a crow, and the hiss of a cat.

Hoisting myself upright in my bed, I rubbed eyes still bleary with sleep. When I could see clearly, I lifted a rough brown curtain to peek through my bedroom window. A smile bloomed across my lips.

"It's about time," I murmured.

Outside, a small flock of lesser gryphons had settled themselves on the cold earth of the yard. There had been a few sightings of their ilk in town throughout the past week — presumably scouts for their flocks— but this was the first full flock of lesser gryphons I had seen around the house this season.

Most of these gryphons had their wings tucked against their cat-like bodies as they pecked and rooted through the grass, but not all. I leaned closer to the cold glass, barely containing a loud chortle as one runtish specimen with the brown coloration of a sparrow, flared his wings out and sprung upon a neighbor of the same variety. Chirping furiously, the two tumbled end over end, locked together in battle.

Their antics caused them to knock into a larger member of the group with the black head of a crow. He let out another caw like the one I had heard before. When that did not deter them, he sprang back and swatted, black tail twitching like mad. One sparrow-gryphon fled back the way it had come without further hesitation, while the other fluffed its feathers and fur, and hissed in return.

It dawned on me that it had been the noises of their arrival that had woken me the first time. If only mother had told me! Had I known it was *gryphons* I would not have tried to get back to sleep. I loved when they migrated south off the mountains, as it marked the true beginning of autumn in my home country of Somerlarth.

The offended crow-gryphon had stalked stiffly away from the rest of his flockmates. He preened busily, as if pretending to ignore them, a leg stuck straight in the air as he ran a wicked sharp beak through the soft white fur of his underbelly.

Bored since his playmate had been scared off, the other sparrow-gryphon that had offended him took a few strides before leaping into the air and out of sight. Butterflies fluttered in my stomach as I watched it go. Even after years of seeing them they still could make my breath catch as they flew overhead.

Lesser gryphons were magic, in a place that had so little. As far north as I lived, I could only ever hope to see a creature like a phoenix in my dreams or in sketches. They hated the cold. As to the other kinds of magic—the type some people possessed— that wasn't any more common. Most anyone with any sort of magical gift to speak of went south, to the capital. That was where the school for mage-craft was. Few made the choice to return to the harsh life of the far north once their training was complete.

Of course, in a sense, I could hardly blame them. Even if they were the sort of person who enjoyed frosty winters, to the people of the Carpathe Mountains, myself included, the lesser gryphon migration was a reminder that their cousins were not far behind. No one enjoyed *them*. My smile shrank a fraction.

Absentmindedly, I drummed my fingers against the cold glass of my window. Every one of the gryphons outside froze, hyper alert. Seven sets of dark eyes scanned the yard for the source of the noise. Flighty creatures that they were, their alarm did not last long. After a short pause, they dismissed the threat and returned to their foraging.

It was hard to remember that these clownish pests in front of me were harbingers for the monsters in the mountains. Still, they *were* related, and the warning they provided was a blessing. Before long, standard gryphons would also be moving down off the high cliffs, and into the heavily forested lands that bordered civilization. If there was one thing we didn't want to catch us by surprise, it was those beasts.

With a last wistful look, I turned away from the spectacle outside. By this time Michael would have already been out with our family's sheep for hours. He had taken the dawn watch, but I was to relieve him at noon. If I didn't hurry now, I'd be late.

I scrubbed my face and arms with the water in the basin by my dresser, wincing at the crisp air on my skin, and dressed hurriedly. The bite of the cold water reminded me that soon I wouldn't be able to leave a pitcher overnight.

It was strange to me that Michael had opened his window at

all last night. Even with the small hearth in my room, I'd soon have to get up earlier to heat the water if I wanted to wash without pain. Michael's room, which relied on the heat which leached through from my hearth and the one in our parent's bedchamber, tended to be even colder.

I dressed, and with expert efficiency, then braided my hair tightly back on both sides of my scalp. The top was twisted back as well, and I finished it off by connecting all three sections into one heavy braid that stopped a quarter of the way down my back. There was no mirror in my room; the only one in the house resided in my parent's bedroom, but I didn't need to look. There was only the sheep to impress on watch days.

I took a moment to shake my blankets into some semblance of order, then all there was left to grab was my work belt from where it hung on the inside of my bedroom door. It was beautiful piece, with impressions of ivy branded into the leather. There were loops for attaching equipment, and several pockets in which I could keep anything I'd need throughout a normal watch day. Today it already held everything I'd need, besides food. I slipped it on across my chest as I made my way down the hall to the kitchen.

Though Mother was already in town doing mending, she had left a large pot simmering over the low fire of the hearth. The rich stew within made my mouth water as I removed the lid. Dinner from last night, became the morning's breakfast.

Once I had eaten, I shod my feet, donned my cloak and bag, and left the house, through the door at the back of the kitchen. My clothes were a nod to the crispness of the autumn weather that met me as soon as I stepped out the door. My feet were jammed into thick tights, with wooly socks layered over them. A moss green skirt was ideal for masking the stains of sitting on the grass and dirt all day, and a knitted sweater with a high neck that had once been black but now was more of a charcoal gray would keep me toasty, so long as I stayed in the sun. Within the house the clothing had been almost oppressively warm, but now that I was outside I was grateful for them.

At my appearance, the flock of lesser gryphons, who had migrated to this side of the house in their foraging, scattered. In a cacophony of shrieks, they ran for a short distance before leaping heavily into the air, lighting in the tall oaks and pines that grew close to the house. Their arrival displaced the sparrows who had chosen to perch there. Those birds fled to the rooftop of the house and from there they scolded me sharply.

"*I* didn't chase you out of your tree!" I called back at them, but it didn't seem to matter. They continued to admonish me, their tiny dark eyes as serious as the town's priest's. I shrugged. "Suit yourself."

While the gryphons themselves weren't clearly visible, I saw branches move as they climbed about the limbs. I gave those trees a wider berth. It was a fine thing to watch them through glass, and for the most part, they were too skittish to bother a human. Even so, an occasional scuffle between two of them could catch a bystander, and that was not the way I wanted to start my morning. For their part, they jeered raucously at me, but refrained from coming any closer.

The barn was a short walk from the house, the dark stained wood barely showing through the trees that separated it and the paddock from the house. Great double doors stood at the front for when the sheep had to come inside. A smaller one served for normal entrances. Inside a flock of geese milled about, honking and beeping at me.

Getting to the pony stalls felt like wading through a river of feathers. One goose nosed my hip with his flat bill, as though he expected me to share my packed midday meal. I shooed him. Mother would have fed them all before she left for town.

When my pony Hale saw me making my way towards her she shifted excitedly and gave a little shake. Her shaggy slate gray coat gleamed in the morning light, and her rich brown eyes were impatient. She was clearly sore at being stuck with the geese. I couldn't help the smile that ghosted over my lips.

"It's a work day," I warned her. "We're not going anywhere fun. We're only going out to the field."

Hale whickered and nuzzled my hand as I slipped on her harness, then her blanket and saddle. She was a veteran at traversing rugged mountain country, and knew the daily routine as well as I did, but I couldn't help but speak as though she could understand me. Sometimes I thought doing so was what gentled her towards me. Anyone else had to use extreme patience when readying her for a ride. She would swing her head to and fro and make the whole process an ordeal, but not for me.

I mounted, and with a companionable slap on her shoulder, I set us off towards the field. The ride took close to an hour. The way there took us over the brook that separated our land from our neighbors. The boulder-laden stream was shallow at the crossing, but if you followed it down as it snaked along the property lines, it yawned wider and deeper. The icy currents in those parts were no good for swimming, but a person could load a basket of fish over the course of a morning.

A flock of lesser gryphons had spaced themselves along the shores by the bridge. A few were hunting minnows in the shallows. As we approached, three of them began a game of chase, leaping from rock to rock. The ones that had been hunting took exception to this as it scared away their prey, and a small tussle sent several of them rolling through the shallows.

Hale shied to the opposite side of the path when their shrill voices alerted her to their presence, and I had to keep a firm grip on her reins. She had been badly scratched last year when I accidently startled one out of the rafters of the barn and onto her back. It had fled as soon as it righted itself, but the damage had been done. She still had a small scar across her left haunch, and was now of the firm opinion that the little critters could not be trusted.

But, it was too nice a morning for such thoughts. Before long, the scent of pine and cold eased them away. As we got farther from home and town the lesser gryphons dropped away as well. When at last I crested the final hill before our lands began my brother came into view, sitting against one of the few trees that grew on the field.

Lying at his side, on full alert was one of our family dogs. Brooks was a shaggy beast—a Carpathian shepherd. Broad shouldered with a short muzzle, he was dark gray across his back which blended out to white on his legs, chest, nose, and around his eyes. His gentle brown eyes were already turned in my direction, soft floppy ears pricked forward in attentiveness. When he saw it was just me he settled back, and his tail gave a small wag in recognition. Brooks didn't miss much. He was five years old, and well-versed in his role as sheep guard. His parents before him had been the same before they got to be too old to make the daily trip to the field.

There were thirty sheep in his and my brother's care, and they were mincing their way around the rocks that jutted from the grass, picking at tufts of green and brown grass. Their "*bahs*" sounded like crying as they talked to one another.

Michael was apparently oblivious to their din. His nose was stuck into a thick tome that I hadn't seen him read before, but then, he was always scrounging up something new from the gods only knew where. His brow was furrowed, and from a distance I could see his lips moving as he read. Unfortunately, being the best reader in a small mountain town could only mean so much. I knew many of the larger books he found gave him trouble.

He looked up at the sound of Hale's hooves. "Taryn!" He pitched his voice to carry across the hills so that he might as well have been standing next to me. "Have you got anything to eat?"

I shook my head in amusement, riding out to meet him as he gathered his belongings into a satchel and used his crook to stand. When I was within a few feet of him I arched my eyebrows in mock disbelief. "Don't tell me you already ate all you packed for the day?"

He spread his arms wide. "It's getting cold, I need an extra bit of padding between myself and the winds."

"If you need a bit, then I need more than a bit," I countered, swinging off Hale in the same breath. "I've no food to spare for someone who is so reckless with his *own* rations."

"Miser." He crossed his eyes at me as he gave me a side-hug.

I hugged him back and let go when Brooks came over to nose my free hand with his cold muzzle. I knelt to stroke him from his crown to his tail, as Michael turned to scan the field a final time. From a pouch on my belt I produced a bit of jerky for the dog to gnaw at. He could hunt small game if he got hungry enough, but I couldn't help but spoil him.

Placing his fingers to his lips Michael whistled sharply twice, with a longer note at the end. Hale shuffled her feet, and Michael reached out to blindly ruffle her fetlock. "Not you Hale."

From behind a hill out to our left came the sound of the bells Michael had sewn to his own pony's saddle. Soon Cherub came within view, heavy in her own hooves, but clearly competent in her trek over the rocky terrain. She was Hale's half sibling, with a honey brown coat in the place of gray, and a sweet disposition rather than a waspish one. Otherwise though, she was identical to my own mount. The sheep moved slightly to let her pass, in the noisy manner that was their way, and Michael smiled softly.

"So," I gestured to the field, "any problems today?"

"The sheep were calm, and I didn't see any markings on my round this morning. Glenn stopped by though, and he says he *thought* he saw something that *might* have been a gryphon." Michael met my incredulous look with eyes that glittered with his own restrained mirth.

A breed apart from the lesser gryphons, standard gryphons were magic I could live without. They were more cunning than any wild cat, just as large, if not bigger, and by all accounts far deadlier. Their heads were shaped like the local birds of prey, like eagles or hawks, and in the areas surrounding the town of Nophgrin their bodies were almost always that of mountain lions. Standard gryphons were serious business, but luckily Glenn was not.

"Oh yes, because a gryphon would really come and take one of his skinny cows." I snorted.

"Glenn is a lonely man who likes to have something of distinction about him." Michael shrugged.

"Glenn tells tales because he is bored to tears since his wife left him for being more of a braggart than the butcher," I snapped.

Glenn also liked to come and bother me when I was on watch in the morning. He always hovered too close, and talked for too long about nothing. I wasn't a fan of when any of the men in town paid attention to me for too long, and least of all him. I was glad he had caught Michael this time.

"That's the truth. Still, it is the season, I saw some lesser gryphons on the way in. Worse than Glenn being right about there being a gryphon would be Glenn being right, and *us* not believing him—"

"And losing livestock over it. Yes, I know, but you didn't see anything?" I hugged myself as a strong gust of wind blew around us.

Michael looked across the field, a silence stretching out lazily before his reply. "No, I didn't see anything."

If left unchecked, a standard gryphon could beggar a shepherd or farmer. They were hard to kill, and known for stealing into pastures and making off with the prized ewe or cow if a shepherd wasn't attentive. Unlike their lesser cousins, they did not fear people, but merely had a healthy respect for us.

"The sheep seemed all right?" I persisted. I pulled my blanket off Hale's saddle and wrapped it around my shoulders at the next gust. Cherub had reached us, and she paused to let me pat her, then nuzzled Hale in greeting, moving around Brooks with the ease of a pony accustomed to a dog being underfoot.

"The sheep seemed fine." He turned back to me. "Am I released from my duty?"

I made an exaggerated bow. "You are free to roam the land beyond these fields sire, as far as your pony will take you."

"So, to home or to town," he joked. Cherub only knew the two routes.

There had been an edge to his voice, but I chose to ignore it. "If you choose the latter you can help Mother with the washing."

"Home," he said firmly. He gave Brooks a scratch behind the ear and swung onto Cherub's back.

"Ride safely. I'll see you this evening." I patted his boot, and his pony jolted into motion.

When he had started his ride back towards home I pulled my longest tether from my pack, and tied one end around Hale's harness, and the other around a small gnarled bush. The shrub was bare but surrounded by enough grass to keep her happy.

The field *was* almost entirely fenced, and generally I let her roam as Cherub did, but with how she had behaved this morning with the lesser gryphons, I decided against it. I didn't like the idea of her getting spooked and bolting.

With her sorted out, I claimed the post by the tree, sinking to the chilly earth with a sigh. The ground in this field was hard, full of rocks and clay and no good for farming, but the sheep liked it fine. Though it was hilly there was also nowhere I couldn't see by climbing to the top of the tree I was leaning against. I had spent my whole life exploring the knobby boulders and twisted trees of this field. Sometimes it felt as though I lived here and not in the warm home I had left this morning.

Brooks trotted back up the hill to lay next to me. His fuzzy body kept my left leg pleasantly warm, and I rested my arm over his back. His ears flicked back at me for a moment, but his almond eyes never left his charges.

2

A strange feeling stirred in my gut after Michael had been gone for a few hours. It was a sharp pain for a moment, and then a vague sense of uneasiness. I knew what it was without having to think about it. It wasn't common, but the two of us sometimes could tell when the other was in trouble. These days Michael was in trouble more often than he wasn't.

A sigh billowed from my lips. I'd be the one to pay for it, like as not. I was always the one who had to smooth things over. There was nothing I could do for it while I was in the field though. With the ease of much practice, I forced myself not to imagine what had happened.

Father was still in the barn when I got home that evening, but Mother was in the kitchen. She was salting a few fish fillets—Father's catches of the day. Her hair, darker than my brother's and my own and streaked with steel-gray strands, was coming untidily out of its up-do. Strands of it framed her face and trailed down her neck.

"Where is my dear brother?" I asked idly, as I removed my outerwear. It was hard to miss the mess across the counters when I came closer to her and the kitchen hearth. "Shouldn't he be here helping you?"

Mother wiped a scale-specked hand on her apron before patting my cheek. I wrinkled my nose, but allowed it. "I'm all right. He does have himself shut up in his room with that new book of his. When I asked if he was hungry he grunted at me. See if you can lure him out?"

I pursed my lips, ready to give him more than a talking to. At his door, I lifted my hand to knock but stopped. Gentle snoring could be heard before I even opened it.

Pushing inside, I found him on his bed, sprawled on his back. His open-mouthed breathing confirmed what I had suspected. Michael had fallen asleep. I rolled my eyes, but at least that meant he hadn't been hiding from Mother when she needed help.

The book he had been reading in the field lay open across his chest, and his fingers still gripped it tightly. It was bound in dark leather. If there was any title pressed into the cover or spine I couldn't see it. Not that it'd be something I'd want to borrow anyway, knowing Michael's tastes.

His bedside lamp still burned beside him. I shook my head. He'd use up all his oil at that rate. On tiptoes I crept across the floor to turn it off. My fingers had just brushed the glass that surrounded the tiny flame when Michael snored again. I turned to smile down at him, and my stomach lurched.

Michael had pushed his sleeves up, either as he read or as he slept. On one forearm, clear even in the low light, were four purple shadows—fingerprints where someone had gripped him roughly.

The next morning, I woke early. I lay in bed listening as Father left for another early fishing trip, and then to the soft stampede of hooves outside as Michael drove the sheep to the field. When Mother came to wake me, I was already dressed.

"This is a surprise!" She beamed at me. Though the bun her hair was pulled back into was neat and tidy she absently made the movements of smoothing it back as she spoke. "Usually I have to drag you from those covers."

I grinned, leaning around the doorframe, to grab my belt and crook. I spoke to the ground as I cinched the belt around my waist. "I was going to go to town this morning. Are you going?"

"No dear." She spoke over her shoulder on her way towards the kitchen. "One of the geese got out yesterday, and I've a mind to find out how he managed it. I was *hoping* to get your help with that." Her tone implied she had *expected* my help.

I followed her as she walked, and I accepted a plate of eggs when she took it off the kitchen counter and handed it to me. "I won't be gone long. I promise."

Her mouth twisted as she thought about that, and for a moment I feared she'd ask me to stay, but then she smiled. "All right. Tell Nai I said hello, won't you?"

It figured mother would guess that it was her whom I needed to speak with. When I had agreed to her request, Mother left me alone to begin her own task. I waited until she was out of sight before I shoveled the eggs into my mouth in a manner she most certainly would not have approved of, still standing and barely chewing. Then I raced to the barn to saddle Hale.

Riding to town was a shorter trip than riding to the field and before long, the brick and stucco wall that surrounded it came into view. It was twice my height and about three feet thick, with two entrances—one on each side of town. It was possible to bypass the town and rejoin the Great Road on the other side, but it meant traversing the woods, which was old growth, and that meant leaving any horses or caravans behind. Typically, that was far too inconvenient for anyone with good intentions.

"Miss Taryn, this is a surprise!" A man's voice greeted me from within the guard's post. The face that poked out the window was beaming from ear to ear. "How are you today?"

Both the north and south entrances were manned by a guard. These men and women were allotted to us by King Lionel and his lady, Queen Amane. They were trained at the capital and sent to the far corners of the kingdom to keep some semblance of order, and to collect taxes. Some guards came and went quickly, and others decided they liked their station enough to settle down there. William, or Willy had been at his post for the past twenty years. He was a good man, who often felt more like an uncle than a guardsman.

"I'm all right," I responded to his question. "And yourself?"

"I can't complain. Where's your mother?

I dismounted, tying Hale to the hitching post. "She's tending to some things at the house. I'm sure she'll be here later this week though. I'm only staying a little bit."

"Well, mark it up, miss." He offered me the log, a small chalkboard that was made to keep track of the comings and goings of people in and out of town.

I did as I was told, exchanging a few more pleasantries with the older guardsman before I went on my way. Hale whickered softly as I left, but I didn't pay her any mind. I trusted Willy to look after her as well as anyone.

Nophgrin was not large, by any stretch of the imagination. There were no extravagant perfumeries or instrument shops, and you could go from one side to the other in under ten minutes if you ran—I knew, because racing back and forth had been a common pastime when I was younger.

For me, its size was part of its charm. If you needed something Nophgrin didn't have you could do what the merchants did. They wrote letters to distant relations in the capital, and waited for one of the guards, or their counterpoints to have occasion to go there. A trader would come through every few months in the summer with great wagons full of parcels for them. For the most part though, the rest of us made do on our own.

The only thing *I* was looking for right now was my best friend. She would know what had happened with Michael, and truth be told she might even know it better than he did. Sometimes I could find her at the washing well, but as early as it was I was willing to bet she was still at home, helping her mother and father with the baking.

I was a few blocks shy of my destination when someone called for me to stop. "Taryn, I thought that was you!" A head with a soft bob had popped out of an upper-story window to my right. The head belonged to Beth, a girl only a few years my junior who had recently attached herself to Nai, and me by extension. "Hold on a moment, would you?" Without waiting for my reply, Beth disappeared, and in a few moments the front door to the house flew open.

"Morning Beth." Carefully, I smoothed the laughter from my voice as Beth tugged at her skirt, which she had shut in the door. "How are you?"

"I'm all right. Are you going to visit Nai?" I covered a smile with one hand. Beth was cute, in a disheveled sort of way. She had rosy cheeks, and large pretty brown eyes, that made her look like a doe. Two thin braids pinned back artfully kept the rest of her bob from getting into her face. Beyond that she did not seem to have much going on. I was pretty sure Nai let her hang around because she enjoyed being idolized—and Beth did idolize my friend.

"I was," I told her. "I wanted to ask her if she saw Michael yesterday."

Beth bit her lip, the picture of guilt. "Um, about that...That is to say, I suppose I should talk to you about that."

I narrowed my eyes. "Did *you* see him?"

She was wringing her hands now, and her words came in a rush, "I did, and I swear I told Corey to stop, but only he wouldn't listen to me—you *know* how he is. You aren't upset with me, are you? I told him *after* that there was no reason to be jealous and that he can't just do stuff like that, and he *did* say he was sorry. Please don't tell Nai!" When she finished her voice had gotten so high and fast that I could barely follow what she was saying.

Irritation flickered in me for a moment. It was too early for her carrying on. Taking a deep breath, I let it out slowly, reining in my patience. "All right, Beth, I'm not mad. I just need you to tell me exactly what happened. Slowly."

Unfortunately, it was in that moment that the other person apparently involved in yesterday's encounter showed up. Corey, a tall young man who could be described as surly at best, ambled around the corner and stopped short when he saw me. He glared.

"I wanted to see if you felt like going for a morning walk around town," he said to Beth, without so much as a hello to me.

That shortened the discussion considerably. Beth had been forthcoming, if a little flighty in the way she first told the story. With Corey looming, she became evasive and less critical of her beau's part in yesterday's events. She was either eager to go for a walk with him, or unwilling to upset Corey by bringing up what had happened.

Corey didn't seem to care either way. He waited for Beth to finish, slumped against the wall of her home. His arms were crossed over his chest, and he glowered, mostly at me. Which just figured. Every time Michael got into a fight people acted as though I had been in the thick of it too—as though I wasn't the one who was always smoothing things over.

Once Beth told me everything she was willing to, I rode straight to the field. My blood was boiling with impotent frustration. If I had been there I would have stopped it before it had begun. Beth ought to have known better. Frankly, they all should have known better—brawling in the streets like a couple of hedge-born lackwits. Mostly I blamed Corey and Beth. She was a flirt, and Corey was always ready for a tumble. However, I couldn't even say as much without them thinking I was taking Michael's part in it all. Which I wasn't. He had been wrong too.

At the field, I reined up beside Michael in record time and dismounted, still seething. Brooks stood as if to greet me, but I signaled for him to sit back down, and he did, though his ears drooped mournfully.

"You're early." Michael greeted me without looking from his book.

"You want to go for a ride around the field?"

He squinted at the page he was reading and flipped between it and another a few times before responding. "Right now?"

"We can talk about it here, just as well as in the saddle," I said trying to keep my tone light and amiable.

"Talk about what?"

I did my best to keep my voice from sliding towards accusatory. "You went into town after you left the field yesterday."

He did glance up then, marking his place in his book with the black ribbon that was connected to the binding. "I needed to get some things for Mother's birthing day gift."

"You ran into Beth."

"Yes."

"And Corey."

His expression soured. "Yes."

"Want to tell me about that?"

Carefully Michael slid the book into his satchel. "Like I said, I was looking for a gift for mother. Beth was there, and I asked her about some ribbons that were for sale. Corey showed up. Corey is a moron," he said succinctly, as though that explained everything.

"Beth says he thought he had something to be jealous of?"

Michael let one shoulder rise and fall. "Like I said."

"She said that you told her in front of Corey that she could find a better purpose in life than marrying the pig farmer's son?"

"Which is true, and I'll tell you, it never fails to please me that you aren't interested in the men in town. They'll live and die here doing nothing more than their fathers before them. It's sad."

"Michael, you can't say stuff like that to people!" I exclaimed, exasperated. I purposefully ignored his attempt at turning the conversation towards *my* feelings about the men in town. "And you know when you do they get mad at me too. It's me they gabble at about it—like they think being twins means we're one gods-cursed person! You should have seen the way Corey was looking at me!"

Michael did appear repentant then. "I'm sorry. I didn't even mean to get into it with him. It just happened. The guy is a brute. No finesse. No self-control." He scratched the back of his head. The movement of his arm reminded me why I had gone into town to begin with.

"So, he punched you?" My tone was gentler this time.

He blinked at me and then looked away. "Yeah. He got a hold of me before I could get out of the way."

"He left your face alone," I pointed out. "Where did he get you?" After a moment's hesitation Michael lifted his tunic to reveal a goose egg-sized bruise on the side of his gut. I gasped in sympathy. "Oh, Michael..."

He let the tunic fall back down. "It's fine. It won't be long before people like him won't be able to come anywhere near me."

We talked for a while after that. Mostly Michael talked —he had much to say about going south and becoming someone's apprentice—while I listened. Michael had been hinting at these thoughts for a few months now, probing for my opinion, but he had become more irritable about it lately.

When he had first asked what I'd thought of *both* of us

leaving I had told Michael in the simplest terms that I couldn't fathom it. I had hoped this was a fancy he would get over, but I was slowly realizing it wasn't going to be that simple.

"Michael," I said, as he paused for a breath, "a great city won't be any kinder to you than Nophgrin. No one in big cities know their neighbors enough to even wish them a happy birthing day. Cities are dirty and cramped." I tallied on my fingers. "Not to mention that the lands surrounding the capital, for example, are clear-cut and ugly. I've seen the sketches. Some of them are from books which *you* own. There aren't any forests to get lost in or secret places you could have all to yourself."

Michael listened in stony silence. When he replied his voice was as earnest as before. "But there are more opportunities for us there. Ones we could never even dream of here in the mountains."

I frowned. He had said 'we' again. "Like what?"

"Libraries full of knowledge, for one. The capital is home to the mage university and it has the greatest library in all of Somerlarth."

"Yes, but you're not a mage," I pointed out.

His eye flashed dangerously. "Trust me, I'd be allowed to look."

"If you say so," I said dubiously, unimpressed by his display of temper.

His expression lightened as he waved aside my dismissal. "Anyway, it wouldn't matter if people were more or less kind in the city. The point is, there are ways in which someone who was clever could rise through the ranks in big cities, and become someone with power to throw around."

I scoffed. "What more "power" could we ever need?"

"I mean power to have whatever we want, when we want it. Power so that if someone irritates us then we can remove them, so that we never have to see them again. Who couldn't use power like that?"

"All I want is for the four of us to be happy, and safe," I said firmly. It was mostly true, and there was no way I was giving him even the slightest indication that I would be understanding if he abandoned us.

Of course, the conversation didn't end there. Perhaps he thought he could make me understand, but no matter how much he talked, nothing he spoke of appealed to me like it did to him. His head was filled with thoughts of the architecture, the foods, and the wells of knowledge just out of his reach here in the mountains. By the time he had run out of steam, his shift in the field had ended, mine had begun, and we were no closer to an agreement.

I was shamefully relieved when he rose to go. I had thought to bring along my harness, which had the canteen attached and Michael still had some jerky which he let me have, so he wouldn't have to bring me anything back from the house. All that was left was to hope Mother wouldn't be upset about my missing out on helping her with the geese. Before he left, Michael promised to make my excuses, and to help her if it turned out she had not been able to solve the mystery on her own.

I glanced at the sky, so blue it almost hurt to look at, with only a few spindly clouds sailing quickly in the wind. The trees at the end of the field were well into the business of gussying up for autumn. Pops of bright red, orange and yellow peeked between the solid rows of green pines. Muscles I hadn't known had been held tight relaxed, and I drew my horse blanket from my shoulder to across my legs. The wool was undyed and a little dirty from use, but it was thick and cozy. I pulled a block of cedar out of my bag and retrieved my knife from my harness. I whittled away at the wood as my thoughts wandered.

Michael wasn't wrong, the capital had some things we didn't, and they were nice. They were *not* worth leaving home for. I had my own issues with small town life, as my brother knew. We had a duty though, to our parents, and to the farm which they had dedicated their lives to. It'd be one thing if he had found love, and was leaving for that. I could understand that. But for stuff?

The facts were that in Nophgrin we were known, and cared for. In the city, his master would only care if he could not perform his work. Here in Nophgrin, he had the status of being the only son of one of the most successful shepherds this side of the mountain. *That* was as much power as he could ever hope for, for all the good it did him. The moment he left the mountains, that power would vanish. In the city, the people purchased their food and clothes without ever seeing the creature it came from. Even if they did care about who produced their purchases, our father had never sold outside the mountains. They wouldn't know or care who he was.

Curls of cedar piled by my right leg as I shaped the wood. Though my mind whirred, my fingers moved the knife slowly, remembering how painful it was when the blade slipped. The sheep were talking amongst themselves, and moving about with the ease of creatures who had nothing to fear. Two of them were burdened with new life, and comically round and cranky. I would help them when the time came, and years from now I would do the same for their babies. So would Michael.

I sighed, and rubbed my forehead. There was no better life in the world for us. He was smart, and sooner or later he would realize that. When one of the girls in town who were eyeing him finally caught his gaze in return he would quit his fighting, quit his talk of leaving, and that would be that.

3

My shift passed without any incident. The sheep meandered, Hale cropped the grass around her, and Brooks diligently stared at them for the next six hours. When it came time to leave the cedar block had taken on the rough shape of a small sparrow gryphon, which I planned to sand, stain and give to my mother for her birthing day next month. Carefully, I wrapped it in a hank of cloth and tucked it and my tools into my bag.

At my "Come-bye!" Brooks leapt into action while I untied Hale and readied her to ride. Brooks's frame was thick, but his legs were long, and with the skill lent to him by five years' experience, he rounded the sheep into a tight cluster with sharp barks and snapping jaws—all for show. His training assured he would never actually harm any of the sheep. By the time he had them ready for me, I was mounted on Hale, and with his help, I drove them across the field, back to the road that led to home.

The sheep yelled their discontent at me and at Brooks, whose tongue lulled out as he grinned, happy to finally be doing real work. True to his breed, Brooks was loyal, and fearless. Some Carpathian shepherds had been known to take on bears and other giant beasts that might attack a flock, making them ideal in gryphon country. Brooks had yet to be called upon to face down a greater gryphon, but at home he took great pleasure in rushing flocks of lesser gryphons. He would sit for hours at the base of a tree if he knew there was one perched up high. Still, I was sure Brooks spent much of his work day in boredom. Sometimes he would get a chance to chase lesser gryphons away, but it was rare for lesser gryphons to come out to the field. There was little cover for them, and even less to hunt.

We were halfway back to the farm when the clatter of hooves preceded only momentarily the sight of Glenn, riding full speed in my direction.

"Hold!" I called to Brooks, and he moved closer to the front of the flock to keep the sheep stationary as I moved over to get out of Glenn's way. To my surprise he pulled up short beside me. His face was pale, and his eyes were dilated. He ran a hand through his thinning blond hair, clearly trying to compose himself.

"I hoped I'd catch you before you turned in for the evening." His nasally voice wheezed as he spoke. "Did your brother speak to you about my visit earlier this week?"

"He told me you thought you saw a gryphon," I said cautiously. Brooks snapped at a sheep attempting to break for the tree line a few feet off the road.

"I was right! I had my boy out getting kindling and I've got markings now—on the northeast side of my property!"

I grimaced. That was the side that bordered our own property. "You haven't had any losses, right?"

"Not as yet, but I expect it'll happen any day now," he all but wailed. "And me, short-handed as I am, I'll be pulling double shifts until the season ends unless I pay for help. Where am I to get the funds for something like that?"

"I appreciate the warning, and I'll let my father know. My brother didn't say he saw any markings when I arrived, but we'll check again in the morning." I clasped arms with him in polite thanks. I winced; his grip was too tight. "When the gryphon sees our animals are well-guarded, it may well move off to the coast."

"I'd have your father go out tonight and check," Glenn insisted. "If you went out in the morning to find a gryphon napping in your tree, it'd be more than a disaster. You, *or* your brother." He added the latter hastily.

Another sheep tried to move forward, and I gave Glenn a hasty wave. "Absolutely. I'll tell him you made the suggestion. I must get the flock home now, and I'm sure you want to get back to your herd. I'll see you in temple."

"Of course, Taryn. You be safe, and I'll see you at temple." His smile looked strained as he turned to bolt off in the direction he had come from, and I pitied his horse.

He would likely come calling again before temple, as unpleasant a thought as that was. Still, I hadn't lied. He had probably given us a warning that would save a sheep in the next month, and for that I was grateful. There were ways to deter a gryphon, and it was best to do them as soon as possible. If a gryphon *was* marking our territory as its own, we would all do best to quickly prove it had made a mistake. I took a moment to peer at the tall pines surrounding us. My stomach did a nasty flip, and I shook myself.

"Brooks, come-by." Brooks, who had been towards the front of the flock, made his way clock-wise back to me. His movement caused the sheep he passed to move into a more orderly shape. When he reached the right side of the flock, I gave Hale a gentle nudge. "Brooks, walk on." At that command, we moved forward.

Gryphons didn't hunt at night. It was one blessing bestowed by their bird-like eyes, but dusk and dawn were fair game for them, and true darkness had yet to fall across the land. The red light of the setting sun filtered through the pines, casting a bloody glow on the white of the sheep, and Hale must have sensed my mood as she set the pace a hair faster than it had been before Glenn stopped us. Periodically I glanced at Brooks, gauging his mood, trusting his superior senses would pick up on a predator. He seemed attentive to his task, but not nervous.

When the barn and paddock came into view a half hour later, I spurred Hale a little faster as the road widened so I could reach the gate first. Using my crook, I hooked the latch and pushed my way through as Brooks drove the sheep in behind me. When I had left back through the gate, I secured the latch.

"That'll do Brooks." Brooks, who was in a stalking position by the sheep, glanced at me and then abandoned them to run to his water dish.

By the time the animals had been put away and seen to, it was solidly dusk, and the brightest light was the one shining out of the kitchen window in the house. It was too dark for gryphons, greater or lesser, but I knew that didn't mean there weren't other predators roaming the woods. I kept a firm grip on my crook and hurried from the barn to the house, shivering without my blanket to protect me from the chill of the evening.

The kitchen door creaked as I opened it, and my mother glanced up from her place by the cauldron on the fire. "Taryn." She smiled warmly, setting down the wooden spoon she had been stirring with to come and embrace me. She was warm and she smelled like lye and baking bread. Her normal bun had loosened over the course of the day. She leaned back from me, hands on my forearms, her kind eyes—the gray-green eyes my brother and I had been passed, searched my face.

"How was watch? No, wait. Is something the matter?" Her brows drew together softly, as she pressed a warm, rough hand against my cheek.

I grinned ruefully. "I'm in the door two seconds!"

"Your mother is good at sniffing out trouble. That's why I married her." My father spoke from our small, round table where he sat next to Michael. Both were set up with a tankard of ale and a bowl of stew, but it didn't look as though they had begun eating yet.

My mother released me to return to the fire. "Well, what sort of mother would I be if I couldn't tell at a glance that something was amiss?" She served me a portion of stew into a wooden bowl. I held onto it even after I had taken my place to the left of Michael, allowing the warmth of the bowl to seep into my weather-roughened fingers.

"Well, I imagine you'd be a fair bit easier to live with," Michael joked, and I grinned at him.

She let that one pass and paused in her questions to finish serving herself dinner. She brought that, and a plate of bread, to the table, with a pat of butter and a knife. The three of us each greedily grabbed for a slice, and lathered our pieces with the butter. Next, she brought the pitcher of ale from the counter, and a mug for me and her to the table. I poured for her as she glanced about, as if to make sure there was nothing she was forgetting. Finally, clearly deciding the table had no room for ought else, she took her own seat to the right of Father and turned her gaze back to me.

"So?"

"Michael told you that Glenn visited the field this week?" I asked.

Father looked up from the spoon which was halfway to his mouth; his eyes met mine with sharp focus. He was a tall, lean man, with dark gray eyes that missed little. Where my mother was soft he was angular, with blond hair that he wore cropped too short for the customary braids worn in our part of the mountains. He *had* let it grow long last winter, but in the summer, he shaved close, and it had yet to grow in.

"He mentioned Glenn running his mouth, yeah," he said.

"Glenn met me, on the way home today. He was going full tilt down the main road. He said he was on his way to the field to warn me—he has markings, towards our western border, he says."

Michael sucked his teeth and I glanced over at him. He was looking covertly at Father, and I would have bet decent coin he was hoping Father wasn't assuming he had overlooked something as crucial as a gryphon marking.

"Great," was all he said, before shoveling another bite of carrot and potato into his mouth. I did the same, chewing on a fatty bit of beef as my father mulled over this piece of news.

"We'll need to do a thorough check of our land in the morning. Taryn that means you're up at dawn with Michael and me."

I checked a groan at the thought of a dawn wake-up two days in a row. It would only irritate him. It was important enough that it *should* irritate him.

"Did Glenn say if he had lost anything?" Mother asked, grabbing a second slice of bread and smearing it with the butter.

I dipped my own bread into my stew, and paused to answer before taking a bite. "I asked, and he said nothing yet, but you know, Glenn is in an absolute panic."

Mother nodded. She finished chewing and swallowing her own spoonful, before she addressed father. "You should ask if he'll let you check the markings—" Michael snorted, and she cast him a sour look. "*Not* because I don't believe him. It's just that Glenn has a habit of—"

"He has the habit of flying off the handle over nothing. Do you remember two years ago Wynny?" I ducked my head to hide my amusement, directed as much at my father's nickname for my mother as it was towards his bash on Glenn.

"*Raynard.*" Mother could do this thing where she pursed her lips and raised her eyebrows so high that they almost touched her hairline.

"You saw the marks, Wynn," he insisted, around a bite of stew. "A lesser gryphon more likely made them, or a stray cat."

Mother's mouth relaxed into a wry smile. "You should hear Gladys at the washing well these days."

"Is she still gossiping?" I asked.

"On the contrary! She's so blissful now that she's with Robert she has nothing to say about anyone. I lost my most reliable source of intelligence when she remarried!"

"If intelligence is what you could call it," Michael muttered.

"Hey, I like Gladys." I kicked him lightly under the table. "She might have been a gossip, but at least she was smart enough to leave Glenn."

"Yeah, after she bore him two sons, and a daughter," Michael countered. "If she was so miserable, she should have left instead of wasting her time and his."

"They're all more than half grown now," I pointed out. "She waited until they were all done with their schooling."

"Exactly." Father said this sternly. He reached into a pocket on his own harness and procured a jar of tobacco, and an ornate long-stemmed pipe. The bowl of the pipe was carved with five-petal flowers, and curling vines, much like my harness. He packed the pipe as he spoke. "You take care of your family. You make a commitment, you honor it as best you can."

Mother rested a hand on his knee. He glanced up from his task in surprise, but when he saw her look he returned the smile. Embarrassed, I tipped ale down my throat, using the mug to block my view of the two of them making eyes at one another. I caught sight of Michael doing the same across the way from me, and when he saw me he crossed his eyes and stopped drinking long enough to stick out his tongue.

When dinner was finished, Father took some of the scraps out to Brooks and the rest of the dogs. Michael and I lugged the dishes out to the pump with a couple of rags and soap as Mother took the task of tidying the house before we tucked in for bed.

Michael and I talked while we washed, trying to distract ourselves from how cold the water pouring from the pump was.

"You know that talk about family having to stick to one another was tripe. Gladys didn't stay," he said to me. Frustration laced his voice.

"Well, no, but she stayed as long as she needed to make sure the family would be ok. Plus, she's still there for her kids, and like Mother said, she's happier now she and Glenn are separated. That's probably better for them."

Michael snorted. "You can justify anything, if you think about it the right way."

"I hate when the gryphons come down," I told him, trying to change the subject as I scrubbed hard at the bread board. "The road is lined so thick with trees everywhere I have to go during the day, one could skulk right up to me and I wouldn't know it."

"Brooks would know. So would Hale," he reminded me, without looking up.

I rolled my eyes. "All right, so they warn me. Then what? Am I supposed to fight a gryphon?"

That made him laugh. "That is something I'd like to see. You whacking at one of those great beasts with your crook—or trying to hit it in the eye with your little slingshot!"

"Hey! You're not much better off. Which is another thing I worry about. You, Father, Mother, and me… We all go about our days on our own, save the animals. If something were to have happened to you on watch this morning while I was in town, I wouldn't have known for hours." My throat felt tight, and I stopped washing at that thought.

"Unless you got a twin sense of it," Michael said, trusting I'd understand what he meant. He nudged me with his knee. "I want to go to bed soon, so don't stop working." I handed off the dish in my hand for him to dry and moved on to wash the next one. "Anyway, there's not a gryphon in the world that could sneak up on Father, nor one that's quicker than his trigger finger."

This was true, Father was an amazing shot with a crossbow. We got to shoot sometimes, but not as often. Though I'd never ask for so expensive a gift, I couldn't help but secretly hope a crossbow would be my birthing gift next year.

"Well what about Mother?" I asked stubbornly.

"Mother…" Now it was his turn to pause in his scrubbing.

I poked him with a sharp finger. "Keep on."

He flashed me a sarcastic smile, and continued. "Mother, I never thought to be worried about in the past. Gladys and her daughter and youngest boy used to walk to town with her."

"But Gladys lives *in* town now."

"Right. I have to think Mother knows enough to stay safe though. She *has* lived here a bit longer than we have. Still, if you want, we can ask her if she wants you or me to walk to town with her in the mornings until the season is over."

Part of me balked at this idea. That would mean getting up at dawn whether I had first watch or not, and when it snowed the trek into town was downright miserable. Like a chastisement, Father's words from dinner played through my head. *You take care of your family.*

I nodded slowly. "I'll do it. She's getting older, and I've never seen her carry so much as a knife. Maybe she's never had to think of it, or maybe she doesn't want to ask it of us, but we should offer."

4

We lugged the dishes back inside the house, carrying the bin between us. Mother was in the main room. It was the one closest to the front door, and where we spent our evenings, doing mending, and passing the time. Father was still out in the barn. He tended to dally out there, spending time with the animals before he turned in for the evening.

Together Michael and I put away the dishes, and then while he went to grab a pair of trousers that he needed to stitch up, I went on to join Mother. She was sitting in her rocking chair, the light of the lamps and the fireplace casting a warm glow on her as she hummed and knitted. I hesitated nervously, hovering at the edge of the sitting area.

"Mother?"

"Yes?" She was over halfway done with my skirt, and the wool draped across her lap, almost reaching the floor. She straightened her yarn as she waited for me to speak.

I spoke in a rush, "I was wondering if you wanted me to walk you into town in the mornings when you have work? I know you used to walk with Gladys, and I thought it might be lonely now. It might be nice to have company."

Her smile deepened. "Taryn, are you worried your old mother is going to get eaten by a gryphon?" At my weak smile, she chuckled. "Well I can assure you I've never felt in danger walking the main road, even in gryphon season—the bigger ones don't tend to go closer to town. Still, I know it worries your father as well." Her gaze fell to her lap where one hand stroked the soft wool. She only contemplated for a moment before looking back at me. "I think that would be nice."

"You're sure?" Michael spoke from behind me, and I jumped. "I don't know if you've encountered Taryn in the morning recently Mother, but she's sort of a monster herself."

I scowled at him. "I am no worse than you are! Just the sheep are your only witnesses."

"I think we'll get along fine. Come sit down you two, you're hurting my neck." We complied, taking our places on the long couch that sat against the back wall of the room. "Taryn, this might be a good thing. We're so far out here, I feel like you don't have much of a chance to spend enough time with the boys your age."

"Such a loss," Michael muttered under his breath, and I jabbed him with my elbow.

"It *can* get a little lonely with only Michael and the other animals to talk to," I said sweetly. "But I spend enough time with them mother."

"When I was your age I had my share of suitors," Mother

said, undeterred. "It's important to know what you want in your partner, and you can't learn that if you don't talk to them."

Michael scowled at the needle he was threading. "It's not as though you'll get much better conversation than what you get from Hale out of anyone in town."

"You know Michael, it wouldn't hurt you to come to town more often either." Mother blithely ignored our picking. From the direction of the kitchen I heard the kitchen door open and shut with a *clunk*. "Beth has asked about you the last two times I've seen her at the washing well."

"I like Beth," Father said as he joined us, stripping his outer coat off and hanging it on one of the hooks by the fire. "She's smart too. I think she could give you a run for your money Michael."

I tucked my lips between my teeth to keep from giggling. A glance at Michael killed that mirth though. He had not taken his eyes from his sewing, but his mouth twisted down at one corner.

"I'll be right back." I stood as I spoke and made my way to my room.

We were at a new moon, and though the stars shone brightly, my room was swathed in shadows. I lit the small lamp that sat on the nightstand by my bed; it sputtered and then shone steadily, casting relief on the small space. I looked around, trying to find something to putter about with.

As I had been gone all day my side of the fireplace was closed, and the room was chilly. Mincing on tiptoes, I went to the doors of my fireplace, and I opened them a shade so the heat could seep into my room. Under the crackle of the wood eating away at logs, I could hear Michael's agitated voice, responding to my mother's cajoling tone.

With a sigh, I resisted the urge to eavesdrop— I knew what they were arguing about. It was the same argument Michael and I had had not even a day ago, and it was the same argument that seemed to crop up once a week.

While it was true that I wasn't trying *very* hard to find a potential match for myself, I also wasn't opposing our parents in their quest to find me a suitable partner. Michael on the other hand... Even if he hadn't voiced his urge to leave town to my parents yet, his mannerisms and his attitude towards people outside of our own family was telling. There had been a time when he had gotten along with the boys his age. He used to get little crushes on the girls in town. However, as his interests had changed, I had watched alongside my parents as he strayed away from those friendships, which he now determined—

"Unstimulating!" Michael's voice rang through the fire, and I winced at the booming response it received from Father.

Determined to try and ignore the three of them, I moved away from the fire. I removed my harness, setting it on the bed as I went to pull the packet that contained my oil and cloth out of the lowest drawer of my dresser. Rather than sitting on the bed, I took a place on the floor to tend to it. The first year I'd had the harness I'd cleaned it on my bed, but of course one evening I had spilled oil across the comforter. I'd found out the hard way that the stuff was incredibly difficult to remove from bedding.

The task of oiling only took about ten minutes, even with extra careful inspection and scrubbing. When it was done, I put the kit away, then replaced the harness on its hook on the backside of the door.

I pursed my lips in thought, my fingers finding their way to root at the base of a braid. What else was there to do? It was still a little early, but there was no reason not to prepare for bed, I supposed. I changed into my nightdress, and then grabbed my comb off the dresser. Carefully I removed my braids and brushed out my hair until it was smooth.

I was combing out the last of my braids when heavy footsteps stormed past my room and then a door slammed in the direction of my brother's room. Only moments later the back door opened and slammed shut as well.

Since there was nothing left to be overheard, I opened the fire door the whole way, and a rush of warmth swamped over my toes. I stood there for a moment, arms wrapped around my middle, eyes closed, letting the heat embrace me. Then I crept back down the hall to the family room. My mother was still there, rocking in her chair and knitting, but her shoulders were slumped, and her eyes looked tired as they focused on her needles. She glanced up as I entered the room and smiled wanly at me.

"I want him to be happy, and I don't feel like he is." She only spoke when I was near enough for her not to have to raise her voice.

I sat on the part of the couch closest to her and matched her quiet tone, sensitive to Michael's closeness, not wanting to rile him more by letting on that we were talking about him. "He thinks he'll be happy in a bigger city," I admitted. "He told me so yesterday."

She shook her head. "Your father and I have been to the capital once when we were young and newly married. We stayed with his sister. For all its excitement, it is a very cold place. Taryn, can't you talk to him? He won't listen to us, but he may well listen to you."

"Michael loves you both," I offered lamely. "He'd go to the ends of the earth for you, and me as well, but I don't think there's anything I can do to change his mind."

"Michael loves us, but to him we're two old folks, set in our ways. He thinks we just don't get it." She sighed. "Well, maybe he's right."

"Then I must be old too," I said stoutly, "because I sure as the gods don't get it."

I did get it though, if I chose to think about it. Michael was smart, and he wasn't smart in the way Father was or the innkeeper was. He was smart enough that when people came to town and they spoke with him their eyes widened. Strangers rarely talked down to him once they had spoken to him. City-folk thought we couldn't tell when they spoke down to us, but we could, and as much as it irritated me, it burned Michael.

Yet, what burned him worse was having to check himself from speaking in that exact same manner to the people he had grown up with. He felt out of place and odd talking to people. I wished I could fix it, but I wasn't good enough with people to bridge that distance between him and the rest. Even the two of us had drifted apart. I could not even attempt to match him in learning, and honestly, I had never cared to, and he knew that.

"Will you please go in and talk to him anyway? I'll speak with your father and try and unruffle his feathers so he's in a state to apologize for yelling, but you know he'll only do that if he thinks Michael is sorry too. I swear the two of them get under each other's skin so badly, it's enough to make me want to pull my hair out." Her frown caused the wrinkles at the corner of her lips to deepen, and she began to put away her knitting.

"I'll go talk to him." I stood before she had finished packing her things away, and paced back down the hall. I knocked gently on the imposing wood that stood between him and myself. "Michael?" I whispered loudly.

"I'm not in the mood, Taryn," came the forbidding reply.

I scowled at his response, "I didn't *ask* if you were in the mood Michael, and you won't throw that moodiness at me."

Michael let out a bark of laughter, and then, "Come in." I opened the door only a fraction and slid inside, "But I don't want to talk about it," he finished.

He sat on his bed, his back against the wall. His knees were drawn to his chest with his arms crossed on top. He looked like a little boy.

"Floor board?" I asked, hopefully.

"There's nothing in it," he mumbled.

"Oh."

Feeling a little disappointed, I sat on the edge of the bed beside him. For a few minutes, I waited for him to say something, but his forehead now rested against his arms. It seemed he had no intention of moving.

"Father only gets so mad because he thinks *you* think what he does has no meaning. This place is his whole life. Well, this place and the three of us." I rested a hand on top of one of his feet. "I know you understand that."

"I don't think this place is a waste." Michael's voice was tight. "I just know it isn't for me."

I scooted backward so we sat side by side, our shoulders touching lightly. I stared at the opposite wall for a moment. "What is so great about a bigger city? You'll be poor and you'll be at the mercy of whoever decides to take you on."

"I won't be poor. I've saved a decent amount, and I'll be able to pick my master. I actually..." he hesitated, "I have someone in mind."

My eyebrows darted upwards. "Who?"

"It's a man who came to town at the beginning of the spring. I'm not certain you'll remember him—Master Noland?"

I shook my head. The name sounded familiar, but I was terrible when it came to remembering the names of nobles. Too many of them sounded alike. Hadn't I heard of a Master Nero? Or perhaps that had been Master Nicholas?

"Did I meet him?" I asked.

"Maybe not. I had gone in to town in the afternoon after my watch because I had heard from Glenn that a man had come from a distant city, looking to learn about gryphons in exchange for coin, or his own knowledge. By the time I got to him, he already had all the information he needed, but I offered to buy him a meal at the inn and got him to talk to me anyway." As Michael spoke, his excitement caused the words to tumble quickly from his lips. "We ended up spending almost three hours talking, and by the end of it he paid for both of us—"

"Michael!" I chastised, appalled.

"No, but it was all right, because as it turned out, he was a *duke* Taryn. The Duke of Oswell— that's to the south-west, towards the capital. He wasn't some academic. He was well and truly wealthy in his own right. He could have had anyone come and collect the information he came for, but he didn't like sending others to do his research for him."

"That must be nice." I murmured. "Still, what does that have to do with you?"

"He said he was in the habit of rooting out bright minds during his travels and taking them under his wing, back at his estate. He said he likes to keep his circle filled with clever men and women who are of use to him." Michael's voice held traces of awe at the remembrance of this great man's approval. "He said if he wasn't mistaken, I fell into that lot. He told me I could come and call on him at midwinter, when his travels concluded. I told him I would send word when I knew my answer."

"You never said…"

He shrugged. "I was trying to figure some stuff out."

I mulled this over, chewing my lower lip. It was a strange feeling to know my twin had kept something from me. We talked every day, about everything. He was the *first* person I'd come to when I began to fear none of the young men in town were going to grow into someone who I would be willing to marry. That had cost me a lot to say, since part of being a good shepherd's daughter was finding a husband, and having children who the farm could be passed on to. I'd still told him. I hadn't waited and brooded about it all to myself.

We had talked about his wish to leave Nophgrin enough. Why had he kept this detail from me? Was there something wrong with this man? The offer he had received *did* seem too good to be true. A nervous voice in the back of my head whispered that it seemed a lot like keeping people as pets. Yet, I knew there were men out in the world with so much money to spare that they could afford to show such benevolence.

"Have you looked into this duke and his lands? Have you asked other travelers if they've heard of him and what they've heard?"

"I'm not an idiot. Duke Noland of Oswell is of very high rank. He's said to be a smart ruler. He's not an exceptionally public man and seems to keep to his inner set. Still, his lands have prospered since the king gifted him the lands—after the previous duke Erraswell fell ill and passed away ten years ago. None of his people or those who have traveled through his land have ill to say about him," Michael recited confidently. I saw his fingers gripped his knees tightly, so that the knuckles were white.

I felt blindsided, and my voice belied that. "Will you go in the spring?" Naturally, midwinter was not an option, which was a bit of a relief. A person would have to *fly* to get through the mountain passes after the snows began. Yet, spring didn't feel like much more time to convince him to change his mind.

He glanced over at me in surprise and then lowered his chin back down onto his arms. "I don't know. I want to, but without them supporting me—without *you* supporting me—it feels impossible."

"I'll support you whatever you decide to do, but I worry." I pulled a hank of my hair forward, running fingers through it.

"What do you have to be worried about?" he asked. "I'm the one who'd be risking it all, and doing that traveling in foreign lands."

"Yeah, you will," I snapped back. "And *if* my twin ever comes home he'll look at me as his backwater fool of a sister, and he won't even know what to say."

He leaned against me a little more firmly. I wanted him to say "that's not true," but instead he said, "You could come with me, Taryn. Getting to him won't be the easiest thing, and you're smart and strong. I could do a lot worse than to have you at my back. I'm sure Master Noland could find something for you to do too. You're wasted talent here, like me."

"I can't." Now my eyes pricked and I shut them, swallowing a lump that was suddenly lodged painfully in my throat. "I can't leave Nophgrin, Michael. This is my home. Especially if you're leaving, Mother and Father are going to need someone to help them look after everything. Elsewise they'll have to hire someone, and Father is more likely to kill new help than wait for them to learn his methods."

Michael laughed wetly. "Yeah, I know."

We listened to the wind howl outside for a moment. We had sat together like this often when we were kids. The two of us used to drag my bed closer to the fire, and eat candy from his secret store beneath the loose floorboard. We would make bets as to how long it would be before Glenn claimed to have seen a gryphon. We'd jokingly guess at how long it would be before Father decked Glenn, but he never did.

"I don't want you to go," I said fiercely.

"I know." This time the words were melancholy, and he brought his forehead back down.

I slung an arm over his shoulder, and he tensed, "But I know you have to at least go and see." His shoulders relaxed marginally. "Promise you'll write and you'll visit, ok? And if something isn't right there, don't feel like you have to stick it out—come home."

He squeezed me tightly. "Taryn, I may not belong here, but you're a part of me. Always."

5

Dawn came too early the next day as Father's gruff voice boomed down the hallway, telling us Michael and I needed to be up and ready. As I slowly obeyed those orders, the memory that Father and Michael hadn't made amends the night before swam up through my groggy mind. I groaned and rubbed my eyes.

After Michael and I finished our talk we had gone together back to the family room, but Mother and Father had not come back inside yet. Though we waited up, their talk must have gone well into the night. I thought we had both fallen asleep on the couch, but when Mother came in and woke me the cushions beside me were empty. Michael must have decided to forgo another chat for the evening and taken to his own bed.

I was not looking forward to being out in the field with the both of them. Michael being mad was one thing, but Michael *and* Father being mad at each other was so much worse. They were like great thunderheads, rumbling and crackling at one another. I sighed. With any luck, they'd be too tired to lay into each other.

Father was waiting for us in the kitchen when we finally staggered to attention. Mother bustled behind him, readying the slightly larger provisions for the long day ahead of us. Both of them were disgustingly awake for the early hour. Mother was humming something lively as she worked, and Father looked crisp, as though he'd had time to iron his cream tunic, embroidered vest, and breeches, though I knew he couldn't possibly have.

"I'm going to ride out ahead of you Michael to take a look at our field and Glenn's markings," he said tersely. "Tess is fast, but try and drive the sheep slowly to give me time to make sure everything is as it ought to be. Taryn, I'm told you're going to go with your mother into town. When you're through there, you can come out to the field and I'll let you know if we have any need of you."

We grumbled our ascent and he nodded curtly. After he hugged his wife, and gave her a kiss on the cheek he accepted the parcel she gave him, and then he was out the door without so much as another word. I yawned hugely, my jaw straining with the action, which caused Michael to echo me a moment later.

"Is there breakfast?" I asked.

"I have porridge cooking, and we have a little bit of honey left and some milk that I got this morning to put into it." Mother set the pot of honey and pitcher of milk onto the table, while I grabbed the bowls. I handed one to Michael and kept one for myself.

"Have you eaten yet?"

Mother shook her head. "Not yet, would you grab me a bowl?"

I handed it down to her; Michael brought us all our mugs. We each served ourselves, and took our normal places at the table. Michael and I both loaded our porridge with the honey and milk, and Mother was only a hair more conservative. I drank a full glass of milk, and poured myself another before I tucked into my food. We ate in silence for a few minutes. I was only adjusting to being awake, but I wondered if the other two just didn't know what to say.

"It's good porridge," I mumbled around a bite.

Michael cleared his throat. "Yeah, it's great. Thanks for breakfast."

Mother took a few bites before responding. She was looking at Michael but he was fixedly concentrating on scraping the last few bites out of his bowl. "I talked to your father last night. He's going to apologize to you himself at some point today. Try not to make it too hard for him." Michael grunted, still not looking up. "Taryn says you want to go to a larger city."

Michael shot me a dirty look, and my heart flipped as I simultaneously cast a wide-eyed one at Mother. "Thanks a lot, Taryn," he spat at me, and shoved his chair back. As he moved to stand Mother stopped him.

"Sit back down Michael." Mother didn't often feel the need to speak firmly, but she did so now, and Michael's bottom fell back into the seat as though the bones had vanished from his legs. I felt very small, and I hunched my shoulders as I sipped more milk and tried to be invisible. "As I was saying," Mother put her spoon down, "Taryn told me you want to see the world outside of Nophgrin, and I spoke with your father last night. We're willing to help you go for a year, to the capital." Michaels jaw popped open at the same time mine did. "We have a little bit saved, so if we need the extra help, we can get it. Obviously, it won't be until the spring, but you know your father's sister married and moved south. She's a possibility, though she has her own children. He has also built working relationships through her, with a few folks who live on the outskirts of the city itself. If all goes as we hope, one of them will let you stay in exchange for some labor. You can work during the day and see the sights of the city in the evening and on the days off they give you."

"How did you convince Father?" I burst out as Michael sat in befuddled silence. I leaned on my elbows on the table, rising slightly out of my chair in my eagerness.

"We don't want either of you to feel as though you're trapped here. That's not good for you or the family—or even the sheep. We work as hard as we do because we want the best lives possible for you. For us, that is this farm, but you should have the opportunity for more, if that's what you want. The roads from here to the capital are busy in the spring, so I won't have to feel too worried about you, and with any luck, one of your father's contacts will be here in the spring and you can ride back with them."

I expected Michael to mention Master Noland at that point, but instead he collapsed against the back of his chair. "Mother, *thank you*. This is more than I could have ever dreamed of."

He had been pale this morning, with dark circles under his eyes that told clearly how little sleep he had gotten. When he grinned toothily, all that blurred away. It was nice to see him smile like that, so I held my tongue about his potential benefactor as well. I'd ask him about it later.

Perhaps Mother realized as I did how hard it must have been to be a black sheep in such a small town. At any rate, the residual sternness vanished from her demeanor in the face of his gratitude. She stood and leaned over to hug him tightly, and he hugged her back.

"There are a couple of months until this is all set up, so don't thank me yet. You know your father is going to drive you extra hard until you go." She began to gather our dishes.

"At that thought, I'd say it's time I get a move on, or else I may be accused of dallying." Now he also stood. I couldn't help but notice he avoided looking at me. "Do you want me to take the dishes out to the pump?"

"No, you go on ahead. Taryn and I have them." She flapped her free hand at him, and after he had hugged me tightly he flew out the back door.

I turned to watch him as he left, and I stayed in that position for a moment, staring thoughtfully at the door. I didn't like that Michael had apparently been hiding Master Noland from me, and now he was doing the same with our parents. If this man was as good as Michael claimed, why not be open about his invitation? The sounds of Mother busying herself, cleaning the table of spilled milk and sticky honey from where spoons had rested, brought me back to the present.

For an instant, it felt strange to watch Mother bustling around the kitchen. She was a part of this home, and this farm; she was as much a staple to the world I knew as the house itself. I had a dizzying moment where I imagined the inevitable day when my own daughter would look at me and think those same thoughts. I'd always thought Michael's future would be much the same, but now it was a great yawning blankness. Would my children even know him? Or would it be much like our aunt, Therese, who sent letters but had never once visited?

"How did you get Father to agree? What if he doesn't come back?" I asked, trying to quell those ominous feelings.

Mother's hand bumped the milk pitcher almost upending it, causing more droplets to slosh out as she swept the rag across the table. She swore crossly. I took the pitcher to the counter and leaned back against the wood while she finished her task.

Finally, she replied. "This is the safest option we have. If we don't do this, he'll find his own way, and there are people out there who will take advantage of a young person with seemingly no connections."

"Michael is smart," I hedged.

"These people are smarter." She stopped cleaning to rub her forehead. Her face was turned from me but her voice sounded tired. "Taking people is what they *do*. It's so safe out here—isolated, some would call it. Especially since his highness took it upon himself to secure the northern borders. You've never known Nophgrin without a guardsman. I've never had to teach you two about this sort of thing. All the visitors who come through must register at the gates; we're so out of the way on the farm that we only see a quarter of those people who do visit town. Michael has *read* about these things, but you're both young, and you think you're invincible."

"This coming from the woman who walks to town alone at dawn during the time of gryphons!" I stuck my tongue out at her and received a weak chuckle in reward.

"Yes, well, on that note—let's get on our way."

We readied ourselves to leave for town. From the closet nearest the front door mother pulled a large pack which was filled with her sewing kit, scrub brushes, rags, and a few other odds and ends. I rarely saw her before she left or when she arrived home, and was surprised by the way the thing bulged hugely on her back. It made her look as though she had grown a disproportionate, and lumpy shell. I offered to carry it, but she rebuffed me.

"You three all work in the fields every day to stay fit, and this is my way." She shifted one strap higher onto her shoulder. "Let's go."

I had mulled over walking Hale behind us, but had ultimately discarded the idea. Hale was so jumpy as of late, and frankly I didn't feel like dealing with her unless I was on her back. As we set off down the road, I did feel a little bit of guilt at this. As her owner, I should have been willing to take the time that was necessary to work her through whatever was causing her agitation.

I looked backward towards the barn for a second, and in that second Mother gained a good lead on me. The quick movement of her short legs caused her plain brown dress to swish and kick up a small bit of dust that swirled in her wake. I hustled to keep up. She was an old hat at the task of carrying her heavy load. Leaning forward slightly, both hands gripping the straps that held the pack she plowed forward. The sun was cresting the tree line, but the cloudless sky bespoke a sunny day to come. The exercise of walking with my own load and my thick clothes made me perspire slightly before long.

When Michael and I had first started our stints in the field, Mother had exulted over having no children to mind. In a matter of weeks, however, she had begun to complain about having to chase around the geese, and some of the chores piled up without her young charges to help. There had been nothing for it. Michael and I *had* to learn how to mind the sheep, and so Mother made do. By the time she had adjusted to working without two extra pairs of hands, Michael and I were trained enough in the field to go on watches individually. With our help added back in, her day suddenly felt full of time, and it wasn't long before she declared she was going to make use of it. She wanted to go with Gladys into town to see what kind of work could be found there.

Up until that point, trips into town had been a much rarer occasion. Our land boasted a small vegetable garden, and near to that was our own well. With those things, as well as the animals, there was no real need to make the walk most days. However, she wanted to see humans that were not her children or her husband, and a place beyond her own yard, and none of us could blame her.

Her parents had still been alive then, and they were the ones who had ended up finding her work in town. Most of the jobs were odd chores for the two wealthiest families who lived in Nophgrin. Merchant ilk, who had chosen our town as an out of the way place to grow their families and fortunes, they weren't nasty by any means, but money made them difficult to approach. There were some in town that scoffed at how little they joined in on town events. Mother didn't mind any of it though; they paid her solid coin for the work she did. That extra coin had gone to necessities over the past year, such as fixing the roof and buying medicines. She also made many friends by doing her own washing as well as her extra work at the washing well in town.

The washing well was simple enough, from an outsider's perspective. All there was to it was a large stone basin that was filled with water from a hot spring that some brilliant person had tapped into long ago. Women in town came to the basin to do their washing, but also to do their mending and gossiping while soaking in the hot steam that billowed off the water. To anyone who didn't know better, it might have seemed like a blended lot, but in reality, many social circles divided the basin. Every one of them as difficult to enter as it was to enter the king's own vault.

Though she had grown up within the town walls, and though they bought our sheep's wool and cheese, and milk, many of the people who lived in town thought Mother had abandoned them to go live off in the woods with my father, who had *not* grown up in town. One-day Mother had come home absolutely heartbroken because she had been shut out of every conversation she had tried to be a part of. Even Gladys had sat on the opposite side of the pool from her, rather than be lumped in with her exile.

Michael and I, young though we had been, did our best to comfort her. She had pretended for our sakes to feel better by the time we all went to bed, but Father knew better. The next day he had gone into town, something he rarely did unless it was on business.

As a child, I had been certain he was going to crack some skulls, as he always threatened. He had done no such thing. Rather, he brought the husbands of those women who had hurt

Mother to The Black Gryphon—the local inn and pub. There, he had bought a round of ale, and made plans with them to go shooting in the lands around our field.

As if by magic, Mother was suddenly welcome amongst her old friends once again. By extension, so were Michael and me. The same women who had scorned her, as well as their families, occasionally came to dinner at our home. Sometimes we got dressed nicely to visit them in town, or to have picnics in the field.

It had been hard for Michael, who resented these new social responsibilities. Though he tried his best, he had never quite gotten the hang of it. I had not adored it all that much either, but it was how I had met Nai. She had taken me under her wing by force, and she had helped in the social aspect a great deal.

As these thoughts rolled around in my head, we walked in the chorus of the wakening forest. Birds called to each other sleepily, and lesser gryphons dove over our heads from tree to tree in their haphazard fashion. A furlong ahead of us a rabbit hopped from the border brush. It froze on the road, eyes locked on us. The trees to its right swayed, and my mother put out a warning arm, staying my movement.

"Don't look!" She warned me, but it was too late.

From the right, a hefty lesser gryphon sprang out of the bushes. The two animals rolled for a moment, but in the end the gryphon carried the rabbit off to the other side of the road. There was a cacophony of screeches as its flock joined it. The shrubbery in which they feasted shook with the flurry of their movements.

We skirted around the blood on the road as we hurried past the scene. "That was awful. They're so cute until you see them hunting something living."

Mother nodded solemnly. "I saw a greater gryphon take a cow once. This was years ago. They hunt in much the same way. No fear of humans seeing them. They leap onto the back and—" she clapped her hands loud enough to echo, which caused a flock of starlings to remove themselves from a nearby pine.

I had jumped about a foot into the air at her clap and glared at her, though I couldn't keep the smile off my face. "Thanks for that. You know, I won't be a very good walking companion if you cause my heart to stop."

"I'm just trying to keep you on your toes my dear girl," she teased.

I held up a hand to stop her before she could move forward again. "Hold on a moment. I think I have a rock in my boot."

She waited as I crouched down to remove and shake out my left boot. When nothing fell out, I dug my hand inside. I kept my eyes peeled, feeling blindly for the stone that had been biting into my big toe. It looked as though the flock enjoying their kill was the only band of gryphons in this area. Any other ground creature we might have seen had fled at the bloodshed. Still, bent over as I was, my neck felt exposed and vulnerable.

"There we go," I said with forced cheerfulness. I tossed the stone behind me, and pulled my boot back on, straightening. "Not far now, right?"

We walked another twenty minutes before town came into view. When it did, we also spotted Willy. He was out from behind his booth, filling the horse watering trough, his belly jiggling as he laughed at something. He waved when he saw us and we waved back.

Willy's face was bright and cheery this morning, his eyes little crescents from his cheeks squishing upwards. I had vague memories of Willy a bit more like what one would expect a guard to be—lean and tough, but that had been when I was a little girl. One would think being gryphon adjacent would make Nophgrin a dangerous place, full of action, but we simply weren't. It didn't help that Willy had married the baker's daughter, and that his mother-in-law showed her affection in the form of pies.

"Good morning ladies, and how are we this fine morning?"

"We're fine William," my mother said. "How are things this side of town?"

"Can't complain. I cannot complain." He bobbed his head. "Miss Taryn, it's good to see you twice in a week. How are you?"

"I'm wonderful Willy, thanks for asking. How's Sarah?"

"Oh, she's a wonder. Cries all the cursed night, but she's perfect." His voice was earnest and I had to laugh.

"You're helping your wife enough right?" I pressed him.

"When she and the mother-in-law *lets* me miss. I tell you it's like they think I'm going to drop her if I hold her." He looked at his big hands in mock incredulity. "I've told them I'm a good catch, but that doesn't seem to put them at ease any. Sign in." He offered us the slate and chalk. Dutifully, we signed our names, the date, and the length of our stay. He skimmed our answers briefly and then beckoned us through the gates. "See you this afternoon ma'am, and you in a little while miss."

When we arrived, the washing pool was already teeming with women, young and old. One set was singing as they worked, their voices harmonizing from much practice, and a few groups were talking, some loud, some quiet.

Gladys was already there amongst a loud couple of women,

although *she* wasn't saying much. She was Mother's age, tall and thin with graying sandy-brown hair that she kept pulled back in one long braid. Wrinkles had begun to spread finely at the corner of her eyes and across her forehead. Mother said she had once been one of the most beautiful girls in town, and it still showed in the confidant way she carried herself now she was grown. She smiled, and nodded along to the story being told as she scrubbed a pair of breeches against her washboard. She gave Mother and me a small wave when she saw us, causing soap bubbles to soar through the air.

"How are you this morning? Taryn too? It's rare to see you under the morning sun." The current piece of gossip died down for a moment as the other women offered their greetings and asked after Father and Michael.

I answered the inquiries about my family first and then turned back to Gladys. "I was walking my mother to town. Did you hear Glenn thought he saw a gryphon?"

"Well, it's fall so I assumed he did." Gladys rolled her eyes and scrubbed a little harder.

"Raynard has gone to check with Michael, but we thought better safe than sorry. I'm not as spry as I used to be." Mother heaved her pack to the rim of the pool with a groan of exertion.

"That is one nice thing about living in town." Gladys lifted her thick braid off her neck with one hand and rubbed the sore muscles beneath with her other. "As much as I loved our walks together, it's nice to only have to walk a few minutes in any direction to get where I need to go. My knees are starting to get bad."

A lesser gryphon with the head and wings of a starling landed on the thatching of the rooftop to our left. My head whipped in the direction of the noise. It stared me down for a moment and then began preening.

"I swear those things get more and more uppity every year," I muttered, sitting down next to Gladys. The warmth of the steam fanned my chapped cheeks pleasantly.

Beth, who had been one of the girls to ask about Michael, shook her head in commiseration, her short bob swinging with the movement. "Just this week I had my windows open and one of the cursed things tried coming inside to see what I was cooking! I got my broom out, and it kept swatting at me until I got a good swing in."

To her right a red haired and freckled girl who was five years my senior laughed. "You might have let it taste what you were cooking. That would have knocked it right over without the fuss!"

"Claire, you want to talk about fuss? You better hope Beth doesn't tell your mother who she saw you with when you were meant to be in temple last Wednesday. *That* would be a fuss." This came from Nai, the last girl in the circle.

Naieed was tall, even sitting down. She had curly hair and a slightly hooked nose and hazel almond eyes. True to form, she had spoken quickly, before the younger girl had managed to form her own retort. Though she was friends with most everyone, she was also sharp as a knife, and few people were safe from her barbs. Beth looked at her as though she thought Nai put the stars in the sky.

Not that I could blame Beth. I had orchestrated no few suppers wherein I spent the courses trying to get her and Michael to interact, maybe fall in love. It was a casual endeavor that had never taken root.

Claire's face paled around her freckles and then flushed hot red. "Nai, who told you?" She pressed the backs of her long fingers against her cheeks, trying to calm her coloration.

As they continued that line of talk, I leaned over to where Mother was setting up. "Are you all right here? I should head back to Father and Michael." Mother was chortling at Nai's reply to Claire's question and merely nodded at me, opening her arms for a hug, which I obliged her with. "I'm off!" I told the rest of the circle.

"If you come again tomorrow, see if you can't stay a little longer so you and I can catch up on a few things," Nai said with a wicked grin in Claire's direction.

"Who told you?" Claire wailed again, throwing her rag to splash in the water at Nai's side and the group broke into more laughter. Beth wiped tears of mirth from her eyes, and Gladys was hugging her sides.

"I'll make sure I do, I miss you Nai. As well as the rest of you ladies," I quickly amended. They gave me a good-natured razzing on my wording. I ruffled my hair ruefully as I moved away from the group.

As much as it was true I missed Nai, there was no way I could stay longer today. Father would be fit to be tied if I did. It was just as well though. I had no interest in who was kissing whom. Especially not when I was pretty sure they were only putting on a show for one another. No one truly cared that much about the boys they were seeing. Butterflies in the stomach, and pining were just some of those things girls exaggerated about. Though I had done my best, I had never gotten the knack of it, and I always felt silly playing along.

6

A few feet beyond the moist air of the well, autumn's chill sank its teeth back into any bare piece of skin I had left exposed. I found myself puffing small bits of my own steam into the air as I hustled back towards the guard's post. There, a group of people had gathered. The sound of discord reached my ears before my feet reached the booth. I slipped around the large press of bodies until I had gotten close to Willy. He was currently engaged in a spirited conversation with a large man whom I recognized as one of my neighbors. A farmer named Daniel.

"So, what are you going to do about it?" Daniel was jabbing a thick finger at Willy.

I didn't listen to the response as I glanced around the group. Perhaps there would be someone not currently engaged in an argument who could tell me what was happening. To my right, I found Glenn surrounded by his own tight group of listeners, his face awash in misery.

"Dead!" He was saying. "Five of my best cows slaughtered, and not even eaten. They were clawed at and left to rot."

I spun back to Willy, now much more eager to hear what he was going to do about it. Willy caught my eyes. His mouth was tight and he gave me a small nod. I pushed my way to his counter, and around the man yelling, who checked himself in my presence.

"Willy, what's happening?"

"Ah, miss," Willy's bushy eyebrows were slanted upwards; his eyes, which had been crinkled with joy not an hour earlier, held none of that light now. "Glenn went this morning to check on his herd. The barn was open, and he found five of them out in the field, dead. The rest was huddled inside the barn, about to die of fright."

Horrorstruck, my hand flew to my neck. "*Five?* But gryphons never kill more than they can eat. That would be a *flock* of standard gryphons!"

"Aye, it would be, *if* any of them had been eaten, but from what Glenn says, they were torn into and left. I've got to get myself and my partner and go out and see the state of things myself, which means passage to and from town will be shut down for the afternoon."

"Well I'm leaving now. I've got to get out there too—that's where Michael and my father are supposed to be." I ran agitated fingers down the length of my braid as I spoke. I gazed unfocused at the long road that led back to the farm, and the field even farther away.

Willy seemed to sense my urgency. "Laura will be here in a few moments miss. I sent the runner after her fifteen minutes ago, and all she needs to do is shut her gate and hop ahorse. You can ride with one of us, and we'll get you where you need to be."

"Seriously?" I asked earnestly. "That would be a godsend!"

He put a staying hand up at my enthusiasm. "It'd make me feel better, rather than have you walk that road alone."

"No one should be walking alone if there's such a damnable flock of gryphons hunting." That was Daniel again.

"Mind your tone Daniel." Willy bellowed loud enough to gain a momentary lull in the noise. "We are going to see what there is to see, and when that has been determined, we will do what needs to be done. Swearing and carrying on ain't helping *anything,* so you'd best all return to what it is you do on an afternoon as fair as this one."

The crowd shifted, grumbled, and then slowly dispersed. A few people clapped Glenn on the shoulder or cast distrustful looks towards the trees. By the time Laura had arrived, the group had reduced to Glenn, his oldest son Martin, Willy, and me.

Laura was a stocky woman with more muscles than anyone I knew, and she kept her dark hair braided tightly away from her face in rows. Younger than Willy by a little under two decades, she had only recently completed her circuit around the kingdom that was mandatory before a guard took up a permanent post. She acknowledged the gathering with a nod and rode her gelding over to Willy, who was finishing the work of shutting down his gate and readying his own mount.

"The runner says we might have a large flock of standard gryphons causing trouble out in the herding quadrant?" She spoke tensely, but her grip on the reins was loose.

I saw Willy swallow a pained look, and I wondered if he got

any say as to who his partners were. "Yes, out in Glenn's land close to Raynard's. This is Raynard's daughter, Taryn." Willy spoke with too much patience, and as he gestured towards me, I gave her a conscious smile. She granted me another jerky nod. "You remember Glenn, and that's his eldest, Martin."

"Begging your pardon, but shouldn't civilians stay out of this matter?"

"They were my cows, and Martin needs to know about this sort of thing!" Glenn burst out.

At the same time, I voiced my own protests, "My brother and father are waiting for me to join them!"

Willy smiled and raised his hands helplessly at her. "You see? It's best not to argue with them."

Laura blinked slowly at the both of us. "Yes, I see." She turned her horse towards the road. At that clear signal that she was ready to go, Willy helped me mount in front of him on Flicker. Glenn and his son mounted their own ponies at the same time.

There was little talk as we rode out to the field. The hooves of the horses barely seemed to touch the ground. Laura's questions on the land we were headed to and about the gryphon attacks of the past were the only sounds that punctuated the whir of the wind as we rode. I was pretty sure she knew all the answers to her questions. Still, I did my best to stave off my irritation. Perhaps she was trying to be thorough.

Father met us at the beginning of Glenn's pastures; I guessed Michael was with the sheep in our own fields when I didn't see him.

"Any sight of the beasts that did this since Glenn came to

fetch us?" Willy asked father, once the pleasantries were out of the way.

Father shook his head. "None. A few lesser gryphons have been flying in close, but I've kept them off the cows."

"And how *are* my cows?" Glenn whined. "The ones that are left *alive* I mean. I'll bet they can't even eat. That's going to hurt their milk!"

"They're spooked," Father acknowledged. "They're eating all right though. They're in the barn."

We took the horses in that direction so Glenn could check on them for himself, and the rest of us could tie up the horses. If they got any nearer to the bloodshed we were about to view they would more likely spook and try to bolt. Father's face was unreadable as he drew beside Willy and me as we were dismounting.

"Taryn, I want you to take Tess over to Michael. I'll come when I'm through here, and your brother and I can ride home together. You can take Cherub home when your shift ends."

I blinked a couple of times, stung despite myself. "You don't want me to stay and help here?"

"There's nothing you can do for this, and it's not something you need to see to understand. Michael can fill you in."

"Your father's right." Willy's feet thudded to the earth behind me as he dismounted. "I'm sure your brother could use the extra eyes for now, anyway."

Father nodded at him over my shoulder and handed me Tess's reins. "Tell your brother things are going fine over here and that one of us will be going to pick up your mother when she's through in town."

I accepted the reins, and mounted once more. Turning away

from them I kneed Tess in an easy trot towards Michael and the sheep. Our land was a scant mile from where the livestock had been slaughtered. We closed the distance in little time.

When we arrived, Michael was in his usual spot. Today however, he was not reading. His eyes were fixed out on the field. Or maybe it was the trees beyond the sheep that held his attention.

Cherub was tied to the bush I had used for Hale the day before. She seemed to sulk as she cropped grass. She was rarely confined in such a way, and as though she knew who she ought to resent for it, she had stretched her rope as far as it would go away from my brother.

Brooks thumped the ground with his tail and woofed softly when he saw me. He rose quickly and ran to meet Tess and me halfway up to the field. He kept pace with us for the remaining distance back, and as he trotted, he kept looking at me, as though he expected me to give him orders.

Tess didn't need to be tethered, as she never wandered more than a few feet at any given time. I left her to her own devices once I had ridden to the tree and dismounted. To be frank, I was more worried about Michael than I was Father's horse, who seemed inclined to join Cherub.

Michael had looked exhausted this morning. Now he was clammy and his skin was a sickly color on top of that. He acknowledged my appraisal with a tight smile. As he went to stand, I put out a hand to stall that and sank next to him and Brooks instead.

"Was it bad?"

"They didn't let you see?"

I shrugged. "Father sent me directly here when I rode in from town with Glenn, Martin, Willy, and Laura."

He shuddered. "Consider yourself lucky. I'm going to be having nightmares for the next month."

"Was it really that bad?"

"You really didn't get to see?" I shook my head in the negative, and Michael sucked at his teeth. "Yeah, it was that bad. I've seen animals that have been attacked before, and this was something else entirely. They were split open at the ribcage." He drew a finger down the center of his chest. "It was nothing like I or Father had ever seen." He paused, fiddling with the hem of his shirt. "It almost made me sick. I had to walk away."

"Then I am extremely grateful to have been spared the sight, I guess."

"You guess?"

I sighed gustily. "It's not as though I want to see a mangled corpse. I just want to know what's happening. I was right there. It would have been nothing to walk another thirty feet over the ridge and see what all the fuss is about. Everyone in town is talking. You were allowed to see it." I added the last part quietly.

"I probably spoiled the privilege for you with my reaction." Michael's nose curled. "If I'd known you were so eager, I could have reminded him you have a stronger stomach than me."

I punched his shoulder lightly. "Again, it's not that I wanted to see it. I just don't like being forbidden to. As though I couldn't handle it."

"Father knows very well what you can handle. You *could* have handled this. Trust me when I tell you this is something you don't *want* to handle. Take the words 'chest cracked open and scooped clean like a shellfish at holiday' and breathe easier knowing all you can perfectly picture is the shellfish."

"Yeah," I muttered, still not convinced.

Michael made a noise of exasperation. "I'm certain if Father had had any real idea of what we were going to come upon, he wouldn't have let me get any closer either. Gods above and below, it *stank* Taryn. Worse than your meat pies!"

I stuck my tongue out, face contorting in disgust. After a moment of thought, I asked, "What kind of beast does that? Gryphons don't attack like that. They take their prey away and eat out all the soft bits. They don't crack ribs open, not like you're describing. They don't leave their kills out in the open, and they don't kill more than two beasts at a time. One, if it's one gryphon, or the flock is small."

Michael shook his head. "All of which are solid points, and things I asked, but we don't know what else to think. There were tracks all over."

I made a noise of understanding. Gryphon tracks were much like those of mountain lions, but unlike true felines, a gryphon could not retract its claws. This meant their tracks came with the enormous talons present in the impression at all times. There was no mistaking them.

I leaned my head back against the roughness of the tree, taking in the thin clouds that had blown across the sky since the morning. I wondered if we would have rain today or tomorrow.

"Whatever it was, it did its killing at night," Michael said after some silence. That sent a shiver of fear down my spine.

"How do you know that?"

"Father says that's how old the kill was. He said based on how cold the cows were and how much the lesser gryphons were already going to work on them, they had to have been there several hours before dawn."

"Do you think we have a mad gryphon?" I didn't want to say it, but it was all I could think.

One of the sheep bleated exceptionally loudly, and was met with responses from its flock. Michael and I jerked our heads up and looked around in unison.

When he didn't answer my question, I went on. "We got lucky this week. I didn't believe Glenn even in the slightest, and even if I had, we wouldn't have locked the sheep up tight over a gryphon attack. They don't hunt at night."

Michael gave me a side hug around the shoulders. "We know now. We'll be more careful now."

"Mother is going to need someone to go with her to and from town every time she goes. I also want to start practicing crossbow in earnest. I'll ask if I can make payments so I can buy my own," I said firmly, glaring when Michael laughed. "This is serious!"

He spoke through a condescending smile. "Don't get me wrong, I'm not happy about this, but I'm also not getting a weapon yet sister. You don't need to have one either. It's one attack. The hunters and the guards will go out, no later than the week's end, probably as early as tomorrow. They'll find a gryphon and put it down. That's what happens."

I pressed my lips together. For a boy who had almost vomited at the sight of what the beast had done not two hours ago, he showed an irritating amount of nonchalance. "If that's how you feel then I won't let you practice with my new crossbow."

He rolled his eyes. "I hardly think I'm going to need that skill where I'm going." A heavy silence followed his declaration, and I pulled at the grass next to me, unwilling to break it. Was this the explanation for Michael's apparent indifference to the slaughter? He wouldn't be here come spring, so perhaps he didn't feel as though it affected him? I felt my cheeks warm in resentment. Before I could spit an angry retort at him he spoke again. "I didn't mean it like that." He scooted back on his bottom so he faced me, cross-legged. "I'll help you buy a crossbow if you're dead set on it. If Mother and Father are helping me get to the city I won't need nearly as much coin. You'll just have to wait until we can both go to town together."

"That reminds me!" I exclaimed, irritation not having faded. "You didn't tell them you already have an offer you want to accept. When are you going to tell them?"

"I'm not," he said matter-of-factly, "And I'd prefer it if you didn't tell them either."

"Why?" I turned to mirror his sitting position.

Michael leaned in, elbows resting on his inner thighs, causing the braids at both of his temples to swing forward. "Taryn, they won't let me go. It's as simple as that. They want me to go all the way to the capital to do basically the same thing I'm doing here. What they have set up will give me only the smallest time to see what I want to see, and that's the way they want it. They don't know Master Noland, and so they're not going to trust him."

"You don't know him either."

He raised his hands in supplication. "I know enough. What he's offering me is of infinitely more value than more farm work."

I crossed my arms over my chest, and glared. At that moment, the sun peeked out from behind a long thin cloud, causing my twin's hair to shine golden. His mulish expression won out over my misgivings. He wouldn't listen to anyone if he felt he was being attacked.

"I want you to be safe, the same as our parents do," I reminded him, and found Mother's words slipping from my lips. "I know you're terribly smart but there are those out there who are smarter than you, and I can imagine someone like that would be delighted to get ahold of someone with as much potential as you."

Michael seemed to think over my warning couched in praise. His eyes slid down and to the left. Finally, he met my gaze with his own unwavering stare. "I'm going to be safe, and I'm going to be smart about this, but I need you to trust me, and not rat me out, because I am going no matter what. You didn't meet Master Noland, but if you had you wouldn't feel this way. He's smart and he's—he's the sort of man I want to grow into, and there isn't anyone like him here for me to learn from. I need this."

I got to my feet, jerkily. Too upset to sit and look at him, I walked around the tree to a lower branch and raised both of my arms to grip it. The bark was rough and cold under my fingers, and I held on tightly. If I was in a less foul mood, I might have pulled myself up to dangle.

"There are good men here too Michael. They may not all care about the ridiculous things you like, but you're not above them all."

"Yeah? And which one are you going to marry if they're so great? Because I haven't seen you spending much time with them either."

"I'll marry whichever one tosses you in the river the most before you leave, you ass!" I yelled, finally losing my temper. How dare he use what I'd confided in him against me!

Michael didn't reply, and I turned to check on him. He had put his back against the tree once more and now stared straight out at the field. Brooks whined, and I peered around the tree trunk at him; his eyes flicking between the two of us and he licked Michael's hand. Michael scratched him roughly up and down his back, without shifting his gaze.

Out across the field the tree line shifted in a gust that had yet to reach us. The crowns of the oak, maple, and pine trees swayed like beautifully dressed dancers, and I wanted desperately to find peace in that sight. Instead, I gritted my teeth, determined to wait Michael out. I wasn't wrong, curse it! I wanted to support him, and I wanted him to be happy, but not if he was determined to make the rest of us out to be uncultured slobs. That wasn't fair, and it wasn't nice.

The sound of footsteps became apparent in our uncomfortable silence, and I turned in the direction of the sound. Father was walking towards us. I couldn't discern his expression from this distance, but he didn't seem in too much of a hurry. Michael must have heard him as well as he gave a lazy wave without turning. Father waved back, and the two of us waited in tense silence for him to reach us.

"What did you all decide upon?" I asked, as soon as he was near enough to answer questions.

His eyes swept over Michael, who hadn't risen, and then came back to me. "We'll hunt tomorrow at dawn. Willy is fairly certain that with an attack of this scale we can get a decent-sized party even on such short notice. We want to beat out the rain that's coming our way. If we don't it'll make tracking the thing more maddening than it's already going to be."

I nodded. Unlike their lesser cousins who tended to travel primarily through flight, standard gryphons normally kept low, and this ought to have meant an easy trail. They were heavy, and there was nothing that left prints quite like a gryphon. However, they were clever beasts, and they had been known on some occasions to fly when they became aware they were being hunted. In such cases hunters were left scrambling to find fur that might have been caught on high branches, and feathers that might have come loose during flight. Rain would wash away those clues, and then we'd have to wait until it ventured close again.

"I can help?" I offered tentatively, sure I already knew the answer.

"I need you to walk into town with your mother again, and then you have your normal watch out here." He seemed to become aware of the churlish tone of his son's silence. "Michael, the same goes for you. You'll have your watch, and then I'd like you to walk your mother home."

I made one more attempt. "You're sure you don't need either of our help?"

"No." As though that settled the matter, Father moved on. "We've an extra crossbow. It needs some fixing, but that'll be both of yours to share as you do your watches from now on. I'll work on it, and then the two of you can shoot it properly this evening."

I blinked in surprise, and then grinned with delight at this piece of news. With Michael going to the city in a few months the crossbow would be mine by default, and I didn't mind if it was old so long as it worked. When Father saw my face brighten his stern expression relaxed into a benevolent smile. There was a silver-lining to Michael's eagerness to be rid of us after all, it seemed.

7

Plumes of smoke rose from Glenn's land as he burned the bodies of the five cows. Though the wind blew the smell away from us I still caught the faintest scent of charred beef and whatever kindling he had used. Glenn would have begun preparation for the pyre as soon as father left him. We burned kills made by gryphons so the ill luck didn't stay or attract more of the same. We did something similar when a life was lost to sickness or unfortunate accidents. If a person was accused of a particularly violent crime and found guilty they would often face the same fate, though that had not happened since I'd been alive. I was glad of that; it sounded brutal.

Father didn't indulge in idle chitchat and spent much of his time walking the perimeter of our field. He found gryphon tracks on the portion of our land closest to Glenn's, but he told me they headed deep into the woods. When he had finished his scouting, he asked if I would mind staying for the rest of Michael's shift.

At my hesitant agreement, he told us he would return with Hale, and set off on Tess at a good speed.

Michael made it clear he had no intention of talking to me. Keeping his shoulder propped between us, he read the same book he had been at all week. For myself, I pulled the gryphon carving back out. The task of etching the details of the wings into the wood was normally soothing. Still, I found I couldn't relax. I had questions about the gryphon attack. I normally would have bounced them off my brother, and instead they pinged about inside my skull. By the time Michael's shift had ended, I had a headache, and Father had returned with Hale in tow on a lead rope. When he was certain I would be fine on my own, they both left.

Although I spent a good portion of my time after they had gone jumping at the everyday noises of the field, the afternoon passed without any further incidents. The younger sheep giddily leapt about, and the older ones tested my patience with their gabbing.

Towards the evening a herd of deer poked their heads out of the woods. They saw the flock and kept their distance, but stayed long enough for me to appreciate how different they were from my wooly charges—how much more still they were.

Once Brooks got to his feet, nose to the air, but as my heart came to pound in my throat he lay back down. Clouds sped across the sky, pushed by the strong winds, coming down from the mountains. I kept myself wrapped tightly in my blanket, which Father had brought along with Hale.

When my shift ended, I drove the flock home and into the barn rather than the paddock. Both Tess and Cherub flicked their ears at me and snorted in clear irritation at this intrusion.

"Not my fault," I told them over the din of the sheep, who were no more a fan of these cramped quarters than the horse and ponies.

When the animals were taken care of, Father, Michael and I practiced shooting with the crossbows until it was too dark to continue. Father had done all the fixing needed for the spare crossbow, and it shot smoothly, though I would need a great deal more practice before I was any kind of marksman.

Dinner that evening was like the night before in many ways, but there was a distinct lack of good humor. Michael snubbed me, and Father was short with Michael. Mother spoke to Father in her most reproachful tones, not knowing Michael had been a bear all day. I did my best to stay out of the crosshairs, and was relieved to finally retire to my own bedroom.

The next morning my eyes were already open and staring at the ceiling as the first threads of daylight creeped through my curtains. The rain had come a few hours after midnight, complete with thunder and lightning that had brought me to anxious wakefulness well before it was time to get out of bed. For several hours, the storm had gone strong, but at some point I managed to sink back into a fitful sleep.

As I rubbed the back of my hand across my gritty eyes, my head pounded dully with the same ache from yesterday that had never fully gone away. With some difficulty, I dragged myself out of bed. Father hadn't called for us to get up yet, but since I was already awake, I figured I would do well to surprise him by already being up, and ready.

As I went to wash, a groan slipped from my lips at the realization that I had not refilled my basin the night before. Below the basin was a wooden bucket with a handle, and I bent stiffly to retrieve it. When my woolen cloak was securely wrapped around the thin material of my night dress, I shoved my feet into my boots without bothering with stockings.

I crept down the hallway so as not to wake my brother, and slipped past the kitchen. Therein the murmurs of mother and father, and the sizzle of something frying over the fire could be heard. I caught a whiff of bacon and my stomach growled. With new haste, I made my way out the front door.

The pump at the gate still held the dishes from last night, and I shifted them aside to make room for my bucket. The cold water droplets that flicked onto my skin as I filled the container made me wince.

Idly, I looked around the yard as the bucket filled; it felt strangely foreign in the weak light of the morning. The grass glistened, and the trees dripped steadily with the last night's rain. A wispy mist threaded through the trees and bushes, cutting some parts in half and obscuring others entirely. Through the haze, in the direction of the barn, my eyes caught on a sight that made my heart stall. A few feet inside the trees was the unmistakable creamy white wool of a sheep, and I recognized the sound of hooves crunching through fallen leaves. A strangled gasp escaped my lips, and the fright that had run through me eased back only slightly as my brain registered that the sheep was on its feet, and seemed to be grazing. Even so, the world blurred as, bucket forgotten, I splashed through the muddy puddles of the yard as I ran directly for the kitchen.

"Father, there's a sheep loose!" I was speaking before the door was completely open.

Father was in motion only a fraction of a second after the sentence left my mouth. He set down the piece of bacon that had been headed for his mouth, and rose to his feet.

I saw him cast a look at Mother who widened her eyes and jerked her head, removing the skillet from the fire. He nodded curtly in response and turned to me. "Taryn, wake your brother. I'll go have a look and see what's happened."

"You shouldn't go alone!" I burst out. "What if it's the gryphon?"

Mother moved to close the door behind me and rest a hand on my shoulder. "I'll go with him. More likely than not a lesser gryphon nosed the door open to get out of the storm, one of the sheep got spooked, and now they've all gone wandering. There's no beast that goes hunting in the torrents we had last night. We'll round them up, and the sooner you get Michael out of bed, the sooner you can help."

As Mother spoke, Father disappeared. When he returned he had donned a thick cloak, his hat, and his boots. He also had his crossbow slung over his shoulder.

"Let's go, Wynn." Mother grabbed her own cloak and shoes. Father nodded at me. "Good eye, Taryn."

My mouth parted slightly and then I nodded in return and spun to go and get Michael as they exited the house.

"Michael!" I banged on his door. "The sheep got loose last night. It's time to get up and get to work!"

Michael flung the door open and glared at me. "There's no need to shout." He stopped and squinted at me. In the span of a moment he took in my pale face, disheveled hair—which I reached to smooth at his gaze—and the mud splatters on my nightgown. He covered a grin with his hand. "Taryn, it's not the gryphon. It rained like an ocean was being dumped on us last night."

I swatted at him. "Shut up. You don't know."

"Whatever." He rolled his eyes. "I'm nearly ready, let me get my harness and my boots."

With a start, I realized Michael was fully dressed and his hair was already braided back. I glanced down at myself and grimaced.

"I'll be just a second. Don't leave without me!"

Back outside I ran, to grab the bucket, which was overfull. It sloshed down my front as I lifted it. Hissing every swear I knew, I tipped the water out onto the grass to make it more manageable, and lugged the thing back inside. I dressed, my morning wash forgone, tossing my soaked night clothes into a balled-up heap in the corner of the room. By the time I had finished Michael was in the kitchen, cloaked, and feet shod in muddy boots—when had *he* had a chance to go outside to get water and wash up?

"Are you ready?" he asked, smiling smugly and crunching a piece of bacon.

I snatched the piece of bacon from his loose fingers, and bit it savagely. "Let's go."

We trudged quickly across the sopping wet yard towards the barn, our crooks made sucking noises as they sunk in and pulled out of the muck. At least the gods had seen fit to give us one blessing. There were no lesser gryphons prowling about. There had been several flocks over at Glenn's yesterday, attracted by the carcasses. It was possible they were staying near to him in hopes of more. I grimaced at that thought—poor Glenn, having that reminder. However, at least that probably meant no new kill had drawn them this way.

The lone sheep I had seen before was nowhere in sight, and I assumed Father wrangled it on the way out. As we neared the barn, a dog came out to meet us, tongue lulling. It was Nag, Brooks's mother, discernable from her mate Benjie only by her smaller stature. Unlike Brooks, both Nag's and Benjie's fur were shot through with the gray of age. Nag's eyes were also starting to show the blue that meant she was losing the sharpness of her sight. When she reached us, I knelt to stroke her face and coo to her.

"Hello pretty girl. What have we found, sweetling?" Nag wagged her tail and tried to lick my face, but I pulled back in time to spare myself the washing. "Come on, show me Mother."

Nag's ears pricked forward and she set off at a trot back towards the barn. Therein Mother was finishing the filling of a trough, which she had dragged towards the center of the open space. A handful of sheep were already digging into the food greedily, and the whole place smelled of wet wool. If my count was right, it seemed twelve were still missing. I looked at Mother quizzically.

"Half of them were already here when we got to the barn," she explained, as she slung the bag of feed back onto its high shelf on the wall, brow flecked with sweat from the exertion. "Most of the other half were milling around right outside. You shut the gate last night, right?" At my emphatic nod she sighed, and rubbed her neck. "The storm must have pulled it, because it was standing wide open. Your father, Benjie, and Brooks have gone to fetch the rest. There were a couple towards the back of the paddock, and we've left those for now, but there's still nine unaccounted for."

Michael and I edged around the sheep, towards the stalls that held our ponies. Hale whickered at me and I smoothed her forelock out of her soft eyes.

"I know, it's been a busy couple of days for you," I murmured as I led her out of the stall.

She glared at sheep as I maneuvered her around them. Halfway through she paused as one blatted at her and I thought for a moment she might snap at the dunderheaded creature, but at the sound of Cherub jingling behind her she shook herself and kept moving.

"Which direction did Father head?" Michael asked, as he checked Cherub's bridle, making sure it was secure.

"He went towards the fields. Usually when they get loose they head in that general direction. You know these silly things only have food on their minds. One of you can follow him and one of you can check the route towards town."

I opened my mouth to respond, but Michael was quicker. "I'll take the town side," he said before mounting and galloping ahead of me out the barn door.

I didn't mind heading in the same direction as Father—in fact I thought it was a fair bit stupid to go searching for the sheep towards town when, likely they had behaved as Mother and Father guessed. I'd probably reach Father as he was driving the rogue sheep home. I climbed onto Hale's back at the barn's wide doors, eagerly anticipating my brother coming home long after

Father and I had finished. I'd be sitting by the fire drinking hot tea, and he'd come trudging in, cold and maybe wet from the drizzle that seemed to want to start again. I allowed myself a mean smile.

"Is he all right?" Mother's words pulled my attention back down to her. "Ever since our fight he has been so distant. I thought our news would make things better but..." Her shoulders slumped.

I winced. "That might have been me. He and I got into a squabble out in the field, after I left you yesterday."

"What about?"

I looked away, not liking how she was frowning at me, as though I was at fault. I almost ratted him out about Master Noland. They had a right to know he was sneaking around, after all. In the end though, I settled with the core of my grievance. "He just acts so stuck up sometimes!"

She tilted her head, right hand absently stroking Nag's soft ears. "Even towards you?"

"He didn't use to," I spoke quietly, still avoiding eye contact, "but these days, yeah, even towards me."

Mother didn't speak for a minute, deep in thought, and I began to feel antsy, shifting in my saddle. Finally, she gestured towards the door. "I'm sorry, this has been troubling me as well. I'll find an answer soon, I promise you. Go and help your father."

"You don't need to have an answer Mother." I leaned over in my saddle to kiss her on the cheek. "What I need to do is whoop him in a fight, like I did when we were kids. If you recall, I'm very good at beating the attitude out of my dear brother." I kicked my heels in and Hale lurched forward.

"Do not fight your brother!" Mother called after me, her voice a mixture of amusement and warning. "I mean it! You're too old, someone will get hurt."

I waved at her without looking back, guiding Hale towards the road. As I turned her right, heading towards the field, I kept my eyes peeled for the familiar dirty-white of sheep. The brush on either side of the road was a few feet back, and for the most part had been cultivated by generations of farmers to consist of thick hedges that would keep all but the most determined beast on the path—or off it. Still, there were places where a sheep might slip through to frolic in the shadowy woods. I wished Nag was still spry enough to come with me. She was a veteran at the retrieval of wayward sheep and her nose was better than my eyes.

The morning was overcast and the rain did in fact insist on continuing, softly but steadily. I found myself wishing that I had brought my broad-brimmed, oiled hat, and that I had my oiled cloak to put over the wool I was wearing. Sure, I was warm, but I would soon be soaked and it was doubtful that my clothes would be dry by the time I had to go out again this afternoon. They certainly wouldn't be if I intended to take Mother to town.

I was more than halfway to the field and there were no sheep in sight, and no Father either. There was, however, water dripping down my leggings and into my boots. Curling my toes rewarded me with a squelching noise. I whined deep in my throat and wiped the rain out of my eyes.

"Taryn." I nearly fell out of my saddle as a shadow moved from the woods. It was Father, I realized, relaxing enough to soothe Hale, whom I had startled. *He* had a hat, I thought sullenly. "Where's your brother?"

"He went towards town, just in case," I stuttered. "Where are Tess, and the dogs?" I looked up and down the road. "The sheep?"

Father smiled grimly, stepping over a lower portion of the hedge to join me on the road. "They're in the field. Brooks and Benjie are keeping them tight, and Tess is tethered. I wanted to be sure I didn't miss anything back in these trees. I thought I saw something on my way out, and we're still missing one. You didn't see one on your way here?"

"No, I'm sorry. I haven't seen any. I was actually starting to get worried."

"Don't be. This was not a gryphon. This is gods all cursed bad luck, but that's all it is. Still, thanks to you we were lucky enough to have an early start."

"But the hunt." I said lamely.

Father smiled honestly then. "The hunt won't suffer too much with my absence, and they'll have to pass us to start it so I can tell them I won't be there, and warn them to look out for our lost sheep. Come on, help me drive the sheep home. Hopefully your brother will have returned with the last one."

Getting back to the sheep and then getting the sheep to cooperate could have been described as grueling at best. We stopped to speak with the hunting party as they made their way to our field—a task which was lengthened as Father was forced to assure Glenn twice over that this was not another gryphon attack. However, despite all of this, Michael had not returned by the time we came home. Father and I got the sheep into the barn, where Mother and Nag had also wrangled the ones from the paddock, and then we joined her inside the house. The bacon from dawn had gone cold, but when we came in, soggy and dispirited she began to fry up the pieces that hadn't had a chance to cook. We shucked our wet clothes to hang by the fire in the family room which she had stoked high, and ate the cold bacon while we waited.

"One gone missing," Mother mused. "That's not quite so bad as it could be."

"We may have one son missing on top of that," Father groused.

"Speak and he arrives," I muttered as the back door creaked open. Twice as wet as we had been, and looking like a cat that had been dumped into the wash, Michael clumped into the kitchen, tracking mud behind him.

"Hey," he said. I had to clap a hand over my mouth to stifle my snicker. How one person could wrap up so much defeat into one word was simply beyond me.

"You are soaked to the bone! Come now, breakfast is almost ready," Mother exclaimed, helping him remove his outer layers so that they could hang by the fire. She pressed a hand to his cheek before he could pull away. "Your skin is clammy."

"I don't suppose you found any of the sheep?" I asked innocently batting my eyes.

He glared, kicking off his boots. "No. I didn't."

"We found all but one," Father said, looking between the two of us. "I'm hoping that one makes her way to the field or to the barn in her own time."

"It could happen." Mother set plates of food in front of our usual spots. To me she said, "I'm not going into town today, not in this weather, so you don't have to worry about walking to and from in your wet things. There will be no one down by the wash, and I'm more interested in being here in case our sheep happens to wander back through."

I slumped back into my chair in relief. "That's great. I'd hate to go back out into this rain just as I've gotten out of it." I shot a look at Michael, but he was pointedly ignoring me, stuffing his face with his breakfast.

"All right." Father sat up a little straighter. "What is going on between the two of you? You've been taking shots at one another since yesterday and it's about time you settle whatever it is."

"They've had a small fight." Mother put a hand on Father's forearm.

"So, you told her—big surprise," Michael spat at me.

"I didn't tell her *everything*," I shot back. Michael bit his tongue and settled for glaring at me harder.

"That's enough. Both of you." Mother raised a warning finger. She had caught my emphasis on 'everything' I could tell by the way she glanced between us, but she didn't press it. "I swear, you're too similar sometimes. I mean it. I don't want to hear another word from either of you unless it's something nice."

Michael made the motion of buttoning his lips. I rolled my eyes and ate another piece of bacon. As though he was the wronged one in this situation. He was the one changing things. He was the one leaving and calling the rest of us simpletons. He was the one *lying* to Mother and Father. To my dismay I felt tears prick at my eyes and I quickly screwed them shut, keeping my head down.

When I had gotten myself under control Mother and Father were eating with purpose. They clearly thought the matter was settled. Michael was—I started. Michael was looking at me in a way I didn't understand. It was not apologetic, as I might have hoped. It was *speculative*, like I was a strange word he was trying to figure out in a new book. I didn't like being stared at in a normal sense, but something turned the expression from odd to creepy. His eyes were slightly dilated, as though the kitchen, cheerily lit with morning light, was dark.

When he realized that I was looking back at him, he returned to his meal as though nothing had happened. I blinked and shook my head. Perhaps I was more tired than I had thought if I was seeing things. Once he finished what was on his plate, he turned to address Father, and the problem with his eyes was gone, if it had ever been there.

"Should I take the sheep to the field?"

Father cleared his throat, and scratched the back of his head. "That's fine. Remember to be extra careful. I want you to bring Benjie as well as Brooks, and you can take my cloak. It's dry."

"Thanks." Michael stood and went to gather what he'd need for the morning. "Taryn, is the crossbow in your room?" He asked from the family room.

I shoved my chair back, rising. "Yeah, I'll get it," I called back.

I ducked out of my parent's too concerned gaze, and into the other room. Michael was leaning against the brick of the fireplace, eyes on the wooden floor. I grimaced and stalked past him, down the dimmer hallway towards my room; I heard him follow behind me. As I knelt and reached my arm under the bed to pull the crossbow out of its hiding place he finally spoke.

"Come on Taryn, what's your problem?"

My fingers twitched on the crossbow and I turned, the

weapon propped on my bent knee. His silhouette was a dark spot in my doorway, "What's my problem?"

"Yeah, what's your issue? You were fine with me going not two days ago, and now it's like I've killed somebody."

"I was fine with it Michael, until you started lying and putting on airs."

"I'm not putting on airs!" he exclaimed. "Why can't I say that I can do better without you taking it as a personal attack?"

"Because that's not what you're saying! You're saying that there's nothing for you here. Nothing!"

He pointed a finger into my face, speaking as I stood to get clear of it. "I told you that you could come with me. You said no."

"Just because you're doing something, that doesn't mean I have to! I happen to know my duty to our parents, and I like our home!" I clenched my fists at my sides.

"Well if duty to my family means being miserable then I refuse it. And you can't tell me Nophgrin has everything you want. I know better."

Those stupid tears threatened to come out again. I shoved the crossbow at him. "Here."

He took it gently, and his eye brows slanted upwards. "Please don't hate me Taryn. I couldn't bear it."

Cradling the crossbow, all his haughtiness gone, he looked like my brother again. I tilted my head to the side. He wasn't though. This was the man Michael had grown into when I wasn't paying attention. He wasn't a bad man, perhaps a little eager to prove himself and a little careless with the feelings of others, but he genuinely wanted to do better for himself. I sighed, and if this was what he thought it would take, it wasn't as though he'd be a treat to be around if I coerced him into staying.

"I don't hate you. You know that. I think I'm scared," I admitted.

"Of what?"

"Of who you're becoming. Of who I'm becoming. I don't know them quite as well as I thought I did."

Michael's eyes widened and then his expression relaxed. "Maybe it's a good thing you don't know who we're growing into. It'll be a surprise." This was him trying to tease me, and I allowed myself a small smile.

"Maybe. I just don't want to wake up in five years and find you a stranger, and me a bumpkin."

"You will never grow up to be a bumpkin," he promised me. "This I know for a fact."

"I'm frightened that you're going somewhere I can't follow," I whispered. "There *are* things I want that aren't here, you're not wrong. I just can't imagine leaving all of this behind, to go out into the world and get them. I'm not ready for that. I don't know how you suddenly are."

"What are you two doing?" That was Mother, her tone a mixture of sternness and concern. It broke through the stillness that had settled over the two of us.

Remembering what I had told her earlier, I bit back a grin. "She thinks I'm wailing on you."

"Can I guess that's because you told her you were going to?" My guilty face told him everything he needed to know. Michael shut his eyes as his face broke out into full smile. "Well then I ought to go and alleviate their concerns. Are we ok?" He searched my face earnestly.

I wanted to tell him yes, but my smile was bittersweet. "No. I'm angry with you, Michael. I'm going to try and be good about it because I know you have to go, but you're going to have to give me some time."

He inclined his head, subdued. "Ok. I get that. Can you at least promise me again that you won't tell the parents about my plan?" At my doubtful look he hurried onward, voice hushed, "I'll think of a way to tell them, I promise, just not now. The whole thing is complicated, and I want them to get used to the idea of me going in the first place."

I exhaled gustily through my nose, eyebrows high, my lips pressed together in what I was certain was an excellent impression of Mother's signature expression. "Ok, but then you can't get mad at me when I snap at you. You have to let me be mad."

He snorted. "I can try Taryn. I'm not *that* good a person."

"Michael?" This time it was Father.

"All right, I have to go. Quiver?"

"Oh!" I crouched and quickly retrieved the quiver full of bolts from the same spot the crossbow had been and handed them to Michael. He pulled me into a hug as he grabbed them, and they poked painfully into my chest, but I didn't pull out of the embrace.

"It's going to be fine Taryn. I've got everything under control, I swear."

His quick exit caused a draft to billow out my door after him and I wrapped my arms around myself. There was still time, maybe he would change his mind.

8

The morning was slow, and dull. I helped Mother clean the dishes, and then we cleaned the floor of muck. Throughout the day we turned the clothing that was by the fire, making sure everything dried evenly and nothing singed.

Father and I worked on my aim for a scant hour before I had to leave. I enjoyed the training, but I found myself grateful when it was time for me to ride out to the field. Father's full attention always made me nervous. He was a serious man, who seemed to be good at most things he put his mind to. Even telling myself that he'd had years to reach that level of skill, I wanted him to be proud of me. Every time a bolt went wide I cringed.

Outside, the rain had yet to completely fizzle out and there was a crisp wind blowing steadily, but everything I wore was toasty from the fire. I kicked Hale into a gallop as soon as I turned out onto the road and we made it to the field in record time. The trees whizzed past us, a sage and russet blur. We were going too fast to even think about the lesser gryphons that jeered from the tree line. Riding Hale at her full speed always felt like stepping out of the world. For the duration of the ride the funk that had settled over me the past few days lifted.

When Michael saw our speedy entry into the field he clambered to his feet and stalked out to meet me, his face a mask of displeasure.

"What are you doing?" he demanded as I reined the pony in.

My mood plummeted. "What?" I asked sullenly, sliding off Hale's back. Michael grabbed me as I attempted to push past him and he gave me a small shake. It was then that I saw the fear in his expression. "Michael, what?"

"You can't ride her so fast Taryn. It's wet out. What if you had fallen and broken your neck?"

"I never—!"

"There's a gryphon prowling." I noted that his knuckles were white on the hand that gripped his crook. "Dashing around like that is like trailing bait past a trout! I don't know what I'd do if you got killed."

My heart thumped painfully, and a hand raised to anxiously rub my collarbone. "I hadn't thought…"

"Well you need to. You're the one worried so badly about the gryphon. You'd never see it coming, and I couldn't stop it if it was dead set on killing you—if it attacked you back on the road. That's out of the crossbow's range."

I shook my head, mind racing over what I had seen of the woods as we had galloped through them. I hadn't seen anything, and not because nothing had been there I was certain. I thought of the rabbit mother and I had seen on the way to town. It had never seen the lesser gryphon coming either. I swallowed.

"Thanks. Michael, I swear I didn't think of it."

Michael rubbed his brow. "Yeah, you know I wouldn't have thought of it either until I saw you ride up. Though, to be fair, I don't ride Cherub at a gallop unless you and I are racing."

"No, you don't." I leaned against the warmth of Hale's side, and stroked her shoulder. "Gods above and below, I'll tell you this— if there was any part of this life that I might understand you wanting to leave, it's gryphon season."

"I'd say so." Michael scanned the field and trees behind a final time before walking back to Cherub. "Of course, there are other monsters besides gryphons."

"True, we don't have dragons out here," I acknowledged.

Michael flicked a glance at me. and there was something I couldn't place in his face. "True," was all he said.

Benjie and Brooks were both at the tree. The older of the two was lying, eyes closed, and I wondered how much longer he'd be able to make even these occasional trips out to the field. His eyes opened as I approached, and he wagged his tail but didn't so much as raise his head. Brooks trotted over to give me an affectionate greeting.

"Beyond my own idiocy, has there been anything of note today?" I regretted mentioning my own failing as soon as the words left my mouth. Still, I reasoned, that was what I would have said before this month of fighting. I was used to being candid with Michael, and I didn't want that to change.

Michael shook his head as he packed away his items. "Nope. Haven't seen the hunting party or any gryphons. Saw a herd of deer a little earlier. They've been hanging around."

"I saw them yesterday. I have to say, I sort of find them comforting. They're so skittish, if there's a gryphon they'll bolt as fast as a sneeze."

"Or better yet, the gryphon will satisfy itself with venison instead of veal." Michael mounted, and shoved his long hair back over his shoulder. His hair needed trimming, I thought. It was getting unruly.

"Now that is a sentiment I can get behind!" I said with forced cheerfulness. "Ride safely, all right?"

"I'll ride like the slowest snail in the garden," he said agreeably. "See you at home."

The carving I had been working on for the past several days was all but finished. Truly, it needed some detail work that I couldn't manage with my fingers stiff from the cold or covered in my mittens, so I left it in its pouch.

Unlike Michael, who could sit reading a book for hours at a time, I took little pleasure in reading. There had also been no mending to bring. I sang some, mostly old shepherding songs, made to echo over the hills. I'd never be a bard, but my voice wasn't terrible either. When I'd tapped all that I had in my repertoire the silence felt deeper than before.

I made myself move about the field then. If there were any signs of creatures that ought not to have been there I would find them. I ended up following fresh boot tracks the whole way around the field. I acknowledged with amusement that they must have been from Michael doing the same check. That warmed me. With his concern at how fast I had ridden in, and these tracks, it seemed clear he was not as aloof as he wanted to appear. He cared about how close the gryphon was coming to our land—and to me.

It seemed that neither of us needed to have bothered looking around. The only animal tracks to be found were that of the sheep and deer, and the only dung was of the same nature and that of rabbits. I knew that if anything else had been on the ground it would show in the muddy earth, and I tried to let that soothe me, but still my chest felt tight.

I also found, much to my relief, that the sheep were not inclined to wander in the direction of Glenn's property. However, they were testing their boundaries for how close they could get to the unfenced portion of the field before I had the dogs bring them back around. It was just as well that Brooks and Benjie were both with me because it was a battle all day keeping the sheep in line. I wondered if the smell of the slaughter to the west had reached their nostrils. It would explain their skittish behavior. The dogs seemed unchanged, but then they weren't prey animals and were more comfortable with the scent of blood.

A bleak drizzle kept on the whole afternoon. It would clear for a half an hour at a time, long enough for me to feel hopeful that I might dry off, and then it would rain again. I had brought my broad-brimmed hat which kept the rain from my eyes, but eventually I had to forsake my usual place by the tree to perch on a boulder, or else face sinking into the mud.

Two hours before dusk the hunting party rode through Glenn's land. They were noisy enough that the sounds of raised, angry voices, the jingling of tack, and the stamping of hooves punctuated the white noise of the rain. A few yells of agreement and disagreement were all I could catch as they faded off again. I gathered up the sheep as quickly as I could, hoping to catch them on the road home, but I didn't. Frustrated as I was, I dared not push the sheep to go any faster, thinking of Michael's warning.

By the time I got to the house, Father and Mother were saying their goodbyes to Willy and Laura, who had declined an invitation to stay for supper. I hurried the sheep past them. "How did the hunt go?" I twisted in my saddle to ask.

Willy shook his head, his expression gloomy. "Your father will tell you."

"Put the sheep in the barn," was all Father said.

When I returned from the barn Willy and Laura had gone; Mother and Father both had withdrawn to the house. They were in the kitchen, finishing the supper preparations; Michael was presumably in his room. The smell of baking bread hit me like a warm hug as I stepped inside and shed my moist outer wear.

"I heard them as they were coming back from the hunt," I said hesitantly. "It did not sound good."

Father had his pipe out and he nodded as he puffed, getting the tobacco to light properly. He inhaled the thick smoke deeply into his lungs and then let it out in a soft, fragrant trail. Mother coughed delicately and waved her hand in front of her nose. He shifted to face me so the smoke blew away from her, and I came to sit next to him.

"Well, did they find anything?"

He went to take another drag, and I made a disgruntled noise in protest. He sighed and lowered the pipe. "They found a sheep. Our lost sheep, I'd say, since no one else reported one missing. It was killed in a similar manner as the cows."

"That's terrible." I slumped. "Michael said that this gryphon didn't even eat sensibly when it came to the cows. Is it the same for the sheep?"

When Father hesitated to speak again, Mother came behind him and rested a hand on his shoulder. "There were deer in the same clearing as the sheep. Two of them, killed in the same way. Nothing finished, everything torn to shreds. Laura looked so pale... Willy could barely speak about it. I don't think they had ever seen anything like it."

I furrowed my brows in confusion, gazing down at my palms. "I doubt anyone around here has. That doesn't make sense. Gryphons don't kill without eating. They don't waste."

"There were tracks." Father spoke through smoke. His own expression was perplexed, as though he, too, was trying to figure this out. "Deep scores in the earth as well as markings on the tree around the clearing. Will has admitted he may be out of his depth. He told the hunting party as much. When Glenn heard that, he told us he had sent his eldest off with a letter yesterday. He's tracking down a pack of mercenaries Glenn knows of. Didn't even consult the guards first. They'll be here within the week if they're on their regularly scheduled route."

"Was Willy angry?" I asked.

Father tilted his head. "No. He seemed relieved, to be honest."

I was surprised that Glenn hadn't gotten into trouble. There was a chain of command for a reason. It was sometimes loose with Willy, but in situations like this it seemed like he belonged in charge. Nophgrin was part of Lord Peyter de Nophgrin's barony—though he had not been to his lands since the estates had passed to him. Even so, *he* should have been the one to call in for extra help. I asked my father why this had not been the case.

He rolled his shoulders. "The baron hasn't been this far north in over a decade. When we've had troubles in the past—that hard winter a few years back, you remember?" I nodded, "We sent him a letter at his estate in Winterstag, asking for medicines and the like. Took a month for a response to come from one of his clerks that his lordship was wintering in the warmth of the capital. We were told a letter could be written to be sent that way if we thought it was 'really' worth troubling him."

That winter we had lost two of my grandparents. Lords, I thought with disgust. They cared for no one but themselves. So, perhaps that was it. If I were Willy, I'd have been relieved to have the decision of whether to deal through them out of my hands.

"Do we know these mercenaries?" I asked out loud.

He shook his head. "Glenn knew of them through Thomas—Claire's grandfather, not the young Thomas. Their barracks are a little more south than us, but I don't recall them ever coming through town. Glenn says they usually come through Goatstrack, or Winterstag depending on the year."

"Supposedly they specialize in this sort of thing," mother put in. "Monster hunters is how Willy described them. He had heard of them before in his circles. He says they're experts."

I thought about this for a moment. "Well, who's to pay these extremely good mercenaries?"

That startled a chuckle out of Father. "My shrewd girl! More than likely it will be paid for by those who think it's necessary, and divvied up between us equally."

I glanced up at him. "You think it's necessary?"

Another smoke cloud proceeded his answer. "Normally I'd say no. If this were a gryphon and its mate that had dragged off a beast or even two and eaten them to the bones, I think we would have had no trouble in putting an end to the issue. A normal gryphon knows when to leave well enough alone." He licked his lips. "However, what we've seen in two days speaks of viciousness. Maybe even madness. If there are professionals close by, I think it'd be just as well to have them come in and be done with it."

"But in the meantime, there is some sort of rabid gryphon— or worse several rabid gryphons tramping through the woods?" I was hard pressed to keep a whine out of my voice.

"We'll keep the herds inside at night and if any more attacks happen in the next few days we won't take them to pasture at all. Still, I don't think we'll see any more attacks. Now that everyone knows there is a threat they'll be keeping a much keener eye on their livestock, and it will move on to easier prey."

"You don't think the gryphon will come to the pasture in the day?" Mother's voice carried a stern quality. She was pulling the bread out of the oven, her back to us.

Father looked back at her. "From what I can tell this beast still has some care for humans. Enough that, for all it marked up its latest kill, the hunting party couldn't find a trace of it in the surrounding area. That sounds like it fled from them. Besides that, it has not even come to our field yet." Mother made an *mmm* noise deep in her throat. "If it will make you feel better I'll take watch with the children."

"I'm not a child and I don't need minded like one." Michael was in the doorway. He had come so quietly that he startled me. "A gryphon would have to come from the trees and cross a fair bit of distance in the open to take one of our sheep in the field.

In the time needed to make that span, I'd shoot it down. Taryn could do the same."

"What about on the road to or from the field?" I asked. He was all over the place when it came to this gryphon, it seemed. "As you said, those are much tighter quarters."

"Right, and in such a case I'd already be dead before Father had turned in his saddle at the *thump*. I'm not trying to be pessimistic." He brought his hands up in front of his chest and hurried on when I open my mouth to point out that he had praised Father for being a marksman not two days ago. "I'm merely saying that Father probably has better things he could be doing than babysitting us each day."

Father appeared abashed when Mother looked to him to deny this. "I *would* like to start doing some scent warding around the house."

Scent warding was one of the more certain methods of driving off a gryphon. Using a spray bottle, and the urine of either another gryphon, or less effectively, a similarly large predator, you worked your way around the perimeter of your land, spritzing the trees and brush with urine. A gryphon that came upon the smell, believing it to be the hunting territory of another gryphon would move off. It was, however, one of the more expensive methods of keeping gryphons out—because there was only one way to get a gryphon's urine, and it was no afternoon stroll. We had a small bottle out in the barn that I could only remember him using one other time.

Mother's eyes narrowed, and he plowed onward. "The field would also do very well with that, which means that I'll be out in the field with them at least one of the days." He puffed quickly on his pipe. The room now smelled richly of cherries and tobacco over top the bread.

I shrugged at Mother helplessly. The world had to continue to turn. I was as scared as anyone, but one bad gryphon didn't mean our lives stopped. If we didn't make sure the sheep fed properly we'd pay for it later when their wool was lackluster and their milk was thin.

"I can still come with you to town," I told her. "I'd feel better doing that, even if Michael is right about it being pointless."

"I didn't mean it was pointless." Michael shot me a warning look. I acknowledged my attitude, pursing my lips and tossing my head to the side. He turned a kinder expression towards Mother. "I can still come home with you as well."

"I would like to go in to town tomorrow. I can't wait to hear what everyone is saying about all of this," she said.

"I don't mind, although I think I'll lead Hale on the way out so I can ride her back."

Mother inclined her head. "That's fine by me, so long as you think she'll be all right. There are a couple of flocks of lesser gryphons nesting close to town, and I know she has never been a friend to them, and especially not since getting swiped."

"It has gotten worse in the past year," I admitted. "She should be all right though."

We settled our plans for the next day. Michael and Father would ride out to the field together, where Father would scent ward. I would walk mother to town, and then help Father scent ward around the paddock. Scenting would make the farm animals unhappy, but there wasn't much else for it. After that, I would go to the sheep, taking the crossbow from Michael before he went to collect Mother.

That evening as I readied for bed my thoughts buzzed with the events of the day. Our poor lone sheep, and the deer that Michael and I had both taken comfort in seeing. They had been ripped open at the chest and then left like there hadn't been a point at all to it. I gnawed at a loose piece of skin around my thumb nail. It was irrefutably a gryphon, everyone who had seen the tracks, Father included, agreed to this. Yet, there had never been an attack like this. I hadn't even known it was possible for a gryphon to contract a malady like rabies. Would it be able to spread whatever was wrong with it to other gryphons?

I climbed into bed and drew my blankets up over my shoulders, lying on my side. If whatever was wrong with this gryphon was catching then this situation had the potential to become horrifying quickly. My mind drew up images of a drooling, sickly gryphon with murderous eyes. Goosebumps raised on my arms as the wind howled through the trees outside. How close to the house had the sheep been when the gryphon seized it and carried it off? If it was hungry enough, would it try to come into the house?

For the first time since I was a small girl I fell asleep with my blankets pulled all the way over my head.

9

Seven days passed. Martin returned with the news that the mercenaries were not far behind. A pig went missing from its pen, and though there was no proof that the gryphon had done it, everyone was positive that it had. Every morning as I dropped Mother off at the well there was more talk of someone seeing a shadow pass by their window in the dead of night.

Willy was looking more and more harassed every morning, and I pitied his position. The hunting party had told their families what they had seen, and those individuals had drawn up their own conclusions as to how much trouble we were in.

The merchant families had declined any future picnic invitations until the matter was solved, but from what I heard they were more than willing to front the entire cost of the mercenaries if no one else was willing. Luckily for them, it seemed every farmer in town had a mind to pay whatever it took to feel at ease again.

On the ninth day, the mercenaries arrived. Mother and I came to town to find a long list of names already written onto the roster for the day. Fifteen people all told, and two names were written in characters which I didn't recognize. The uniform hand writing suggested that what we were looking at was a copy made by Laura and sent over to Willy by a runner.

"They came early this morning," Willy said as he took the slate back from us. "Actually, their caravan was waiting at the gate when Laura went to open. After they signed in, three of them came to meet me."

"What are they like?" I asked leaning forward so my arms were on the booth. Behind me Hale snorted. Mother took the reins from me and led her to the post to be tied until I returned for her.

Willy propped a fist against the front of his chin as he thought. "They're hard folk, miss. Not the kind of people you'd want to live with, but they seem decent. It was good of them to stop by before they'd even rested their heads. I wouldn't mind taking a meal with them and listening to what they've seen. Their leader, Aedith, she reminds me of my captain back at school. A real hard ass, but she seems to be fair."

"Are they staying at the inn?" Mother asked.

Willy grimaced. "I asked Aedith, and she said they brought tents. I told her it seemed like it'd be cold and wet and that the inn would give her a good price, but she was insistent. They're set up with their caravan over towards the southern entrance to town."

I felt a small thrill in my stomach at the thought of warriors in town. With them here, at last the threat would be squashed and things could get back to normal. Not to mention, they'd have stories, and hopefully one or two of them wouldn't mind sharing them with us.

"Mother can we have supper in town tonight?" I asked eagerly.

She gave me a knowing look. "Ask your father, but I don't see why not—although, you know it's going to be crowded. Everyone is going to want to get a look at these people, and they might not even feel like coming out tonight."

"They'll want to meet your husband and Glenn." Willy's voice was oddly glum now. "As well as the rest of the hunting party who saw anything as soon as possible. Aedith seemed to be a down-to-business sort of woman."

I inspected the guardsman carefully. At first, I'd thought he seemed less tense than he had been the last couple of days, but his voice didn't sound that way. Upon closer inspection, his eyes were bloodshot, and the furrows above his brow were deep. I imagined it was hard to have to outsource for the protection of the town when it was his whole job. I opened my mouth to say something kind, but I didn't know what to say, so I shut it again.

"Taryn, are you walking me to the well?" Mother was already moving in that direction.

"Coming! Willy, I'm glad *you're* here to handle them," I said quickly, and then turned to dart after Mother. I didn't dare to wait to see what response he had for such an awkward comment.

Today the washing well was packed with everyone who might have come out. We made a beeline for Mother's usual group. Gladys, Naieed, Beth, and Claire were all in attendance. There was one other addition, Francine. She was a larger woman with red hair, who was related to Claire on her father's side.

Francine didn't often come down to the well, though she was often the hostess when gatherings were held. She had married a fur merchant and could afford to have someone else do most of her laundering. Today it seemed there had been enough incentive to come down herself. Like everyone else, she was a little scarce on laundry to be washed due to her help coming down every day this week to gossip. She scrubbed delicately at a handkerchief as she spoke.

"They've completely churned up the earth on the south side of town, setting up their tents and their fire pits. I don't know why they can't stay in the inn. It's right there, and the gods know that it would help the town to have their business."

Beth wiped her brow. "Benjamin says they're probably afraid of leaving their caravan too far away," she said, naming her stepfather. "Who knows what kind of weaponry they've got hidden in that thing."

Naieed gave me a wicked grin, flashing teeth as she saw us arrive. "I'd like to see what kind of weaponry they've got hidden away. Right Taryn?" I flushed.

"Naieed curb yourself," Mother said dryly as she sat, and Naieed let out a peel of laughter.

"I'm sorry Mother Wynn. I only mean that Taryn is a weapons enthusiast. Everyone has seen her ogling at the blacksmith's and we know that's not about anything but the steel in his window!"

Claire was sitting to Naieed's right today, and she nudged her with a toe. "But you were up this morning when they arrived right? What did they look like?"

Naieed was twirling a stocking that was clearly clean in the hot water. "I was getting some lamb from the butcher when they rolled through. One large wagon, driven by a tall man from the south east—dark hair, gorgeous," she made sure to add. "Twelve a-horse, surrounding the thing. One woman was at the lead. I'd take her for their boss, and I'll tell you, she was scary! She saw me gawking and she stared me down until I had to pretend I needed to retie my boot laces!" There was a murmur at that. Naieed's nature did not lend to her scaring easily. "There were five other women that I could see, the rest men. They're all brutish, strong looking, and clad in leather armor."

"If you saw thirteen, then that means two were either in the wagon or elsewhere in town already," I said thoughtfully.

Francine turned her sharp gaze on me. "How do you figure?"

Mother spoke for me, seemingly pleased to have a bit of news to share. "We saw the roster as we came in this morning. There were fifteen new names. Willy says the leader is called Aedith."

The group next to ours had picked up on this information, and I heard it slowly spiral out to the rest of the men and women. Little echoes of our words came back to my ears, not always entirely correct. I smiled. You couldn't beat the small-town rumor mill for its efficiency.

"All right," I braced my hands on my knees to stand, "I have to go. I've got Hale waiting."

"Oh no! Stay!" Naieed protested. "We've barely had the time to talk."

"You can always come with me to the gate, but I have no washing to do," I told her.

She sighed gustily, and addressed Claire, her lower lip jutted out. "Will you watch my laundry? I promise not to tease you for two days if you do."

Claire rolled her eyes. "Don't make promises you can't keep, Naieed, but do go. It will make it so much more peaceful here."

"Oh, I am wounded! You can't mean that. After all we've been through!" Naieed clutched at her heart and threw her body against Claire's, who laughed and shoved at her.

"*Go!* Maybe while you're walking you'll catch more of the newcomers, and if you do, I want to be the first to hear about it."

"No, I do!" Beth shot her hand up.

"You'll both hear it at the same time, same as the rest of us," Gladys said, and she and Mother shared an exasperated look that screamed, *Kids, what can you do?*

"Let's go." I tugged my friend to her feet, and together we left the steamy circle, our arms linked. When we were out of earshot a glance at her reaffirmed my suspicions. "You've done your hair up." I giggled as she ducked her head. Her long hair, a brown so dark that it was almost black, smelled of rose oil and it was braided and looped into an intricate bun at the back of her head.

"I have. I thought the occasion called for it." She gave her russet colored skirts a quick twitch with her free hand.

"What occasion? They're only mercenaries, and they're not staying."

She shrugged, smoothing the front of her dress with her free hand. "That doesn't mean they won't want to enjoy a little bit of the local culture while they're here."

I rolled my eyes. "Nai, don't you know by now that I have my heart set on you marrying my brother?"

Nai put a finger to her lips and hummed thoughtfully. "Michael? I think I've better luck getting a mercenary to stay in this place than your brother." My smile fell, and I let our arms fall apart. "Oh, Taryn, has he finally told you lot that he's going?" She stopped walking, pulled me to the side of the road. Grabbing my hands to stop me, she searched my face earnestly.

"He told *you?*" I tried to pull my hands back, but she held on firmly.

"No!" She wrinkled her nose. "Only," she paused again and I cleared my throat with some impatience. She obliged in a rush. "You know how I'm so good at being in the right place at the right time. I was helping in the pub when he met with that creepy character who rolled through a few months ago. I was refilling Fred's tankard behind them when I heard him make the offer. It was all hushed tones. Michael turned around and saw me eavesdropping and he made me swear not to tell." She bit her lip. "Please don't be mad."

I tugged at my hands again and this time she let go. I rubbed my itchy nose. "So, the man was creepy?"

Seeing I wasn't upset with her, Nai's pinched features relaxed marginally. "He was completely sinister, but it was because he was old, you know, bearded and hooded, I think. He tipped fine, and it's not like he killed anybody." We started walking again.

"Do you know anything else about him?"

She shook her head. "No, I'm sorry. It was spring and we were busy with travelers. I didn't even get his name. Hey!" We were at the corner by the butcher and instead of turning left she spun me right. "Want to see if there's any of the mercenaries at the inn now?"

I moaned. "Nai, I have to get back to the house, to help Father scent-ward."

"Not for another three hours or so! I *know* your schedule. So, we pop in, and if someone is there, we buy a round and then you leave when it's over."

She was already dragging me in the direction of the inn, and I wasn't fighting her hard. I was curious who would be skulking the lands around the pasture. I wanted to know if they were as fierce as everyone was saying. Besides, it was past breakfast, and not quite lunch, so it was unlikely that they would be eating at the inn. It would also have set a fairly bad precedent if they were drinking, so I couldn't imagine they would be doing *that*. In fact, it was doubtful that they would be present at the inn at all.

10

We wound our way down the street, our boots crunching on the dirt and rock road. Our conversation ranged from who Nai had seen that morning to what it was like for me, living and working so close to the forest right now—Nai lived inside the town, a solid wall between her and true deep forest. Usually the idea of being trapped behind the walls each night was not something that I envied. Yet, those drawbacks didn't seem so bad with the recent gryphon attacks.

When the inn came into view our talk stalled and we glanced at each other. Children who were still going to daily lessons were forbidden from going to the pub on their own—the rule was meant to keep youths focused on their studies, rather than on socializing. Or perhaps the owners didn't want the messes that children tended to leave. Either way, Nai and I had been allowed on our own inside The Black Gryphon, since we had turned fifteen a few years ago, but going without our families was still so rare that it had yet to lose its charm.

The inn was modest compared to one which might have been found in a city, but it was a large building for our town. Nai's mother ran an eating establishment in town called Sweetlings, but it was much smaller in both menu and size. If a person wanted to hear news from out of town or host a large gathering, The Black Gryphon was the place to go. It was two stories, with small staff quarters on the first floor situated next to the stables that protruded out the back side. The outer walls were white and received a fresh staining at the end of every winter, so the deep walnut of the whirling detail work on the carved wood stood out crisply in the morning light.

The front desk, where a person could check in to stay upstairs, also served as where locals could request an eating table. As Nai and I came inside the bell attached to the door jingled cheerily and the woman posted there came plainly into view. Maude was sound asleep and snoring. At the noise of our entrance she bolted upright and wrested herself from her chair with some difficulty. With great suspicion, she squinted blearily in our direction.

Maude was the sister of the inn keeper. Old, and more than a bit crotchety, she was the kind of woman whom the young children in town lived to play pranks on. I never had, but I had heard stories. I didn't know that I'd have her manning the front door if this place was mine, I thought as she glared at us over her spectacles.

"Are you ladies here to eat, or do you need a room?" she asked imperiously.

My chin jutted forward in automatic irritation, but Nai elbowed me squarely in the ribs before I could say anything.

"Maude, you look wonderful this morning. Have you been getting extra rest?"

Maude's gaze darted to the chair she had been dozing in and then back at Nai's sweet smile. "We're serving lunch. I'll show you two to a table."

"That would be great."

Nai and I followed Maude out into the dining room. It branched off from the front entryway and was filled with several long tables, as well as a few small round ones tucked into the corners. A few of the smaller tables held patrons and as we walked by those, people pointedly avoided looking at the largest table. There sat the hunting party, my father and Nai's father Anwar were included, as well as three strangers. None of them took their attention away from their conference as we entered.

Maude sat us a fair distance away from the hunters, at the leftmost side of the room. The small table was as near to the fire as a table could be. Even in the middle of winter the low ceilings confined the heat so well that no table could be within five feet of it.

"We've mutton and beans for lunch, or I'm sure there's still eggs and toast from breakfast if you like it." Maude spoke through a smile that looked like it hurt.

Nai waved her off. "Give us a moment, please?"

"As you like."

If looks could have killed, we would have been stone dead. I ducked my head to focus on the table, tucking my lips under my teeth to contain my grin until Maude had stomped back to the front room.

"She is going to spit straight into your mutton!" I hissed when she had gone.

"She won't," Nai said dismissively. "She's going back to bed, and we'll probably have Thomas coming out to serve us. He'll be nice. He likes you."

I shushed her and cast a covert glance over at the long table. A couple of the men from town had noticed our arrival, and gave us friendly nods of acknowledgment. Anwar and my father were bent over a map. It was spread open, facing the woman who they sat gathered around. On either side of her were two other newcomers.

Nai and Willy had been right about Aedith—as this must have been her. She was intimidating to say the least. Somewhere in her mid-thirties, she had the aura of someone who was used to being obeyed. The skin of her face was weathered and tan; a three-pronged scar ran from the right corner of her thin mouth across her cheek and disappeared down the collar of her leather jerkin. Her brown hair was wavy and coarse, and she wore it long and braided down her back. Small eyes moved quickly from the map to each man as he spoke. She did not speak, though her two men asked many questions.

Both of those men were younger than their leader, though by how much it was difficult to say. The impression I got was that they were in their late twenties, but like Aedith, they each bore lines and creases on their faces that bespoke a hard life. The man to my father's left was clearly tall—he sat higher than anyone else at the table. His thick muscles were covered in mahogany skin. He wore his curly hair cropped close to his skull, and when he spoke the words seemed to rumble from his belly.

The man on Anwar's right, seemed to hail from the Spiral Islands to the south west. He had hooded eyes, and his hair, blacker than any I'd seen before, was caught back in a low ponytail at the nape of his neck. His comments were more sparing than the first man's and harder to catch.

Neither man had any obvious scarring on their faces, but the man closest to my father had a few elsewhere; they stood out starkly against the skin on his forearms. More talon marks, at about the same stage of healing as the woman's. Still pink, but no longer painful looking.

"That's the man who was driving the wagon," Naieed mouthed at me behind a hand which she pretended to rest her cheek on. She pointed to the man next to her father with a less than subtle finger.

I nodded my acknowledgment. "He is handsome," I mouthed back, though I didn't know that I would call him handsome. Impressive perhaps—both men were, but not handsome.

The kitchen was located through a small door behind their table. Constantly swinging open and shut when The Black Gryphon was busy, it was best to be avoided at all costs in the evenings unless you wanted a black eye. When it was flung open now, I watched with interest as the two men shifted ever so slightly so that they could see who had entered without ever seeming to take their focus from the conversation.

It had been Thomas. Not Claire's grandfather, but the innkeeper's son. He made his way to our table, a pitcher of water in one hand and a basket of bread in the other. When he caught my gaze, he smiled earnestly, and I smiled back. Thomas was a year my junior, and like many of the locals he wore his fair hair braided back in multiple strands. The tunic he wore was an unobtrusive faun that matched his leggings and boots.

Nai was giving me a knowing smile, clearly thinking I was looking him over. I had not had a chance to tell her that, nice boy though he was, Thomas was not my type. I had thought perhaps I'd change my mind, but now I was certain that I would not. In that moment, with Aedith and the other mercenaries in view behind him, something about him came across plain, in an unpleasant way which I had never before experienced.

"Hey, you two, don't usually see you this time of day." Thomas set his burdens down on the table. As the pitcher *thunked* my father looked our way and raised an eyebrow at me. Thomas swore. "Rats! I need to grab you two cups. I'll be right back!" He hustled back towards the kitchen, and Father beckoned me with a tilt of his head.

"Nai," I said, "I'm sure you'll be pleased to hear that I've been spotted."

"Is that so?"

Nai searched until her eyes found my father and then she gave him a big cheerful wave. I saw him shut his eyes for a brief moment as if to gather strength, and then he smiled thinly and nodded at her as well.

Anwar followed my father's look, and his expression was far less welcoming, but still Nai rose with me as I made my way towards them. She knew better than I did that her father's serious countenance masked a man who doted on his family.

The talk at the table slowed to a halt as we approached, and Aedith raised her eyebrows high. When she spoke, her gaze did not shift from the map, which seemed to include ours and Glenn's lands. "Is there a reason that you have stopped explaining the last kill, Master Anwar?" Her voice was higher than I would have expected, with the faintest rasp.

"My apologies. May I introduce my daughter, Taryn?" my father started.

"And my daughter, Naieed," Anwar added.

The weight of the rest of the table looking at us was nothing compared to when Aedith turned and fixed us in her stare. I felt about two inches tall, and I shifted, waiting for Nai to say something clever. When she didn't, I glanced at her and was nearly floored. She was studying the ground, looking for all intents and purposes like a child that had been caught spying on something she shouldn't.

"It's nice to meet you ma'am," I squeaked out. Emboldened by hearing my own voice I managed to continue. "Is it all right if we sit and listen to what's happening?"

"I'm not in the habit of feeding the gossip farm," Aedith said crisply, "and I've doubts that what we are discussing here would be deemed suitable for your ears regardless."

My cheeks warmed at this rebuke, but Father's expression told me he didn't necessarily disapprove of me asking, and I managed to push on. "Please, I work the same fields that Glenn and my father do. I probably helped to birth the sheep that was lost. I'd like to know what your plan is."

The stranger at Anwar's right chuckled throatily. "Let her stay, Aedith. There can be no harm if they are quiet and their fathers do not mind." He smiled at me, his wide nostrils flaring with amusement. I mustered up a grateful smile for him in return.

Aedith looked at him skeptically, and then shut her eyes and shook her head as if to clear it. "Fathers of these girls, do you mind if they join the table?" Our fathers both responded in the negative. "Then, I honestly could not give two turns beneath the dirt. Sit or don't, whichever you please, but be quiet either way. If you need anything from me," as we hurried to follow her orders, she jerked a thumb first left and then right. "These are Dai, and Kaleb. You talk to them. They're my seconds."

We nodded without speaking, eyes huge in our faces. Thomas returned and deftly noticed the change of seating. As the topic of the slaughter resumed, he moved our bread and glassware to our new places. Though he smiled at me, he didn't dare say another word while the hunters were speaking. The bread basket at this table had been emptied. My guess was it had been for a long time, as our new dining companions reached blindly for our pieces as they listened. We had to move quickly or risk going without, filling our glasses with water after we had served ourselves.

We were at the end of the table, farthest from the fire now, not to mention Aedith, but it allowed me a better view of who was there. Counter-clockwise from Aedith there was Anwar, Dai, Glenn, Martin, Fred, Robert, Daniel, who was a farmer with pigs, as well as his son Corey, then Kaleb and my father. I wondered if Laura and Willy knew about this meeting, but I had to assume that Father would have told him on his way in, if they hadn't been the ones to send for him to start with.

"Now, from what I understand, all of the animals were killed in a fairly similar way." Aedith steepled her finger in front of her mouth. "Could you tell me about that, Glenn?"

Glenn started. "I'd have thought Martin would have told you

all about that," he stuttered as he spoke, and he quailed under Aedith's stern gaze. "Yes. It is best I tell it. You see, my cows, when I got to them, they were on the ground. They had—they had been laid out on their backs and their ribs had been cracked apart. It was like the gryphon started eating and then moved on to the next one. The same went for the sheep and the deer."

"But in each instance the animals were grouped together."

Dai hummed. "It is strange. In the forest it makes sense, if that clearing were a den where the beast was dragging each prey back to before feasting. Out in the open field..."

"It's not how they operate," Aedith agreed. "It would have had to have killed them all at once and then fed on each one in turn. Or else it killed one then chased down the next, brought it back and so on and so forth. Are the bodies still there for us to inspect?"

"Certainly not!" Glenn sputtered.

Aedith could raise one eyebrow. That was a skill I wanted. "Well where have you buried them? Or where were they killed? I'd like to look at that land." Kaleb shook his head. Something about the way his lips pulled down in the corners bespoke amusement at her mistake. Aedith redirected her glare to him. "Yes, you have something so say?"

"He'll have burned them and the land they were killed on. Nophgrin is a town that burn things that are unlucky. Yes?" Kaleb looked around for confirmation.

"Well don't say it like we're strange for it," Fred muttered.

"He's right though," Robert said. "Otherwise there's no telling what kind of evils something like that will attract."

"It is the belief that like attracts like, but it can be purged and cleansed by fire," Anwar agreed. He knew and abided by Nophgrin's ways as well as anyone, even if he had been raised with the different customs of the lands to the south.

"It is unlucky for us that you did not have the forethought to save something we could have used to gain a better picture of the situation. Tell me, are the sheep and deer also ashes?" The hunting party exchanged guilty looks and Aedith rested her head in her hands. When she spoke again, her slow speech was too controlled to be confused as anything but incensed. "All right. In the future, if before this is over another animal is found—your pig for example, Daniel. I must kindly ask you not to burn it or the land it is found on before I get a look."

The men, save Anwar, grumbled unhappily. It was one thing to call in a stranger to help with the gryphons. It was another thing entirely for those strangers to deny the rituals that kept us safe year-round.

I looked at Nai through the corner of my eye. She was already doing the same to me. Her lips pressed tight, her eyes crescents. It wasn't surprising that she thought this was funny. I rolled my eyes away from her and up to the window. The sun was climbing higher. Though it seemed we would not be scent warding today, I knew that I would still have to leave soon if I wanted to reach my watch in good time.

Nai seemed to sense my thought and reached under the table to grab my arm. She shook her head in an almost invisible sign to stay a little longer. I leaned back into my chair with a sigh that might have been permissible if the chair hadn't creaked in chorus with it. Aedith was on me in a flash.

"Do you also have something to say against not burning

evidence young—Taryn, was it?"

I sat up straight again. My palms felt sweaty. "No ma'am."

"Are you saying you think we shouldn't ward off the gods-cursed luck?" Glenn protested. "I'm not going to invite bad luck into my home if another of my cows gets killed."

"Begging your pardon Glenn, but I'd think," I said slowly, to my own surprise, "that if another one of your cows gets killed, then bad luck will already have come, and proved burning was pointless."

Nai let out a bark of laughter, and Glenn turned white with fury. The rest of the table erupted with protests much on the same train as Glenn's. My shoulders shot to my ears as I realized what I had said.

My father said nothing, nor did Anwar. They were quieter men, content to keep their peace until everyone was calm. It was why they got along. Both sat with their arms crossed and watched, like the men that Aedith had brought. I realized with some surprise that this similarity between our fathers and the mercenaries pleased me.

"Enough!" Aedith bellowed when she had had her fill of the bickering. Silence fell almost instantly, though no one appeared happy to bite their tongues. "You may burn whatever you like. I couldn't give *three* turns beneath the dirt. All I'm asking is a chance to look at them before you do! Gods above and below—be easy! They won't be on your land for more than the time it takes me to ride to them, and that's only if we don't catch this gryphon before it strikes again. Where is the staff? I need food and tea if I'm going to be yelling all afternoon. Let us take a moment. Go relieve yourselves if you have to, and someone go tell the guardsmen what we're about."

Glenn gestured to Martin, who rose reluctantly to his feet. He glanced at Nai and me, and I saw him mutter some kind of protest. I guessed he was saying one of us should go. However, Glenn's dark expression and low response sent him speeding out the door.

Thomas must have been hovering at the kitchen door because his appearance quickly followed Aedith's inquiry. He brought a pitcher of water and refilled everyone's cups before he took orders. Most at the table, including the mercenary men, wanted the mutton with some of the black tea which The Black Gryphon got in a few times a year. Father and Anwar stuck to their lemon balm tea.

When Thomas promised Aedith he would return with tea, he spoke to his shoes rather than her stern face. "Do you take anything with it?"

Aedith rubbed her forehead. "Heaps of honey." When he turned to leave she called after him. "Bees ought to find it a little sweet lad!" Dai chuckled and when she looked up she caught my open-mouthed stare. A wry smile ghosted across her lips. "My throat gets sore from all the yelling."

I shut my mouth with an audible click of teeth, and she turned back to speak with Dai and Anwar. I could barely take my eyes off her even as Nai addressed me.

"She is something else, isn't she? I mean, we have Laura, but even the guard are usually men, aren't they? She's got almost half her group as ladies." Nai took a sip of water and when she had swallowed, we bent our heads together so that we could speak more quietly, our lips barely moving.

"Even of the guards that are women, most don't get to be leaders. Looking at her I can't imagine why. Do you see her muscles?"

They weren't hard to see. Like her companions, all but her forearms were covered, but her clothes could not hide bulk akin to what the blacksmith had—and I would have bet serious coin that she knew how to use it better than he did. I took a gulp of my own water.

"Plus, she's not as mean as she seems, I think," Nai said, and I snorted. A few men glanced over but clearly decided we didn't warrant more attention as they immediately went back to their conversations.

"How do you figure that?"

"Well, I don't mean she couldn't make a boar turn tail and run, but look at the corners of her eyes and her lips? Those wrinkles mean she smiles and laughs a lot. You can also see it in the way her seconds speak to her. They're not afraid to rib on her."

I nodded thoughtfully. I hadn't thought to look for those things, but Nai was right. She had deep laughter lines. Watching Aedith hold a hand up to stop Daniel from talking over her, I felt a stirring of jealousy. "She's not afraid of telling this lot to shut up either. I like that."

"You basically told Glenn to shut it," Nai pointed out. "His face was priceless. I can't believe you did that."

I fiddled with my braid. "I just didn't want the mercenaries to think that we're all insensible. I really need to go now."

Nai ignored the last comment. "Michael may care what strangers think, but you don't. You're a lifer for this place. What do you care what they think of us? Our ways work fine, and it's not like they honestly care either way. They want to get the job done and leave, like you said."

Usually I liked being described as someone solidly planted in this town. It made me feel as though I was getting things right. This time though, it did not make me feel light—instead it was as though a rock sat in my gut. I twisted my mouth, considering this.

"I don't know. Maybe they'll think they can cheat us." Thomas came out of the kitchen, his little sister trailing after him, both loaded with plates of steaming food. I pushed away from the table. "I do need to leave now. I'm going to say goodbye to my father."

Nai blew a strand of hair out of her face. "Oh fine. I suppose I won't stay much longer either. I'm sure Claire will have left my clothes out to be snatched up for gryphon nests by now. I'll let you know if anything else gets said before I leave though."

"Thanks." I hugged her from behind and moved around the table to my father. I waited to speak until a natural lull in the talk came as Thomas served the four at the front of the table. "I'm off to relieve Michael. Do you want me to have him come here?"

Father shook his head. "We should be wrapping things up by the time he would arrive." He glanced at Aedith for confirmation and she nodded. Thomas had not brought out the cutlery yet, and she was using her fingers to peel off a piece of mutton from the bone. When she stuck a piece in her mouth, she murmured in approval. Father gave me a look that forbade me from saying anything. As if I would have. "You can tell him that I'll be riding with your mother home though, so he's free of that duty."

"Mother agreed we could have dinner in town tonight." I glanced at the mercenaries then back at Father meaningfully.

"All right, duly noted. We won't have time to do scent warding today, but I'll see you this evening." He twisted awkwardly to give me a one-armed hug over the back of the chair.

I passed Maude on my way out. As Nai had guessed, she was dozing in her chair by the small stove that warmed the antechamber. I smiled, rolling my eyes, and pushed out the door into the overcast street. The bell tinkled behind me, and I heard her snort and the chair scrape as she stood to attention.

11

The sight that I was met with outside brought me up short. A girl, who couldn't have been much older than myself, leaned against the molding of the alcove that surrounded the front door. What was surprising was the striking resemblance she bore to the mercenary captain. When she felt the draft of the door opening she looked up sharply, lower lip between her teeth, her dark eyes wide. The expression was the work of an instant, when she saw it was only me she relaxed and gave me a once over.

Not liking the smirk that twitched on her lips as she took in my plain clothes, I smoothed my right temple braid and returned the stare. She was dressed as the mercenaries: a finely made leather jerkin over a tight, undyed cotton shirt, the sleeves of which stopped at the elbows. On her legs and feet respectively were dark breeches and sturdy brown boots. A belt around her hips held a pouch and a dagger. Like Aedith, her hair was sable brown and thick. Unlike the older woman, this girl wore it loose and it curled slightly at the ends. She pushed it back away from her eyes now, and it immediately fell back once she removed her hand.

"Are they finished in there yet?" she demanded.

My smile was my best impression of Nai, as I stuck out a hand. "Good morning, I'm Taryn, and *you* are?"

She took my hand, in her gloved one and pumped it once. "Aella. Are they finished?"

"Can't you just go in and see for yourself?" I asked innocently.

Her scowl could have stripped the paint off the building at my back. After a moment, it lifted. She ran a hand through her hair and kept it at the back of her head. "I'm sorry. The group sent me to find out what's happening, but if I go inside when we've all been specifically asked to stay behind, Aedith will let me have it."

"Even if you weren't going to stay?"

"Aedith is big on rules, especially when it comes to her and me."

I squinted, and tilted my head. "Because you're related?" It had been a gamble, but she hesitated and then nodded. "Does she do the same with your father, or is he one of her seconds?" She didn't look like Dai or Kaleb, but one never knew.

When she glared, her mother shone through her face strongly. "I don't have a father, but if I did, yeah, he'd have the same regulations as me. Are they done in there?"

Belatedly, I realized I'd been rude. These mercenaries seemed candid and blunt, but that didn't mean I could ask about their personal lives.

"Yes—well, I mean, no," I hurriedly attempted to backtrack. "I'm sorry, what I mean to say is that they're pausing to eat midday. I apologize. I shouldn't have..." I trailed off, flustered by her unwavering stare.

She rolled her eyes, and let her hand fall back to her side. "It's fine. I'm not sore about it; townies always ask."

Wounded in spite of myself, but determined not to show it, I crossed my arms over my chest. "Townies?"

As I spoke, I moved so that I was no longer pinned between her and the door. I didn't like the trapped feeling of being in her shadow. Something about it made my heart race uncomfortably. The street around us was empty. Although, down towards the corner the butcher had come outside his door, arching backward slightly and yawning hugely.

"Yeah, you know, all you folks from the backwaters are always concerned about that sort of thing. I guess there isn't a whole lot else going on." She shrugged casually.

I sputtered. "I wasn't concerned. I was making idle conversation! Which, for the record, I didn't mean to offend you with, which I think you know, which means you are being deliberately unkind."

She could do the Aedith eyebrow quirk, and my stomach flipped. "Big words."

"Better that than a big mouth," I shot back.

Her jaw clenched and she shifted slightly so she was no longer leaning. We stared each other down and then... She laughed, hard, collapsing back against the wall. The tension eased all at once as I broke into nervous giggles as well.

"I'm sorry," she said, wiping her eyes with a delicate finger.

"Your face! What were you going to do—fight me?"

"If you swung first there was a chance I would have ducked, hit you hard, and run like mad," I said agreeably.

"So, you *are* scared of me little town bird." She raised her eyebrow and tilted her head with a devious look.

"Only in the most sensible way." I straightened my skirt with exaggerated stiffness, making my face prim. "You know, you being a seasoned warrior, and me being a very fast runner."

"I'd have had to let you get away with it. We're not actually supposed to stir up fights with the locals. Leastwise not until we're on our way out of town." She winked at me, and I glanced over my shoulder at the empty road, feeling tongue-tied and hoping I'd have a witty reply when I turned around. "I was defensive. I didn't mean it about the townies thing," she said when my reply took too long.

I turned back. "Isn't being defensive a tool of the trade?" I gestured to her outfit. "I can hardly blame you, can I?" That garnered another chuckle.

"Anyway, people from towns like these can be real asses, and it's best to scare them quiet before they can start in on me or my ma."

"Nophgrin's not like that though. I mean, you don't have to worry about people being unkind to you here. This is a nice place."

"So far as you know," she said dubiously. "They have to deal with you the rest of their lives; who's going to be mean to you?"

The door opened behind her, and she jerked around. It was Nai and she seemed to take in the situation swiftly before speaking. "I thought I heard you laughing out here, Taryn." At my quizzical look, she shrugged and made her face comically forlorn, "Father asked if I had finished the washing, and when I admitted that I had left it at the well there was nothing for him but for me to go back and retrieve our things. A mercenary is eating the rest of my lunch. Weren't you meant to be headed back to the field?"

My eyes darted to the sun which was making its steady way upwards. I pursed my lips. "I am, and likely I'll be late."

"That's fine, Michael is probably dying to cram in all the extra time he can with the sheep." Nai shrugged. "Hello to you." She gave Aella an appraising look.

Remembering my manners, I performed the necessary introductions. "Aella this is Naieed, my closest friend. Nai, this is Aella, daughter of Aedith."

Nai and Aella shook hands. "I can see that—you're like a spitting image of her. Is your father one of...?" she trailed off lamely as I shook my head in what I thought was a subtle manner and made my hands into an 'x' at my waist.

Aella gave me a wry smile, clearly having caught my signaling. I blushed, taking a half step backward. "He's from some town in the west where my mother lived for a few years. Out on the coast."

"Isn't that interesting?" Nai smiled warmly as they clasped hands, and though Aella seemed to look for it, there was no trace of sarcasm in her voice.

The two were striking side by side. Both of them had darker hair and skin than was common this far north, and both were taller than me. However, where Aella's skin was a ruddy olive like her mother's, the tone of Nai's was slightly warmer and darker. Aella's nose was also sharper and straighter than Nai's, sloping only slightly and ending in a point. Her lips were thinner, and her hair was a shade lighter than Nai's, and it curled a little more. My friend also had a half a head of height on the new girl, and she was built leaner. Aella had the body of someone who worked hard, with strong legs and thick arms. Nai prided herself on her svelte figure, choosing to wear scoop necked dresses that called attention to her long neck and smooth skin. These were the kind of girls that got stares—*I* was staring. I blinked and looked away. At least it seemed to have lasted a short enough time that they hadn't noticed.

"Excuse me." I dipped lightly, not quite a curtsy. "I really will have to run if I'm to make it before my brother is purple in the face. Aella, it was nice to meet you and your mother. I hope we'll see you all for dinner. My family and I will be at the inn tonight." Aella returned the sentiment, and I set off down the street at a brisk pace that was just short of a trot.

"Your mother's scarier than a gryphon. Nice to meet you though," Nai said to Aella, then she ran to catch up with me. "Taryn, wait up!"

I glanced behind me. "I can't stop. Catch up."

She did so quickly; her legs were longer than mine. As I pumped my arms and puffed, she made the speed appear easy. "So that's the unaccounted for fifteenth member. Aedith has a daughter," Nai mused. "She seems as tough as the rest of them."

"Plus, she's gorgeous," I said. "She has a good sense of humor too, like you guessed her mom does. I thought she was going to slug me and then we were just laughing."

"Why was she going to slug you?" Nai's voice was appalled. "Violent group, aren't they?"

"What, mercenaries?" I deadpanned. When she didn't laugh I sighed. "No, it was my fault. She's sensitive about her father and I blundered right into it. That's why I waved you off the subject."

She made a noise of understanding. "I bet she gets bothered for it all the time. If they were married at all—"

"I'm sure they were!" I protested, scandalized.

Nai continued as though she hadn't heard, "Mother and Father say that in other places in the country divorce is more frowned upon than it is here. Some places it's not even allowed."

I shook my head and my braid swung, brushing softly against my back. "Why? You can't stay with someone who does your head in. That's not good for anyone involved. Look at Glenn and Gladys. I think she was a few months away from setting the barn on fire, living with that man."

Nai shrugged. "There's no accounting for people, but I imagine she has gotten to see all types in her travels. Aedith didn't seem to know about us burning to keep off bad spirits, and that's as wild to me as anything. They layover only a few towns west of here."

"True enough. Maybe it never came up. It's not as though we've had a big burning here since before I was born, and it's not exactly good conversation." We were nearing the gate and Hale was already pricking her ears at me. "I wonder what they do in other places for bad luck. Do they let it do what it wants?"

"Back where Mother and Father are from some people practice as we do. Still, they say their home city was so big and not everyone believed in it, so it wasn't a city or-or," she groped for the word, "*ordinance*. Criminals got burned sometimes still, but the rules were a little different. It was not about the luck exactly."

"I can't imagine such a place."

"You're the one who sassed Glenn about burning the cows."

"It wasn't about the cows!" I shook my head emphatically.

"Well what does that mean?"

I was appalled at the idea that someone could think I *didn't* believe in burning away ill luck. "We didn't know there were going to be more attacks at that point, nor that we'd be calling in mercenaries. I know he *had* to burn the cows, especially since they were on his pasture, and near our own. All I meant was that now that the mercenaries are here, he could wait to burn anything new. At least until they've all had a good look at it."

Nai's face was thoughtful. "Glenn did know the mercenaries were coming though. He sent Martin after them right after his cows were killed, isn't that right?"

The sides of my lips turned down as I thought. "No, you're right. That's Glenn for you. Even when he panics rightly he does it wrong. Though, can you imagine leaving those bodies out as long as it took Aedith's group to get here? Gross."

We had reached the gate, and Willy smiled out his booth at us. "Ladies. Miss Taryn you've had a bit of a late start, haven't you?"

"Yes, we were listening in on the hunting party. Nai will have to tell you all about it though. I have to leave in a rush."

"If she wouldn't mind?"

"No, not at all. I imagine they'll tell you a great deal more when you meet up with them, but it can't hurt to know the general idea, now can it?" Nai sidled up to the booth, eager to share her news with the guard.

"No, it cannot Miss Naieed. Ride safely Miss Taryn!"

12

Normally if I was late I would ride Hale at a gallop and get to my destination with time to spare. Today however, Michael's warning kept sounding in my head. The woods looked dark, and with the gray skies casting no extra light into their depths, I couldn't bring myself to put Hale to more than a trot.

Up in the boughs of the trees at the edge of town were two separate flocks of lesser gryphons: sparrow types and grackle types. They had camped out on either side of the road where standing puddles of water provided good bathing pools. I patted Hale's neck and murmured praise as she walked rigidly but stolidly towards them. They seemed to be at leisure. A few were playing on the ground by the path, pouncing and shrieking at one another. As we neared, one rolled onto its back. Acting as though a hated enemy had dropped from above, it batted at a falling leaf with quick paws. I giggled and felt the uneasiness in me lift.

We were almost past the flock when a lesser gryphon with the head of a sparrow and a body all in brown galloped towards Hale's hooves, intent on a gryphon on the opposite side of us. As I yelled a curse at it, the grackle gryphon it had been in pursuit of flared its wings and clawed at the air. Whipping around, the first gryphon darted back the way it had come, making a trilling noise. Clearly the little monster was tickled with itself.

Unfortunately, it had not reversed its course soon enough. Panic stricken, Hale let out a squeal. At the noise, every one of the gryphons scattered into the bushes, many contrarily crossing the road to do so. Hale veered from side to side, her eyes rolling backward as she tried to avoid the beasts. I pulled hard at the reins, trying to regain control. By the time I had her calm again, there were no gryphons in view to shout at. I let out a shaky breath.

"I'm so sorry Hale," I murmured, truly feeling it, as I stroked her sweat-soaked neck. "I wonder if Father knows of any way to help you with this," I mused aloud.

Hale let out a deep whicker. Her sides were heaving with labored breath, and I felt pricks of real concern. If her fear got much worse, she would become dangerous to ride in the winter and fall—not that I blamed her. Still, I could have fallen. In the winter, I probably would have fallen

I had to stop in at the house to grab my supplies, so by the time we arrived at the field I was more than a few minutes late. Michael was up and waiting for me. Cherub was already loaded, and he was standing with her, his eyes intent on where I'd come in from. He mounted as soon as he saw me.

"I'm so sorry," I said, riding up to meet him. "I lost track of time. I was listening to the mercenaries and the hunters talk in town."

"It's fine. I was honestly just worried." Michael reached across the gap between us to grip my hand. "Maybe we need to train the dogs to carry notes so we can let each other know we haven't been eaten."

I laughed, surprised, but pleased to find he wasn't mad at me. "Well, here I am, definitely not eaten, only tardy and sorry. Can I trust you'll get home without being eaten as well?"

"As soon as I pick up Mother," he agreed.

"Oh, no you don't have to do that." I remembered. "Father says he'll take Mother home when he's done at the meeting, and then we're all going back into town tonight for supper."

Looking up through his bangs he made lips like a duck, and nodded appreciatively. "That frees up the whole afternoon for me."

"You can work on Mother's gift."

His expression was blank for a moment, and I prompted him with an incredulous stare. He shook his head, as if to clear it. "Her birthday! Yes, it's coming up fast."

"What is it that you're making for her?" I asked.

"It's a surprise." He tried to wink, but it looked awkward. "All right, you've kept me in the field long enough. I'm going home, sister. Be safe."

"You as well!"

When he had been gone not ten minutes the rain started again. This wasn't pleasant by any means, but the day father checked for markings around the field he had also brought the supplies to make a collapsible shelter in anticipation of the autumn rains. Michael had set it up while Father worked. The shelter consisted of two large pieces of canvas, sewn together and oiled, then stretched tightly over four poles. Beneath this was a small wooden platform, only big enough to sit cross-legged on. The uncomfortableness of this seating assured that I was continually getting up to stretch over the course of the next several hours. The shelter wasn't tall enough to accommodate me standing fully. Most of the time I'd straddle the wood, lean over with my hands on my knees, then straighten my legs, and arch my back.

The ponies had a similar structure that was stretched over a taller branch on the tree. Hale glared at me disapprovingly from under it; she'd have much rather have been in her stall where it was warm and dry. Brooks lay next to me on the driest patch of dirt the shelter provided. Benjie had been too exhausted to join us for a fifth day in a row and was being given a break. If he could have made the walk out to the field, he wouldn't have had much to do. The sheep were inactive and sulky from a week's worth of rain. Their skittishness from the first few days after the attack had also vanished, and I thought maybe the rain was keeping any nasty smells tamped to the earth.

It wasn't a bad shift. For all it rained and the wind blew hard against me, I was nicely bundled up under my wool blanket. I spent a lot of the time thinking about the mercenaries, specifically Aella who seemed to be the only one of them who was close to my own age.

She was so different from the other young women in town— we had our share of prickly people, but there was something about her that I couldn't put my finger on. It made me not mind her defensiveness. I wanted to talk with her more, actually. Would she and the rest of her company come to the inn for supper or would they take their meals privately? From what I had seen of their group, I liked them. Dai, Kaleb, and even Aella had seemed to be good-humored. Though Aedith had certainly owned her formidable presence, she and her daughter had made an impression on me, and I wanted to know more about them.

They would probably have good stories to tell, and they'd be the sort I'd like. They would know if raiders were crossing the border more often to the east, and what new illnesses were important to keep an eye out for. They would also have tales to tell of different lands and older stories about the magical beasts within them. I coveted those above all others.

It was said that hundreds of years ago magical beasts had not existed. Not anywhere. Humans had the run of the world, unmatched by any animal. Then, a guild of the greatest mages of the time had decided to test their magical strength, and together they created a handful of monsters— amalgams, Michael had called them, of creatures from land, air, and sea. Their reasons were wildly speculated upon, but most people thought they wanted familiars.

A normal animal, made into a familiar could be drawn upon when a mage was in need of extra strength. It made sense that people concerned with power would wish to create stores of extra strength greater than any that could be found in normal animals. The thing was, no one knew *how* they had managed to do such a thing.

Being one of the largest countries on this side of the Western Sea, Somerlarth had once been the home of enormous libraries.

In those buildings, there had been great scrolls and volumes, detailing any magical theory Michael might have wished to read about, or any story that I could have hoped to read about gryphons, dragons and the like. Those archives were now little more than overgrown ruins.

Legend had it that the gods saw the creation of the new animals as blasphemy and struck every mage in the guild stone dead. It didn't end there though. As punishment for their hubris, and as a warning to all mankind, they didn't just let those creations live, they caused them to thrive and multiply. They shielded their adopted children from the effects of most magics, and then? They cast them throughout all the lands to wreak devastation.

No one really knew the truth of it. We didn't even know when exactly they had first begun to show up. When King Lionel's great great grandfather, King Richard, road his armies across the seven kingdoms in what would later be called The Great Burning he had, well, burnt a great number of old libraries and artifacts. Somewhere amidst the smoke and flames, the truth of the origin of gryphons, phoenixes, dragons, and the rest was lost. These days most of the knowledge and stories we had from those times were reduced to what was passed from town to town through people like mercenaries and bards.

Michael was not nearly so infatuated with what he called "old wives tales." He wanted to know *how* the creatures were put together, not why. Which was folly, in my opinion. Knowing however a bird and a cat came together to form a gryphon would not stop it from stealing a sheep.

He also liked to hear about new imports and magical

inventions. I could understand that, but whatever innovation swept the kingdom, nothing of that nature reached us until a solid twelve months after the fact. Even then, pleasant indulgences, such as chocolate, or charms to heat bath water, were a rarity.

"I might move to the capital if I could get chocolate every day," I admitted to my listener Brooks. His tail thumped the ground a few times in agreement.

The exciting stories were the battles that made the hair on my arms stand on end. Not the parts Michael liked, such as learning that Prince What's-his-face had been usurped by His Highness So-and-so of the kingdom next door, in order to take part of his kingdom. I'd rather learn about the daring heroes who served them—the ones who triumphed against all odds. Who cared who was in charge? It all amounted to much of the same for people like us, as far as I could tell. I liked the ordinary people, who did extraordinary things for those for whom they cared for the most.

When I finally made it home that evening my parents and Michael were ready and waiting to head to town. I had left a little early so that we wouldn't be reaching the inn too late. Even so, the sun was barely hovering over the crowns of the trees by the time I had washed and pulled on something a little nicer than field clothes.

Over a cream colored, long sleeved shift that hit at my knees, I had on a dress that had once been a vibrant cornflower blue, but had faded after many washes. Despite its altered state, it was my favorite dress. The fabric was soft and the full skirt reached my ankles and pleated prettily. It was one of the few things in my wardrobe that made me feel delicate and feminine. I'd paired it with my usual boots—it was muddy outside after all, but I thought it still looked all right.

The dress covered broad shoulders, a long torso, and strong thick legs— I was no lithe beauty like Nai. Pretty, yes; strong, yes. I could admit to being that, but I was in many ways a female form of Michael. Dry skin from being out in the weather. Cupids bow lips centered on a strong jaw. Gray-green eyes set under thick dark eyebrows. Where these things might make Michael ruggedly handsome, they sort of just made me look rough. I liked my sturdy physique, but with a friend like Nai who was diligent about her appearance it was easy to note where I lacked.

Remembering the onceover Aella had given me earlier, I moved into my parent's room to take a quick look in the mirror. It wasn't that I cared what she thought, but I made a face at what I saw. My hair was one of the few things about my appearance that I could truly say I loved, and it was a windswept mess. With the little time I had, I rebraided it, smoothing the flyways and twisting the braids anew with deft fingers. I used a small dab of sunflower oil from the slender jar on my mother's dresser to make everything sit right. The scent of it draped around me pleasantly. Mother wore the oil often and the smell was like carrying a piece of her around on my shoulders.

"Taryn, are you ready?" she called from the kitchen. "We're heading to the barn."

"Coming!" I yelled back. Carefully I replaced the items I had borrowed back where I had found them on my parents' dresser, and with a last nervous glance at my appearance, I darted back down the hallway.

My family was filing out the front door, and I quick-stepped to keep up with them. I noted with some amusement that Michael had brought his crook, but I checked my urge to tease him. If he thought he could hold off a gryphon with it, then who was I to stop him? After all, I had heard Father muttering that he was bringing his crossbow, and at least Michael wouldn't have to check his "weapon" at the gate.

Mother rode with Father on Tess, who was more than strong enough to bare the load of both of them, whilst Michael and I both road our own ponies. We might have walked to town and still made fine enough time, but it was simpler to ride. Getting to town in a timely fashion meant we would not have to worry about having to stand to eat, or coming home in the dark and wet. As it was, it ended up being lucky that we got in as early as we did. In the summer months when the light stayed longer, Willy kept the gate open later, but with the dark of fall, he locked his town up tight when he could no longer see a mile down the road. He was closing his booth when we arrived, and his next step was to lock the gate.

"Raynard and kin!" he greeted us. "You're just in time. I was about to lock up."

"Will we be able to go home this evening if we come in?" Mother asked teasingly.

Willy bobbed his head. "Yes ma'am. I'll be back out here for another hour or so after I take my supper, then we'll shut down for good for night."

It was protocol more than necessity that drove Willy's routine. While we still saw the occasional party of bandits, the days of yearly raiders were several decades behind us, along with the previous rulers of Somerlarth, King Theron and Queen

Mary. Opinion was always split when it came to the old king and his wife. They were the first monarchs to invest in the education of their common subjects, not just the wealthy ones. They were also the first rulers of Somerlarth in centuries who reigned in total peace. However, that meant that they let a lot of slights and inconveniences go—which was to say they let raiders do what they pleased, so long as they didn't make *too* much of a fuss.

When they joined The Dark Lady—the goddess of death—in her court, too early, some had said, their son Lionel had come to power. His first act as king was creating a taskforce—a group of warriors and mages who patrolled our borders. They stamped out the overreaching tendrils of our neighbors to the north and the east.

King Lionel was also the one to increase the number of guards deployed throughout his kingdom. It was directly because of him that we had Willy. He had won the hearts of his people with his dedication to their safety. Though, if you asked some people, he might have been sick of losing his revenue to thieves, and he didn't concern himself nearly enough with making sure that education continued to flourish.

I tilted my head, squinting in the dusk to get a better look at Willy. As before, his shoulders drooped and now I detected the strain in his smile and the faint purple thumbprints under his eyes. Between his new babe and this mad gryphon nonsense, I wondered if he would be writing for a substitute from the capital. Maybe he already had. If Father were in his place, Mother would have already demanded he take time to raise his child, and leave the bulk of this mess to someone younger. I raised my eyebrows at the thought. What would the town be without Willy there to greet us at the gate?

We dismounted and walked our mounts in past him to tie up at the inner horse post as Father signed us all in. A few other horses and ponies were already strung there. I noted Glenn's mount, as well as Daniel's and a few other farmers who lived outside the town's walls. Together, the five of us walked to The Black Gryphon. Under the remaining light of the sun, which trailed weakly over the slanted roofs, and the slightly stronger light of the torches lit on each street corner, I saw Beth with her parents and a few others I recognized. Thunder rumbled off in the distance, promising more rain. I looked apprehensively at the sky. Without a word, we quickened our pace.

Inside The Black Gryphon, a harassed looking Maude directed us to the long table by the far wall which the hunting party had occupied earlier in the day. Now that table, as well as the majority of the other tables, were all but filled. Great hulking men and women were clustered at the center long table, and I recognized Aella, Aedith, Dai, and Kaleb amongst them. They were laughing with their neighbors as well as drinking and eating with gusto.

The sound of foreign accents laced the familiar speech of what was known in mountains. Places like our own village, and it seemed the homes of many of the visiting warriors, spoke specific dialects. Because of that, it was important for anyone who was traveling to know a little bit of all the languages that ran throughout the land. Some of the mercenaries like Dai spoke the south-western way, quickly, gutturally, from their throat. A few had the slow cant of the midlands. Like most people in the country, it seemed the mercenaries could speak the common tongue—it was taught in schools along with simple mathematics, so that made sense. However, every so often there was a hitch as someone fumbled for a word. Only large cities relied on common tongue for day-to-day conversations, so all of us were rusty.

I made a mental note of who seemed to be from the midlands and vowed to steer clear of them. Midland accents drove me crazy. Those from the far north and deep south spoke very different languages, but we spoke them in the same way. Whether we were freezing in the snow or burning in the sun, we understood it was best to spit out our words and be on our way as quickly as possible. On the other hand, midland folk had no ken of weather rushing their speech, and they took *forever* to get to a point.

Willy's wife Nadia stood when she saw him. A timid but good-natured smile spread across her lips as she wove back and forth in order to be seen through the ever-shifting crowd. She was a small woman, younger than Willy by a decade. Though the years had been kind to her, she still carried a few white streaks through her light hair. Willy stooped to kiss her forehead when he reached her, and she curled her arms around his back in a brief embrace.

"Where's my daughter?" Willy asked.

"She's with my mother. I think you'll agree this would be a little much for her," was Nadia's tart reply. Despite her soft appearance, Nadia was like any woman born and raised in the wintery mountains—more than tough.

"Of course, my dear. How has the day been?"

We moved off, to give them time to catch up. Father took us towards Aedith. When he stood behind her, she turned to greet him. Though she was still clearly a woman to be reckoned with by point of her muscles, this evening she had relaxed. With cheeks flushed from wine, she beamed up at my father.

"Raynard!" She glanced at me, "And Taryn! How are you this evening? Lads, these are a few of the folks who live and work on the—on the lands we'll be hunting." This incurred a cheer, and I noticed with interest that none of the women seemed to take offense at being called lads.

"Aedith, this is my son Michael and my wife Wynifred." It would have been ungenerous to describe my father's tone as disapproving, but he was, in his own words, "a busy man," and not one to imbibe to the point of carelessness.

Aedith shook both of their hands. "It is wonderful to meet you. This is my daughter Aella. You lot!" She barked the last part abruptly, not giving me time to say that her daughter and I had already met. She gestured at the three women and Kaleb who were to her right. "Scoot down, will you?" When the two men on the other side of those four grumbled, she gave them a mean smile. "It won't kill you to go and make nice with the townspeople. You know as well as I do that this place is full because they want to get to know us." They hesitated a moment longer, and her next word was said in a tone that made my spine tense. "Move."

They gathered their plates and cups without another grumble and moved to the other long table where Willy was sitting. Introductions were made, and their voices carried none of the resentment I would have expected. When I checked I found them to be smiling and shaking hands as though making the rounds had been their intentions all along. Those at their new table amiably made room for the mercenaries to sit. Aella caught my eye and waggled her brows at me. I covered a smile.

"That was very kind Miss Aedith. You didn't need to go to such trouble," Mother said demurely, taking the seat next to the larger woman. Father took the seat next to her, then me and then Michael.

"Aedith likes any excuse to make us socialize. She thinks the road makes us uncivilized." Kaleb flashed white teeth at us.

Aedith grinned into her tankard. "He's right. Besides, I find they work harder when they have memory of local faces swamped in admiration at their stories."

"You make them feel as though they've something to prove?" Michael asked.

"Something to live up to," Aella countered from across the table, before her mother could reply. "Seeing you lot and talking to you reminds us of the standards we should already have." She practically glowed when Aedith nodded approvingly.

"It's easy for us to forget in the thrill of the hunt or the doldrums of the marches that we're fighting for the lives of people, and not just the chance to see a little bit of coin and our own warm beds again," said the man next to Aella. There was a melancholy note in his voice that surprised me.

He was a slim man who bore deep wrinkles across his forehead and at the corners of his eyes. His scalp was bare and speckled with sunspots and it gleamed in the firelight. A little girl, bouncing on the lap of a mother who hadn't been able to find a sitter for the evening, waved and babbled some baby nonsense at him. He smiled and waved back. The smile caused the cloudiness in his green eyes to blow away and they sparkled. It showed a faint echo of the man he must have been when he was younger.

"I'm sorry, I don't believe we have your name sir." Mother leaned forward on the table to address him.

"Victor, mum." His movements bespoke stiff joint as he reached across the table to shake hands. "It is a pleasure to be of whatever service I can be."

Over his shoulder a panicked Thomas stumbled through a clutch of bodies. He seemed to be searching the room for something, or someone. Mother caught sight of him, and with a look like a cat with a canary she flagged him down.

"Have you even said hello to Thomas yet?" Mother asked me as he came closer, a wicked smile on her face.

I wrinkled my nose. She knew I hadn't. I hadn't left her side. "No Mother, not yet. Good evening Thomas. How is your night going?"

"It's *busy*. You didn't go to the seat Maude pointed out for you," he said, voice half a whine and half apologetic. "Where did everyone who was sitting here go?"

I pointed out the four in question, who had moved down. "There are two more who moved over there though." I gestured to the table the others had moved themselves to.

Thomas made another small moan. "What can I get for you? We've a fine roast pie tonight, with potatoes and carrots, or a stew, which to be honest is much of the same mix." Thomas's gaze darted to the front door as he spoke, as it swung open and a few more bodies poured in. He practically wilted, clutching his small slate and piece of chalk to his chest.

"I'd like a refill on my wine," Aedith said. "Aella, more wine?"

"A little, please."

After conferring with us for a moment, Father asked for four portions of the roast pie, as well as two glasses of wine and two tankards of the ale. Thomas took a few more orders from the rest of the table who all wanted refills on their drinks, and then, with a parting beg for us not to switch tables at least until things settled down, he fled back to the kitchen.

The stocky woman to Aella's left watched him go. "Poor lil lad. Don't they have anyone else to help?"

I gestured to Thomas's little sister. She was about fourteen and shorter than most everyone in the building. Darting between tables, she served from a too large platter which she balanced on a hand held high over her head—often the only part of her that could be seen. "That's Thomas's sister Maria. Their mother and father work kitchen in the back, and their aunt is the one up front."

"She was foul! Does she have to pull the stick out if she wants to sit down?" This came from a laughing man to the left of the woman who had spoken before. She guffawed her agreement, then stopped abruptly with a contrite glance at my family.

Father shrugged. "She doesn't take kindly to strangers.

"Or anyone," Michael muttered to me, and I grinned at him.

The burly woman shrugged, not seeming to have heard him. "Can't blame her. I'm Tess, by the way, and this is Harold."

"Very good to meet you two."

"And the same to you," said Harold. He had a plate in front of him already, the same as the other mercenaries, and he was stabbing a potato with his fork and bringing it to his fat lips. I looked up from them to find him watching me watch him. He met my stare with one of his own. As he took a bite with a bit more force than necessary, I dropped my gaze.

"But," Tess went on, either not having seen Harold, or ignoring him, "are there no others to help? There must be half of the town trying to squeeze their way inside. It must be a madhouse in the kitchen."

A quick survey of the room proved Tess to be right. Every chair had filled as we talked, and now some people were standing at the ends of them. The large room was warm with the press of bodies and loud with conversation. The pleasant sound of good natured discussions rolled across the floor, punctuated by laughter and some people had to shout in order to be heard. Anwar and his wife Salma had taken the seats next to Willy and Nadia. Naieed was missing from their party, and there were no empty seats she might have momentarily vacated.

"It's likely," I said, "That they're wrangling up help even as we speak. You remember Naieed from earlier today?" I asked Aedith. She frowned as though she didn't, but nodded. "Her parents are here, but she is not, but she wouldn't have missed this for a new dress. So, Thomas has likely conscripted her to help."

As if on cue, Nai exited the kitchen. She was tied into a splotched apron, and her hair was pulled out of her face in a bouncy pony-tail. She used a toe to kick the door open and those nearest to it moved back or were struck. As she cleared the doorway, both of her hands came into view, balancing full trays of drinks. Despite the veritable sea of people, she made a beeline towards us with such grace that the trays never so much as wobbled. When she reached the end of our table she set the trays down and made a show of wiping her brows.

"Taryn, look at the state of me! I come to get a hot meal and you see what happens? Poor Thomas saw me and he was practically on his knees begging. What's a kind-hearted girl to do?"

I snorted, pretending not to notice Aedith's appraising look. "Maybe tell Thomas that his parents should admit that they need to hire you on full time?"

"Good evening Nai," Mother said to Nai with an affectionate smile. "How are you holding up?"

"'Lo Mother Wynn, Mister Raynard, Michael. The kitchen's like an oven, and you lot must all be looking to match your body weight in liquids, for how quickly I've been running in and out those doors." There was no real reproach in her words. She smiled as she passed wine glasses and tankards to us. "Aella, it's good to see you."

"Yes, you're looking well— is it Naieed or Nai?"

"It's Nai, unless you're mad at me, or you're my parents." Moving counterclockwise as she spoke, Nai refilled the empty cups of the others at the table, going through the remainder of both a bottle of wine, and a pitcher of ale. "That's me. I'll be back sooner than later."

With that farewell, Nai made her way back the way she had come, pausing at a few of the smaller tables and making notes on the slate she had fished out of her apron. Giggling at the little comments made to her at each stop, complimenting, and teasing, she smoothed any discontent about the slow service and left smiling faces in her wake.

"When did you have a chance to meet her?" Aedith placed both forearms on either side of her plate to skewer her daughter with a look. Her voice was clear and easy to hear over the din. "I know you weren't skulking by the door this afternoon like an eavesdropping child."

Aella froze in the midst of a bite of roast, then she swallowed thickly. "No, Ma."

Tess and Harold exchanged a knowing look. When Tess opened her mouth to say something I thought I saw Harold move as though he had kicked Tess. Certainly, she elbowed him back.

"Nai ran into Aella and myself on the street. After I left you all, I came upon her and we got to talking," I supplied.

Aedith would not be deterred. "Where did you run into each other?"

"Near the butcher Ma. I saw her and I asked if she knew where I might purchase some soap. I was getting a lay of the area."

I nodded my corroboration, and Aedith shrugged and took another swig. "Just making sure. You know my rules."

"Yes," Aella agreed. She spooned a potato and a carrot into her mouth at once, not meeting her mother's eyes.

Outside, there was a flash of light and then the crack of thunder that tore a cheer out of those in the crowd who had already had too much to drink. Following that came the shushing noise of steady rain on the roof of the inn. Those around me raised their voices to be heard over the sound, and it became too difficult for me to follow any one conversation.

Around that time, Maria came out of the kitchen again. This time she deposited full plates in front of me and the rest of my family, much to my empty belly's pleasure. The food was steaming hot, and the smell of the rosemary which the meat and vegetables had been cooked with was enough to make my mouth water.

When the initial downpour slackened and it became possible to be heard again, I returned my attention to the mother and daughter mercenaries, though I didn't stop eating. The wine seemed to have removed some of Aedith's edge, as she had already moved on from grilling her child. At present, she was addressing a man to her left in an animated fashion.

Aella caught my attention and mouthed, "Thank you." I shrugged.

Michael caught the display and leaned over to whisper in my ear. "Helping the little mercenary stay out of trouble?"

I spoke out of the corner of my mouth. "It's honestly nothing worth her getting into trouble over. She wanted to know what was happening, the same as Nai and me. Her mother's a bear about rules, I guess." I cut at the tender meat on my plate.

Michael glanced at the mother mercenary, who was slapping her companion on the back, mid chortle. "That, I can see."

"She's not like this sober. She's actually sort of amazing." My shoulders rose a little so that they were almost touching my ear.

He shrugged. "I'm sure. She's a brawler. This is how they are, right?"

"How do you mean?" I popped the meat I'd been worrying into my mouth.

"I mean they fight and get bloody all day. They keep serious and stalwart through all of that, and then in the evenings they cut loose and act like animals. I'm sure Nai will go home with one of them tonight. Or to his tent rather."

My eyes widened in shock and I was grateful that it was too

loud for his dining companion to the right to hear him. It was Kaleb, and I liked Kaleb from what I had seen. "That's a nasty attitude to take. They're here to help, and Nai can do what she likes. It's not like you've taken up with her."

He rolled his eyes. "I'm not judging her or them. I'd get drunk and belligerent too if my only purpose was to beat things bloody until I couldn't stand anymore. If I had as little to do and was as pretty as Nai, I'm sure I'd get around as well." I wondered if my glare could melt the metal of the spoon he was twirling between two fingers.

"Certainly, we live a gruesome life, put into those terms young Master ... Michael, was it?"

Michael sat upright in surprise, and my gaze flew over his shoulder at Kaleb, who had us fixed in his sights. One long finger traced the rim of his wine cup delicately. He had heard. I blindly grasped for mine and took a sip that drained half of its contents. Across the table, Aella perked up. She hadn't heard what Michael had said, only her fellow's response, but it seemed her warrior instincts gave her a good sense of when a fight was imminent.

Surprise caused my brother to fumble for words at first, but then he donned that haughty expression I was growing to hate, and he pushed a braid back over his left shoulder. "You don't take offense to it, I hope. You're a fighter who isn't affiliated with the official guard; there must be a reason for that. Also, the chances of you striking upon something lucrative enough to let you settle down comfortably is incredibly slim. Taryn, stop pinching me."

"I'll stop pinching you when you shut up," I hissed.

"That's all right Miss Taryn. Master Michael shares a very

commonly held opinion, which is that those who choose to travel and fight for seemingly random causes have no other discernable skills that they might capitalize on. Is that right, Master Michael?"

Michael blinked, and I knew he had not expected such vocabulary from someone whom he considered to be a grunt. "I believe that is generally safe to assume, yeah."

Kaleb's voice was soft, and though the smile never left his lips, I felt a chill creep up my back, turning the sweat from the warm room into ice droplets. "I would say that it is a dangerous thing to assume that a person is only the sum of what they appear to be doing when you can see them, wouldn't you?"

Michael's mouth hung slightly ajar. His smug expression had vanished. I had the dubious pleasure of seeing Michael at a loss for words. "I suppose so," he managed, then, "I apologize. I was rude."

"It's a family trait. I don't think we can fairly blame you for it." Aella was grinning sympathetically at me. Her earlier attitude at my questions made much more sense, given my brother's outburst. Despite what she had actually said, she didn't seem upset. Somehow, I managed to relax enough to smile back.

A glance at Michael told me he was still wire tight. He shoveled food into his mouth a little faster than he had before, not looking at anyone else. He was embarrassed, I realized, noting the flush in his cheeks. Michael had been getting into more of these little tiffs lately, but it was a rarity for him to be put in his place— verbally at least.

None of our parents had noticed anything amiss. They were engaged in conversation with the next table, turned in their seats so that they could interact with Willy, Nadia, Anwar, and Salma.

I glanced back at Aella, she was pushing a stringy carrot around on her plate, and her companions were talking to the table on the other side of them, where Dai sat. Kaleb was now turned away from us, towards a tall black woman with a shaven head who was one of those who had made room for us. Many patrons around the room had finished their meals and were lighting up their pipes. The air above our heads began to fill with the fragrant smoke.

13

When I pushed back from the table. Father glanced up but I waved him off. "I'm just getting a little air."

The sound of the rain had ceased to be discernable over the noise of the tavern. If it was still sprinkling, I was willing to brave it. Normally I might have passed an awkward meal talking with Michael, but these days...

I weaved my way through the chairs that had been pushed up against the ends of tables and had to apologize as I bumped into no small number of other patrons. I was not the best in crowds sober, and the wine had been strong. When I finally made it out into the night, I saw that the rain had soaked the streets thoroughly but had moved on as quickly as it had arrived. I took a gulp of the crisp air and reveled at its lack of taste, save for the faintest hint of wood smoke that swirled out of the chimney behind me. A wooden sign thumped against the door as I closed it behind me. It read, *At Full Capacity, Thank You.* The wood still had a few pieces of dust clinging to the grooves of the words scored into its surface.

Leaves scraped along the road, pushed by a mountain wind that moaned. Accenting that eerie, yet so familiar sound was the plinking of the rain dripping from the awnings. There were low murmurs as well; I wasn't the only one who had chosen to get some fresh air. Beth's back was against the wall of the inn, and a mercenary whom I hadn't been introduced to leaned over her, with one arm propping him up, the space between them negligible. She was blushing and fluttering her eyelashes coyly, with a hand pressed against his chest.

So much for Corey, I thought ruefully. Corey was Beth's current courter, or so I had thought. He was inside, as far as I knew. It'd be a fight if he came out and found her like this. He wasn't the most levelheaded young man. I shrugged and turned away. Not my problem.

On the other side of the door, Maude was puffing quickly on what I guessed was her usual roll of sweet leaf and tobacco, but the smoke was blowing away from me. There would be no more customers for her to seat, but still I couldn't tamp down on my ire entirely. Nai was working when she ought to have been allowed to sit and eat, and Maude got to smoke outside in the cool night? I smoothed back a few strands of hair that had blown into my mouth, and shook myself. I'd tell Nai tomorrow. I moved out of the doorway. Rather than stand next to Beth and her "friend," or Maude, I decided to take a walk around the block.

Halfway down the road, I was shivering. I hadn't planned on a walk when I had risen, naively assuming stepping outside would give me privacy enough. I'd left my cloak back on my chair. I exhaled gustily in exasperation. I'd look silly coming all the way out here and then going all the way back in, only to come out again. Plus, there was a huge chance that at some point in that production I'd get stuck talking to someone, and frankly I didn't feel like it. I walked on.

More and more I was thinking that it would be a relief when Michael left for the city. People were always saying we were alike, and we were in many ways, but being compared to him in terms of rudeness had given me pause. I shook my bowed head, as the wind blew against my back. Some of the folks in town had started to treat me differently in the past year. I'd thought maybe it was something I'd done, but I never *meant* to be hurtful when I erred. Could it have been because of something Michael had said? I chafed my sleeves against my arms.

The sound of boots crunching on gravel and the creak of leather on leather caused me to turn quickly. Aella. My chest loosened. Silly—what danger did I think could befall me in town? She waved my dark cloak above her head. "Michael thought you might want this. He was going to bring it, but I said I'd do it since I had to run back to camp anyway."

I met her halfway, immediately accepting the cloak and swinging it around my shoulders. The instant blockade between my chilled body and the wind was a godsend, and I thanked her profusely, trying to squash my guilt at thinking poorly about Michael not moments before he came to my rescue.

"I can't tell you how ridiculous I felt in all this wind and just my dress," I said.

"Aw, the dress is nice." Aella grinned at me, stooping briefly to pluck at my skirt. "It makes you look pretty." I snatched the fabric away from her, blushing. Aella held up her hands in surrender.

I tucked my hands into my armpits for warmth. "Well it is certainly fine for sitting in that roasting inn, but not so much for an autumn walk in the dark."

"I'll agree to that. Why didn't you come back for your cloak?" I made a face, and she began walking. I followed, keeping at her side. "Come on, tell the scary mercenary what's on your mind."

She wasn't looking at me, but I thought she was smiling. I didn't *think* she was mocking me. "My brother is a horse's rear more often than not these days, and I'm worried that I might be one as well," I said, surprising myself with the truth.

Aella's lips turned down at the sides, like a fish's mouth as she mulled this over. She linked her arms loosely behind her head. "You're talking about what I said—about being rude as a family trait?" I nodded. She tilted her head to the side and made the fish mouth again. "Is this something you've been thinking about? Or do you have thin skin?"

I slapped her lightly on the side with the back of my hand. "Don't laugh!"

She rubbed her ribs where I had struck, giving me an accusatory look. "There's no need to get violent Miss Taryn."

"I thought mercenaries liked violence," I teased, hoping to lighten the mood. "And it's just Taryn, please."

"All right, Taryn. You probably do judge folks." I stopped to gape at her, and she hurried on, "But I don't think you mean anything nasty by it!"

"That doesn't make it any better." I sighed, pulling the edges of cloak more tightly around me.

We were at the end of the block now. Aella would continue forward to get to her camp site. I'd need to turn right to loop around the block. Or else I could turn around and go back the way I had come.

There were some thin gray clouds scooting across the sky above us, but it looked as though the storm had sailed by us with only that small dousing. The stars were brilliant and a bright quarter moon beamed down on us. When my eyes came back down to Aella, she had a peculiar expression on her face.

"I think," she said, haltingly, considering her words, "that there is a great deal of difference between immediately assuming a stranger is lesser than you," she paused again; she still hadn't taken her gaze away from my face, "and meeting a person and assuming that they are like you, and then wondering if that's good or bad when you find that they aren't." The wind blew her thick hair around her face, and I had the urge to push it away so that I could better see the way she was looking at me.

"That's nice to say. I think." I put my hand to my throat. My voice was raspy. I hoped that wasn't an indication of a cold coming on. I cleared my throat, and went on, my tone light. "Still, you've only known me less than a day. You could ask around and find that I'm the worst person in town, with a nasty habit of tripping toddlers."

Aella chuckled and turned away from me to dig into the pouch at her hip. From it she produced a skinny strip of leather. She wound that around her mass of hair, securing it back, but for a few shorter strands which could not be caught. Those danced merrily in the wind, tickling her cheeks. "That could be, but I doubt it."

"And why is that?" I asked.

"Well for one, my mother thinks you have a certain something about you, and she's rarely wrong when it comes to people."

I blinked, surprised and flattered that the mercenary captain had spared me a second thought. "A certain something? What does that mean?"

"Like a spark." She motioned towards the direction of her tent. "Walk with me a little ways farther?"

I looked back over my shoulder at the bright light that was the inn, and then in the direction she was headed, lit only by the stars and a few street torches. The distance was about the same as if I were to loop the block. I started walking in answer to her request, and she joined me.

"When did your mother mention a spark?"

"She didn't use the word 'spark' exactly. She just mentioned you when she came back to the tents. Not by name, but she said a braided blonde girl and her friend acted pretty bold for mountain girls. I assumed she meant you."

"Perhaps, but truly it was Nai that wanted to see—" My boot caught in a divot in the road and I stumbled slightly. In the same moment, Aella put an arm out and I clutched it tightly. My fingers dug into the loose cotton of her sleeve. I was surprised to find the fabric was soft over hard muscle. Once I had righted myself, I dropped my hands and she resumed walking again. I continued, watching the ground for any more small pits. "She's the one who has a 'spark' to her."

"Yeah, maybe if we had gotten to you a little bit earlier. Now you're probably only good for herding and wedding."

I gasped indignantly and whipped my head around. She was smirking. I let my scowl wilt into a plaintive pout. "You don't think that, do you?"

"Does that bother you?"

"Well, yes! Not because I want to go off and travel like Michael does, because I don't. I love my parents and my work." I felt like I was assuring people of that too much as of late. "But I don't like the idea that I couldn't if I wanted to."

"It's not for me to decide that. *Can* you do anything else?"

"Well I," I bit my lip and thought quickly. "I'm a decent shot with a slingshot, and I'm learning the crossbow. My father says I'm going to be great. I'm an ok reader, though I'm nowhere near as good as Michael. I can sew, I can cook, and I can fish. I'm fantastic on horseback—or rather, pony-back."

"But those are basic skills for anyone who minds herds and homes," Aella pointed out. "What sets you apart?"

I let my hand creep out from under my cloak, to stroke a braid. "I don't know."

Aella raised a shoulder and let it drop. "So, marry a farmer boy, and herd your sheep. As you said, you like it."

I rolled my eyes. "Oh yes, it is so simple. Let me pick one and get on with it."

"I know that I saw the serving boy giving you looks across the table. He's pretty, as boys go. Marry that one," she said, as though it was as simple as picking a piece of meat at the butcher's.

"Nai says he likes me, and he is fine looking, but she sees goo-goo eyes where there are none."

"Nah, Nai is right," Aella interjected with a wicked grin. "He looks at you like you're 'a plate of very fine roast.'"

"I think there must be something I'm not seeing in him... and the rest of them," I said, my voice gloomy. I punted a stone a few yards ahead of us, and the echoing noise of it bouncing forward filled the silence that followed my statement.

"Do you think you're too good for them?" Aella asked finally. "Isn't that why your brother hasn't found a steady sweetheart?"

I glared. "No. It's not that. I mean, I don't think it's that."

"For you, or for your brother?"

"For either of us. Or, all right, at the very least, for me. Trust me, I've agonized over that thought, especially watching Michael these days. It's more than that though. Thomas, for example, is handsome and kind. I like his family. I can tell Mother likes him. I can see why he would make a good match. I can see that. It's just..." I trailed off, suddenly self-conscious.

It was too easy to talk to Aella. Naturally I had said these things to Michael, but I hadn't even confessed any of these thoughts to Nai, and she was my closest friend. She was so in the dark that I allowed her to set me up several times with boys I knew I had no interest in, to avoid the conversation.

"Maybe the person you're destined for is from elsewhere," Aella suggested, oblivious to my thoughts. "Some fine lad could ride into town any day now looking to try his fortune at sheep herding. Your ma and da will be thrilled. Your brother will take him for a pint at the inn. Beautiful wedding. Beautiful babies. No more worries."

"Maybe," I said glumly.

"Or maybe you'll wake up one day and realize what you wanted was here all along. Don't ask me. I move around too much to know anything about waiting around for someone."

"I *don't* want to leave Nophgrin, but if I'm honest I can almost understand why you like that sort of life and why Michael is itching to be somewhere else. There's no work I'd rather do, but you're right, I don't even know if I'm missing someone great because I don't know what else is out there."

"I think lots of people feel that way."

Nai didn't. Nor did Beth or Claire. My mother hadn't, and even Gladys had married twice from the crop provided. Aella had been all over though. Perhaps she could provide some insight, and if not, well, wouldn't she be gone in a week or so? Who would she tell?

"Aella do you have a beau? In the company, or that you write to?"

Aella's voice was sly. "No, I most certainly do not. Why?"

"Do you ever feel…" I stopped again. This was hard.

"Yes?" She prompted me.

I found I couldn't look at her and say this. I ducked my head as it came out in a rush, "When the other girls in town talk about a boy they're interested in, I can tell how much they like him. They can't wait to see him again. They exchange notes. They pine over him when their parents keep them too busy to see him every waking moment. I never feel that way. The few times I've kissed a boy it's as though there's a wall there. When I get through the wall then the kissing is fine, but I always think… this can't be what they're mooning over."

"Perhaps you just haven't been kissing the right boys?"

"I've kissed all the boys in town I'd care to," I said sourly.

"Then I suppose you'll just have to wait until someone new moves to town. Since you don't want to leave."

I groaned in frustration. "I wish I was like you."

"What do you mean?" She sounded genuinely curious.

"No one expects anything of you. All you have to do is follow your captain on great adventures. If you marry? Wonderful. If you don't? No big deal."

"But that's not so for you?"

I sighed and rubbed my forehead. "My life is supposed to go a certain way. My family is meant to stay together, and take care of one another. We're supposed to take care of the farm together. I'm supposed to marry and have children."

"Well, why can't you?" We had reached the stone I had kicked before, and this time Aella shot it forward.

"Michael already wants to leave, so that's one thing out the window. Nothing I say is changing his mind." I scowled. "What if that person that would make me feel the proper way never rides into town? If they don't, then how will I ever get my life … right? Will I have to leave like Michael, if I want to find love? It'd break my parent's hearts if we both did that."

We were in the housing quarter of town towards the south side, and there were far fewer torches to light the way. I found myself grateful for the lack of light. At the very least it made it difficult to discern what Aella thought of my confession, which was just as well, because I didn't know what else to say. The only other person I had admitted these fears to was my twin, and even we hadn't spoken of it since he had started talking about leaving. These days he only ever used it to prove that it was ok for *him* to leave.

We walked in silence until the tents came into view, taking turns kicking the rock. Aella was the one who finally spoke. "I don't have any siblings, so I can't speak to your problems with Michael. Have you tried hitting him?"

I snorted and shook my head. "I'm not supposed to."

She grinned, but continued on in a more serious tone. "I do understand when it comes to courting the wrong people ... It's sort of like wearing a fancy gown that's made to someone else's measurements. It'll fit in a pinch. It's pretty on your friends. You'll be pretty, and you'll probably be fine for the night, but it wasn't made for you. The shoulders don't set right, and the hem is too short. It's not comfortable." I looked askance at her ruggedly outfitted body. When she noticed, it was her turn to take mock offense. "I do know about lady things, thank you. These aren't my only clothes. Sometimes we get hired by nice gentle people and have to attend dull dinners."

I laughed but didn't respond, taking a moment to survey the mercenary camp as I thought over her remark. The tents themselves were a thick canvas, and stretched at an angle over each one was rectangle of skin, which I assumed had been water-proofed. Most of the structures were not tall enough to stand in. The mercenaries would have room to kneel or crouch inside. While there was room for them to spread out lengthwise when sleeping, clearly these were not places in which they spent a great deal of time. Only one differed from this, and that one was in the back row on the far right. Tall enough to stand in and big enough around to hold two of the other tents was the commander's tent.

Aella nudged me. "I'm two down from my mother's tent. Come on, and try to step lightly. A few of the men had an early supper and came back to pass out already." A ragged snore sounded from one of the tents, confirming her statement.

We strode quickly down the aisle between the left-most and middle tents, without speaking. There were no torches lit in their camp, so we had to rely on the light of the moon and stars, and the straightness of the mercenary's rows. I winced as my boot stuck for a moment in a particularly wet patch of mud; I could feel the chill of it through the sides of the shoe. Francine had been right, they had churned the yard with their horses and heavy feet. A glance at the base of the tents to my right and left proved that they had linings underneath them as well, to keep them from getting soaked.

When we reached the last tent in the line, Aella crouched. She set about undoing the tiny hooks that secured the front flap shut with practiced fingers. Then she crawled inside, leaving me in the dark.

"What did you have to come out here to get?" I whispered.

She popped her head out, beaming. "My flask. I figured we could drink it on our way back to the inn. It'll keep us warm." She disappeared back into the recesses of her tent.

I blanched. "You had us walk all the way out to your tent so that we could get something that would make coming back from your tent slightly more pleasant?" I bent over to peek into the dark shelter. "Are you joking with me?"

Aella had found the item in question, and she jiggled it at me. "It's honey whiskey."

"It's cold!" I squeaked. Someone snorted, and Aella shushed me.

"Come in here out of the bluster for a second then, if it's so bad. These things are so small, they actually retain heat pretty well, especially if there's more than one body in them."

"Yeah, I'm sure," I muttered, but I crawled in after her anyway. There was, in fact, a noticeable difference between the night air and the temperature inside the tent. The constant wind dropped away, and I found that I could feel my cheeks again. I plopped next to her on her bed roll.

"So, did you want this?" My eyes adjusted to the comparable darkness of the tent and I saw she was offering me the flask with an innocent smile. I snatched it from her and took a generous swig. I gasped as the sweet liquid burned my throat and curled its way heavily into my gut. I clapped a hand over my mouth as my stomach instantly rebelled. "Do not get sick in my tent," Aella warned, taking the flask back from me.

I closed my eyes, and shook my head. "I'm not going to. It took me by surprise, is all. I've barely eaten yet today." There was a beat. "Oh, gods above and below. Aella I can't stay out here much longer. I've a meal on the table, and my parents are going to be wondering where I am. We can drink this on the way back like you said."

Aella put a restraining hand on top of my right one. It was as calloused as mine was from labor. "Aren't you all going to be staying there until late, hearing stories drunkenly told by my friends?"

"Yes…" I hedged, "But…" Her fingers were wrapped all the way around my own, and I could feel them through my skirt. They were warm, and they made it hard to focus on what I was saying. I took back the flask and had smaller sip of the whiskey, trying to think of a good reason to head back in a hurry. I passed her back the flask.

"Do your parents truly think you could get into any trouble? I bet there isn't even a town drunk in Nophgrin."

I inclined my head. "Sometimes Daniel gets a little belligerent on feast days, but no, not as such." She passed me back the flask, and I sipped, then returned it.

"And do greater gryphons swoop into town at night and lift off maidens?"

"No," I drew the word out, "but I am hungry."

"Yeah, I'm a little peckish myself." Aella's dark eyes were on my lips.

It was then that I became aware of how close Aella and I were to one another. We were touching from legs to shoulders; she hadn't removed her hand and I could smell the one drink she'd had of the whiskey on her breath. The way she was looking at me ... I flinched back, pulling my hand out from under hers. "You're making a move on me!"

She let her head fall backward, and silent laughs wracked her body. "Gods, I thought you'd never catch on."

"You like women?"

Aella cocked her head to the side. "I like people, but in my line of work, women tend to be a bit safer. My mother will be the first to tell you how unpleasant it is to get stuck in one town long enough for a babe to grow up. Have I completely misread you? You and Nai never...?"

"*No!*" I had to remind myself to keep my voice down.

"What a pity. I suppose it's just as well she was working tonight." When I didn't laugh, she rolled her eyes. "You've never wondered what her lips felt like?" She overplayed a sultry voice, clearly trying for a laugh.

My heart thudded painfully against my ribs. "No."

The tent felt uncomfortably small, but somehow, I didn't feel like leaving yet. I yanked the flask back from her, reveling in the coldness that slid down my throat as I took a drink to match my first one. My stomach didn't roil as badly this time, much to my relief. Instead, the whiskey brought up a valid thought.

"So that talk about your mother thinking I have a spark, was that just to get me back to your tent?"

"Well, I probably wouldn't have mentioned it if you weren't cute, but no, she did seem interested with you at supper."

"Do you do this with a lot of people?"

"I don't take someone back to my tent every time I come upon a new town, if that's what you're asking." Aella drew away from me. "I'm sorry— have I really upset you?"

"I'm not upset," I said, my voice still a little strident. As I went to take another drink, she took the flask back.

"Enough of that. This stuff is strong, and I saw how much you drank at the table. I'll go ahead and assume you don't have a lot of practice in the art of drinking yourself under the table. There's no need to start on my account."

My head felt a little airy. In Nophgrin, the healer had a husband, and they were both nice men. Other couples of the kind had traveled through, looking to start new lives in new towns. I *knew* it was an option. I'd just always thought of that sort of relationship as an indulgence for those who could afford to be without children to take care of them and their land when they were too old to work. Certainly, it was not something I'd ever considered for more than a fleeting moment. Not even when I had complained to Michael about not liking anyone in town.

"What even made you think you had a shot?"

"Besides cockiness?" she asked, and I nodded. "You sounded like me, a couple of years ago. That dress metaphor is how I explained it to myself, back then. Me preferring girls. I sort of thought you were trying to tell me that."

"But I was talking about traveling versus staying at home," I pointed out.

She squinted at me, and I jutted my chin out stubbornly. "All right, so maybe I was doing a little bit of hopeful projecting." She shrugged. "Is that so bad?"

I studied my hands, and shrugged. "I suppose it doesn't matter either way."

"No, I suppose not," she agreed.

I thought about the times I had spent in the field, picturing my future. Had there ever been a man in it? There was a home, and children, but my partner was always a shapeless blur. Did that mean I was meant to have a woman in my future?

I waited as long as I could manage before I asked, "So I've done an awful lot of sharing with a stranger. It's your turn, I think. When did *you* realize that you liked girls?"

She gazed at the tent wall in front of us, eyes unseeing, remembering. "I was something like twelve? It wasn't a big deal to my mother. A couple of the women and men who are in, or have been in, our merry band have been the same way. Da though, he was from a pretty fanatical town out by the western sea."

"I thought you didn't know your father," I said, tilting my head.

"I said I don't *have* a father," she said, harshly. "But I knew him, well enough. The place I grew up. The people there mostly worship a sun god. Artuos, The Burning One." I bobbed my head again. The Burning One was an extension of our own sun god, Hearth Father—the violent part. It was said by some that King Richard had been a chosen hand of The Burning One. Aella continued, "They think sex is for making babies and that women ought to stay in their place, which is right under their husband's or father's boot. Tending to the hearth fire."

I winced. I had heard of such places. For the most part, here in Nophgrin it was about who was most qualified, not what was under a person's clothes that determined who was in charge. However, though the kingdom officially took stances against the behavior she was talking about, the capital and its laws were a long ways away from the outskirts of the kingdom. There was no rule against a guard returning to their home city and working there, turning a blind eye to "old ways." Guardsmen could be and often were bribed to allow local custom to reign above the law of the land. I knew that Beth and her mother had come to our town seeking refuge from such a place. Their bruises had told stories I'd never dared ask about.

"I can't imagine your mother living with someone like that."

"You don't know her. She was a different woman back in those days. She was a mercenary for a while, but she says she had taken a break from it before she got pregnant. She was working at an inn, trying to save enough money to go north. Then I came along and trapped her." Aella took a drink from her flask before she spoke again. "She didn't have enough money to leave yet, and then she couldn't work whilst she was pregnant or lugging around a babe."

"Why not ask for help from those who raised her?"

Aella shook her head. "She said she burned that bridge when she first left to be a mercenary. I've never even met those people. I asked her why she didn't take an herbal remedy when she realized she was pregnant, and she said she hadn't felt like it. A real thinker, my mother."

I imagined a lot more thought went into Aedith's decision than her daughter gave her credit for, but I held my tongue on that thought. It wasn't my place to tell her so. "If the town you grew up in was so harsh, what possessed you to tell your father that you liked women?"

"He was arranging these dinners with terrible boys who I had grown up with. All of them shared my da's warped opinions, which my ma had worked her hardest to keep from rooting in my own head. I knew my father was setting me up to marry one of them."

"Twelve seems so young to start the marriage process," I mused. "Though I know it's common here too. In the mountains, so many boys and girls still believe their best chance at a full family is to start young."

"For places like my home, it was to keep children under thumb as thoroughly as possible. I thought I'd save him the trouble of having marriage negotiations fail. I guess, honestly I panicked. I thought," she inhaled and laughed shakily, "I could see my life narrowing down to my home and my hearth, and after hearing stories of my mother out in the world fighting, I couldn't bear it. I thought I was his daughter, and that that would matter more than his ideologies."

"But it didn't." It didn't come out as a question and she nodded.

"He slapped me across the face so hard I hit the ground before I knew what had happened." She rubbed her chin lightly, as if remembering the feeling. "He'd never done that before. Sure, he had been scary and he had loomed and glowered, said if I didn't shape up and act proper then the fires would get me, but he had never hit me. I couldn't believe it."

"What did your mother do?"

"She didn't know I was going to tell him. Maybe she would have stopped me. By the time I got my feet under me again, she had come into the room and seen what happened. She got right in his face. Which, you don't know him, but nobody did that. She was yelling at him too. I remember being scared, because he *would* hit her, and I didn't want him to hurt her. Then he got tired of being yelled at, and he went to strike her, and I swear Taryn, I saw her eyes go cold. I've only seen that expression one time since that day. All the stories she had told me about being trained to fight, they weren't stories anymore."

I motioned for her to pass the whiskey back. She obliged without looking at me. This time I took a more moderated sip. The tent smelled of wet canvas and earth; I was warm now. "What happened then?"

"We left that evening—took every piece of coin he had. Then we holed up in the next town over, and Ma paid an old hedge witch a hefty sum to scry for her old guild. They were in Port Orion, another sea town, celebrating from a stint of work in Threece that had taken most of the previous season. The job had been settling a dispute between two families."

I made a noise of understanding. Threece was a small country, and what little land it had was divided amongst... I wanted to say, five families, though I couldn't quite remember at the moment. Each spring as soon as the fields thawed, one family or other was bound and certain to declare that their neighbor had encroached upon their borders and declare a feud.

Aella chuckled. "That was the first time I saw Kaleb. I guess when the witch scried for him, our faces turned up in his drink and he swore and spilled it. We had to have her work the magic again. That time we appeared in the ale left on the table. It was then he told us that the second in command from when Ma was traveling with them had become the commander. That was good news for us because they had been mates. We met them halfway between Port Orion and Threece, and I immediately began training to be of use to them, and to be one of them. The rest is history."

"Gods," I murmured. "You're not putting me on, right?"

"Nope. That's my life. Some bits and pieces left out, sure, but that's the gist. So, you see," she said, her tone teasing once more, "if you do harbor same-sex tendencies, you don't have half so much of a reason to be afraid to explore them as I did."

I groaned and shoved her. "I'm not afraid. But you're right, Nophgrin doesn't care about that sort of thing. Two men, Andrew and his partner David hand-fasted in front of half the town not two years ago. I just never thought of myself in that way."

"Well, I won't push you then." Aella rolled to her knees and crawled around me to the door flap. "It's hardly my place." She climbed out into the night and hissed. "Man alive, I'd forgotten how chilly it was."

I followed the trail of cold air streaming into the tent,

somewhat reluctantly. "I'll admit I've never said a lot of the things I told you."

"Strangers are like confession booths." Aella tugged her jerkin straight and smoothed loose strands of hair, only to have them blow back where they'd come from. "We roll into town, you unload your sins, and then we leave. We're safe."

We began walking back the way we had come, passing the flask between us. "So, I guess each town you come through is a lot like that. How many times have you unloaded your past onto a girl in your tent?" Was that jealousy that I felt burning in my gut, or the whisky?

Aella licked her lips, catching the lower one between her teeth and gnawing a piece of chapped skin free. "I don't tell my story to everyone. I'm sure you can imagine how we are otherwise occupied. Tonight, you asked so I told. If it had been your friend, I might not have."

"Yeah, you might have gotten farther with Nai than with me." I said, punting a rock a few feet. "She likes guys, as far as I know, but who's to say? She's way more adventurous than I am."

"Nah, I'm glad it was you I brought back to my tent— if we did do any talking she wouldn't have let me get a word in edgewise, I think."

"Is that why?" I laughed, and she nodded fervently.

"Don't get me wrong, she's pretty," I took another drink, nodding as I did so, "but you're interesting, Taryn of the sheep."

"Nai is interesting too," I said stoutly.

Aella took the flask back. "Take a compliment."

"It's not nice to imply that my closest friend isn't as interesting as I am. Especially when she is." My words slurred together slightly as I spoke, and I scowled at them.

"Gods you are a peevish girl, has anyone told you?"

I put my arms out and spun in place, then paused as I waited for my vision to refocus. When I did speak, I did so slowly, enunciating carefully. "I am peevish, but you like me." I spun again, enjoying the way my skirt rose and fanned out above my knees, not minding the cold air that hit my tights as my feet stumbled across each other.

Aella caught me by the right arm and pulled me to her, chest to chest. With my hands pressed between us I could feel how solidly she was put together. I worked hard every day, and my body still had a little jiggle to it. Aella was like a rock.

The hand she had on my arm slipped down to take my own hand, and the other one rested lightly on the small of my back. My free fingers creeped up to grip her shoulder for support. She grinned down at me, and without a word she proceeded to dance us lightly in a circle. Our clasped hands were out like a tea kettle spout; we dipped backward and forward as we swirled, and the movement and wind caused my skirt to wrap around and between her legs.

I laughed in surprise, and clung to her to stay upright. She twirled me out so that our arms were fully extended. My other arm was flung back behind me for balance. She spun me back in towards her, and I let the momentum take me with little care for how my feet kept up.

"I do like you." I tilted my head back, surprised by the admission. She lowered her head so that her lips were inches from my own, and I felt a magnetic pull between us. I let my heavy lids drift shut, expecting her to close the gap, but then the warmth of her breath left my face, and we were dancing again. "Sadly, canoodling with drunk farm girls is a sure way for a mercenary to gain a bad reputation."

My eyes flew open. "I'm not drunk."

"You're hardly sober. You've let me dance you around without once mentioning the fact that you need to get back to the inn to get your supper."

I dug my heels in, halting us on a turn, and my eyes darted to the faint blaze of light at the end of the street where The Black Gryphon sat. At this distance, I couldn't even hear the noise from within. "Horse dung."

Aella snickered. "That's one way to put it."

"Why'd you let me prance around like a lackwit?" I demanded, tugging her by our joined hands in the direction of the inn. She let herself be dragged without resisting.

"It was fun, and it didn't take that much time." She let her boredom at my concern ring clearly through her dry voice.

The row of houses we were on had only one torch, a few feet down the street from us. It was because of that low light that I almost stumbled right past Michael, who was in a narrow alley to the left. When my mind registered him crouched there, I jerked myself backward, opening my mouth to say hello. A shriek left my open lips as my brain registered Beth's prone form beside him and the dark pool of liquid by her skull. Michael's head swung up, fear in his eyes, even after he recognized us.

"It's Beth," he said, his voice high and hurried. "Quickly. Get help— she's been bludgeoned!"

14

I covered my lips with my free fingers as more incoherent noises tried to tumble forth. At first it didn't appear as though Beth was moving at all, but as I stared in abject horror I saw her chest rise and fall in shallow breaths. Or was my vision playing tricks on me? I rubbed my eyes, but it didn't help. The edges of the alley wiggled like it was made of worms. My legs shook as though they might give out beneath me, and I tore my gaze away to cast a helpless look towards Aella.

"I'll go," she said, squeezing my other hand tightly, and then she let go, running at full speed towards the inn.

I was rooted in place, eyes transfixed on my brother, and my friend. I thought of earlier, seeing her with the mercenary and worrying that Corey would see and become upset. "You didn't..." My throat felt thick, and my voice refused to work. I tried to think of how to ask if Corey had done this. I attempted to speak again. "Michael, you didn't..."

Michael seemed to misread my unfinished question. His eyes were desperately wide in his pale face. They flashed with ire and then impatience for a moment, before settling on fear. "No! This wasn't me. I came upon her like this."

I took a few stumbling steps forward and sank next to Michael. "Of course not. What happened?"

He shook his head helplessly. "You're guess is as good as mine. I was having a terrible time in there, so I came out here to track you down and to make sure Aella got your cloak to you." His eyes never left Beth's pale face as he spoke. "I got to this point and I heard moaning."

"She didn't say anything to you?" I reached out to smooth the hair back from Beth's forehead but let it drop halfway there.

"She was conscious when I got to her, but I couldn't make her stay that way, and she couldn't say anything. I think her jaw is broken. The way it's sitting…" he trailed off, and I rubbed his shoulder roughly. His shoulder was freezing, and his cheeks were flushed red from the cold.

There was the distant sound of several pairs of boots on the gravel and cobblestone. I stood with difficulty, using the wall to help me up, and moved to peer around the corner of the alley. From that position I saw a whole parade of bodies arrowing towards us with Aella at the lead. Laura, Beth's mother and stepfather, my mother and father, Aella's mother, as well as the medics Andrew and David, and another mercenary whom I didn't know. I flagged them down, and when they caught sight of me their pace quickened further still.

Benjamin and Anne pushed past me without a word to kneel by their daughter. Benjamin pulled her into his lap without minding the sticky blood.

"What is this? Who has done this?" He demanded ferociously of Michael, but softly, as though his daughter was asleep and he feared disturbing her.

"Careful of moving her," Andrew chided gently, as he came to kneel beside them.

I had moved to press my back against the brick wall behind me, so that Andrew, David, and the mercenary could get by. Michael rose to join me, but not before grabbing his crook off the ground. He seemed almost hesitant to touch it, and I could see why. Beyond the normal muck from laying on stone and earth, the wood had also picked up some of the blood seeping from our friend. The whiskey in my system made it hard to focus, and I forced myself to breath slowly and evenly, willing my stomach not to reject what little it contained. I couldn't believe Michael hadn't puked already. He kept switching which hand he held the crook with, and scrubbing the free one along his breeches. They'd have to be thrown out, with how stained they were. No amount of hot water would get them clean.

Andrew took one of Beth's wrists, and she breathed in a shuddering gasp but her eyes didn't open. Gently Andrew felt along the fingers. "Pulse is steady, but slow. I think she has a few broken fingers. We'll need to get her to a lighted area, out of this wind."

Behind him David sat the large medical bag he carried onto the ground and popped it open. A bit of digging procured a tightly folded length of canvas. Michael and I moved entirely out of the alley to make room. Mother put her arm around me and I nuzzled into her shoulder, but still I couldn't take my eyes off the scene in front of me.

David and Andrew lay the canvas smoothly and as closely to Beth's prone form as possible. I squeezed my eyes shut. She looked like a doll that someone had thrown at a wall and then left.

Andrews gaze flicked to the hovering mercenary. His voice was cool. "A third medic isn't necessary, thank you."

The woman was silent for a moment, then crouched to speak quietly to both men. With her back to me, I had to strain to hear her. "I'm a healer. If she has a concussion I can reduce the swelling around her brain and prevent any further damage."

David had struck a match, with his other hand he cracked one of Beth's eyelids open. He waved the match back and forth in front of her, and without looking up from his inspection he said, "It can't hurt, Andrew, let—" there was an expectant pause.

"Belinda," she supplied.

"Let Belinda help. Beth won't thank us for turning down assistance."

Andrew looked conscience-stricken at Beth's prone form. "Fine. But we need to get a move on. This chill isn't helping her any."

Consciously, Belinda ducked her head in her own nod. As she tucked her glossy brown hair behind an ear, she glanced backward as though collecting her thoughts. There was relief in her voice when she spoke. "Ito."

"I'm here," a soft male voice came from behind me.

I jerked my head around to find the man who spoken. I had not realized he had come upon us. Before I could get a good look at him, his back was to me as he conferred with Belinda.

Glancing at Nophgrin's medics nervously, she gestured to the new man. "This is Ito. He is not a healer, but he is a mage." When they didn't immediately rebuff this, she spoke to Ito again. "Can you move her? I cannot tell yet how deep her injuries go. It would be safer."

"Of course," he said simply.

Without preamble, Beth's body rose evenly from the ground. My eyes bugged out. Her hair and clothes barely brushed across the bloody cobblestones, as what I had to assume was Ito's magic smoothly shifted her onto the canvas.

My eyes felt dry as I stared, but I didn't want to blink. To move a girl as though she was as light as a feather was a big deal to me. Of the two medics, only Andrew had magic, and he did not do stuff like this. Andrew had once explained that he simply didn't have enough of it to waste on anything but healing. If he even moved a few logs across the room, he might not have the strength to burn out a winter cold. He could get a familiar to expand his powers, but here in the mountains we didn't possess the instructional texts that would teach him the process.

If Andrew was resentful about this show of power, he kept it in check. He and David moved to take opposite ends of the canvas without comment. Ito waved them off, and with the motion of his hand lifted the makeshift stretcher into the air until she floated at waist level.

"To our home?" Anne's voice was reed-like, as though she couldn't get enough air into her lungs.

Andrew shook his head. "It's too far. Even with the help, I want to begin work immediately."

"We can't take her back to the inn. It'd be a madhouse," Laura said shrewdly. She seemed to have taken this show of magic in stride, though her hand was on her sword hilt. "My home is near, and it's safe. We can take her in there." She surveyed the crowd. "It's not a large home though. Medics and family only, if you please." She fished her keys out of her pocket and handed them off to Andrew, then recited her address to him, though everyone knew where the guards lived. It was one of the thatch roofed, one-story homes that Aella and I had been dancing in front of. Laura did not immediately follow the procession that carried Beth. Instead, she turned to scan the bloody alley. "I need to look at this, and I'll need torches, if someone will fetch them."

Michael was staring with unfocused eyes at the ground, so I raised my hand. "I'll go."

Mother looked sharply up at me. "Not on your life. We don't know who did this. They're still out wandering the streets. Your father will go get some."

"As will I, and while I'm at the pub, I'll tally up my people and put them to their bedrolls. Aella, you stay here with guardswoman Laura until I come back." Gone was the jovial Aedith from earlier in the evening. Her face was drawn and tired.

"Yes ma'am," Aella said in equally formal tones. She stood ramrod straight, her feet shoulder width apart, and her hands stacked loosely in front of her. Aedith and my father sized each other up soberly, and then turned to stride quickly back to the inn in silence.

Mother chafed my shoulder. On her other side, she did the same to Michael, though he stood almost two feet taller than her and she had to reach up to do so. "As soon as your father comes back and Laura clears us, we'll go home."

I nodded dully. Beth had been with a mercenary when I left. Had he lured her out into this shadowy alley? What could possibly be the point of beating a girl you only just met? Had Corey come out, and seen them as I had feared? But he was more likely to fight the mercenary than Beth, wasn't he? Unless he decided he was too outmatched by the mercenary, and went after an easier target. I bit my tongue and hoped desperately that someone else would mention seeing Beth and the mercenary together. Certainly, Maude wouldn't withhold the information. Then they could come up with their own conclusions.

I snuck a few glances at Aella, but she wasn't looking at me. In fact, she hadn't moved from where her mother had left her, and her eyes stayed fixed on the dark stain on the cobblestone, her mouth a grim line. Had she seen her companion and Beth pressed against the wall of the inn when she came to follow me? A worse thought: had she seen them in the alleyway and kept me from returning sooner?

Down towards the housing district, noise began to pool and torches became lit. It seemed someone, my guess was Willy, had diverted those who were leaving the inn to the next road over to get home. This meant that they didn't pass this scene, although those who lived near the alley craned their necks in curiosity, trying desperately to get a look inside the alley. Laura stood in front of it, her arms crossed and her face a foreboding mask that drove them into their homes with their heads bowed.

Not much later, Father returned. Behind him was Aedith and her troops, in varying states of drunken disrepair. Tess and Harold were weaving slightly as they walked, and Victor moved with painful deliberation, as though he wasn't certain about his footing. Kaleb and Dai moved more easily, and they also carried torches like my father and Aedith. When they came closer, I could detect a glaze over Dai's eyes.

Towards the center of the group I recognized the man I had seen with Beth. Probably in his mid-twenties, he had a scruffy beard and long lashes. His face hadn't been roughened by years of service, and his hair was luminous—it was no wonder Beth had chosen to idle with him rather than pimply Corey. He was the sort of fighter bards loved to write about. At this moment, I imagined those story-tellers would be in raptures. As his gaze darted about at each scrabble of stone or *chink* of curtains opening, I wondered if his nervousness stemmed from fear of rightful or wrongful retribution. Across the whole group hung a feeling a trepidation, and from the way they occasionally glanced at him, I got the distinct impression that they knew their comrade was the last person to be seen with Beth.

Aella moved to stand to the left of her mother, and Laura finally acknowledged them. "You understand that your lot will be blamed for this."

Aedith nodded, and I was impressed that her expression didn't change, though her hand fiddled with something in the pocket of her cloak. "So long as you understand that we're professionals here to do a job. Though I'm sorry the girl was badly hurt, my people did not do this."

Laura ran her tongue across her top teeth, and pulled out a pocketbook and a bit of charcoal from her waist pouch. "That remains to be seen. You, and Taryn." She pointed between Aella and myself. "You came outside a little over an hour ago, I saw you go. Did you see Beth then?"

I started, and Aella flinched at being addressed. She spoke quickly. "No ma'am. There was no one outside when I left."

"Taryn?" Laura's voice was stern.

My eyes flicked to Aella, but still she wasn't looking at me. Mother gave me another encouraging squeeze. Hesitantly, I spoke. "Yes. I saw Maude," Laura jotted down a note, "And ... I saw Beth, with that man." I lifted a heavy hand and pointed at the nervous mercenary.

"Did either of them seem agitated?"

"No, they were, erhm ... talking." Laura speared me with a look, and I blushed crimson before adding, "Closely."

Laura turned her glower at the young mercenary. "Well? What were you *talking* about?"

He gazed wide-eyed at me, and then turned to Laura. "I swear I didn't harm Miss Beth. You have my word. I came outside to have some fresh air, and she followed me out. We got to talking, yes, but that was it!" The man's companions wouldn't look at him, and his voice was strangled coming out.

"What's your name?" Laura asked, harshly.

"It's Lucas—Luke ma'am. I swear, she was fine when I went back inside." His words toppled over each other.

"Lucas you'll need to come with me this evening. It's as much for your protection as the town's. When word gets out about this, I can imagine no few of my neighbors who will be out for blood."

Finally, one of the mercenaries spoke up. "We can protect him fine." It was Victor, and Luke looked at him gratefully.

Laura shook her head. "This is not a negotiation. There has been a serious crime committed here, and Lucas was the last person seen with the victim. I have to take him in."

Aedith's lips had pressed tightly together during this exchange, and when she did speak her tone was regretful. "Luke, I'm afraid guardswoman Laura is right. This is not the first time someone has capitalized on our presence to commit atrocities." To Laura she said, "At no cost to you or yours I would add on to my task rooting out who did beat this poor girl."

Laura met her gaze without backing down. "It all depends on if the town is willing to let you stay. You understand. When that's decided I'll tell you whether or not I will accept your help." Her words were clipped, and I could tell she had taken offense at the mercenary captain's offer.

Footsteps drew my eyes over the shoulders of the mercenaries. It was Willy, with a sour looking Maude in tow. "Clear a path. Excuse me!" Willy's voice was good natured, as though he was speaking to friends, not extremely on edge mercenaries. "Ah, Laura, there you are. I've scrounged us up a witness."

"William, Taryn saw Beth with that man, Lucas, before she went on her walk this evening, though mercenary Aella denies it." Laura gestured to Lucas. I saw Aella bite back an objection with impressive restraint. Lucas opened his mouth as if starting to declare his innocence again.

Willy waved him off. "Maude, is that the mercenary you saw with Beth?"

Maude squinted at Lucas, taking him in from boots to hair, and I almost groaned— it didn't take that long to identify someone you had stood right next to! She curled her lip in distaste. "Yes, that's him guardsman."

Lucas went to protest again, and again Willy forestalled him.

"Taryn, you came outside and saw them together, and then you went where?"

I blinked stupidly but was more than willing to aid him in whatever scent he was dogging. His smile had a hard glint to it that I rarely saw from him. "I walked south, towards the mercenary camp. I had planned to circle the block, to get some air."

Willy turned to Aella. "But they were not there when you came outside?"

Aella shook her head. "I saw Luke right before I left, he was joining a table that was," she glanced at her mother, then gave Lucas an apologetic look, "throwing dice." Lucas seemed to try and shrink in place and I saw Aedith's nostrils flare and her lip curl ever- so- slightly with displeasure.

"And Beth?"

"I didn't see her, but I wasn't looking for her either, sir. I'd never met her before I saw her here tonight."

Willy nodded. "Laura, from what I gather, sometime in the minutes between Taryn leaving and Aella joining her, Beth vanished."

"Are we going to trust this girl when she says she saw her friend inside? She knows if he's found guilty they won't be paid. Why wouldn't she'd defend him?" Laura sputtered.

"My daughter is no liar." Aedith's words were a low growl.

"Well, young women do not vanish in this town, and turn up with their heads bashed in!" Laura's face was turning a mottled purple color.

"You can ask the men I was throwing dice with!" Lucas was yelling now.

"You think I won't?"

"Willy," my mother's soft voice carried, and the shouting paused. "I'd like to take my children home."

"Yes. Just one more thing, before I can conclude here. Luke, will you please step to me?" Lucas looked between Laura and Willy, his distrust clear. Reluctantly he did as he was told, and the other mercenaries parted for him to get through. Willy gave Laura a meaningful stare, and then he beckoned my father closer with the torch and knelt in front of Lucas. To my confusion, he tugged to lift one of Lucas's boots. Though it surprised him, Lucas obliged. "Do you see his shoes?" He stood, and circled Lucas, pulling at and inspecting his clothes. "Do you see his clothing?"

Laura was beginning to look sullen. "What's your point?"

"There is no blood on his boots or clothing, no scratches on his skin."

Michael was glaring at Willy now, his shoulders tight. It seemed he had given up wiping his bloody hands. There was so much blood on his breeches that it did no good. I squinted, and swayed. Would that make Michael a suspect? But of course, that was ludicrous, I was sure. There would have to be some blood on him. He had been cradling her. I shook my head, ruefully. I wasn't about to let my fear and drunkenness make me suspect my own brother. Resolutely, I returned to attending to the conversation at hand. Willy was asking a question.

"Luke was in the inn when all the mercenaries were gathered together and had been for some time, if my memory is to be trusted. Taryn, Aella, did you see Master Luke at any point during your walk?"

Laura spoke over my attempt at a reply. "This alley opens on the next street over. If he and Beth had walked that road and entered this alley from the other side, then Aella wouldn't have seen them. He could have then returned to the tents when they were on the block he came from! If he ran from here he would have been back before anyone saw them."

"Actually," I said, my shoulders level with my ears, "We were at the tents, and I didn't see him or hear him. Everyone there was asleep."

"Why were you at the mercenary tents, Taryn?" my father asked, his face was blocked from me by flames. I bit my lip.

Aella spoke into the silence. "I needed my flask. Taryn agreed to walk with me since I don't know the town yet. Much the same as Luke doesn't know the town." This time Aedith's disapprobation was cast on her daughter, who staunchly ignored it.

Luke ran both hands through his hair. "I swear, I didn't beat her." He looked small. "I swear it." He repeated this a few more times, but more quietly until Victor put a comforting hand on his shoulder.

"Laura, it seems unlikely the lad did this," Willy said. "Look at the blood here. As much as it pains me, we're searching for someone within the town, or else another guest. We'd do better tallying who *wasn't* at the inn at all tonight."

Laura shook her head. "We need to hold him and question him."

Willy turned to Aedith. "Are you going anywhere?"

She shook her head. "We've a job to do. We don't get paid unless we complete it, and if someone is setting my people up to take the fall for their own evils, that's more of a reason for us to keep on."

"This is absurd!" Michael burst out. His voice bordered on hysterical. "One of them—maybe not this Lucas fellow, although I doubt it, but *one* of them assaulted Beth. They can't be allowed to meander the town and the lands as though nothing is amiss!"

"Watch your tone, boy. There's a thing called due process." Aedith's nostril flared.

"Yeah, and there's a pretty good reason for why mercenaries can't find work in real armies!"

The mercenaries were muttering amongst themselves. On a good day, I imagined they weren't inclined to take such insults. Now, with the accusation and their guts full of drink they were becoming agitated.

Again, Willy spoke. "Michael, this doesn't appear to be the deed of one of our new acquaintances, however there is no way to know that for certain, and I've doubts this situation will get any better as the moon climbs higher. If the morning comes and the mercenaries have vanished into the woods then we will call their guilt confirmed and bring the law of the capital down upon their guild." More grumbles came from the mercenaries. "If, however, they stay, and it can be proven that someone else committed the offense, we will all be satisfied, I think."

Aedith looked nonplussed, but also a little impressed at Willy's diplomacy. "My men are exhausted from an evening that came just short of being perfect. We will go nowhere, this I swear." Luke seemed less than pleased by this, but he bobbed his head along with rest of the group.

Though Laura didn't look happy about it either, she nodded. "Aye. That does seem all we can do in this moment. But Lucas should still go into lock up!"

Lucas took a step backward, but Aedith forestalled his protests with a hand. "Guardswoman Laura is right. For your safety, you should at least spend the night there. Elsewise, we risk a brawl from which no one will find themselves the victor."

Willy agreed as well. "With that settled, Laura, would you escort Aedith and her people to their tents, then wait for me there as I walk with Raynard and his family to their horses? We'll walk Lucas to lockup together."

As Aedith spoke quietly with Lucas, we walked in silence back to the gates. Glenn and a few others were impatiently waiting to be released. Once we had gotten out of sight of the other group, Willy's confident smile had withered away, and now he ignored the questions the farmers bombarded him with. It seemed to be all he could manage to collect signatures and to open the gate. When Daniel found the guardsman unreceptive he turned his ire on Father.

"What in the name of the gods happened back there? I was having a strong drink at the inn and then we're all being told that we have to return to our homes. Then we find we have to wait here in the dark and the cold because the gate is locked and we can't go home! Where the blazes were *you*, Raynard?"

Father waited until he had mounted Tess to reply. "There was a problem in town. I am more than certain everyone will know all the details by noon tomorrow. Rather than giving you information to blow out of proportion tonight, I'll ask you wait until then." Daniel sputtered a protest but without pause, Father reached down to give Mother a hand up so she was settled snuggly in front of him.

"You will tell me right now! Or I'll not move from the spot!"

Daniel crossed his arms over his chest in defiance.

Michael and I exchanged a weary glance and slung ourselves onto our ponies. Cherub and Hale were in a bad state. Between the late hour and the reek of the blood that stained the front of Michael's clothes and his boots, we were lucky they didn't toss us and run. Father and Mother seemed to notice, because they waved to Willy, who waved back. Then they led us out through the gate.

Behind us the fight continued. "Daniel, you may plant yourself wherever you like, but that gate is only staying open the next two minutes! I'm going home to my wife and babe."

I peeked over my shoulder. Daniel glared for a few moments more, but good sense seemed to win as he finally hustled to mount onto his own speckled gray pony. "I'll be writing the capital. Mad gryphons, and whatever has happened here tonight. You're slipping William!"

"Go home and take to your bed Master Daniel. Threaten me again tomorrow when I've had my sleep."

Daniel might have growled a parting shot, but we were out of earshot. The dark trees looked like looming ogres, and I huddled into my cloak as our mounts took us quickly home.

Mother made Michael leave his bloody boots outside. I didn't see what he did with his soiled clothes. All my energy went into getting myself into my own bed and ignoring the gentle probing questions my parents were asking him about what had happened. Even if he had left anything out from his report, I trusted that Michael would let me know if there was anything left to tell.

It could have been Nai. The thought came unbidden after I had tucked myself in for the night. Or it could have even been me. We'd had strangers come through town before, a few had been unsavory. Never had something of *this* magnitude happened. I couldn't help wondering when things would get back to normal. How could they ever get back to normal?

15

The hunting party arrived at our home before the sun had finished creeping over the horizon. The firm knock on the door came as I was shoveling porridge into my mouth. Mother was in her room, Michael had gotten up early to clean his boots and was in the barn preparing for the field. Father was out there as well, getting ready to hunt.

Swallowing my last bite, I pushed back from the chair, wincing at the scraping noise it made against the wooden floor. On stockinged feet, I padded to the front door. For the first time since I was a small child I paused to peek through the peephole before I opened it. Aedith's stern face was fish-eyed through the small round glass, and I unlocked and opened the door. I was still in my nightgown, and though her body blocked me from the rest of the hunters, I couldn't help but cross my arms over my chest.

"Good morning mercenary Aedith." I bobbed a lame curtsy, not quite looking her in the face.

"Taryn … Miss Taryn, is your father ready to join us?" I looked up at her first utterance of my name. There had been regret in her voice, but her face was as much like a stone as it had been when I'd first met her.

"Yes ma'am. I believe he's saddling Tess now, out in the barn." I hesitated. "Would you like to come in and wait for him?"

She shook her head, a small smile twitching at her lips. "I'm afraid good manners would dictate you then let the rest of that lot in." She jerked her head at the company of near thirty men and women assembled on the road. "And forgive me, but I don't believe you have enough chairs."

I couldn't help but smile in return. "No ma'am, I believe you're right. One or two of us would have to stand." Another pause, then as she turned to leave three words left my mouth in a rush. "Was it him?"

She stopped short, and her eyebrows lowered as she stared at the ground, and then she brought her gaze back to me. "Luke is new to my company in comparison to the others, but he's been with us a year and a quarter. I feel confident in judging his character. He's a pretty lad, and he picks up a bedmate in each town we pass. He probably has bastards across half the country, but every time a lady has said no to him, he has moved on as quickly as a blink. There's always a more willing partner around the corner. He did not do this." She met my eyes with her own brown ones and enunciated the last sentence clearly.

I thought of Luke's panicked face last night, lit by torchlight. "But you can't be sure."

"Surety is for the gods. We cannot be sure that a gryphon

killed your livestock, but for the signs it has left which are typical of a gryphon. The same is true for any beast that hunts. It leaves tracks which those who are experienced can read. I know what marks an opportunist."

I rubbed the fabric of my nightgown as I mulled over her words. The draft from the open door caused the hem of the skirt to press against my shins. "You truly believe it was someone from Nophgrin?"

She ran her tongue across her front teeth. "I believe it is possible that someone who had eyes for Beth saw her with Luke, and punished her for it when she was alone."

"Who though? Beth wasn't tied to any one boy. She was seeing Corey some, but he wasn't the only one. Gods, my mother even said she was asking after my brother on occasion, and no one came after him." Corey had, I realized, but I kept that thought to myself.

Aedith seemed think about that for a moment. "It could have been one of her beaus, it's true, or it could have been her father, if he didn't like that behavior."

I schooled my face carefully as I thought of Aedith and Aella's own experience with disapproving fathers. The details were a little muddled, as was everything from last night, but I knew they weren't good. "The man you saw her mother with, he's her stepfather, and he'd never hurt her. Beth and her mother sought sanctuary here a few years ago. She only remarried recently, but her last husband is ancient history. There's no way he'd come here."

"I wouldn't think Willy and your wall could provide such assured safety." Aedith spoke carefully.

I looked away, unsure if she knew and was being coy. "Nophgrin is a northern town that burns all of those murderers and rapists who are caught and tried, ma'am. It's the only way to keep the bad energy from continuing. It's what the flame symbol burned into the gates means."

Through my lashes I saw her eyes widen in surprise. It was a fraction of a second, but it was there. It was a harsh rule, some called it barbaric, but the general opinion was that it was no more barbaric than committing the crimes to begin with. There was always the option of being shipped to the capital's justice, but that fate was a grueling and bleak one. A march on foot to the capital where a judge almost always sided with the town's judgment, and then the sentence was hard labor until death. Few criminals argued for the right to it.

She looked over her shoulder at her people. "What if you get it wrong?"

I shrugged helplessly. "I don't know. There hasn't been a burning since before I was born, and you'll understand I was not told the details."

She made a noise of understanding. "Where Aella is from, they burned those who dared disobey their sun god Artuos. I suppose given my druthers between the two, I'd pick your village's way but..." Her eyes went over my shoulder and I glanced back. Michael was emerging from the light of the kitchen. He must have come in through the back.

"I wanted to say goodbye to you and Mother before I went to work." He spoke to me, but his eyes were on Aedith. "Father's headed this way now. You should take to your horse, mercenary." He didn't add her name to the title, turning it into a slur.

I didn't chastise him for it. Michael had found poor Beth and had to sit with her alone in the dark as she slipped closer to The Dark Lady. I couldn't even begin to imagine what he was feeling towards the people he believed to be responsible. Still, I felt the insult and looked to the mercenary captain to see if she had taken offense.

The blank mask Aedith had adopted when Michael entered the room did not waver. She merely nodded to him, and then to me. "It was good to see you this morning Miss Taryn."

"You as well, ma'am. Hunt well, and stay safe."

She saluted me and turned to stride towards her horse. Without her form blocking my view, I could see the group that had been gathered at the inn. Had that only been yesterday? Were there also all fifteen of the mercenaries? No. I scanned their faces one more time. Aella was missing. Michael came up behind me and shut the door.

"Hey—" I protested, then stopped short at the look on his face.

"You're letting the cold air in, and we don't need that mercenary seeing you and targeting you next." Michael's voice was cold.

I flushed, glancing down at my nightgown. "Aedith says she doesn't believe it was him," I said softly. "She says he has been with them over a year, and it's not the kind of man he is."

"We've known the people of this town for over *seventeen* years now." Michael was moving back to the kitchen, and I followed him. "Can you say that you could imagine any of our friends and acquaintances doing that to Beth?" He scrutinized my face, and I was the one to look away. "Exactly."

"You think she flatly lied to my face?" I sat down and scooted the chair closer. The porridge had congealed into one gelatinous mass. I poked at it with my spoon.

"People do that. She probably doesn't want to have to take the time to replace this Lucas fellow." He saw my perturbed expression, and he sighed, tucking a strand of hair back behind an ear. "I think she's looking out for her men. The gods only know, maybe she believes him and thinks she's speaking the truth to you."

"Maybe that's it." I spooned a piece of porridge into my mouth and swallowed without tasting it.

The scent of sunflowers and lye swept into the room ahead of Mother. She smiled, but her eyes held concern that made me wonder how much she could hear of the rest of the house from her bedroom.

"You're on your way out?" she asked Michael.

He came over and embraced her in the doorway between the family room and kitchen. "Yes, I just wanted to say goodbye before I went. I love you. Be careful to and from town."

She cupped his cheek with one hand. "I love you too dear, and I want you to practice that same care. You never know, the hunting party could spook the gryphon and drive it towards field rather than the mountain."

"I'll keep a sharp eye out. Taryn," he stooped and hugged me around the shoulders, "I'll see you this afternoon."

"Ride safe, brother dear." My tone was mocking, but my hug was earnest.

When he had gone and my porridge was finished mother and I took the dishes out to be washed. The only sign that the hunting party had been to our home was the churned road. Father had not stopped inside to say goodbye before he left. Mother told me she and he had said their farewells before he went out to the barn.

"He's anxious to get this over with," she said, scrubbing at the stuck on oats in the bowl she was working on, with more force than was necessary.

My hand slipped as I rubbed hard at my own bowl, and water and foam squirted onto the grass. "It's from this onto the next catastrophe. He's probably hoping to stay ahead of whatever bad luck we've called down upon us."

I saw out of the corner of my eye a large tomcat of a lesser gryphon creeping out of the hedges. His body was gray with darker stripes across his back, which blended up to the head of jackdaw. His eyes were intent on a bowl that still held a few yellow streaks from Father's egg yolks. Casually I began to fill the bowl I was washing full of water.

Mother continued, oblivious. "He and I spoke last night after you two went to bed. He says it's as likely to have been Beth's father as one of the mercenaries. That's not new bad luck. That's old luck that didn't get dealt with properly."

"But how could he even get into town? The gates were shut tight, and Willy knows not to let him in. They have his name, right?" I swirled the water gently. The lesser gryphon crept closer, his thick tale swishing slowly.

"That's true, but nothing is completely certain." She echoed Aedith's sentiment. "He could have slipped in during this confusion of the past week or used a fake name. Even Beth's mother could have had a moment of weakness and harbored him" The jackdaw gryphon inched one paw forward.

I shook my head. "That I find hard to believe. We all saw her when she first came to this town. She was bruised from eyebrow to ankle, and both she and Beth were meeker than mice. She'd have to be crazy to let him into town."

"Sometimes the heart can be blind to the faults of other— *don't.*" Her stern tone caused my arm to scoop back in the middle of tossing the bowl of water on the jackdaw gryphon. As a result, the water made an unsatisfying splat a few inches in front of me, and the startled creature leapt into the air, as dry as ever.

I glared at Mother. "It wouldn't have hurt it any, and I'm starting to hate the cursed things. They're annoying."

"It didn't do anything to you. Now finish with that bowl and plate so you can get dressed and we can go."

I had been uncertain whether Mother would be willing to go to town today. I was relieved that she was. Beth might have regained consciousness. If she had, I could only wonder how much Nai had already discovered since the sun had come up. Not only that, Aella had not gone on the hunt with the other mercenaries, and it occurred to me that I wanted to see her again. Very much so. These thoughts quickened my scrubbing and I finished my stack of dishes in record time. I even took Mother's clean stack from her to carry inside and put away.

Without thinking about it at first, I tried to dress with close to the same amount of care as I had last night. I could not bear to wear the blue dress a second day in a row. Though I knew it shouldn't, it seemed to me that it smelled of blood. The green skirt which I had worn earlier in the week was the least dirty, and I chose that one and a clean sweater to go over it.

It was as I was taking a little more time to fix my braids that I realized what I was doing. Twisting them and pinning, I managed to set the hair into a neat square at the back of my head. Staring at my reflection in my parents' mirror, I told myself my primping had nothing to do with the possibility of seeing Aella. The fact that I had to tell myself that made me doubt the truth of it.

When I was ready to go, I met Mother at the barn. We had agreed that we would ride together on Hale this morning. Mother's knees were causing her pain, and frankly, we both wanted to get to town as quickly as possible to see what news had developed over night.

Willy did not stand at his usual post at the gate. Instead, Nadia was there. She was small compared to her husband, but the grim line of her mouth was determined. Behind the counter leaned a sturdy quarterstaff capped in iron with mean looking knobs. It was almost her same height.

"Names on the list," she said a little too loudly.

"Good morning, Nadia," Mother said as she scrawled her name. "How is the baby?"

Nadia smiled softly. "She's just fine, ma'am. She's with my ma."

"And how is Willy?"

The smile shrank a fraction. She gestured for me to step up and sign. Her voice was loud again. "He's just fine ma'am.

Mother didn't press her, and after I had tied Hale to a post we made our way towards the center of town. We exchanged a small look, but Mother didn't say anything, so neither did I. At the washing well, I was taken aback to find how quiet it was.

Quite a few of the usual people were missing. I'd expected the place to be packed. This surprise lessened slightly as it became clear that it was all the younger women. Kept home no doubt by worried parents. Even Nai was absent from the waterside. All of Mother's friends were present though, and once she had settled in, I asked to be excused.

"Nai's not here, and I want to make sure she's all right after last night. She's closer to Beth than I am."

"You'll stay on the main roads?"

"Yes, Mother."

"Then I see no reason not to," Mother said, dipping her rag into the warm water and giving it an idle swirl. "Give my love to her. I'll see you this evening."

"Have a good morning. Good-bye ladies," I said to the other women, who smiled at me, and said their own farewells.

I rubbed my arm nervously as I turned away. The dark circles under their eye belied the worry that their lips weren't discussing. The empty spaces where my friends ought to have been told of the unspoken tension still more.

Usually the day before temple was busy, as everyone ran about to get anything they might need for tomorrow when the shops were all closed. Today I was joined on the street by only a handful of other people. That more than anything else nailed home the seriousness of the night before. The suspicious glances the other people shot at their neighbors made my stomach flip painfully.

To get to Nai's place, the fastest path was the road that passed in front of where Beth was found. Instead, I took the long way— the parallel street, one block over. By this time, those in town would have soaked both buildings adjacent to the alley in water, and doused the alley itself in purifying oils. They would have lit the oil on fire, banishing the monstrous energies that came with such crimes, singeing mortar, wood, and clay. I couldn't bear to look at the scorched bricks that would mark where Beth's body had been found. My alternative route also happened to take me past the mercenary camp, but if Aella was there, then she was sitting quietly in her tent. The place was as deserted as the street on which I walked.

Nai's home was not far from there. It was no more splendid than its neighbors, and certainly not as extravagant as the merchant's homes at the top of the hill, but unlike the houses on either side it still looked brand new. Where other people might have allowed the thatching to go thin, or the paint to peel, Anwar put a great deal of whatever spare time he had into improving the home in which he lived. Nai's father had commissioned for their home to be built a half a year before he had arrived in Nophgrin. He spent another half a year living in it as it was being built, and furnishing it before his wife and young daughter joined him.

I knocked on the bright red door, which stood out from the plainly stained doors along the rest of the block. There was some clattering inside, muted by the walls. A few moments later, Salma opened the door. She was close to my mother in age, tall, with wide hips and a prominent mole right above the right side of her thin mouth. She kept her thick hair pulled back under a bright green kerchief. The scent of the sharp spices and herbs that she grew in a small glass hothouse at the back of the house rushed past her to envelop me.

A streak of flour contrasted starkly against the dark skin of her forehead as though she had carelessly wiped a hand across it. She did a great deal of baking for Sweetlings in the house, especially when she was agitated as she appeared to be now.

"Taryn!" Salma's accent was like those from the southeast, and it was more prominent than Anwar's. Her tongue seemed to caress each word before releasing it. "What a lovely surprise. Come in."

I obliged, slipping my boots off at the door. "Is Naieed here? She wasn't at the well when I dropped my mother off, and I wanted to make certain she got home ok last night."

"You are a sweet girl. Yes, she is upstairs in her room, sulking. She wants to go be help at the inn again tonight, and I will not let her. As though I would let my daughter out so late after something so terrible." She stopped short and seemed to remember herself. "You are not staying after dark, Taryn?"

"No ma'am. I'll be headed to the field before noon and back to my home before dusk."

She bobbed her head. "This is good. You know, I like William, but I was glad to hear Francine talking about writing the capital as we were being herded home. He cannot be everywhere."

"Francine is going to write the capital?"

Salma wagged her index finger at me. "I will leave something for Naieed to tell you, or she will be even more cross with me. You go up the stairs, I am certain she will be happy to see you. No. Wait." She gestured for me to pause and hustled into the kitchen. When she returned, it was with a small plate of pastries that were still steaming. "Take these up and give them a try. They are a new recipe I'm trying."

"Thank you, ma'am." I accepted the plate from her, surprised to find it heavy. The fragrant scent of cinnamon and nutmeg flooded my nose, and my mouth watered. She was the only one in town who ordered those spices from the south. They were expensive.

"I cannot remember. You are not sensitive to nuts?" She asked as I made my way towards the steps.

"No, not at all."

"Good, these have pecans and pistachios. I got them off the last merchant who came through. Very delicious." She kissed her fingers.

"Thank you," I said again, and she smiled and turned to go back to her work. As I made my way up the steep staircase that lay in front of the mudroom, I kept one hand on the bannister. Anwar waxed the steps once a month, and I was never sure which day it was. I ran my tongue over my chipped left incisor.

At the top of the stairs there was a tiny landing, onto that three doors opened. The center one held a ladder which led to the attic, the one to the left belonged to Nai, and the right one belonged to her parents.

Nai's door was shut, and I didn't bother to knock before I twisted the door knob and pushed in. Her room held the smells of baking, which wafted up through the floorboards from the kitchen below. It was oppressively hot in the summer, and cozy in the winter. The walls were covered in brightly embroidered hangings that depicted beautiful creatures and romantic scenes. Her aunts sent them to her every year for her birthing day. Before Michael and I switched shift times, I used to love coming in the afternoons after sheep watch. Nai would trace the figures on the fabric and tell me the stories her parents had told her of the place of her birth.

Nophgrin had gryphons, but Nai's family on her mother's side came from the homeland of dragons. According to her father, they started small like lizards, but if you didn't catch them, they continued to grow. If they were left unchecked they could get bigger than houses, but unlike the Carpathe mountain range, there weren't large wooded areas for them to hide in. Supposedly the city had a complex array of tunnels below it that carried away waste and they had to be swept frequently for the creatures.

A glance around the room told me Nai was not where her mother thought she was. The barely cracked window clued me in to her true location. I set the plate of pastries reluctantly on her dresser and moved across the floor, my toes digging into the carpets she and her mother had woven together.

I pushed the window open enough to pull my body through, and then carefully minced my way along the small decorative ledge that ran along the side of the house. It was painted the same shiny red as the door, which made it easier to see in my peripheral vision. Holding onto the edge of the roof was a strain on my fingers, and I moved as quickly as caution allowed. When at last the roof and supporting wall slanted close enough for my elbows to rest on the edge, I managed to heave myself onto the roof.

The back side of the roof wasn't visible from the road, and Nai's family had no neighbors behind them besides the mercenaries, whose camp curved along their neighbor's property, and then behind both houses. It was for that reason that I didn't fear flashing anyone my underthings as I kicked my legs like a frog to get up properly.

This path had been terrifying the first couple of times that Nai had made me come up. My dress always felt apt to tangle around my legs, and once I nearly fell. I would have if Nai hadn't caught me. After growing a foot and getting a lot of practice in chasing Nai up here, I had become pretty good at it. Still, there was always a heart fluttering moment when all that was keeping me suspended were my arms, which I hated.

As I pulled myself up, I spotted my dark-haired friend on the far edge of the roof. I knew she must have heard me climb up, but she didn't crack an eyelid. She was sitting cross-legged and practicing what she called "mindful breathing." Which, as far as I could tell simply meant she let herself take deep breaths as opposed to the usual shallow ones that let her whip out such quick retorts.

"Nai, your mother sent pastries," I said coaxingly in greeting.

Her breathing stuttered. "You can tell her that I won't be her test subject if she's going to act like I'm too fragile to work."

I crawled on my hands and knees until I was next to her and then sat back. "Nai, don't be like that."

"*Your* mother let you out of her sight."

"You can't blame your mother. Did you see Beth?" She opened her left eye to look at me and shook her head. "She was a mess. My brother found her." Quickly I recounted everything I had seen from the time I arrived on the scene until the time we left.

"Poor Michael." She opened both of her eyes, and levered herself onto her elbows. "That must have been so hard on him."

"Yeah, he doesn't have much of a stomach for blood. I'm surprised he didn't throw up."

She gave me a shrewd look. "No, I mean because of the way he and Beth have been flirting lately. I thought maybe she was moving on from Corey on to him, and now this. It's more reason for Michael to want to get out of here."

I reared my head back with an incredulous twist of my lips. "Michael has not been flirting with Beth."

"How do you figure?"

"Because I would have known? Beth has been asking about *him* and he hasn't been interested."

"Well," she fiddled with some of the thatching, "I wouldn't believe it either, but she has been asking your mom about him more recently. Then I saw him give her a flower about a week ago. A little blue one."

I gaped. "You never said anything."

"You're always so keen on him finding a nice girl. I knew you'd jump all over him or her and ruin it."

"Poor Michael," I whispered. "No wonder he was so angry with the mercenaries."

"And no wonder madam Francine was yowling about writing the capital for more guardsmen. It's a wonder she hasn't gotten more than our two here before now."

"Francine is writing the capital?" I asked, as though it was the first time I had heard it.

Nai brushed her hair back as a strong gust blew it over her eyes. "Yeah. She says we need more protection. I suppose it can't hurt, can it?"

"I guess not, so long as they're not going to blame Willy for all the trouble we've seen lately."

That got a forlorn headshake from her. "Maybe someone

didn't cleanse properly and we're paying for it? He can't be blamed for that."

"I guess so. People are so ready to be furious with the mercenaries though. It's not going to help anything to drive them out of town."

"And why is that?" Nai asked.

"I don't think they were the ones who did it. Now I'm thinking more than ever that it was Corey. I think he got jealous seeing Beth flirting with Michael and then the mercenary, and he saw an opportunity to get away with something awful."

"Or," Nai dragged the word out, "the mercenary Lucas lost his temper at something Beth did or didn't do, and he used his mercenary strength to bash her skull."

We sat quietly for a moment, watching the horizon brighten to a cheery blue as the sun began its climb. The hothouse's steamy ceiling was barely visible from our position. The pricey panes of glass glinted in the morning light. Birds flitted across the sky, punctuated by the heavier flight of lesser gryphons who chased them.

"What do we know about Corey anyway?" I asked. "He has always been a bit of a bully, hasn't he?"

Nai stuck out fingers as she tallied. "His father is pig farmer Daniel. He'd love to be a blacksmith. He spent some time with Claire, but now he thinks Beth is sweet, and ... Gods, I don't know, Taryn! He's *Daniel's* son. I stayed clear, but he isn't someone who would beat a girl! We *know* him."

Stroking a hank of my hair, I nodded in sympathy. "It's just, I saw Luke's face last night, and it was scared."

"Right. He looked guilty." Her tone made it clear that this

should have been obvious, but I didn't see it that way.

"No, not guilty. It was like he knew he was about to be blamed for something and he knew he couldn't stop it."

"You can't decide another person feels a certain way," Nai admonished. "You don't know this mercenary. His innocent 'oh no' face could be very similar to his guilty face."

"But then I talked to Aedith..."

"Aye, right, the captain of the mercenaries. A good, impartial choice. Say on."

I glared at her blithe expression. "She's a good woman. Before I ran across Michael and Beth, I was walking with Aella. She told me about her mother's past, and from what I can tell, she isn't someone who would put up with woman beating from any of her people."

This gave Nai pause, and she tilted her head back to watch the clouds above us. Her neck made a perfect curved line that ended at the collar of her yellow day dress. I blinked and looked away. Down at the mercenary camp I could see Aella's tent from this position. It was so still that it might as well have been empty like the rest of them.

"What exactly do you mean by that?" Nai asked. Her tone was idle, but I knew her curious heart was straining with the effort to appear disinterested.

I made a face. "It's not my story to tell."

"Well, either way." Nai lifted a finger and recited primly, "A woman may have little tolerance for misconduct in her own sphere and not care at all about it in another's."

"Is that from one of Claire's grandmother's lady-manuals?"

She grinned. "It might be."

"Well, in this case I don't believe it applies. Trust me," I hesitated then continued, "her own husband used to beat her, and he hit Aella. That's why they're both mercenaries now."

"Perhaps she took the charge seriously, but she can't see everything. Everyone makes mistakes."

"Exactly, and accusing someone of beating a girl with no evidence except for his profession as hirable help seems like a big mistake to me— especially since his current job is to help us. Plus, if Aella's behavior is any indication, this lot places stock in consent."

Nai pounced on this tidbit. "What is *this?* Did the mercenary captain's daughter make a move on you during your little stroll?" She looked absolutely tickled by this prospect.

Heat rose from my neck to swamp my cheeks, and I couldn't keep a smile from creeping over my lips. I'd hoped she would ask. "She might have."

She turned to face me, taking my hands in hers and leaning in. "Tell me everything." The look in her eyes told me she regarded this as the highest caliber of information. I could trust her with it though. Nai knew what to share and what to keep under her hat, clearly. My mind darted for a moment to the thought of Michael and Beth. Why hadn't he told me? But then I returned to the present discussion. I could ask Michael for details of his own flirtation after I got advice on *my* predicament.

"All right, I'll tell you. Keep your voice down though? She didn't go on the hunt with the rest of them."

"Maybe her mother is overprotective too," Nai muttered darkly, before regaining her previous train of thought. Her attention turned to the encampment below. "So, she's down there. What happened?"

"Well you can ease back a hair, I told her no last night." I told her everything that had happened, sparing no detail. "So now, I'm a little ... confused." I concluded.

"Because you thought you felt something." It was not a question, and she hummed thoughtfully. "You know this makes you biased on the Lucas issue as well?" I waved her onward, dismissively. "Well, honestly, Andrew and his partner could probably give you better insight from a romantic perspective." I nodded glumly. I'd had the same thought. "But I've kissed a girl, if that helps."

"Who?" I sputtered.

"Claire, at last new year, after your parents took you home— vomiting off the back of your pony, if I recall correctly. Claire and I were tipsy and we kissed on a dare. It was no big deal."

"So—but—do you like women?"

"Nope," she said easily. "What I'm saying is that sometimes when you're drunk you feel things, it's ok to act on them. It doesn't have to mean anything."

"I don't think it was the alcohol." I shut my eyes, struggling to find the words. "It was *her*. She was charming, and she made me feel interesting." If I thought about it, she had made me feel *something* before I'd drank at all. It had felt like I had been lit up from the inside, but you couldn't say things like that.

Nai held up a finger. "Those well-versed in the art of bedding women often have good tricks up their sleeves."

"Is that the lady-manual?"

She shook my shoulder lightly. "You don't have to believe everything someone tells you about yourself. Besides, it's not as though she's staying. So, practically speaking, what girl in town have you ever had feelings for?"

If I were to have feelings for any girl in town, it would have been Nai. She was beautiful and funny, but no. It had never been in that all-consuming way that girls had crushes on boys and vice versa. I didn't lose sleep over it, or get jealous when she kissed boys. How I felt about her had never been like what I felt last night. She was my friend. I shook my head and said, "I know you're probably right. I mean, I notice when a girl is pretty, but that's normal."

Nai shrugged. "Sure, I'm always coveting what other girls are wearing or how they've done their hair."

That wasn't quite what I'd meant, but I didn't say so. It seemed Nai didn't understand, despite having more experience kissing girls than I did. Not that I understood either. So, what did it matter? I had the mad urge to defend the idea that I knew that I liked Aella, but at the same time it felt fraudulent to say so, and I wanted to deny it. All of which pointed to it being useless to continue to talk about any of it until I wrapped my own head around how I felt.

"Have you heard any news about Beth since last night?"

Nai allowed the switch in topics without comment. "Andrew came by this way close to dawn. He looked done in. I was waiting up, and I think I nearly killed him, jumping out the door as I did. He said she'll live, but she hadn't woken yet. One thing I will say, we were real lucky the mercenaries had that healer with them. Andrew said she studied at the mage school in the capital." She yawned hugely and leaned back on the sun-warmed thatching.

"Did you want to see if they'll let us visit her? I've got some time before I have to go to the field."

She nuzzled her head back into the thatching. "Honestly? No. For one, I doubt momma will let me go, and for two, any blood that's not coming out of my own body makes me queasy. I'll faint and crack my head open and then Andrew will have two head wounds to tend to. Bad idea."

Below, Aella's tent shivered, and then a hand stuck out through the top and began to work the hooks open one by one until her whole upper body could stick out.

"Are you sure?" I asked, trying to keep my voice casual.

"Mm." Nai still hadn't opened her eyes, and I waved at Aella. Her eyes caught the movement with trained quickness, but her wary expression didn't dissolve. I realized with the sinking feeling in my gut that I had expected a different reaction. She gave an exaggerated eye roll, complete with a complimentary toss of her head. When she gestured for me to come down I glanced at Nai.

"Are you sure?" I asked in a wheedling tone.

"Gods above and below Taryn—yes, I'm sure. I promise I'll see her with you tomorrow, but honestly I'm still in a foul mood." Her eyes opened so she could glare at me, but she didn't sit up. From the corner of my eyes I saw Aella making her way towards the road.

"All right! I was only making certain!" I was a little taken aback at her outburst, but maybe she needed a little space. Ignoring the thought that I was excusing myself to go see Aella, I scooted over so that I could give her a quick hug. "I'll give you all the details I can tomorrow."

She hugged me back briefly. When I pulled away her eyes were over bright. "Please don't think I'm being cold. I do want to see her, I just—I'm afraid of what she'll look like." She ducked her head away from me, as though the words had cost her something to say aloud.

I sat back. "You know, last night I kept thinking of how grateful I was that you ended up working at the inn last night." I hugged her again and this time she squeezed me tighter before letting go. "It could have been you," I finished.

"I know." She rubbed her hands down the top of her thighs, staring at them without speaking for a moment. "It can't have been someone from Nophgrin. You have to know that. If it was, then it ought to have been me who got attacked, not Beth. She's younger, and she—she asked my advice when it came to Corey. She said she liked him, but she was getting other offers. I told her to look around. To have fun." A fat tear drop rolled down her cheek.

"Hey, hey, hey," I shushed her, rubbing her back firmly. "This is not your fault. This isn't even Beth's fault. The fault of what happened to Beth lays squarely with whoever hit her. Not with you, and not with Beth. There's no law against flirting with two men at once, but there is one about beating a girl till she bleeds."

She scrubbed at her cheeks furiously as more tears fell. "That Lucas and I were talking before Thomas asked me to help with the dinner rush. Gods, Taryn!"

It became useless to wipe her cheeks as the tears drenched them. I made more noises that I hoped were soothing. When she moved to rest her head on my shoulder, I let her soak my dress front.

"Nai, you know why we burn the attackers and not anyone

else," I said. She hiccupped an agreement, but I said it anyway. "It's because that person alone carries the bad energy. If that person didn't exist, then the crime would not have been committed, regardless of any other circumstance." She sniffled and I felt her nod.

We stayed like that for a few moments, and the worst part of me felt impatient to leave her and try and catch Aella. My eyes strayed to the path the young mercenary had taken towards the road. I told that part of me to shut up and stroked Nai's hair. She smelled like her mother, all spices and flour, and she was warm on the comparably cold rooftop. It was comforting. When she moved again I almost felt sorry for it. She dried her face with the edge of her skirt, and laughed wetly at me.

"I feel silly," she said.

I shrugged. "It's scary, and I'd rather this than you acting as though you didn't care at all. I was a wreck last night."

"I guess you're right." She looked at me speculatively, and my hand creeped to my neck.

"Do I have something on my face? Did you get snot on me?" I tried to joke when she didn't answer immediately.

"About the Aella thing. You know you're overthinking it, right? I've never seen you this confused about any of the lads I've set you up with. That alone says to me that this is something. Think about how it felt when she almost kissed you. It could be better if she actually did."

"Well, now I know you're feeling better if you're up for meddling in my love life." I realized my fingers were touching my tingling lips, and I forced my hand back to my lap. "Gods, I don't know. She's not staying. Can't you and I just live together?

Sleep in separate beds and take care of each other in our old age? It'd simplify my life quite a bit I think."

She flashed me her teeth. "I *know*, right? Unfortunately, my parents expect grandbabies."

"Please, I'd never marry you," I grumbled. "You'd walk all over me, we'd be penniless in a year, with sheep balded from all your new outfits."

She seemed to consider this, "Now that you mention it, I do find you wildly attractive." She batted her lashes at me.

I sighed ruefully. "I don't want to talk about this anymore, is that ok? It's too confusing." It was easier to focus on my hands than her face.

She shrugged. "That's fine. I'm sorry, I didn't mean to make things weird."

"You didn't, trust me," I took her hands and squeezed them reassuringly. "I'm the one that brought it up in the first place. However, I really do have to go. You're sure you won't come with me?"

She placed her forearm across her forehead and flopped backward again. "No, I can't come with you, but I promise I'll pine in your absence!"

I ignored that. "I'll leave the pastries in your room. Try not to sulk too long. Your mother means well, and she could do worse things to try and help you."

She grinned at me toothily. "Be safe with your merc girl!"

Without commenting on that, I carefully eased myself back onto the ledge and back in through her window. I almost walked past the pastries, but veered back to snag one. I popped it in my mouth and moaned in delighted surprise. Eyeing the plate, I grabbed two more, leaving Nai three, and then jogged down the steps.

"Is that you going, Taryn?" Salma's voice emanated from the kitchen.

"It's me," I agreed.

"Such a short visit?"

"I have to get on to the field ma'am. The pastries were amazing though. I'm taking one along with me." I hid the other behind my back in case she poked her head around the corner, but she didn't. The curve of her back was visible around the doorframe and it sounded as though she was rolling out dough on a counter. The pin made a slight squeak as it rumbled back and forth.

"That is very good. They will be available this week at the shop—tell your friends!"

"I will ma'am. Have a blessed day."

"You as well dear. Stay on the main roads!"

16

Back out in the pale light of the morning, a breeze immediately swept my skirt up. I pushed at it with both hands and scanned the road. In the shadow of an awning, Aella leaned against the corner of the house opposite Nai's. She saw me but didn't move, so I walked to her.

"Good morning," I said when I was close.

"Morning," she said. Her eyebrows were low, and her mouth turned in a frown. She wouldn't look at me full in the face, her gaze sliding to the right or left of me.

"What? I thought you signaled for me to meet you. Did I get it wrong?" My heart sank at this reception. Nai had gotten me excited to see Aella, and now it seemed she did not share my enthusiasm.

Aella opened her mouth and then shut it, twice. Finally, a smile replaced her frown. "You look like a kicked puppy."

Her smile still carried an edge. It was my turn to frown. "You're angry. With me?"

She ruffled her hair from her forehead backward. "Some, but it's not all you. I'm sure you saw the hunting party left without me this morning. Ma had me stay here as a sign of good faith. Like I'm a token, not a warrior."

"How did that happen?" I offered her the spare pastry, which she took. "Shouldn't it have been Lucas who stayed, not you?"

"We had a few women follow their men to our camp as we were getting ready to go. They were carrying on, swearing that if we did anything to their husbands while we were out hunting they'd sic the gods and the law on us. Luke is a more experienced hunter than me, so he was needed in the hunting party. Nothing would shut them up until Ma promised I would stay in town with them until the party returned. Like any of you could hold me if I chose to go." She flashed me a mean smile.

"They're scared," I said softly.

Aella's reply was sharp. "That's not my fault, and it's not Luke's fault."

"That's why you're upset with me."

"You're cursed right! Why'd you rat him out like that last night?" she exclaimed.

I spoke in a heated whisper, glancing around to check if anyone was around to hear—there wasn't. "I didn't rat him out, I said honestly what I had seen. If I hadn't then Maude would have, and I'd have been caught in a pointless lie."

"You should have seen him this morning. He's going to sleep in my bedroll tonight since he's petrified you lot are going to drag him from *his* bedroll and burn him on a stake!"

Uncomfortable and unexpected jealousy sparked in my gut. I glared fiercely at her. "We don't kidnap and burn people, Aella."

"But you do burn them. No one here seems to much care what the truth is if the truth is that someone here is responsible." She was close, her head cocked to the side, her arms crossed over her chest.

"If he's innocent the gods won't let him burn."

"That's not how fire works Taryn!"

We were shouting. I realized my hands were fisted at my side. I unclenched them and took a deep breath, letting it out slowly. "I don't believe Luke hurt Beth." Aella blinked and eased back. "I think it was her beau. Many people think it could be her father." I glanced up, and saw Nai's head quickly duck back behind her rooftop. I rubbed my forehead and sighed.

Aella leaned back against the house behind me. She seemed to consider my words. I was grateful that no one seemed to be home to hear our argument. "Are these persons prone to violent outbursts?"

"Her father, yes. Corey? Not any more than any of the lads in town. Still, he's Daniel's son—Daniel is the pig farmer—and he sure as the sun could be called aggressive."

"Have you told your parents what you suspect?" She took a bite of the pastry, blinked in surprise, and then murmured in appreciation.

I scuffed a foot. "Well... no, not yet."

She scowled again. "Of course not."

"My parents have already considered her father, but he has less than half a chance of getting into these walls. Corey and his friends will hate me if I pick a fight with them. What if I'm wrong?" I tried to keep the whine out of my voice, but I knew I didn't succeed when she wrinkled her nose at me.

"Then, I don't know, the wrong man burns for a horrible crime. What a tragedy, right?" She snorted. "Lives on the line, and you're worried about your reputation. Typical." She finished her pastry.

"If you don't like me, then why invite me over to talk?" I burst out in exasperation. "Because I was having a fairly stressful morning already without you telling me all the ways I'm lacking. Just to be clear."

"Yeah, I gathered that, thanks. Who else am I supposed to talk to, my horse? It's a close race, but she's even less of a conversationalist than you." She sneered.

I stared at her a moment and then turned on my heel to stalk down the street towards the north gate. At first, only the noise of my hurried *crunch-slap* on gravel and packed dirt cut through the chilly silence. Then an exasperated sigh dragged out from behind me, and I heard her trot to regain her place at my side.

Her hand grabbed my arm. I yanked it away, but I did slow down. "Come on—I don't think you're terrible. That doesn't make you perfect though."

"Oh, like you are?" I whirled to face her, and jabbed a finger in her chest. "Beth is my friend. You can't even imagine how I'm feeling right now, and you don't care. You're just looking to get—" I made a strangled noise of frustration and resumed my walking. Aella followed, close.

"You think I want to bed you?" Her voice was soft and incredulous. "Newsflash Taryn: you're not that pretty, and there are easier lays in town, I guarantee."

I flushed hotly, not slowing. "So, what is it that you want?"

"I ... was hoping you might help me sneak out of town."

That stopped me dead in my tracks. Again, I turned to face

her, but this time more slowly, my face screwed up in disbelief. I spoke deliberately slowly. "Are you *serious?* What in the world makes you think I'd help you do that?"

She held her hands in front of her chest, palms forward. "It's not to join the hunt or skip town, I swear. I go stir crazy if I stay inside walls too long—and so does my horse, Juniper. Please, Taryn, I'll go mad being watched and whispered about all day."

I had gone slack-jawed as she spoke, and when she finished, I closed my mouth. I looked around surreptitiously for open windows. Finding none, I spoke in a low whisper. "If it was just you, *maybe* I could sneak you out, but you and your horse? You're a loon. It can't be done."

"Look, I've scoured about every inch of the town walls, and I couldn't find a crack that could slip a horse out, but I *know* there has to be something. You all didn't stay in at night as kits, did you?"

I crossed my arms stiffly over my chest. "I've no idea what people from town do to leave at night, *if* they do. I don't live in town."

Aella opened her mouth to reply and was promptly cut off by an airy voice that drifted down from the roof to our right. "I know how to get out of town with your horse."

Both of our heads whipped backward so that we could look at the top of the roof. There, Nai sat cross-legged, looking as smug as a lesser gryphon with a mouse in its mouth. I scanned the rooftops leading back to Nai's home. Even the ones farthest apart were close enough that a determined girl could leap the divide with relative ease. She had never shown me *that* trick. I glared.

"Come down off Miss Raina's roof—you'll get in trouble!" I hissed loud enough for her to hear.

She grinned, the whites of her eyes showing as she rolled them. Without another word she disappeared back over the roof. For a few minutes there was silence, so I finished my pastry. Aella wiped her hands on the sides of her thighs, whether from nerves or to dust off crumbs, I wasn't sure. A series of soft thumps came from around back. A few moments later, a slightly disheveled and out of breath Nai trotted out from the alley separating the two houses next to us. When she saw us staring, she paused in the shadow of the house behind her. She licked her lips and grinned.

"Pretty cool, right?"

"How didn't I hear you?" Aella peered at her incredulously. "I heard you both back on your own rooftop, carrying on. How in the world did you make those jumps," she gestured towards the gaps that were the alleys, "without me knowing?"

Nai shrugged carelessly, moving towards us once more. "One, you were very taken with yelling at my friend. Two, I am excellent at that." She jerked her head back towards the direction she had come from.

"How is that?" I demanded. "You've never showed me that!"

She had reached us at that point. "The short of it is that you wouldn't have liked it, and you would have told Michael." She held a stalling hand up as I went to protest and met Aella's eyes. "Do you want to get out of town, or do you want to hear why I know that Taryn can't be trusted with half the secrets I keep?"

They shared an infuriating grin, and Aella shook her head. Her gaze flicked down the length of Nai's form so briefly that I let myself hope I'd imagined it. "I'd like that secret passage please, and you can tell me when we've made it out."

"All right, your horse is in the inn's stable, right? Taryn, you'll want to go out the regular way."

I bit my lip and nodded hesitantly. "All right. I'll meet you on the road?"

"That will work. I'll move us as quick as I can."

Aella smiled at me, and then she and Nai left. Feeling at a loss as the two of them moved off, I stared after them for a moment before abruptly turning on a heel and walking double-time. Aella's smile had caused my pace to quicken uncomfortably. I only slowed when I became viewable from the guard shack.

As I was unlooping my mount from the post, my hand paused for a moment. Aella had heard Nai and me on the rooftop. My cheeks burned, and I felt woozy with embarrassment. Nadia took my sign out signature mutely. If she noticed my face, she didn't let on. She wasn't quite the talker that her husband was.

There was no sign of Nai or Aella near the gates. They hadn't said if I was meant to wait for them, or if they were going to go a ways down to keep from being seen. I kept my pace slow as my thoughts whirled around the two women whom I considered my friends, even if the title was dubiously given to Aella.

Was it even safe for Aella to be let loose? I felt as though she could be trusted, but her mother had good reason to keep her in town, however unfair it was to Aella. If any of the women in town found Aella missing when it had been promised she would stay, they'd have more than a fit. They'd accuse Aedith of lying, and I doubted that their minds would come up with good motives for the disappearing act.

Nai had been adamant that the attack had to have been committed by a mercenary. If she didn't trust the mercenaries why would she help the captain's daughter? Was Nai trying to buddy up with the new girl to learn more about Lucas? Or worse, was she trying to sabotage them? I couldn't think Nai would do that, but lately it seemed like everyone kept more secrets than they shared.

I stroked Hale's neck lightly. That thought was too depressing. Perhaps this was a scheme with me in mind? Initially she had insinuated that whatever feelings I'd had were influenced by the alcohol and Aella's skills as a flirt. Then she had told me to go for it.

My head hurt, and I shook it to clear it of the cobwebs of thoughts gathering. It was times like these that I missed the days when it was just Michael and me. People were too confusing, and they made me wish I had gotten more sleep.

17

I was about ten minutes out of town when Hale made a nervous noise in her throat. Something rustled in the trees to my right, heading fast in my direction. My blood burned cold in my wrists as I wheeled Hale to face the noise. She snorted and pawed at the ground beneath us, her body squirming between my thighs as she backed up a few paces.

A horse head broke through the leaves first. It was a chocolate flax mount, the pale fetlock contrasting sharply with the rich chocolate color of the horse's snout. Next came the riders of the beast, perched on its back. Nai sat in front of Aella who had her arms looped around Nai's waist to grip the reins. They both grinned, clearly pleased to have startled me.

My heart thudded in my chest from the adrenaline that had yet to leave my body completely. I lowered hands that shook from where they were poised over the crossbow that was strapped to my own mount.

"How did you make it out?" I demanded. "Did you lead the horse onto a roof and jump?"

Nai shook her head, her curls bobbing with the movement, and Aella reared her head back to avoid getting slapped with them. "There's a cellar under The Black Gryphon. They use it for wine now, but Maude says it was originally built to hide the women and children when the town was first built. Back then we had a lot of problems with raiders—mountain-men—there needed to be a way to hide or get out of town fast. There's a tunnel that comes out about a mile into the woods."

"They don't mind you using it for your own pleasure?" I raised my eyebrows at her in disbelief.

"Matthew—the inn keeper," she added for Aella's benefit, "He once told me his grandfather let him in on the secret back when *he* ran the inn. I guess it's customary to leave the thing unlocked for younger folks to slip in and out of. There's no clear-cut path once you get into the woods, so someone has to show you the way first."

"Our parents probably used it too," I mused.

"Well, not mine," Nai giggled, "but yeah, probably your ma and da. I'm glad no one thought to lock it with everything that has been happening this past month."

"They wouldn't lock it for a gryphon." I pointed out, "And whoever hurt Beth was already in town."

"I think it's nice," Aella said, maneuvering her mount around the wall of shrubs to join me on the road. Her horse minced carefully, not stepping on anything taller than its ankle. It was a funny thing to watch. She was so much larger than Hale, and even my pony was more likely to barrel through the flora. "Back home we didn't have a closed wall like this place, and people could mostly come and go in and out of town as they liked, but there was no understanding between the adults and children."

"Aella is actually from somewhere north of where my family hails from." Nai gripped the saddle horn to stay steady as we moved onward down the road in unspoken conjunction.

Aella nodded. "A little more to the west as well, but yes. The pastries your mother baked were so good. They reminded me of the ones my mother used to make when I was a girl. Sweet and spicy. Everything here in the north strays towards savory—salty."

It was my turn to chuckle. "Well, it's cold here, Aella. We need food to keep the winter from our bones."

"It's true," Nai agreed, "I love my momma's cooking, but no one here wants a curry—they want a thick piece of roast smothered in gravy."

My stomach growled, and we laughed together. When silence fell, I found it wasn't strained, and we road comfortably in it for a few minutes. The sun had risen to almost the crown of the sky, meaning I'd be late to relieve Michael again. He'd be mad, but perhaps not when he saw I had brought Nai. I blanched at my next thought. He would not be happy to see Aella. He might even tell Mother that she was out in the field with me.

I turned to look at her. "You two seemed to have found some common ground to speak on. Are you coming with me out to the field, or are you going to show her the forests closer to town?"

Nai twisted to confer silently with Aella. "Three is a nice group," she said. "If you wouldn't mind, I'd love to see where you work. Besides, if the hunting party spooks the gryphon, it may flee towards you, and I'd be an outstanding asset in that scenario."

My hand crept up to twist a braid around my fingers. Nai caught the nervous gesture and nodded in understanding. "You're worried about Michael."

I tilted my head in regretful ascent. "He'll flip if he sees Aella."

"Not a problem. We'll hang back in the woods while you two say your hellos and goodbyes." Nai looked backward at Aella who shrugged wordlessly.

"Just…" I paused to consider my words. "You have to be very quiet and still. I don't want him to hear something strange and fire off a bolt into the woods. Or worse, realize it's you and run to tattle. It would complicate things where they don't need to be complicated."

Aella snorted. "I promise not to let your brother catch us. I'm trained at concealment and so is Juniper."

"And I think I've proven I can be quiet enough." Nai said with fake haughtiness that seemed to be mocking Aella. Our new friend caught the jab; her mouth twisted into a self-conscious smile.

"We'll be careful," she amended in a softer tone. "We got out of town with none the wiser, didn't we?"

"Ok, then it should be fine." I wriggled my shoulders to try and shake the tension from their muscles and let out a sigh. "So why have you never told me about the tunnel?"

Nai shrugged, unfazed. "You don't live in town. What were you going to use it for—sneaking *into* the walls?" She spoke as though such a thought was ludicrous, but I could remember many nights when I would have liked to have been able to sneak off to see my best friend.

"You could have smuggled some ale out to her and her brother. Drank yourselves silly," Aella supplied.

I spoke at the same time Nai made a snort of derision. "Michael would never have gone along with that. He works in the morning." I flushed in embarrassment.

"You see?" Nai waved a hand at me in dismissal. "So, you would have had no use for the tunnel, and it was fun to use it now in a big reveal."

"We could do something tonight." Aella's voice was hesitant, and she glanced between us as though she expected to be rebuffed.

"What?" I asked.

"If you think your brother won't approve, he doesn't have to come. You could say you feel ill tomorrow morning and beg off for the day. I've some mint leaves you can chew so your breath doesn't smell too foul. If your friend has never insisted on a reckless night out, then that's something that needs remedied."

Go without Michael? Well, I'd have to do a lot of things without him soon enough. "I could do that." I said, a little hesitantly at first. Then more firmly, "That sounds fun. But, well, what would we even do?"

"The normal nonsense. Get ourselves tipsy in the woods." Do dares, and tell secrets and stories."

Nai laughed. "Yes, that's about right. A few years ago, Beth, Claire and I found a nice spot for us to go to. Although we usually go in summer, not autumn. We'll have to dress more warmly."

Hale whickered at the trees, and I made a regretful noise. "The gryphon though. It's only safe to go out if the mad gryphon is caught today on the hunt."

"You see?" Nai scoffed. "This is why I never asked you to come along with the other girls. You'd always have a reason not to come."

"A crazed gryphon is a good reason not to go into the woods at night! Not comparable to any other 'excuse' I might have given you if you had ever even asked me."

Aella broke in before Nai could respond. "Taryn, Nai's right, there's always going to be a good reason not to go—but half of the fun is the excitement of what could go wrong. Plus, you and I have at least some weapons training, and from what I understand, this creature hunts in the daylight." Nai nodded her agreement. "There has been no news of any person being mauled, not even travelers, so it's likely that it is afraid of humans still, despite whatever else is wrong with it. A hunting party alone is often enough to scare off these smarter monsters."

Nai and Aella, were fearless for such different reasons, and then there was me, Taryn the shepherd, who was going to spoil the only little adventure she'd ever been offered before it even began. It wasn't as though I'd ever even seen a greater gryphon up close before, I reasoned. They did tend to stay away from people. My mother had only seen one once in her whole life.

A million "buts" ran through my head. Michael would be upset if he found out. Aella and Nai gazed at me expectantly, but neither girl rushed me. There'd always be a reason *not* to do the exciting thing.

"Ok," I said.

Nai squealed and wriggled in her saddle causing Juniper to flick an ear back and huff. Aella looked amused, and patted the horse's neck. "There you have it."

My heart thrummed in my chest, and I made a concerted effort to keep my hands loose on the reins. I glanced at Aella, and when I saw her looking back at me an involuntary grin bloomed on my face. She returned it with a nod of understanding. The road was narrow enough that her bright eyes were easy to see. They were amazing, I realized. Despite how close we had been all of the night of the attack, it had been dark, and I'd been too drunk to properly see them. They were hazel. A starburst of gold surrounded the blackness of her pupils; beyond that was a green the color of oak leaves shifting to their fall colors, and all of that was ringed with a thin sliver of umber. They seemed to pull me in, and I had to tear my gaze away from them to better listen to what Nai was saying.

"... and it would be good if you brought an extra blanket, that way you have something to sit on." She gave me a shrewd look. "You got that?"

"Yeah, I can do that," I agreed hastily.

"Are we almost to your field?" Aella asked, clearing her throat. I thought she sounded dazed. Or was I only hoping that I'd had the same effect on her that she'd had had on me? I was too afraid to look.

I kept my attention turned straight ahead. "We're close; probably about a half mile away." I looked at the surrounding woods and hummed thoughtfully, trying to place exactly where we were. "Probably in the next few minutes you both should duck into the woods. After that, the trees start to thin out the closer you get to the field, and it'll be harder to hide. I'll continue on, and once Michael has passed, you can join me in the field."

They both nodded, and once again Nai's hair brushed against

Aella's face. She crossed her eyes at the back of my friend's head. I caught a giggle in my throat, and Nai glanced at me.

"What?"

"You keep hitting Aella in the face, and she's too polite to say anything," I explained, giving in to my giggles at Aella's noise of embarrassment.

"It's fine. It's to be expected with the cramped seating." Aella said.

"You should have said something!" Nai whipped her head around to look at Aella apologetically, succeeding in having the whole of her hair fly across Aella's face. Aella, for her part, sputtered, and I laughed harder.

"I can't imagine why." Aella picked a few strands of hair from between her lips.

"I mean—" Nai dug in the satchel that hung around her shoulders, procuring a leather strand, "I could have tied it back." She did so, deftly twisting the bottom half of her hair into a loose fishtail braid.

"All right, well I think we'll take this moment to pull off into the woods," Aella said to me. "Better safe than sorry. Send your brother on his way quickly though, will you?"

"I'll do my best." I saluted her, and she chuckled and steered Juniper towards the shrubbery with the most space on the opposite side.

"Hold steady for a moment," was the only warning Nai was given before Aella kicked Juniper into a quick trot, and the horse leapt over the foot of bush. Nai gave a tiny squeak as Juniper went airborne, but when they had landed and turned to face me again, her face glowed with pleasure.

"We'll see you in a little bit," she said.

"Be safe in the woods," I replied.

"So long as you do the same on the road."

Aella just nodded to me, and I bobbed my head in return, then I road on, not waiting for them to disappear into the foliage. I pushed Hale a shade harder than when I was with the other two women, excited to get to my post and send Michael on his way.

He was peevish at my lateness and in no mood to chitchat with me. In fact, the most I could get from him that was more than a grunt were terse one-word responses. I was a little hurt, but much too excited about getting to spend my shift with friends to let it ruin my mood.

I was finishing setting up my blanket under the shelter that served as shade from the sun when it wasn't a roof from the rain, when the sound of hooves piqued my attention. Aella and Nai were trundling up the short path from the road to the hill where I was perched. I waved to them, smiling broadly. Brooks stood, piercing the newcomers with a stern look. I reached down to stroke his soft ears.

"It's all right, Brooks," I murmured. "These are friends. You know Nai."

Brooks sneezed and trotted to meet them halfway. I gnawed my lip as Juniper eyed my shaggy dog, but it seemed Juniper had experience with canines. After a moment's pause, wherein Juniper graciously lowered her head and Brooks gave them all a good sniff, she continued towards me, undaunted.

"Hi puppy," Nai cooed. When they had come to a stop, she dismounted and knelt to massage Brook's head.

"That beast's no puppy—he's a full dog." Aella protested.

"All dogs are puppies," Nai replied seriously, then in a sugar sweet voice, "Aren't you, sweet puppy?" Brook's tongue lulled out of his mouth, and he half-closed his eyes at her ministrations; he was the picture of doggy bliss.

"You didn't run into any trouble, did you?" I asked.

Aella shook her head

"Good—Nai, let Brooks alone, he's working."

Nai stood and joined us. "Are you ready to plan out this party?"

18

My shift in the field had breezed by as Aella, Nai, and I plotted out our plan for the evening. Aella had easier access to alcohol than Nai or myself, and so she would be bringing enough for the rest of us. Nai and Aella would meet by the inn and slip out together. If Claire could get away, she would be with them. Claire was Nai's friend, not necessarily mine. Still, I didn't want to be a spoilsport, so I refused to complain. They would meet me a half-mile from my home, and together we would continue to Nai's hideaway.

At home, I completed my chores quickly. I listened with one ear as I worked, as Father told us of the days hunt.

"We searched until an hour before dusk," he said. "We found no trace of a gryphon, mad or otherwise."

"No one spotted any trails at all?" Michael asked.

Father shook his head. "Besides the markings that Glenn found already, there weren't any others."

Michael made a noise of acknowledgment, and returned to his own chores without another word. Father's pithy recount did not include how the mercenaries behaved, and I didn't want to be the one to ask. I'd hoped Michael would think of more questions, but he seemed almost uninterested in the hunt after that.

Father did tell us that they had swept the woods adjacent to our field and Glenn's, for several miles. It was a lot of ground, and for them to have found nothing boded well. Perhaps the gryphon had receded back into the mountains. I mused later as I scrubbed the day's dishes, muttering noncommittal replies to my brother as he asked about my time in the field.

When that task was finished Michael went to his room to read, and I went to bed early as well, feigning a headache. My parents, though concerned, were distracted, discussing the gryphon, as well as Beth. Mother spared me an inquiring look, maybe wondering if Michael and I had fought again, and I shook my head with a soft smile. The crack under Michael's door glowed with candlelight, and I thought about asking him along, but before my hand touched his door knob I turned away and continued to my room.

A few hours later, when the hatch for the other side of the fireplace clunked shut, I felt my stomach dance. My mother and father made their way to bed not long after. When their door *clicked* shut I swung my feet off the bed into the boots that lay waiting. I paused, and slipped them back off, to carry them instead. I was no expert at sneaking about like Nai, but I knew my stockinged feet were a fair bit less clunky than my boots on the hardwood floors of the house.

The hallway was already chilly with the fireplace closed off. The other two doors at the end of the hallway were shut to contain the heat from their own small hearths. Already wrapped in my wool cloak I didn't mind it.

I'd chosen the kitchen door to make my exit through, since the draft wouldn't be as noticeable from the bedrooms. Outside, I shod my feet once more, and took off at a light jog to the barn. We were almost at a half moon, so I didn't feel afraid that I would trip over an errant stick or mole hill. The sheep, skittish beasts that they were, bleated at me when I pulled the small side door open to slip inside. I hushed them, my heart pounding giddily. They knew me, even if they didn't approve of how late I had chosen to visit. With the exception of the few more gluttonous of the flock who followed me around the perimeter of their pen, begging for food, they quieted.

Hale was another matter entirely. She sensed my pounding heart, and her excited responding energy made it a chore to saddle her. I fumbled in the dimness of the barn, swearing as I failed to hitch her harness twice before finally managing it. She especially objected to the cloths I tied over each hoof. Those had been a suggestion from Aella, which had delighted Nai. They would muffle the sound of her hooves on the ground.

"Easy," I murmured. "It's only until we get out of earshot from my parents. We don't want to wake them, do we?" She snorted, and fidgeted.

With as long as it took for her to be ready to go, I feared Aella and Nai might have assumed I had been caught or chickened out, and gone on without me. As I turned out of our property a bobbing light down the road allayed that fear. Aella carried a small lantern that cast a warm relief on her, Nai, and Claire. I mustered up a nervous smile for the lot of them

Aella hefted a burlap sack with her free hand, and inside, bottles clinked as they knocked together. "You ready farm girl?"

Conscious of how Claire raised her eyebrows at this nickname, I lit my own lantern, pilfered from the barn, so that the four of us were surrounded in a shuddering circle of light.

My reply was full of more bravado than I felt. "As easy as breathing."

Collectively we turned our mounts in the proper direction, as Nai relayed their escape from town. "I had to convince Thomas that it was just Claire and I and that it would be all right for us to go. He was worried about the gryphon, of course, and the attack on Beth. He heard the hunters found nothing though, and I reminded him that only town folks know the secret way out. No one would expect us to be running amuck in the woods right now. I convinced him in the end. Everyone is saying that maybe this gryphon was gorging. Maybe it was with child or something and retreated with all the fuss."

"My papa says the mercenaries are stalling so that they get paid more," Claire said snidely, then she seemed to recall Aella's presence, "Not that I'd blame them."

Aella rolled her eyes, and chose not to comment. Pursing my lips, I cast a subtle glare at Nai, who missed it. She was riding with Aella again, behind her this time, and reaching for the bag of alcohol.

"Is this place we're going far?" I asked.

"No, not at all," Claire said. "It's actually along the river, right up here." She pointed to the point that I normally crossed on my way to the field. "I haven't been here yet this fall but Beth..." she faltered.

Nai passed her the flask that Aella had given her, after she tired of my friend rooting through her sack. "Here, take a drink."

Gratefully Claire took a delicate sip, then she continued, her voice a little rough. "Beth said someone she knew was out here a few weeks ago and there's a mass of bluebells blooming."

"This late in the season?" I asked.

"Yeah, she said she heard they cover the whole forest floor. That's what we're looking for."

"If she didn't hear if from you two, who did she hear it from?" Aella asked shrewdly.

Nai and Claire exchanged a look, and I sighed in exasperation. "My brother. Right?" Did everyone know about this affair but me?

Claire nodded. "Beth said he gave her a bluebell, and then invited her out for a ride. He told her he wanted to show her a whole field of them. She was very impressed. It's a shame she never got a chance. I don't know why she'd pass up someone like your brother—or even Corey, to mix with riffraff."

"Enough Claire," Nai said firmly. "You've made your sentiments about our guests abundantly clear. You're not exactly subtle."

I bit my lip. That was what I had *wanted* to say.

"Oh, don't stop on my account," Aella said coolly. "You might as well get it all out now before I get drunk. Let's see, you've called us cheats and riffraff. Anything else?"

Claire rolled her eyes. "Some people are so touchy. You act like you don't know what folks say about you people."

"People say you're a stuck-up brat, but you don't see us bringing it up every time you're about," I muttered. The words came out too loudly in the night.

"What was that?" Claire asked, her voice sharp, the whites showing around her green eyes. "Didn't she call you a farm girl? Why is that ok, but I can't call her for what she is?"

"Because she wasn't saying it to be nasty," Nai said before Aella or I could form our own replies. "You are. Now stop. I wouldn't have invited you if I knew you were going to be such a rain cloud."

"I'm not—" Claire pouted.

"You are," Nai insisted. "Now stop it. Aella is good people. If she is a mercenary so what? We don't hold your merchant's blood against you." That got the laugh she had been garnering for, and the tension between us all eased slightly.

There was a small game trail that followed the river in both directions. It saw enough use from fishers and hunters that we could ride for most of the way. Eventually though it narrowed and we all dismounted and led them the rest of the way. About a mile in Claire stopped us and gestured towards the trees.

"The bluebells ought to be this way. It's too tight to bring the horses, but there's still a trail to follow. We could tie them up out here?" The questioning tone in Claire's voice bordered on uneasy, but I couldn't blame her.

I swallowed, the back of my neck prickling. Taking a breath, I closed my eyes, gaining my bearings. The forest wasn't unduly quiet. Now that we were paused, I could hear small animals moving off in the trees, cracking through the undergrowth. Those noises comforted me more than they didn't. They meant the prey animals didn't sense anything to fear. Still, I didn't like the idea of leaving the horses any farther away from us than necessary. Together we looked at Nai, who typically made decisions like this.

She tossed her hair, imperiously, smacking Aella in the face, who grinned, used to it by now. "I'd rather not leave the horses behind. It'd be one thing in day light—I wouldn't worry at all then, but a gryphon isn't the only predator out here. I don't want to spook them."

"I should say not," Claire rushed to agree. "I was thinking the exact same thing. We can always run out to the field in a little while, but after we've made a fire."

We staked the horses and immediately took up the task of rooting for firewood. None of us was a stranger to searching for kindling, though I was least experienced at hunting for it at night. As a mercenary, Aella was familiar with finding wood in dark, unfamiliar territory, and both Nai and Claire had participated in several night time bonfires. Before long, we had a decent fire burning off the path on the river's side. The trail had curved as we had gone along it, so none of us feared being seen from the road, but we kept it small so we wouldn't burn through our fuel too quickly.

When at last the horses were moved close enough to the water to drink and the fire was burning steadily we all settled around the flames. Everyone had brought their own blanket, which was just as well, because we hadn't been able to find any logs big enough to sit on but small enough to move. This was nice, I realized, looking across the fire at the glowing faces of my friends. It was exciting to be out in the night, and I liked knowing that I shared a secret with these girls.

"So," Aella said, her smile wicked, "What would we all like to drink?" She upended the sack carefully and several glass bottles slid onto the dark earth. A couple I recognized. There was mead and whiskey, and also what I guessed was vodka in an elegant, tall bottle. There was another bottle of clear liquid that was squatter than the others. The label that wrapped around the shiny container was in a language I couldn't read. The same went for a liquor in a brown glass bottle.

"Vodka. Pass the bottle," Nai said instantly, and Aella complied. Claire accepted the bottle from Nai when she offered it after a swig.

"Taryn?" Aella asked me.

"Do you have any of that honey whiskey? I liked that."

She grinned. "That's what's in my flask again." She took a drink from the flask and then passed it to me. My sip was moderate. I wasn't sure how drunk I wanted to get yet.

"Actually ladies," Nai said, her voice dramatically arched. "If you care to, I have a game in mind."

"What sort of game?" I asked suspiciously. Even sober Nai's "games" could run the gambit from innocent to plain wild.

"I wish the boys would get here. Your games are always so much more fun with them," Claire sulked.

"Boys?" I squeaked. Aella echoed the same one-word question, but her tone was much more forbidding than my own. I looked at Nai. "You never said boys were coming, I thought it was a *girl's* night."

Nai had the decency to look at least a little sorry. "I know, but Claire suggested it, and I thought it would be a good idea."

"How?" I hissed, taking another drink from the flask, which

Aella then delicately removed from my grasp.

"You've never been able to come out on a night like this. I figured why not go a little bigger? Let you have some fun, since that's what you've been missing out on. Plus, it was one of the ways we convinced Thomas to let us leave at all."

"It is a good idea," Claire said firmly. "Four girls drinking in the woods is not just boring, it's unsafe. My mama would lose her mind, and she'd be right to."

"Yes, because your mother would love you out in the woods at night with boys better?" I asked. "And we have Aella! She's an actual warrior."

Aella put a hand on my arm, surprising me into silence. "It'll be fine, Taryn. I'm sure we're not the only ones who need to blow off a little steam. Nai, do you know when they're supposed to be here?"

"Yeah," Nai drawled, her eyes on Aella's hand, which she let fall away, casually. "They were going to leave about a quarter of an hour after we did. Since they didn't have to wait for Taryn, they ought to be here any second now."

"How about you explain this game to us so we'll know how to play by the time they get here."

Nai was more than happy to oblige, and I listened in slightly sullen silence. The game was simple enough. Everyone sat in a circle around the fire and the turn order went clockwise around it. Whoever's turn it was, was asked by the person to their right 'truth' or feat?' They would then either be asked to tell a scintillating secret, or ordered to perform a daring or embarrassing feat. The person could forfeit the turn by taking a healthy swig of alcohol. As Nai was finishing explaining one of the limitations to Aella, we were alerted to new arrivals by the sound of hooves on dirt.

Before long Thomas, Martin, as well as a man who was a little older than Claire named Christopher had settled themselves amongst us. I was relieved that they had had the good sense not to invite Corey or my brother along. Neither were feeling exceptionally warmly towards the mercenaries, and I wanted this to be a nice time for everyone. I didn't know Chris very well, but Martin was Thomas's best mate, and he was alright company, even if he was Glenn's son. He was tall and gangly, with braided blonde hair and wire rimmed glasses that glinted in the fire's light.

Introductions were made, and the rules were explained to the boys, who grasped the logistics quickly, having played their own version in the past. Though Chris seemed surprised to see Aella, he kept any thoughts he had about it to himself, and soon I found myself relaxing, as general banter played between everyone. To be honest, it *did* feel a little safer to have a larger group gathered, and some of the fear I hadn't realized I was still hanging onto slipped away.

"So, who is going to go first?" Martin asked, clapping his hands together and rubbing them eagerly.

"It should be Nai, since she came up with the game," Claire pointed out.

Nai stuck her tongue out at the redheaded girl. "I have no problem with going first. That makes my questioner ..." She turned to her right. "Christopher!"

"All right, truth or feat?"

"Feat," Nai said promptly.

Christopher looked thoughtful for a moment. His ice blue eyes glittered as he clearly came upon what he thought was a good challenge. "All right," he drew out the words slowly. "I challenge you ... to ..."

"Go on—ask me! I'm not afraid," Nai said impatiently, bouncing in her seat.

He shushed her. "I dare you to jump over the fire."

Claire crowed excitedly, clearly impressed. The boys had gathered their own wood and despite our protests, had built the flames a little higher than we had. It was now burning at least half of Nai's respectable height.

Nai smiled thinly and stood. "All right. You lot on the other side, clear the way. I don't want to land on you."

Claire and Thomas moved apart to make room for Nai as she bound her dress up immodestly high. I blushed for her, but she didn't seem to care. She backed up a few feet, as Martin and Chris egged her on. Thomas kept telling her she didn't have to if she didn't want to. Claire watched, fingers in her mouth. I leaned back. If there was one thing I knew I didn't have to worry about, it was Nai's ability to jump.

As she ran and leapt over the flames, Claire squealed in fright. She needn't have, Nai easily clearing them by a few inches, and landed to applause. She shook out her skirts and whirled to reclaim her space between Chris and Martin, looking smug.

"Your turn Martin."

Martin pushed his glasses up his nose to squint through them at her. "Ok. I'll take a truth."

Nai screwed up her face in disappointment. "Really?"

"What, did you have something in mind?" he asked.

"No, but truths are harder to think of." She huffed and gazed thoughtfully upwards. "Honestly, where would you go if you could live anywhere else—besides the north?"

He considered this for a moment. "The midlands, I guess. They're still a fair bit more normal than far south."

If either of the southern-born girls at the fire thought anything of his opinions on what was normal, they held their tongues. Claire's turn was next, and Martin asked her why she had gone steady with Corey the year prior, only to drop the relationship when it seemed he was getting serious.

She shrugged, studying her fingers. "Corey is actually fairly sweet in private, but his father is a terrible boar. In the end, my aunt advised me to break it off. She has ideas about a different match for me. Someone from Forklahke."

"Our guild is based out of there," Aella said, sounding surprised, but pleased.

"Oh? Well, I doubt you'd know him. He's a clerk, from a *nice* family. Truth or feat, Thomas?" Claire posed the game question coolly, before Aella could form a rebuttal. I resisted the urge to reach out and give Aella's hand a squeeze. She was tough, but Claire was formidable in her own way.

Thomas glanced between the two women, before timidly asking, "Feat?" causing Claire to grin toothily.

"For your feat, Thomas, you have to kiss Taryn—on the lips, obviously."

My eyes widened. Thomas had turned as red as a radish. Nai tossed her head back and laughed. "Oh, perfect!"

Thomas cleared his throat, and I stiffly turned to face him. "Is that ... I mean, I can take a drink if you want?"

I didn't want to kiss Thomas. I also didn't want to embarrass him by saying no or be the first one not to participate in the game. "Sure—no, it's fine." My smile felt too thin.

Thomas leaned forward. I knew I was meant to lean forward too; I did so, feeling awkward and like I didn't know what to do with my limbs and my nose. Our lips met, but as he kissed me, I realized that I was not swept up in the moment. I was aware of everyone watching and laughing. I was aware of his hands gripping my shoulders. I was aware of just how much of a lump I must have looked like, hands limp in my lap. I pulled back, breaking the kiss. He opened his eyes as I moved back to my original position. I stopped myself from wiping my lips on the back of my hand.

"Um, truth or feat Taryn?" His voice was rough.

"Truth," I said quickly. I was *not* ready to be part of another feat.

"Do you like anyone in town?"

This was what came from drinking with boys, I thought, frustration making my back tight. I wanted to take a drink, just to get a little more drunk, but I knew the others would take that as an indication of forfeit, unless I waited until after I had answered my question. Twisting a braid, I sighed gustily. "Yeah."

"Who?" Claire exclaimed. "Is it Thomas?"

I saw Martin beam at Thomas, giving him a thumbs-up. Thomas grinned back. Chris seemed amused, but not invested.

Nai beckoned at me. "Well?"

I glanced at Aella, briefly. She was looking at me like the rest of them, but her face was impossible to read. I didn't dare let my gaze rest on her longer than that. "That was not the question." I cleared my throat. "Aella, truth or feat?"

The circle erupted in groans and more laughter. Claire, Nai, and Martin attempted to get me to fess up for a few more moments. They cajoled, threatened, and bargained, but I remained immovable.

Eventually Chris put his foot down. "She got around the question, fair and square. If you want to ask her again properly you'll have to wait till it's your turn again."

"We *ought* to have had it so you could ask anyone you wanted," Claire pointed out.

"I thought it would be more fair this way," Nai muttered. "I didn't know Taryn was going to be so particular."

I smiled cheekily at her and motioned for Aella to pass me her flask, which I sipped from victoriously. "Aella?"

She nodded. "How about this, me and," she paused, looking at to her left.

"Chris," he helpfully supplied.

"Me and Chris take our turns, and then we open it up so that anyone can ask anyone?" When everyone agreed to that—however reluctantly, in my case—Aella inclined her head. "Ok, then I pick truth."

I was a little surprised. I had expected a mercenary to pick feat. Maybe show off a little. I had to think about a question for her for a moment.

"Maybe you could ask her if that Lucas person was the one who attacked Beth," Thomas murmured into the quiet.

I gasped, shocked. "Thomas!"

"Thomas we're all out here trying *not* to think about that," Nai chided at the same time.

He ducked his head. "Sorry—"

"He has a point," Chris said. "They are her people, and she is the captain's daughter. If anyone would know, she would."

Everyone stared at Aella. She closed her eyes, as though gathering strength. When she opened them, she spoke. "What I know is that Luke is my friend, and I don't think he hurt anybody." Aella's voice was even, but it was then I realized that unlike the rest of us, Aella was not seated cross-legged or with legs curled to the side as Claire did. She sat with one leg tucked under her, and the other bent. It was the perfect position to spring to her feet from, if the mood turned sour. Her eyes were deadly serious when she continued. "Beyond that? I can't tell you. I'm not responsible for him, but if it turns out he did it then I'd welcome your punishment of him. A man like that, I would not fight beside. I wouldn't be able to trust him. I'd kill him myself if he tried to run from your justice. Are we good?"

There was silence. Everyone had felt the heat of her statement, as she fixed each of us solidly in her gaze throughout it. Finally, Martin took a chug from the bottle of whiskey he had brought along. He hacked when he pulled in too much, and Nai pounded him on the back.

When he had caught his breath he said, "You heard her lads. Can we get on with the game?"

"I think that makes it my turn to ask truth or feat." Aella said through a razorblade of a smile. "Chris?"

Chris did not meet her eyes. "Feat."

"Try and do a hand-stand, please."

He did try, and he failed. Several times. He had been quietly sipping away at his bottle throughout the first part of the evening, and it did not make for good balance. His persistence and comical toppling all over the clearing garnered a few laughs and helped to break the tension that had ghosted over the gathering.

After that the game opened so that anyone could ask anyone. Claire got dared to hike up her skirts and wade into the river— she took a drink instead. Chris then kissed her on a dare. Nai admitted to skipping temple one week a few months prior to spend time with a bard who had passed through. Martin drank to avoid a feat that called for him to lick his horse's muzzle.

It was Martin who brought it back to me. "So," he said, pointing, the alcohol making his gaze waver slightly, "is it my boy Thomas that you fancy?"

Thomas chuckled and tossed a pebble at his friend, but I could tell he was excited. He took a small drink from the bottle of mead, pointedly not looking at me.

I rolled my shoulders, trying to loosen them. There was no use dragging it out, it would only make him feel worse. "No. I'm sorry Thomas," I said as gently as possible. His smile vanished, making my heart hurt. I didn't want to cause him pain. I *liked* Thomas, just not in that way.

Hastily he took another drink from the bottle of mead. "Nothing to be sorry for, Taryn. I was pretty sure you didn't."

"You're like Michael, right? A little too clever for anyone in town." Martin asked. His tone was light, but his lips were curled in a sneer. He had meant it to sting, and it had. I bit my lip against a hasty reply. His friend's pride was hurt. I could let it slide.

"Alcohol makes you a bit deaf Martin." Nai, it seemed, could not let the comment pass. "She said she likes someone *in town*. She just doesn't like your friend."

"Nai." I groaned.

"So, who is it? Why the secrecy?" Claire asked, clearly exasperated. "Is he married or something?"

"No, they are not married! And who cares who I like?" I exclaimed. "It doesn't matter. Nothing is going to come of it, and I am sick of being asked about it!"

"Gods, Taryn, it's the game." Claire rolled her eyes, and smirked at Martin. He shrugged in return with one shoulder.

"Well no one is asking who anyone else likes," I said lamely.

"Well I'm sick of this game anyway," Nai said when no one else replied to my outburst. Who wants to go with me to check out the bluebells?"

Now that everyone was drunk, they were fearless enough to enter the pitch-black woods. Weaving, and stumbling slightly, they gathered the lanterns that had been brought. I volunteered to stay with the horses and the fire. The truth was, I was embarrassed. I knew I was right. It wasn't anyone's business, but it felt like I had spoiled the mood, and Nai was covering for me.

"I'll stay with you," Aella said.

I tugged at my braid. "You don't have to do that."

"Yes, I do. You shouldn't be here by yourself," she said firmly.

"Ok, that's fine," Nai said agreeably. She squeezed my shoulder as she passed me. "You'll be ok?"

I fluttered my hand at her. "Go. Stick together. No wandering off into a secluded glen with anybody."

When the last lantern in their line had shrunk to a pinprick, I turned to Aella. "I'm sorry that this night has been so weird. I mean, I think it's weird. Maybe it isn't?"

Aella crooked a smile at me. "It's definitely not the least awkward gathering I've been to."

"Sorry," I said again. It was a little colder without someone on both sides of me. I chafed my arms.

"You don't need to be sorry," Aella said as she stood. She moved around the fire to grab another few logs for the flames, building it back up. "I think it'd be stranger if they didn't say anything. Besides, it's not like I was ever in any danger."

That surprised a peel of laughter from me, and she jumped and raised her eyebrows at me. "You're that strong, huh?" I asked. "Three farm boys are nothing to you?"

Her face relaxed into an amiable grin. "I might be. Plus, it wouldn't have come to a fight, I don't think," she said as she returned to her place next to me. A little impressed, I noticed she was not wobbling nearly as much as my friends.

"Why's that?"

"Well, because you like me, and maybe because of that, Nai seems to think I'm all right. You two are the ones who made them settle down, after all."

I swallowed hard. "Who says I like you?"

Her eyes danced with withheld laughter. "I mean purely in a friendly sort of way, farm girl. Or did I get I get it wrong? Are we not friends?" She clutched over her heart, screwing up her face in a pained expression.

I shoved at her shoulder, not putting much strength into it. "Don't tease me! Can't you see that I get enough of it from that lot?"

She tossed her head back and laughed. Reaching out, she

caught my hand before I drew it completely back and gave my fingers a squeeze, then let me go. "Poor Thomas. I don't think he'd ever have had the guts to ask you on his own. He might have held onto his little fantasy until he fell for someone new, if it weren't for his friends."

I rubbed the back of my neck with the hand she had squeezed. My fingers were tingling. "You're not wrong about that. I had hoped that I could get away with never dealing with it."

"Well, never mind that. What's done is done." Slyly she inspected her finger nails. "Might *I* know who it is that you like? It's not as though I'm going to be here much longer."

My heart flipped, painfully. "It—it doesn't matter. Honestly, I meant what I told them. Nothing is going to come of it. We don't exactly run in the same circles. I barely even know them. It's just—"

In the distance, someone screamed. My mind registered it as Claire as Aella surged to her feet. In a flash, she had retrieved her axe from Juniper. I was still rising clumsily to my feet when she was back by my side. With an outstretched arm, she carefully moved me behind her, placing herself solidly between myself and the trees.

19

I felt sweat break out on my brows. Desperately I wished for the crossbow, or even my crook which could have been used as a weapon in a pinch. In my excitement, I had forgotten both. Slack-witted. I was completely useless as I was.

"What do you think...?" I trailed off. From within the woods a racket had started as though multiple bodies crashed through the undergrowth and branches.

Soon the lights of the lanterns appeared. Then, all five of those who had gone to find the field of flowers burst through the trees in quick succession. When they saw a mercenary levering a battle axe at them, they stopped short.

"We have to go. Now." Nai said, without preamble. "Help us douse the fire and then we're quickly and quietly getting out of here."

"What is going on?" I had to lean around Aella to see Nai clearly. Martin and Chris had clearly decided Aella wasn't going to take a hack at them and were already kicking dirt over the fire, and spreading the logs apart. Claire and Thomas were readying their horses.

"There's a kill amidst the bluebells," Nai explained, moving to grab Juniper. The horse, for her part, refused to move until Aella clipped the axe to her belt and came to take her reins.

"As in a gryphon kill site?" I felt lightheaded. We could have been killed. It could yet be prowling outside of the firelight.

"As far as we could tell with only a few lanterns. We're not sticking around to find out if it's denned nearby or if it feasted over here and moved on."

"What did you find, exactly?" Aella asked. She had grabbed Hale along with her own mount and led the pony to me. With shaking fingers, I undid the tether that had been tied around her bridle.

"It was unbelievable," Martin said, shaking his head. The fire was out, and now only the lanterns lit the clearing, so it was hard to see his expression. "There were rabbits, squirrels—I think I saw a raccoon! All of them flayed open like we heard the livestock were. We almost stepped right on them."

"Enough!" Claire shuddered, her whole body shaking with the movement. "I want to go. *Now!*"

Thomas was ghostly pale in the lantern light, his voice was hushed. "Come on. I'll lead the way out." From his own mount, he had retrieved a crossbow.

In a single-file line, we made our way back down the path. Thomas took point, then Martin, Claire, myself, Nai, Chris, and Aella at the rear. No one spoke. When we could ride at last, we picked up the pace only slightly, afraid to become targets of a predator.

Though it might have been from the commotion of the others running, the woods now seemed eerily quiet. I could hear the harshness of Claire's, as well as Nai's breathing, under the jangle of tack and the sound of hooves on pressed earth. When at last the opening to the road yawned in front of us I thought I would swoon from relief. It wasn't real safety, but it *felt* a lot better than being boxed in as tightly as we had been.

"I need to tell my father about this," I whispered abruptly as we prepared to mount up. "The hunting party needs to know of any leads, and if this is fresh…"

"No," Aella interrupted.

"No?" I asked, bewildered.

"Why not?" Chris looked backward at her, his eyes narrowed in suspicion.

Aella raised an eyebrow at him. "Because then all your parents will know that you went out frolicking with a mercenary when a mad gryphon is running amok, and a girl was just bludgeoned by a yet unnamed assailant."

"I wasn't going to say anything, but she has a point." Nai inclined her head. "Still, Aella, Taryn is right. The hunting party has to know about this."

"I'm going to tell my mother that I was out scouting on my own," Aella said grimly. "She won't love it, but it's not the first time I've gone wandering. She might even appreciate my initiative. All right? This way no one gets in trouble, and the information still gets where it needs to go."

"That's pretty decent of you," Martin said, only slightly grudgingly.

"Yeah, but they'll see the fire, and the hoof tracks," Thomas pointed out shrewdly.

"I'll tell her ... I'll tell her I orchestrated the get together, to try and get information from a bunch of tipsy mountain folk. To see if I could get any leads on Beth's attacker." She linked her fingers loosely behind her head. "Hunting parties always split up. She and some other mercenaries can go to the bluebell field, and maybe they'll cover for me, and by extension, the rest of you lot."

"It's a good thought," Nai ventured. When I glanced over my shoulder I saw she was looking back at me, concern coloring her expression.

"A very good thought—who could have guessed that you were so devious?" Claire said darkly.

They dropped me off down the road from my home. Before they left, I dismounted again and covered Hale's hooves once more. It was easier this second time. Perhaps the pony sensed that I was in no mood for antics.

"Do you want me to walk you the rest of the way?" Aella asked. "I don't mind riding to catch up to the rest of them on my own."

"No." I shook my head. "I'll be fine. Thank you—and thank you Nai for putting together this little gathering. Even if it did end a little scary."

Nai pinched my cheeks. "But what a story to tell our children, right?"

I ducked away, swatting at her. "Sure. Ride safe everyone."

By the time I had reached the barn they had gone around a bend in the road and were out of sight. With a wistful sigh, I shook myself and used both hands to pull the barn door open wide enough for Hale and myself.

"Where have you been?"

I muffled a squeak, nearly jumping out of my boots as I did so. "Michael—by the gods! What is the matter with you?" I hissed.

He was leaning against Hale's stall swathed in shadows. When he leaned forward into a beam of moonlight, his face was dark with anger. "Taryn, tell me you have not been off gallivanting with Nai at this hour. I thought you had more sense than that."

I scowled, leading Hale past him and into her stall. "You're not the boss of me. Clearly, I am fine, so what do you care what I was doing?"

He grabbed me by the shoulder, and I jerked it away from him. "Taryn, what has gotten into you? A little time spent with a mercenary, and suddenly you think you can't be killed?"

"No." My movements stiff, I unsaddled Hale, who shifted in place. She was as nervous here as she had been out in the woods.

"Then what? Beth gets almost killed, so you feel like you have to prove you're alive by doing something stupid?"

"No!" I spun to face him. A sheep blatted. "I wanted to go out and have a little fun. I know this isn't news to you Michael, but we work *all the time*. My best friend didn't even think I'd be interested in spending time with other people, because you're stuck up and because I'm so cursed boring!"

Michael glowered at me. "Is that what you think?"

I rubbed my face. It was so late. "I don't want to fight, Michael. I don't. I am exhausted, and my head hurts."

His tone softened. "What is it? Tiredness? Or—" He sniffed. I peeked through my fingers. He was making a face. "Drunkenness?"

I pressed fingers to my eyelids once more. "It was me, Nai, and … some other people. We went to have a fire in the woods and drink a little. I'd never done it before. I thought it would be fun. Then some of the others went off into the woods because they had heard there was a field of bluebells still in bloom. They found a gryphon kill. They think." Michael was silent, and I removed my fingers to look at him. He was rigid, and his eyes were wide. "Michael?"

"Were you one of the people who saw it?" He took me by the shoulders to peer closely at me.

Touched at what had to be concern, I squeezed his right arm with both hands. "No, Michael. I stayed back at the fire. I kind of embarrassed myself, and I didn't want to go along."

"You'll want to wake Father and tell him when you get inside," he said.

I shook my head. "No. Aella was there." Not waiting for him to voice his displeasure, I rushed to continue. "She's going to tell her mother. She's going to try and keep our names out of it so we don't get into trouble for being out in the woods at night."

"That's good. That was good of her. Gods. I don't know what I would have done if something had happened to you tonight Taryn." Suddenly he seemed distracted; he wasn't looking at me as he spoke, but out the window.

"She's a good person," I told him earnestly. There was something strange about his tone, but I was pleased that at least he hadn't gotten upset at Aella's presence. "Actually, when we heard Claire scream, she jumped up and grabbed her axe—she was so fierce! You'd have … Michael?"

Michael had wandered away from me, seemingly heading out

of the barn. He stopped at his name, and turned back to me. There was something about his eyes. They looked so dark in this light, almost as though they had gone completely black. His hand gripped the barn door as though it kept him upright.

"It's late. I was only out here because I had a strange feeling, and when I went to check on you, you were gone. Since you're fine, I'm going back to bed."

I bit my lip. "I'm sorry I worried you. Honestly. Next time, when all these messes have been cleaned up, you can come with us. What do you think?"

He cleared his throat. "Sure. That'd be fine."

When he left, he shut the door behind him. The barn felt creepy in the dark, with the glittering eyes of those sheep who were awake. I was sorry that Michael had woken and worried about me. That had never been my intention, and now he knew I went off to have fun without him. Guilt needled me especially when I thought about how we had gone to a place *he* had found. My head cocked to the side. Had that played into his fear? Clearly Michael had been to the bluebell field on his own, at least once. If he had gone there recently he might have stumbled right upon the gryphon.

I hurried to finish putting Hale away. I wanted to ask if he had seen anything suspicious there, the last time he had gone. By the time I crept inside, Michael was already back in his room, presumably asleep. I'd talk to him about it more in the morning.

I lay in my own bed, feeling strange, like I was floating above my own body. Adrenaline had burned out what little alcohol I'd had in my system. The gryphon, Aella, Michael— it was all a lot to process.

I liked Aella. That much was clear to me now. I liked when she looked at me, and I liked when she said my name. She seemed to like me too, at least a little. She made excuses to touch me. That was what people did when they liked someone, right?

Perhaps I could have found out more tonight, if the gryphon kills hadn't been stumbled upon. It was a good find though, and I couldn't be too upset by it. Now that we knew where it was lairing it could be stalked and killed.

With the gryphon gone, Aella and the rest of the mercenaries would leave. My breath hitched. That was what I wanted, wasn't it? She was nice—wonderful really—but nothing could come of any of the feelings I was having. A relationship with a mercenary couldn't last, and it wouldn't bring a new generation to the farm. Wouldn't it be better for her to be gone?

I took a deep breath, steadying myself. At least no one had been hurt tonight. Michael had not even had a chance to go searching for me, so he had stayed out of harm's way. He blew so hot and cold these days. *Something* was going on with him. I just didn't know what. Did it have to do with Beth? Wouldn't he have told me, if it did? I squeezed my eyes shut tighter, but sleep didn't come for quite some time.

20

The next morning, I woke to the sound of sizzling bacon, and wood tapping on metal. Mother was cooking in the kitchen. I yawned hugely, and stretched. Since I hadn't gotten drunk as planned there was no reason not to go about my day as normal. I was a little saddened by that, but it would be nice to do normal things after last night's excitement. I'd walk Mother to town, catch up on how the night had wound down with Nai. If Aella was still bound to the town, I could ask her what her mother had said about our little escapade.

"Taryn?" Mother called. "Are you up?"

"I'm up!" I sang back, agreeably. I felt good. Refreshed. Perhaps Michael and I *should* have been spending more time with the other youths from town. Breaking the monotony of my routine made me feel lighter than I had in a while. I hopped out of bed, twirling my way to the wash basin. Hurrying through my dressing, I practically skipped my way to the breakfast table.

Mother raised her eyebrows at me. "You seem to be in a good mood," she said, smiling wryly. "Any plans for the day?"

"Nothing special." I kissed her on the cheek as I reached around her to snag a few slices of bacon that had already cooked. "Walk you in. See Nai. Watch sheep."

"Well, I love the attitude. Leave a few slices for your brother though!" She tapped my hand lightly with the wooden spatula.

I grinned, licking the bacon grease off my fingers as I danced backward. "I can't believe he isn't up yet."

"Well, I don't think he slept well last night. I woke towards midnight and I thought I heard him moving around in his room."

I made a noncommittal noise, taking my mug out of the cupboard. The kettle sat on its metal stand near the fire, and I grabbed it, pouring the still hot water over some lemongrass tea. The steam rushed to meet my nose, invigorating and clean.

"Could you go and see if you can't wake him? I'll serve up in here." I took a tentative sip of my tea and blanched. Too hot still. When I didn't reply, Mother turned to face me, the spatula bouncing anxiously between her fingers. "You two aren't fighting again, are you?"

"No," I hurried to reassure her. "I'll do it."

She smiled and cupped my cheek, affectionately her eyes crescents. "Thank you, dear."

Michael didn't answer when I knocked. He also didn't answer when I said his name. I pushed the door open, getting resistance as the wood hit a pile of clothes. I rolled my eyes. Gross. The whole floor was covered in clothes and different bric-a-brac. How had he managed to have *any* dirty clothes? Mother had been taking a load in every day this week.

"Michael, brother dear, Mother made breakfast. Past time to be up," I sang in a wheedling tone. My eyes wandered to the bed. It was empty. I blinked. "Huh."

Shutting the door, I padded back to the kitchen. Mother was putting the last plate on the table. The smell of the crispy bacon and fried eggs was enough to make my mouth water. When she saw I was by myself, Mother laughed. "Is he being stubborn?"

"He's not there. Maybe he's in the barn?"

Her lips pulled down at the corners, and she looked perplexed. "I went out there before I called for you to check if your father had time to eat before the hunt. Well. Perhaps I didn't see him."

"He'll come in when Father says goodbye." I shrugged, slinging myself into my chair. It scraped roughly against the floor.

"Easy." Mother chuckled. "The food isn't going anywhere."

I was a few bites in when the door open behind me, and I turned in my seat. Father was grabbing his wide-brimmed hat off the hook by the door. He donned it, covering his fair hair. "Wynn, I know I said I wasn't going to, but could you— ah, thanks." He accepted the satchel she held out. She had bundled away a hearty cold breakfast for him to eat on the road.

She kissed him lightly. "We can't have you fainting in your saddle because you didn't eat."

He smiled sheepishly at her. "Thanks, Wynny. Taryn?"

I sat a little straighter, "Yes, Father?"

"You feeling better?"

I stared at him, confused. Realization dawned on me as he

stared back. I'd said I was feeling ill before going to bed. "Yeah. Yes. Much better. Thanks." My words fell over each other as I rushed to get them out.

"Good," he drawled. "Have either of you seen my son? He was practicing with my crossbow yesterday, and I'll be needing it."

Mother and I looked at each other, stumped. "He wasn't in the barn with you?" she asked.

Father shook his head. "No. I haven't seen him since last night. I think we missed each other when he grabbed his pony. Never mind, I'll get him." He moved towards the bedrooms.

"He's not there," I said before he could leave the room. "I was just in his room."

"That's strange," Mother murmured, alarm stirring in her voice. "You said Cherub wasn't in the barn?"

"Well, no. I thought he moved her to the front so he could eat and leave." Father strolled to the front door. He yanked it open, going so far as to step outside when he didn't see a pony.

I stood to follow him, but he was coming back inside when I got out from around the table. "No Cherub?" I asked.

Father shook his head. "No."

"The sheep were still in the barn?" Mother asked as Father stalked down the hall.

"Michael?" Father banged on Michael's door, and then opened it. I waited for him, back by the entrance to the kitchen. "He's not there," he said. He looked put out. "Where is that boy? He knows he needs to take the sheep to the field, and I need my good crossbow."

I was starting to get an awful twisty feeling, deep in my gut.

The cheery mood I'd started the day with was curdling there. Michael had said he'd had a strange feeling when I was out by the bluebells the night before. Surely if anything had happened to him I would have sensed it. Right?

"I'll check around the yard." I strode to the door, shoving my feet into my boots. I was swinging on my cloak when Father stopped me.

"I'll look," he said. "You help your mother clean in here. It could be Glenn needed something, and he saw Michael as he was pulling Cherub out. I'll ride over and see."

He was gone before I could protest. I shifted from foot to foot, and Mother smiled wanly at me. "No use fretting about it. He was here last night. It's probably as your father said. Finish your breakfast, and then we'll clean up."

Breakfast had been finished, the dishes and kitchen had been cleaned and tidied, and Mother was beginning to anxiously embroider the skirt she had been knitting, and Father still had not returned. Neither of us had wanted to leave for town before he got back.

I excused myself to check outside. There wasn't anywhere for him to hide close to the house— besides the vegetable garden, but he wasn't there. I walked the perimeter just inside the woods, calling his name. It seemed unlikely that Michael would take Cherub into the woods, but him disappearing wasn't something I would have expected either.

Had Cherub been in the barn last night? I wondered suddenly. Yes. I was pretty sure. I gnawed my lower lip. However, I hadn't seen Michael make it to the house. Had he run away? What if whoever had hurt Beth had—what? Knocked him over the head and taken Cherub from the barn? I swallowed hard and redoubled my efforts.

My voice rang through the quiet morning with no response. There was no sign of him. The dawn sun was weak, but it was enough to light a yard in front of me before the trees clustered too densely.

Eventually I gave up and returned to the house. I felt jittery, and one of my knees bounced erratically as I sat on the couch. I wished I could have worked on my gryphon figure, but it was a surprise for Mother, and I didn't want to leave her alone just to work on it. Her face was a shade too pale for me to believe she truly wasn't worried. A quarter of a candle mark later, Father finally returned. I heard the hooves of his horse, and rushed to open the door.

When he saw me, Father pulled up short. "Glenn hasn't seen Michael, though the cursed fool is certain he heard gryphon cries early this morning. I went a little ways in the opposite direction, in case he took a spill on a morning ride. I'll wait for the hunting party to get here. Willy will know if he has been to town."

"I'm sure that's it." Mother didn't look up from her sewing, her eyes were focused on the patterns she was picking out with her needle. Little snowdrop flowers, it looked like.

"I'll be back. I'll need to find the spare crossbow for now." He backed back out the door.

I tugged at a braid. Perhaps that was it. Michael could have decided to talk to Nai about our adventure last night. Perhaps he had been more upset by our close call than I had thought. But why? None of us had been hurt, and we had learned where the gryphon was nesting. Why would he be upset about that?

Not long after Father had gone to the barn, a knock sounded on the door, and I hurried to answer it. Mother didn't rise from the couch; she continued to work at her embroidery. I peeked through the eyehole before unbolting the locks and throwing open the door. Mercenary Captain and daughter stood, their arms behind their backs, looking serious and foreboding in a way I had long stopped viewing them.

"Captain Aedith, Aella—have you seen my brother?" I asked before they could get out as much as a greeting. "None of us have seen him since last night. It's not like him to disappear. We're becoming a little worried." I knew it was my nerves that made me talkative. Mother's needle paused, but she didn't look up.

"May we come in?" Aedith wasn't exactly meeting my eyes. It was as though she was speaking to my forehead. I realized the hunting party was not on the road behind them.

Feeling confused and a little hurt, I stepped aside to let them pass. "I'll put the kettle back on."

"That won't be necessary. It would be best if your father were here, if you could find him."

Mother still hadn't spoken, but she had stopped rocking her chair. She was watching the mercenaries now, an odd light in her eyes.

"He's in the barn. I'll be back shortly." I looked to Aella, but she was inspecting her boots. I took off at a run.

In the barn, Father was at his work bench, carefully oiling his spare crossbow. His face was drawn and he looked so old in the feeble rays of light streaming through the dusty windows that my heart ached. He glanced up when he heard the door open, hope blooming and dying on his face in the work of a moment.

"Father, Captain Aedith is here. She says it would be best if you joined us for whatever news she has."

When we returned, Aedith was leaning against the door frame that led into the kitchen, her position deceptively casual. Aella stood next to her mother, her eyes trained on the floor. When the door to the kitchen shut behind us, Mother finally rose, moving to stand beside her husband.

Aedith looked both of my parents squarely in the eye before speaking. Her low voice filled the hollow silence strangely, and I shivered. "Wynifred, Raynard, it is good to see you again. I'm sorry it must be under these circumstances. What I am here to say... I take no pleasure in it. You have all been welcoming, to me, and to my daughter."

My parents said nothing. My heart strained against my chest, and the breath caught in my throat ached. Michael was hurt. Michael had been killed. Michael had been kidnapped or—

"Michael is the one who attacked the girl Beth. I have evidence of that, as well as a witness—the victim herself. She woke, and our healer mended her jaw enough to speak. Breaking it and her fingers ... I believe his motive was a distraction, meant to foist my mercenaries from your town. He didn't count on us having a healer."

Mother let out a bark of something too rough to be considered a laugh. "And why would he do that?" Father pulled her close to him.

"We believe he has been the one killing livestock."

An argument erupted. Mother's sharp denials punctuated the back and forth between Father and Aedith. The actual details of what they argued over came to me through what felt like cotton covering my ears. My mind whirred, flitting from one thought to the next, connecting dots I should have seen. The proximity and time of the kills; the times in which Michael was alone. The flowers surrounding the gryphon kill; the flower gifted to Beth. Michael's muddy boots when he hadn't been outside yet. Michael's deal with a strange man in a dark corner of the inn. Michael outside the inn, covered in Beth's blood. Michael's large leather-bound tome that he seemed keen to keep hidden from me. The loose floor board in his room where he used to let me hide my sweets but no longer let me near. How messy his room was when Mother had been to town to do the washing almost every day for the past few weeks. The loose floorboard. The dirty clothes. The loose floorboard. My thoughts caught. I backed away from the fight, slowly. No one glanced my way. When I reached the hallway, I ran, my feet slapping the floor, loud in my ears.

Michael's room was a mess. His bed was unmade and dirty clothes were in a mound at the center of the room. With how much cleaning Mother had been doing, how could his clothes have gone unwashed? With a foot I shifted the pile, revealing the dull wood of the floor. I knelt, and carefully began to push on the different pieces, listening intently.

"What are you doing?" I jumped, but I didn't turn to look at Aella. The last panel had squeaked.

I pulled my knife from my boot and inserted it into the crack between it and the next piece. The floor board lifted away delicately, and from the darkness beneath I pulled a journal and a stack of loose papers from where they sat within. I felt blindly for the book, but there was nothing else. I turned to sit on the floor.

"Are they still going at it in the kitchen?"

"Your father is starting to listen, but your mother is…" I could tell she was looking down at me, but I didn't take my eyes from my discovery. "She's crying. Are you all right?"

"No." I scanned the loose pages first, but they didn't make sense. I began to flip through the journal.

"I know this is sudden. If I'd had even a clue last night I would have told you. I told Ma what we had planned. Then Beth woke early this morning. It all just fell together. We're not sure *why* he'd do all of this. That's what doesn't make sense."

I felt sick. I offered her the loose papers, flipping towards the end of the journal. Michael's tight scrawl crammed the pages. Diagrams and bulleted lists punctuated paragraphs of notes. I held the book close to my face to better read.

Aella murmured to herself as she read what I had given her, and then she stopped short. The hand holding the papers fell to her side. "I can't be reading this correctly." She waved the papers at me. "This is lunacy."

"Yes." I agreed, my mouth dry. It was. Michael's notes detailed a procedure. Master Noland had given him a book that listed the methods it took to harness the mind of another creature. Specifically, Michael was altering it to apply to a gryphon. Master Noland had hinted it was possible. Through blood sacrifices and offerings to the intended target, Michael believed he could command one of the great beasts of the mountains. His most recent journal entries alluded to a specific beast, one he called Zehya. She was a female gryphon with the body of a snow leopard and the wings and head of a snowy owl. She was young—malleable, Michael noted. Over the past five months he had lured Zehya down the mountain with the hearts of animals. First with the offerings of wild beasts, then domestic—chickens, then pigs, then cattle and sheep.

I felt gutted. Where had my head been? There had been moments that should have clued me in. The morning the sheep went missing Michael's boots were already muddy before he went outside for the day. I'd thought how much blood was on him the night Beth was attacked was strange, but I hadn't wanted to see it. I'd known Michael had been hiding things from me recently. I'd known something was wrong, but I hadn't followed my instincts. I had been too afraid that if I pushed him too hard I'd lose him.

Aella crouched beside me and put a hand on my shoulder. "We have to give these to my mother and your parents. Your brother is dangerous Taryn."

"My brother is *in danger*." I countered in a harsh whisper. "If the gryphon doesn't eat him, then the village will burn him. This list..." I pointed at the right side of the journal with a finger that trembled, "It says the gryphon has to consume a human heart and a part of him for the ritual to be completed."

Sitting amidst the mess in Michael's room had given my nose time to adjust; I finally placed the coppery scent that permeated everything. Setting the journal down I reach to my left and flipped Michael's clothing pile over. I choked on my own noise of shock. Aella's quick intake of breath sounded in a hiss. The lower layer of clothes was caked in the brown of dried blood.

I flipped the pile back over and drew my knees up to my chest, resting my forehead on them for a moment. I breathed slowly, in through my nose and out through my mouth. Like

Nai did when she was trying to calm herself. It was hard to breathe. It was hard to think. The warmth of Aella's hand was like an anchor, keeping me from floating away.

When I looked up, Aella smoothed the hair from my face. "What do you want us to do?"

My heart stalled and then thumped once against my chest, and I searched her face. Her expression was fierce and defiant. She was my friend, and she didn't share the town's belief in burning away ill luck. Was it possible she would do what I wanted to ask of her?

"I have to save him. From himself, and from the town. Something is wrong with him."

"But..." Aella bit her lip, conflicted, "he still did it, Taryn. He has to face justice. It's the whole reason I'm here."

"I know that." I covered her hands quickly with my own. "I think a man who came through town months ago somehow poisoned his mind. The town won't want to cure him of whatever is afflicting him. They'll want to burn him. They'd be right to," I said hastily, "but I can't just let it happen. If I can get to him first maybe I can get him to see reason. We can take him to the capital to be tried there rather than burned. Maybe we can even set the crown's justice on the man truly responsible for all of this."

"Who is the man you believe is responsible for this?"

"One Master Noland," I said grimly. Aella's olive skin drained of color. "What?"

"Master Noland?"

"That's who Michael said had offered him a place. *What?*"

"Master Noland is one of the old king's brothers, Taryn."

"The old king's brother? I thought he only had the one?" I felt offbalance and confused.

"Master Noland isn't exactly the sort of relative you brag about. He's the most dangerous necromancer from the hill lands," Aella had dropped her voice to barely a whisper, and she glanced around the room as though she expected someone to step from the shadows.

"A necromancer? But Michael asked around about him—he did his research. He wouldn't align himself with someone like that. He said that Master Noland is a trusted member of the crown's court."

"As he well is, and anyone who says differently wakes up dead. He scours the land for promising protégés and has the most impressive backing of mages in the whole of the kingdom besides the mage school itself. If the crown needs magic done, they send for one of his disciples. Everybody knows though," she swallowed hard, and again her eyes scoured her surroundings. *Everybody* knows he dips his hands in blood more than any man ought to. And that's coming from a mercenary."

"Michael would have told me if the man he wanted to apprentice under was the old king's brother," I said, but I knew I was trying to convince myself more than Aella.

"Maybe he didn't know. Or maybe he lied. People do that."

An annoying voice in the back of my head reminded me that Michael had said something similar, recently. "Michael is no mage," I said, frustrated. "If this is the same man, why would Master Noland have chosen him?"

"These notes detail a magical working. How do you know he isn't one?"

"Because if he is one, wouldn't I be? I'm his twin." Admittedly, I wasn't sure how magic worked, and I'd never had a call to learn. Magic wasn't the business of a shepherd; I'd had real work to do.

"You're sure? You never saw anything in a cup of water or moved things without touching them?"

I glared at her. "I'm sure, Aella. I'd tell you if I had. We're not mages. We're shepherds!"

Aella shook her head. "Mage or not, Michael believes he can do what Master Noland bade him. For whatever reason Master Noland has encouraged that belief and now Michael is dancing dangerously close to the realest test of if he can."

"We have to find him, and I think I know where he'll be." Aella looked at me expectantly. "The field of bluebells. Michael disappeared *after* I told him what we found there. His notes mention a main location for big parts of the," my lips twisted in a grimace, "spell."

I watched Aella make the same connections I had. Swiftly she stood, offering a hand to me. "If we ride fast, we can be there before noon. We may get to him before the town hears the news and rallies against him."

"Only if we don't wait and explain everything all over again to my parents and your mother. They might let you go after him with the rest of your company, but they'll keep me on house arrest."

Aella mulled this over. "Ma might be willing to bring him to the crown."

"Maybe, but Michael doesn't trust her. If he does something foolish now, he could be killed."

She inclined her head. "Agreed. He'll listen to you?"

I furrowed my brows, and stroked my braid. He was my brother. My twin. Despite everything we believed he had done in the past month, he had always made it clear he wanted me to stay safe. "He won't hurt me. If nothing else, that much I think I can be certain of."

She nodded curtly. "Leave the book and notes out and in the open. My mother will know what to make of them. You'll leave through his window. I'll tell everyone that you've taken to your bed and need some time to calm down."

"Smart," I said, impressed with her quick thinking. "All right, and you?"

"I'll tell my mother that I'm headed back to camp to prepare everyone for a potential pursuit. Or a hasty exit from town, if your guardsmen don't like that we went around them to get Michael," she added ruefully.

"Do your people need that warning?" Despite the urgency with which I wanted to get to my brother, Aella and her mercenary crew had been good to our town; they had been good to me. I didn't want them getting into any unnecessary trouble.

"They'll all be ready on their own. My mother will think I'm excusing myself from an awkward situation."

"She'll be angry with you."

Aella gave me a little shake. The grin she wore was fierce, and a little frightening. "Only if we don't bring Michael in, and we're going to."

I met her eyes. They glimmered with excitement. My reserve firmed. "Ok." I nodded briskly. "Let's get a move on."

I crept to my room, a step ahead of Aella. The noise of the

adults arguing had reduced. Mother was still quietly weeping, but Aedith and Father seemed to be having a proper discussion. I grabbed my cloak and harness, longing for Father's missing crossbow. I didn't dare take the spare from the barn and risk leaving them with no defense. In its stead, I grabbed my shepherd's crook. As my fingers touched the cool wood my thoughts flew back to the night we had dined at The Black Gryphon. Michael had brought his crook that night. I closed the bedroom door firmly behind me. The conversation in the kitchen paused, and I held my breath, but then it resumed once more.

The window in Michael's bedroom opened to the back of the house. There was a path to the barn from there, just inside the line of trees. It could be traversed without being seen from any part of the house. Some part of me detached from the rest. It recalled that I had known he'd had his window open recently, despite the autumn chill. I just hadn't made the connection. The trodden earth and bent grass beneath Michael's window showed that this had been his path many a night. It chilled me worse than the morning air.

21

The two of us met on the road a few tense minutes later, and without a word, we kicked the mounts into a gallop. If our suspicions were correct, then there was no danger of a mad gryphon leaping from the woods, at least not until we got closer to our destination. The wind whipped my hair backward and lashed it against my face. Hale was all nervous energy, but she was happy to be running and did her best to keep pace with Aella's mount.

Juniper was an avalanche of a horse, and she seemed to roll over the road without touching it. A glance to the left at Aella showed her as the warrior that had only been hinted at in her time in Nophgrin. Body hunched low over the neck of her mount, her cloak streamed behind her to show her leather jerkin. Her eyes were cold and focused on the road ahead, and her mouth was set in a grim line. Her hair was braided tightly back, and unmoving for the first time since I had met her. Even the wisps I had grown accustomed to were slicked back and contained. A crossbow was strapped to her back, and the hilt of her axe showed over her left hip.

I was uncomfortably aware that my skirt was meant for sitting at home, not even suitable for field work. There hadn't been time to change, and my legs were cold. I was fiercely grateful for Aella's presence. I bent to mimic her pose on my own pony.

In record time, we reached the path that led into the woods where only the night before we had been laughing and drinking. Aella signaled for us to slow and dismount.

"I'm going to have your back in there Taryn, but it's for you to calm your brother down. I'm going to hang back. Seeing me might spook him and cause him to do something stupid. I've seen it before." She noted my wide eyes and hard swallow. "If something seems even slightly off, I'll come in firing. I swear it." She reached across the gap between us, her leather gloves wrapped around my forearms and squeezed, comfortingly.

"Ok," I croaked, and then grinned sheepishly. "Ok, let's do this."

I led Hale into the comparable dimness of the woods. True to her word, Aella hung back, fading behind me until I couldn't even hear her. I was grateful for the strengthening daylight that streamed through the canopy of the trees. Soon though, the dancing shadows of the leaves above had my nerves wrung out, enough that I had to stop and calm Hale who could sense that something foul was happening.

"I know," I murmured to her, "I don't know how I got myself into this situation either, but we have to find Michael and Cherub, don't we?"

At the sound of her companion's name, Hale steadied, but when the narrow path for the bluebell field came into view she stopped in her tracks and refused to go onward. Back the way I had come the path curved and Aella was nowhere to be seen. I rubbed my face wearily and tied Hale off on the nearest pine tree. Part of me had hoped to keep her with me the whole way, even if I couldn't ride her. I should have known better. Hale was much too skittish for this type of task.

I hugged her neck gently. "I know you did your best. Be good, and I'll be right back for you." Hale whickered at me, and her ears flicked forward and back.

Shaking myself and taking a breath that shuddered coming back out, I pressed on. The debris of fallen pine needles, as well as all matter of assorted bracken crunched under my feet. I used my crook to nudge the bigger pieces out of my way, and I winced each time a particularly loud *snap* emerged from beneath me when I missed one.

There were no birds to break the otherwise oppressive silence, nor were there any squirrels or rabbits. Either they were afraid of me or there was a bigger predator they had already fled from.

Gradually, and then all at once I was surrounded by bluebells. Where the flowers grew the thickest the trees were dispersed the thinnest, and the ground seemed to glow blue. When I was surrounded by the trembling blue flowers I swore I heard the tinkling of bells from their delicate forms.

I turned in a slow circle. "Michael?" My voice was barely louder than a whisper. I shut my eyes, disgusted with myself. Louder. "Michael? Are you out here? I've come to help." Had that been a noise? I paused, not daring to breathe. Again. "Michael?"

A groan, faint, and weak. "*Taryn.*"

My feet were already carrying me in the direction of the sound of my brother's voice. It didn't matter what he had been accused of. He needed help. It sounded as though he was through the next clutch of trees. "*Michael!* I'm coming, hold on." I burst into the next clearing and my feet staggered to a stop.

The next groan came with a horrifying new context. Michael was heaving the body of a second sheep onto a boulder where a first already lay prone. They were alive still, but bound very tightly. Their shallow breaths were evident in the quick rise and fall of their chests, and their dark bright eyes darted about the clearing. By Michael was our cart—I hadn't even realized it was missing. It was hooked to a trembling Cherub. Within the cart was more rope, a wicked-looking knife as long as my forearm, a heap of canvas, and the book he had been reading for the past few weeks. Slightly behind the cart, almost within the trees was what appeared to be a wet pile of furs. I became aware of a buzzing noise in my ears. Flies. When the sheep was placed to his satisfaction Michael cut the bindings on their muzzles, releasing their plaintive cries. My stomach roiled.

He turned to greet me. "I'd hoped you'd be able to find me." His smile was nothing like his normal soft smile. He had dirt streaked across his face, and his hair, though combed and braided, showed more traces of filth.

"You can't be out here, Michael. Neither of us should be, especially not with those sheep carrying on. The gryphon will come."

"Of course the gryphon will come." He spoke as though I was being tiresome, his smile fading. "You said you've come to help.

Tell me you found my notes. Did you bring them?"

"Michael," I spoke slowly, "Beth woke up. She told the mercenaries what you did, and soon the mercenaries will tell the rest of the town. You're in terrible danger... from more than just the gryphon."

Michael's eyes dropped to the right as he considered this new information. "Yes, I thought that was coming. This does rush me considerably. Even more than your little party," he muttered.

I crept forward tentatively, hands open in a plea. "Michael, please let the sheep go. Come home. Let us all find a way to fix this."

"Yes, I'll have to let the sheep go. There's no time for anything else." He was still muttering, his eyes trained on the ground, almost as though he wasn't responding to me at all.

I was close enough to touch him, and I did, as softly as I would a skittish lamb. His gaze swung to me and I almost jerked my hand back. Steeling myself, I rested it more firmly on his shoulder. "It's going to be ok. You've never hurt me, and I know you wouldn't hurt anyone else if you didn't feel there was no other option. Master Noland did something to you—threatened or bespelled you, but we're going to figure it out. Together."

Michael flicked his eyes between my face and my hand, and little by little his wire tight muscles eased. He turned to face me and put a hand on each shoulder, his expression earnest. "Listen carefully, Taryn, because this is important. Master Noland did nothing to me, and I regret nothing I have done." A rock sat in my gut. "But it's true. I could not let harm come to you, sister. You're a part of me." Ice shot up my spine; before I could blink he struck me across the face. I went down like a rock, my hands instinctively flying up to catch me. As I moved to roll to my feet he kicked me in the temple. Blackness rushed up to meet me.

The details of the next few moments were foggy. Distant. Through a haze and a dull pounding in my head, I felt myself being dragged and heaved upwards without care. Fire burned and faded down each of my arms in turn. When I returned fully to myself, my cheek rested against the cold surface of a flat boulder. The flat boulder that the sheep had rested on, my brain registered unbidden. Unlike them, however, I was not bound. He hadn't had the time. I didn't move, attempting to take stock of the situation. My arms stung where they touched the dusty boulder, and a careful glance at them proved I sported fresh slashes that bled sluggishly. Something to make me more tantalizing to a gryphon? They were shallow. That was a blessing. I wouldn't bleed out from them at least.

I pushed myself quickly into a sitting position. My hands, which I had skinned on the ground, stung. The clearing spun. When it righted itself, Michael was by the cart, untying the second sheep. The first one was nowhere to be seen. Perhaps the thing had more sense than I did and had run. I rubbed my skull tenderly and winced at the sharp pain. Michael looked up at the noise I made and nodded absently. The second sheep, free, made a break for the trees.

"That kick was a little unnecessary. Revenge for the last time I made you wait on me in the field?" I quipped. I attempted to stand, and my head swam. I sank back to a bended knee, my hands braced on either side, my head bowed. Where was Aella?

Michael pulled Father's crossbow from where it rested on his back. The bolt he notched he pointed at me. "Zehya will be here soon. You will sit still until she arrives."

"Michael, this is insane. Even if this gryphon comes and she eats me alive, you're not a mage and she will turn on you!"

"I'm not a mage yet," he admitted. "Master Noland will train me."

"It's not something you can learn." A sheep screamed in the not far distance. I broke out in a cold sweat.

"I will never achieve the success of a natural mage. I'll allow you that, but I've read enough. I've done enough already under Master Noland's tutelage to know that it is possible for me to bend and subvert the laws of nature to suit my needs." He used one hand to tap the book behind him. He practically glowed with pride. "It is hard work, but I am not averse to hard work."

"It's monstrous work." I spoke hurriedly, my eyes darted around the clearing. My crook was back where I had fallen, a foot from the edge of the boulder. "Michael, if you let a gryphon maul me, you will regret it. You will not only have lost your sister, but you will be caught and you will be burned."

"When Zehya has killed you, she will be completely mine. My research supports that the entirety of a twin's being is more than equal to a single part of me. Zehya consuming you will take care of the last two parts of the ritual at once. Meaning our bond will be stronger than what even the spell would have originally given me. With her in my control, I will leave this very night for Master Noland's estate. By flight."

There was a noise to my right. Slowly I turned to look. Michael did the same, delight rippling across his features. Beak red with the blood of the sheep she had slaughtered and impossibly huge, there was Zehya, and *she* was looking at *me*. I shuddered.

She chirped, the noise somewhere between a bird's trill and a cat's purr, oddly gentle coming from a beast so terrifying to behold. Zehya, I had the ability to admit, was gorgeous. Her white and gray coat looked soft and luminescent. Her wings, heavy and huge, were folded neatly along her sides, and the shoulders where they connected were thickly muscled. She tilted her head and squinted her yellow eyes. They held intelligence in a way that lesser gryphon's did not, and she flicked them between my brother and myself.

She took a pace forward, and an unbidden moan of fear bubbled past my lips. My eyes burned as I tried to keep them open, afraid that if I closed them, she would be on me. Breath whuffled through her mouth and nostrils as she took in the scent of the blood still oozing from my arms. Her beak was slightly agape as she breathed in the scent to taste it on her tongue. Beyond that there was a deathly silence. No birds, no rustling of rodents in the underbrush. I couldn't speak, even to plead for my own life. One thought screamed through my mind: *I am going to die today.*

From the corner of my eye, I saw Michael muttering and his hands flashing in complex patterns. It pulled my attention for the merest of moments. When Zehya sprung, it was instinct alone that sent me rolling off the boulder and onto the hard earth. My hands clapped against the dirt, breaking my fall, and I pushed off with them, my eyes on my crook. I spared Michael one glance, to ascertain his whereabouts. He had stepped back, by the cart his face impassive. Seeing he was out of the way, I could and did grab my only defense, not pausing in my desperate beeline towards the trees.

Zehya had cleared the distance between the tree line and the rock in one smooth leap, and she wheeled to follow me as I scrambled to get away. The thickest grouping of trees seemed to be acres away to my panicked brain. My head reeled, and a misstep brought me to my knees in the midst of the bluebells. As green and blue smeared across the knees of my skirt, Zehya dove through the air where my head had been. At last a scream ripped from my throat, as I cowered, arms over my head. Zehya landed in front of me, her tail swinging as a counterbalance. She growled, low in her throat, and I screamed again.

This time my scream was answered. As Zehya stalked towards me a bolt *thunked* solidly into the earth by Zehya's right haunch, causing her to pause. She twisted to look in confusion at what had almost struck her, and then her eyes locked on a shape above us. *Aella.*

"Taryn," Aella snarled, "Get up and run!" She was situated on a thick branch in a tree by the path out. Perched close to the trunk, she kept her crossbow trained on the gryphon.

Zehya glanced between the two of us, then turned fully to face Aella. The questioning noise she made was not gentle. If she was a person, she would have been asking, "Who the blast is this?" I clapped my spare hand over my mouth to smother the hysterical giggles that threatened to slip free.

Shakily, I stood. As I did so Zehya's gaze flicked back and she started to turn towards me. A second bolt sailed through the air and would have hit her this time if she hadn't sprung to the side, wings flaring to give more air to her side-step. It was Zehya's turn to snarl.

"Come get me beastie. Try for something that isn't weak and

beaten down!" Aella taunted. Zehya made a guttural noise and danced out of the way of another shot.

"I can't believe you brought the mercenary." Michael was watching Aella with disgust. She continued to lob insults at his pet, and had struck her once, but just a glancing blow on the shoulder. Zehya was closing in, using the nearby cover and the tree's large circumference to give herself time to dodge closer while Aella shifted around to find her, aim, and shoot. "She's going to get slaughtered."

My blood ran cold. He could have been talking about the outcome of a race … but he was right. Gryphons were huge and clever, and any hunt I had ever heard of involved at least three fully grown adults. Even that was pushing it. Without someone to flank the gryphon, and keep it guessing, the beast would close the gap between it and its attacker. Once that gap closed, a gryphon used its superior size and strength to overpower any human that came calling.

I had a moment to acknowledge that I was not a gryphon hunter in any sense of the word before I shouted. "Zehya! Leave her!" I made a series of loud hoots and squawks, trying to draw her attention. It worked; Zehya's gaze found me, and then, for all her bright color, suddenly she was out of sight.

Aella whipped her head around to look at me, and made a motion for me to cut it out. I swallowed my last hoot. A lull came in Zehya's dogged attacks after she vanished into the trees, and there was no sign of her for a few tense moments. Swiping at the buzzing next to my ear that had to be flies, and glancing periodically at Michael I edged towards Aella. He made no move to stop me.

When Zehya reappeared, it was in the line of trees closer to Michael and me. She eased out of the dwindling shadows and stalked towards me, intently.

She was bleeding from the shoulder that Aella hit, the red standing out in stark contrast to her frosty coat and she was panting lightly now. I almost felt bad for her. If Michael hadn't interfered she might have never encountered any creature that could have been considered a threat. She might have had a peaceful life, found a mate, and raised a kitten. Now her life would be more of this. More violence and killing whoever Michael or Master Noland decided, and if Michael was any indication they'd leave her to the fighting unaided, even if someone was shooting at her. Even one of her own kind would have helped her.

I blinked. Zehya had stopped. She inspected me, her head tilted. Could she—could she understand my thoughts? That was crazy. The stress of the fight made it hard for me to focus on this line of thinking. I'd never heard of a gryphon—of any creature that could read minds. Still ... if Michael communicated through a magical link, and if I was more than a part of him, didn't it follow that I could do as he did?

"Zehya—kill." Michael said smoothly, and the gryphon shook her head as if to rid herself of a gnat. Then she was moving once more.

I brought my crook across my body. "Zehya," my voice quavered, "Please." Desperate, I tried to project to her what life could be. A home, a child, warmth and affection, though I didn't know if that was something a gryphon ever aspired to. Images of my own mother and home mixed amidst the future I imagined for her. Though she didn't stop coming, Zehya slowed, snorted, and her head twitched side to side. Her eyes were intent slits. Instinct screamed through me to turn and bolt, but I refused to give in. I knew if I ran, any control Zehya had would be lost to predatory drive and she would kill me.

To my right Michael had rekindled his mutterings, coupled with hand movements that were too quick to follow. Zehya let out a terrible noise, this time it seemed laced with pain more than hunger. She moved to pounce, her tail twitching madly, her bright dilated eyes fixed on me.

My brother screamed, and I whipped my head around to look. An arrow protruded from his left shoulder, and he stared at it, eyes bulging, mouth gaping. My own shoulder ached in automatic sympathy as my hand flew to cover the phantom wound. His hands hovered around the shaft but didn't quite touch it.

My gaze returned hurriedly to Zehya, but she was no longer preparing to leap. She was looking around the clearing, as though she didn't recognize where she was. When at last her eyes fixed on Michael, who was making small panicked noises, she licked the blood from her own beak, and emitted a low, thoughtful growl. He tore his eyes away from his own wound.

More words I didn't recognize tumbled out of his mouth, and Zehya obediently stilled. Michael's eyes scanned the clearing, and I followed suit. Aella was no longer in the tree, which made sense. She couldn't have hit him from that angle.

"Mercenary!" Michael called, in a rough voice, "Show yourself. Don't fight from the shadows." He did his best to sound condescending, even with a cross bolt stuck in his shoulder and it rankled me.

Behind me, Aella laughed harshly, but she did as she was bidden and came into the clearing. I turned my whole body so that I could keep the other two in my sight as I watched her. Like the gryphon she breathed heavily and she was coated in a sheen of sweat from dodging about. The crossbow hung casually at her side. Her hair was mussed but still firmly pulled backward. Aella met my eyes, and I felt a jolt in my chest. She was so young— as young as I was, and here I had been thinking she was going to come in and save the day. As much as I didn't want to die today, even more so I wished I hadn't dragged her into this as well. The faintest of smiles tugged at her lips, and she raised her right brow. I returned the smile weakly. She turned cold as she faced down Michael.

"You lure your sister to her death with no defense— you set up a ward so there's no hope of rescue, and you judge how *I* fight?"

"A ward?"

Michael looked smug, if a skewered man could look smug. The expression was wasted on Aella. She appeared more irritated than impressed.

"It's like a boundary. You walked straight through it, and I had to break through. That's why I was late. Your brother is more trained than we thought, or else this master of his is investing an awful lot in him and his gryphon."

"The ward is my own. As I've said, I have power in my own right now. I'd like very much to know how you got through it. Are there more of you killers for hire running around the woods?"

"There might be, but why would I tell you?" Aella jerked her chin up defiantly.

"I suppose it doesn't matter. You'll be dead before help arrives. Zehya—"

"I will plug you full of holes before she even passes Taryn, Michael." Aella had her cross bow trained on my brother, notched and ready to fire. I blinked rapidly. Gods. She was as fast as Father with that thing. Perhaps faster.

"We have a stale mate," I burst in, "Can we not lay down our weapons and mythical beasts and walk away?"

"Don't be foolish. I can't leave without finishing the ritual." As he spoke, Michael's voice rose in pitch. "Master Noland will not accept anything but a gryphon for my entrance, and it must be willing to answer to me and no one else!"

I blinked. "Do you think this Noland will take your gryphon and toss you out on your ear if you don't bind it specifically to you?"

Michael was pale now, and red dripped along the bolt in his shoulder, and spread across his shirt front. He wiped a hand across his clammy forehead. Zehya watched him, unblinking. "No, don't be foolish, but at this point, entirely thanks to your idiocy, I must flee the mountains as soon as my business is completed here. If you leave... well, I reek of prey. Zehya is already under a compulsion to seek my flesh to finish the ritual..."

"She'll kill you if we leave. She won't just take a piece if you try and offer your own body," I whispered.

"Not our problem, Taryn," Aella reminded me. "He brought this entirely upon himself. The ritual always called for a human heart and a piece of him, and magic will have its way."

"What do you know about magic?" Michael took a step

forward, but the movement pulled at his wound, and he stopped short, wincing in pain.

"Clearly more than you do. I know better than to meddle with it when it wasn't granted to me by the gods."

"The gods appreciate those who struggle," he countered.

Zehya chirped almost plaintively, reminding the other two of the presence of the beast waiting to tear my throat out. However, she wasn't looking at me, or even at Michael. Her gaze was fixed on the path from which Aella and I had arrived. We turned our attention in that direction. Aedith, and an entourage of mercenaries stood there—but not all of them, I noted. I let my eyes sweep the circumference of the clearing and spotted four more in the trees surrounding us. My gaze returned to Aella in time to see her nod to her mother, who nodded back firmly, her eyes gleaming with pride.

Relief and concern swamped me, making my bones feel light and airy. She had told them. She had planned this. We were safe, but now Michael was destined for the pyre.

"Aella…"

She looked at me, and the smile on her lips shrank, but when she spoke, it was to Michael, and she turned to fully face him. "Michael, shepherd's son of the Carpathe Mountains in Nophgrin, you are hereby charged with the slaughter of your neighbor's and father's livestock, the brutal assault of Bethany, daughter of Susannah of the Carpathe Mountains in Nophgrin." Aella's voice was emotionless and formal, and my stomach churned at her final charge. "As well as the attempted murder of your sister, Taryn, shepherd's daughter of the Carpathe mountains in Nophgrin."

Michael's eyes darted wildly from one mercenary to the next, and his tongue flicked over his dry lips. "I have been chosen as a student of Master Noland, a trusted advisor of the crown—all I've done has been after his teachings!"

"Master Noland, servant of the crown though he may be, takes under his belt projects that the crown does not condone, Michael," Aedith said.

As she spoke she closed the gap between herself and her daughter. Zehya snarled uncertainly at all the new humans entering her space. Aedith raised her eyebrow dryly as every armed person surrounding us raised their weapons. Michael spared her a sulky glance and emitted a soft whisper. The gryphon looked to him, to us, and back to him once more. Then she lay down slowly, tail twitching.

Concerned that Michael, wounded as he was, would not be able concentrate well enough to keep Zehya from panicking and attacking us all, I did my best to lend my own soothing energies to the beast. She looked at me, large eyes contemplative, head turning back and forth. I gulped. I couldn't tell if I was really doing something, or if it was coincidental that she had settled more solidly into the earth just then.

"I know more of Master Noland than you do. He's a killer and a master manipulator. Likely he *has* done something to your pea brain, causing you to effectively destroy any place you have except by his side." Michael opened his mouth to protest, but Aedith cut him off, continuing. "Whatever the case is, the crown's justice will not spare you. If we brought you to Master Noland in shackles, he would deny you, and he would 'confiscate' your gryphon as a dangerous magical experiment."

"Which is likely what he intended from the beginning." Kaleb had stayed at the mouth of the clearing, but his smooth voice rumbled across the distance between us easily.

"You're wrong!" Michael's voice cracked as he yelled. Zehya's wings flexed uneasily, and the feathers along her neck raised. I made hushing noises to her, kneeling so that I was at eye level. Bound as she was, she was more like a frightened cat than a vicious monster.

"We are not wrong, boy." There was no malice in Aedith's intonation. Rather, something like pity shaded her eyes. "We have seen a great deal more of the world than you have. You have been duped—and duped proper."

Tears welled up in Michael's eyes as despair or frustration gripped him. Perhaps there was still part of him that was … him. My own eyes watered, causing my vision to blur. Consequently, it was a smeared version of Zehya that I saw strolling towards me. Hurriedly I wiped my tears away with the back of my hands.

"Michael," Aella growled in warning, her crossbow leveling on Zehya.

"I'm not doing anything," Michael said hurriedly. "Zehya, leave off!"

Zehya ignored him, and her gaze locked with mine. Something like a static shock, but bigger, 'zinged' through my chest. Somehow, for the first time since I had found Michael's notes, I was unafraid. I could *feel* Zehya's thoughts. There was something like the lightness of falling snow in my mind, and inside of that, a jangling note of discord.

I kept one hand on the ground for balance and raised the other, signaling for Aella to wait. She made a noise of displeasure, but I didn't dare take my eyes away from the gryphon. Zehya was a foot away from me when she stopped and sat, looking expectantly at me.

22

Tentatively, not believing what was happening, but seemingly compelled to do so. I reached out and cupped Zehya's beak in my free hand. It was cool, and tacky with sheep blood. I did my best to ignore that last bit.

I was having the strange feeling of realizing the buzzing noise had been gradually becoming louder the longer I had been in the clearing. It was in my mind, not my ears, as I had previously thought. Touching the gryphon crystallized that knowledge. I thought—no, I knew—it had some sort of connection between Zehya, Michael, and myself.

Sweat dripped down my back. This was as harebrained as anything I'd ever done, but I couldn't pull back now. The contact confirmed what I had suspected: the snow that I had sensed was Zehya, and the uneven note ringing throughout it was Michael.

"What's happening?" Aella muttered. Aedith hushed her.

Thoughts that were not my own told me the jangling note confused Zehya. It filled her with a fury that was foreign to her. She wished to be free of it. Or perhaps that part was me who wished to take it away from her. I couldn't tell. These thoughts were less distinct than words; they were more like feelings, and they flowed between the two of us with no clear beginning or end.

What I could tell was that Michael's will was imposed over hers. The more I exposed my mind to hers the more I could feel it. My breath hissed in. It wasn't just uncomfortable. It was *wrong*. What was more was that I was certain what she was feeling—what *I* was feeling—was constant. This jangling note was not something she felt because of a direct order.

I let myself glance at Michael for a moment. Even from this distance, I could see that his eyes were dark. The black of his pupils nearly overwhelmed the hazel. A jolt leapt through my heart at the malice in his eyes when he looked back at me. How long had he been like this?

Zehya made a questioning hoot, calling my attention back to the more pressing issue. Taken aback, I realized she hadn't just hooted. Through our bond, she had asked me a question. I bit my lip.

"I don't know," I told her honestly, speaking out loud. I didn't know if she could understand my words as well as my intentions, but I also had no idea how to direct my thoughts at her in that way. I turned my eyes up to Aedith. "I think she believes that I can help her... That I'm," I grimaced, "that I'm like Michael, or connected to him somehow. Do you—"

Michael made a choking noise that was something like a

scornful laugh. It seemed that this revelation was too much for his pride, even if he was being aimed at by more than a handful of weapons.

"Never mind that you absolutely *can't* wield the forces I do, but you ask the mercenary to tell you how? Zehya—Zehya, come to me," his voice was half a coo and half an order. His skin seemed to become even more sallow as he spoke. It was as though whatever he was doing was draining his body of strength that it did not possess.

Zehya's eyes rolled backward in their sockets. Her body shuddered, turning like a puppet on strings towards my brother. Even though this broke my physical contact with the gryphon, in that same moment, pain lanced through my own skull. It did not take a trained mage to understand that it was tied to what he was doing to Zehya to procure her obedience.

"Stop it!" I gasped, clutching my forehead. "Michael stop!"

He did stop, causing the gryphon to collapse onto the earth, but it had nothing to do with compassion for me or for Zehya. Another bolt protruded from his opposite shoulder. He screamed in pain, sinking to the ground, unable to lift his arms high enough to use the edge of the cart to ease his fall. I glanced wildly about for the origin as he gingerly touched his newest wound.

Kaleb gave a small wave, baring his teeth in a humorless grin. "We mercenaries might not have all the knowledge of great mages, but we know enough to *shoot* the mage."

I couldn't smile back, despite the immediate cessation of the agony in my head. Michael was making a guttural noise, panting in pain. My heart went out to him. I didn't know how he had gotten to this point, but a part of me felt as though I should have seen it and stopped him. Whatever was happening here I knew there had to be an outside force guiding it. My twin was many things, but he had always loved me, just as I loved him. Perhaps it wasn't too late. If anything could jar him out of this mad state, I'd have thought a few bolts to the chest would do it.

"You'll all pay dearly for this. I swear it," he spat, ruining those optimistic thoughts. "Taryn, you had best enjoy your time with Zehya while it lasts. She'll be feasting on you soon enough and then I'll be—"

"Shut it," Aedith said sharply. "Or I will shut it for you. We have been incredibly lenient with you. However, make no mistake, you are living on borrowed time. If you move to exert your control over the gryphon one more time, I will put you down." He gaped at her like a fish, but she was already looking at me. "It is possible that you can do something to help this creature... but it is something that I've no experience in. Ito!" To me she said, "Ito is our battle mage. Good for things we don't want to waste our healer on."

Down from a tree behind where my brother sat, swung one of the men I had seen the night Beth had been bludgeoned. He was tall and svelte, with fair skin and dark eyes; his black hair was pulled back into a low pony tail. Ito gave Aedith a mocking smile. "This thing you want done is actually almost like a healing. I can maybe guide this task, but only if the beast will let me."

Two other mercenaries made their way to Michael and began the process of hobbling him and removing the bolts from his shoulders. He cursed them and me and the gods above and below. Once more Zehya had the confused, dazed look of returning to control of her own body. Seeing Michael struggling pathetically against the mercenaries, she snarled and took a step forward. Her bond with Michael, incomplete as it was still insisted she defend him.

Without meaning to, I lurched forward, burying my fingers in the feathery mane around her shoulders. "*Be* at *ease*," the words came unbidden, and out loud they sounded like a language I had never heard before. Long vowels, and deep tones. I felt power ripple through them, "*This* conflict *is* not *about* you." Zehya turned back to me; her eye lids drooped, and slowly she lowered to her belly. Finally, her head dropped onto her paws.

Ito rested a hand on my shoulder, and I flinched in surprise, withdrawing from Zehya clumsily. Sparing him a wan smile at my own jumpiness, I gently reached out to touch the gryphon's energy once more. Instantly, my mind was flooded to the point of being overfull with the thoughts and feelings of another creature. She was frightened. Images of the crossbows and the grim faces of the mercenaries, slightly distorted to appear more monstrous from Zehya's perspective poured into my mind like a flood. Looming behind them all was what must have been Michael, a human, swamped in an inky darkness much bigger than himself.

I sat back on my heels, dumbfounded. The villagers had paid a hefty sum for the death of this gryphon, and regardless of why she caused the destruction, gryphons were never friends of mountain folk. If Master Noland had been the one to command her capture, would he care to collect her, even if Michael himself was unable to deliver her?

"If you return to the mountains, my people will not harm you." Ito said this out loud, but I also felt it ring precisely through my mind. Once again, the words didn't sound like the common tongue, but I understood them. Zehya did not appear impressed.

"You can hear her? You can speak to her?" I asked, excitement coursing through my body.

"I hear her through you," he said simply, eyes still on the great beast in front of us.

I looked from Ito, to Aedith, to Aella. "Why can I hear her at all?"

Ito looked at Michael with disapproval. "Your parents told Aedith the two of you are not mage born, but your brother wields magic. His notes indicated you were to be a substitution for a self-sacrifice. He planned to erect a ward. As you walked through, you were hooked into the ritual. It is likely that you share his link with the gryphon because of that. Sloppy." Michael glowered at him, gagged and blessedly silent.

I sensed a swelling of animosity from Zehya. She was more intelligent than a normal animal, and she was listening. She shifted as though planning to rise. My throat tightened. "My brother will face the justice of our people," I said in that strange tongue.

She mulled that over, her tail swishing unhappily. It seemed I could speak to her, and she was able to reason. She also didn't hate me as she did Michael. Still, she could decide she didn't want to talk, and I couldn't compel her, as Michael did. I didn't know how. I felt my heart jitter at that thought. If she decided to turn on us, she'd lose the fight overall, but Ito and I were closest to her claws.

"It is the way of our people," Ito said firmly, and she snorted, glaring at him. A short staring match ensued. If I hadn't been close enough to Ito to smell the sweat under his green tunic, I'd have thought he was in a battle of wills with a kitten, not a gryphon. Regardless, it was Zehya who looked away. Ito took a moment before he cleared his throat. "Are we ready? Michael must be taken to the town to face trial and see those wounds properly tended."

My heart was racing too fast. This was nonsense. I was no mage. We should be trying to get Michael to see reason. He could fix this if only he'd come to his senses. I screwed my eyes shut against the mad scene in front of me.

"It's ok." Aella whispered. "It's going to be ok. Just breathe."

I opened my eyes; she was crouching next to me, crossbow still at the ready. I took a deep breath, and let it out slowly. She and the rest of the mercenaries were relying on me to unhook this deadly predator from my brother's control. If I could do that, then no one else needed to get hurt. Not here, and not in the village. It was the least I could do to make up for what Michael had done. I nodded to her. I didn't trust myself to speak. Part of me was scared the strange language would come from me rather than common tongue. I could feel something humming inside of me, begging to burst out.

I didn't have any frame of reference for what I was about to do, but I sensed Ito would know what needed to be removed and would be doing most of the removal. If I was understanding properly, Ito merely needed me to touch Zeyha's mind since Michael's magic connected us. I took a deep, shaky breath and opened myself to both of them, one hand on Zehya, Ito's hand on my shoulder.

Behind my eyelids was bright yellowish-white light. *Draw that into you, I can't see.* That was Ito. Speaking in my mind. Panic bubbled up, and I tamped it down. Mentally I gripped the edges of my own light—sheep and the fields, wood shavings, the smell of hay and leather. *Yes, that's right. Like a cloak,* he encouraged me. I drew it closer to myself. With it more tightly compressed I could better see that which was Zehya. The snow, and pine trees; the sky and that harsh jangling.

Does everyone have this? I asked. My mind's voice was tinged with awe.

Ito chuckled from his physical body. *Yes, to some extent or other. Make no mistake, you are no mage. You cannot take the earth's magic and work it. Michael stole the strength of other living beings to connect to the well of power. Otherwise what he wanted to accomplish would have killed him. Because he is a novice he allowed some of that stolen magic to leak into you through the connection he forged in order to make a sacrifice of you.*

Explanation complete, I felt Ito step *through* me and into Zehya. The discord within the snow moved back from him, then returned to batter against him. I sensed a grimace in his next thoughts. *Nasty thing wants to bind me too. Greedy.*

Can I help?

No, stay as you are.

Ito was a true mage. Wherever he set about it, the discord could not stand against him for more than a few moments. Like a soothing wave he rolled through Zehya's being, driving the foreign energy out of her and into another metaphysical hand where it gathered, an inky darkness.

"Here comes the tricky bit," he said out loud as he came upon the last bit of wrongness. "Everyone, weapons up. She's about to be unbound."

All around us there was the soft sounds of mercenaries shifting into fighting stances. Those behind her moved to give her room to exit.

"Warn her," Aella whispered to us. "Make sure she knows we don't want to stop her."

I waited for Ito to say something to the gryphon, but he seemed to be waiting on me. Hesitantly, I reached out and spoke to her, with my mind, as I had with Ito. *You're about to be free. Go home. Let us deal with the man who bound you. No one will stop you. I promise. Turn and run home. Don't look back.*

There was a swelling of excitement from Zehya. I was frightened to open my eyes and leave the strange space I was suspended in, which wasn't quite on the same plane as the forest clearing. This was a gamble, but she deserved the chance to live. It wasn't her fault that Michael had roped her into this mess. I just hoped she wouldn't decide to eat me instead.

"Do it." I said.

Zehya screeched triumphantly when the last bit of Michael's magic left her. I opened my eyes as she reared back on her hind legs, her impressive wings beating hard. They came so close to my face that they almost grazed me. Then she was wheeling away from us, her amber eyes scanning the clearing. Searching for a target or a way out? For a breath, her gaze locked on Michael. I saw his eyes widen in terror, and he tried to scoot backward on his bottom, but the mercenaries behind him blocked his retreat.

I squeezed my eyes shut, waiting for the sound of her pouncing on him. It never came. When I opened my eyes again, she was gone. I realized I was crying. With shaking fingers, I brushed the tears away. I was alive. We were all alive. I shook my head at Ito in dumbfounded relief.

"We're not done yet," he reminded me. "It is likely the magic that has bled into you will dissipate, but it is probably best to gather it up with the rest while we are thinking of it." He spoke as though the errant blood magic was simple tidying that needed done.

Trusting him, I shut my eyes once more. "Ok, what do I do?"

In a flash, Ito had rejoined me in my mind. With the presence of his experience, I could more clearly feel the layers of the magic that sang through my veins. The magic itself was pure, like boiling spring water, but Michael's energy and the blood magic he had used sat like a film over top of it. I shuddered. It was gross.

Not to worry, Ito said. Now that the imminent threat of being mauled by a gryphon had passed, his mind's voice was much more relaxed, though slightly tired. I wondered how much strength it had taken to undo Michael's working. *The magic is like a bit of gauze running through you. Michael has pinned it in place. All that needs done is to take hold of the pin, and draw the whole thing out, and put it with the rest of the magic he used on Zehya, so that I can take it apart.*

As he spoke, Ito reached out to grasp the magic that coated me. When he pulled at it, it was as though a floodgate had been opened. But something was wrong, and we both realized it too late. Rather than the magic in me being pulled to join what he had already gathered, the magic he had gathered from Zehya rushed into me.

I shrieked and clapped my hands over my ears. The buzzing roared within them. It felt like lightning was in my veins. I couldn't breathe. I opened my eyes, but I couldn't see past the bright light that covered my vision. I squeezed them shut again—or at least I thought I did, but the blinding light was inside my eyelids too. It felt like my skin was blistering but from the *inside*.

My body was convulsing. I could hear people yelling but I couldn't understand what was being said. Impossible as it was, the light was in my ears. I could hear screaming and I knew by the roughness of my throat that it was me screaming. I couldn't bear it. No one could take this pain. It was too much.

Then, all at once cool, delicious darkness replaced the fire that had been consuming me. My breathing was shallow. I didn't dare move for fear of breaking the silence in my own head. I realized I could feel my pulse once more in my scraped palms. I was laid flat on my stomach on the cool earth. I could feel the grit of the dirt under my cheek. I could hear my own breath. I could hear someone else's breath. I opened my eyes. Aella was crouched beside me, her face a mask of fear.

"Taryn?" she asked tentatively. "Can you hear me?"

"What?" I croaked. "What happened?" I attempted to sit up, and she moved forward to help me. I noticed a split second of hesitation from her before she touched me.

To my left, Belinda was propping up Ito. He was haggard, sweat dripping down his face and soaking his tunic. He looked like I felt.

"I'm so sorry Taryn. I never thought—I didn't expect ..." His voice sounded raw. I wondered if he had been screaming too.

"The magic reacted in a way he did not expect," Belinda explained, handing him a flask. "Both of you are lucky to be alive."

"Did Michael do something?" Aella asked, glaring at my brother.

He was staring at me, I realized. He appeared thoughtful. Not frightened, or guilty. That frightened me. Resolutely I turned away from him. Whoever that person was, he wasn't my brother.

Ito shook his head. "No. The magic was drawn to itself more powerfully than I expected. I'm afraid I was a little overconfident. I did not take into consideration that magic acquired in this way would behave erratically. You are all right?"

I thought about that. The gryphon was gone. I could no longer feel that foreign fire rushing through my veins. Someone was offering me a flask, and I took it. When the first sip proved it to be water with crushed mint leaves, I drank deeply before replying. "I'm ok."

"Good girl," Aedith said. She was the one who had handed me the flask. "It's time to move. Can you walk?"

There was approval in her eyes. That bolstered my spirits enough for me to give her what I hoped was a confident nod. She nodded curtly in return, and began barking orders at her company.

At her command, Michael was steered bodily between two of the men, back down the path. Cherub, who was still attached to the cart, was led behind him. I'd have pitied the poor animal if I'd had any energy left.

"Aella," I murmured quietly as she rose from her crouch. "I don't think I can get up on my own." With an apology, she knelt back down and let me loop an arm around her shoulders. My legs felt like they were made of jelly as we rose together.

"Ok?" she asked.

For a moment, I stared, at the field of trampled bluebells, not truly seeing them. Then, with a headshake, I jerked myself back to the present. "Get me to Hale, and I'll be fine from there."

23

The walk back to the main road was surreal. Part of me wanted to run to the front of the line; I wanted to grab Michael by the shoulders and demand he explain himself. I kept waiting for the moment when I would wake in my own bed, and realize it had all been a dream. Already the exact details of the fight were becoming hazy as my nerves and body succumbed to exhaustion.

When a mob of our neighbors met us halfway back to the house, a commotion broke out. I was at the back of the line of mercenaries, a position I would never have thought would have felt safer than being near my own people. It did though. There was a grim darkness to their expressions that frightened me, almost as badly as Zehya had.

"We are taking Taryn home," Aedith attempted to explain, her voice almost drowned out by the people blocking our path. "Then we are taking Michael to the capital."

"I'm afraid that will not be the case," Willy said, amidst

jeering agreement. Of all the people in front of us, he looked the most like himself. There was a hesitance in the way he glanced back at the mob, as though he was checking that he really had to do this. "We're taking Michael to stand trial in town."

A short discussion ensued, but ultimately Aedith conceded to Willy's authority. This was what they had been hired to do, after all. They had found the monster that had been attacking livestock, it just turned out that monster was my brother. When she indicated the men holding Michael were to give him over, Kaleb moved quickly to the front of the column of mercenaries. He bent his head low to speak with Willy but what they said was lost to me as the crowd shifted then, blocking them from view.

"What was she doing out in the woods with...?" one voice, that sounded like Glenn's hissed. I flinched, ducking my head.

Another voice, which sounded like Benjamin, said, "She was out on the street... the night Beth was attacked."

There were more mutters. Each time the amount of malice with which it was spoken sent a bolt of terror into me. I couldn't stand the way some of the town's folk were looking at me. It was as though they thought they ought to grab me as well, though they didn't.

Michael didn't look back at me once. I didn't know if I wanted him to. The last glimpse I got of his face showed it held an air of strange disinterest—even boredom. After that, I kept my stare on Hale's mane. Eventually the whole crowd rode off, Michael at the center. When they took Michael away I expected to hear my own voice, demanding they let him go. I wanted to tell them not to touch him. I wanted to say that what was happening was wrong—all wrong, but I didn't.

Once they had gone it was just me and the mercenaries. Aella reached across the gap between our horses to squeeze my wrist once, but let her hand drop away when I didn't look at her. When we reached the house, Aedith's seconds took the majority of the company back towards the village to settle up.

Mother and Father met us in the front yard. I practically fell out of the saddle into their arms. As I breathed in their comforting scent, I broke into silent sobs that racked my body. It was too much. I couldn't speak. Aedith told them what had happened as my mother stroked my back and hushed me.

Inside, Mother set me up on the couch with a cup of tea and a blanket, since I refused to go down the hallway to the bedrooms. Within moments I was dozing listening to Mother and Father, who talked in hushed tones to the mercenaries in the kitchen. Every so often, I'd awaken and one of my parents or Aella, or the mercenary mages would be looking in on me. They'd give me a tight-lipped smile, and then I'd close my eyes and they'd be gone again. It wasn't until I heard the sound of a horse at a gallop that I was startled into full wakefulness.

"Don't move," Father said to me, opening the door a crack to look out. Only when he saw who it was did he open it fully.

I looked backward, out the window. It was Nai. She swung off her father's horse before it had come to a full standstill and came straight to the house at a run without tying him off. Her hair was undone and wild. Farther down the road behind her, a wagon and horses kicking up dust, headed this way.

"Nai, this isn't the best time—" Father began, but she cut him off.

"You've got to get Taryn out of here. Beth woke up, and she

said it was Michael who assaulted her. She said he's got some sort of plan to trap a gryphon, and she said he said Taryn's involved. Now they've *got* Michael, the gods only know how. There's a group of people getting ready to come get her to put her on trial too. Such as it will be, with the state they're all in," she said, her tone stating clearly how just she thought the trial was likely to be. "Those dung heap mercenaries are right behind me but we can still hide her and then maybe we can stop them from…" she trailed off, taking in the armored guests, and finally seeing me on the couch.

"Hey," I said dryly with a small wave.

Nai pushed past Father, rushing to embrace me tight enough to hurt. "Are you all right? You look like you've been rung out and hung to dry." She rounded on Aedith and the three other mercenaries present. "You can't have her. She hasn't done anything. She wouldn't hurt anyone!"

I wished I could have laughed, but I couldn't. To my own ears, my voice sounded brittle. "Nai, don't yell. They've just finished saving my life. It isn't polite."

She looked back at me, suspiciously. "What?"

"Nai, you said they're coming for Taryn?" Aella interrupted.

Nai seemed to see her for the first time. "Yeah. Laura, Martin, Robert, Daniel, maybe some others, I don't know. Willy tried to talk them out of it, but they wouldn't listen. Michael is talking in riddles, but he's making it seem like she was in on everything. As soon as they started talking that way, father helped me sneak away to the stables."

I felt dizzy. I hadn't done anything, but would that matter? They were scared, and they were angry. If my essence was close enough to Michael's to complete a spell, then wouldn't they be right to assume that I'd been infested with the same ill luck he was? They'd burn me too. They'd have to, to protect their crops, livestock, and families.

When illness had swept the Nophgrin mountains a few years prior it had taken many lives. My grandparents had been included. The town had watched from a distance as the bodies had been burned, to prevent the tainted luck of sickness from spreading. The fire had raged so hot and steady that when it was over there had been barely enough ashes for each affected family to scatter a handful. A wave of nausea rolled over me.

"*Ma,*" Aella murmured urgently.

The two of them were staring at one another. Aedith's eyes flicked to the side. She looked to Ito and Belinda in turn. They each gave the tiniest of nods.

Outside, the mercenary wagon had drawn up next to the house. Around it swarmed the rest of the company. Kaleb ducked inside with a nod to my father who was still by the door, looking lost.

"Time to go," the tall black man said. "Things are getting a little too exciting in town for my tastes." He looked from my father to my mother. "I'm sorry, for both of you. This trial is all but over. Michael confessed outright as soon as we ungagged him. There may yet be time for you to say your goodbyes if you leave now."

To my shock Mother shook her head. "No. Michael made his choice."

"Mother," I protested.

Father's eyes were bleak. "You take care of family, and

Michael is no son of mine. If they're coming for our daughter then we must focus on that. She can't stay here."

"We don't have much to offer. Most of our wealth is in sheep," Mother said. "But you're leaving now. We'll give you anything we have if you take Taryn out of the mountains with you."

The bottom dropped out of my stomach, and I felt like I was falling. Nai was holding my hands and I could see my wide eyes in her own. Leave Nophgrin? Run away with mercenaries? But it was that or face almost certain death by fire. Nai squeezed my hands, and I squeezed back.

Aedith didn't keep us in suspense. "There isn't much time to waste. Gather what you think you'll need, Taryn. We ride as soon as you've packed."

With Nai's help, I stood. Father grabbed his overnight bag from under his bed. It had barely been used in the past, and the leather was still stiff. It fit a few dresses and other articles of clothes. Nothing in my room seemed like it belonged with me on the road. My crook might have, but it had been left back in the clearing. I wasn't about to request we go back for it.

My work belt I looped around my waist. Father had commissioned a matching set for my brother and me, when we became old enough to take solo watches. I stroked the cool leather thoughtfully, tracing the patterns. Had Michael been wearing his when he was apprehended? I couldn't remember.

In the blur of packing I found the little wooden gryphon that I had been whittling. Mother was hovering in the doorway, and I gave it to her.

"For your birthday," I said. "I'm sorry, it's not finished."

She cupped my face in her hands. "I love it. I love you."

When her face crumpled and tears began to fall she turned away from us with a muffled apology. She strode down the hallway and then the sound of my father comforting her in the family room came to me faintly.

I looked back at Nai, knowing this would be where we said our goodbyes, and unsure how to. "Thank you," I finally said to her. "Your warning probably saved my life."

Her smile was as bright as ever, though tears were streaming down her cheeks like the rest of us. "You're my best friend. What else was I going to do?"

"I wish you could come with me," I said, and when fear flashed in her eyes, I quickly amended, "I know you can't. I'm not asking you to. I just think I'd be less scared if you were with me."

"With a girl like her at your back, you'll forget me soon enough." Nai jerked her chin over my shoulder. I didn't look, I knew she meant Aella.

I hugged her, hard. As I did so, an intense feeling struck me, and before I let go, I whispered into her ear, "In Michael's room there is a journal of notes. Take it. Hide it away. Ok?" I pulled back to look her in the face. She nodded, eyes wide. I had so rarely asked her to keep secrets, but I knew she would keep this one.

In the kitchen, I said my goodbyes to my parents. "Be brave," Father told me. "It could be that they'll calm down and it will be safe for you to come home."

"Write us when you've reached somewhere safe to stay." Mother pressed a coin purse into my hands, and a parchment with a list of names. "These are our contacts from the capital. The people we thought Michael might," she faltered, then went on. "Try and get to them. That way we know where to write to you. You'll be safe with them until we can tell you when you can come home."

I knew I wouldn't ever be able to come home. My luck was tainted with what Michael had done, wasn't it? Even if the town changed their minds, I knew better. I could never come home to poison them. I didn't say as much. Instead I hugged them tight, for what I knew would be the last time.

Then I was out the door and mounting Hale. In one breath, I was waving goodbye to my parents. In another, I was riding alongside Aella, and Lucas was sympathetically telling me it was going to be all right. In a third, we were cresting the first part of the mountain pass, and I was looking down the slope at Nophgrin. It was so small that I almost didn't see the plume of smoke that curled up from it into the afternoon sky.

STAY TUNED
FOR THE NEXT
INSTALLMENT

Of
Dragon Warrens
and
Other Traps

I was on a pyre. My legs and feet were bound to a long, thick piece of wood. Idly, I wondered how many of these we had on hand and where the guards kept them. It seemed odd to think we had a stockpile of stakes laid up on the off chance that someone needed burned.

To my right, William was using a torch to light the smaller pieces of kindling. He looked up and met my eyes with his own regretful ones. The wood began to crackle as the fire burned through the smaller pieces of fuel and then eat into the bigger logs. He shuddered and turned away from me. What did he see, I wondered? Not just a shepherd, that was for certain. A mage. A powerful sorcerer. Someone to be feared, and respected.

I was gagged in deference to that fear. A charm had also been placed around my neck. The mercenary Kaleb had given it to William. I didn't know exactly what it was, but I knew that it made my magic feel as though it rested just outside of my fingertips. Strange how used to its presence I had become in such a short amount of time. Without it, I felt half empty. It was no matter. Soon enough it would be back within my grasp.

The fire was coming closer to me now. I could feel the heat through my boots. Still, I wasn't afraid. I shut my eyes against the smoke that was beginning to thicken, and sting. My master would not invest so much into my education only to let this ignorant horde kill me. He would come for me.

Over the sound of the fire, I could just barely hear the crowd that had gathered. There was some muttering, as some that had thought they had known me debated my 'motives.' Mostly a heavy sort of silence prevailed.

I knew Beth was out there somewhere. I had seen her as they dragged me to the platform. She had been supported on both sides by her mother and stepfather. I couldn't imagine how much it had taken for her to drag herself out of bed to attend. I was flattered, in a way. The terror and hatred I had seen in her face as she gazed at me had been breathtaking. More was the pity that I hadn't used her as I had initially intended. But I had gambled, and I had lost. That happened sometimes, even Master Noland had said so. Eggs and omelets, after all. I knew better now. Next time I would not lose.

Fire licked my ankles; it was more than hot through my breeches. I could smell my leg hair burning. My heart fluttered slightly. Ruthlessly, I shoved the fear aside. He would not let me burn. Think of something else.

My twin. I had hoped to have her here with me when my master fetched me. It would have simplified things. However, neither she nor my parents seemed to be in attendance. I swallowed, and the smoke burned my throat. Where was she now? I had heard no word of her being caught. Yet, if they had not arrested her when I indicated she had been involved in my plan—well she would have been here, to say good bye.

It had been difficult to decide to use her in the spell, but Master Noland had been right. Ultimately, using her would have worked far better than some random girl. It had been worth it to try. If she could have only grasped all he knew, she might even have seen it for the honor that it was. To be in service towards his greater purpose...But there had been no time.

White hot pain snaked through my thoughts, and panic blanked my mind. I was burning. The fire had eaten through my breeches and was charring my boots. My eyes sprang open, onto a wall of white smoke.

Shocked, I screamed hoarsely as the fire raced up my leg. My body convulsed on its own, attempting to pull me away from the pain that was eating away at the bottom half of my body. There was nowhere to go. The ropes had been soaked in water, and they were as thick as my arms besides. Pain lanced through the wounds in my shoulder as the movement pulled at them. Agony on top of agony.

The fire was crawling up my chest now. Soon it would be over my head, enveloping me entirely. He wasn't going to let me burn. He wasn't going to let me burn. He was—

The rope from which the charm hung burned through. The small token fell from my body; it bounced off a log that had yet to be consumed and rolled away from the pyre into the wet grass beyond it. I wouldn't have noticed it amidst the anguish, but my magic rushed back to me then. For a moment, elation struck me, but the feeling was quickly extinguished. There was too much pain. I could never grip the magic firmly enough to wield it. Not now.

Tears rolled down my cheeks, little tracts of cool on skin that felt as though it was blistering. Which it probably was. I was more than certain that I could smell myself cooking. I was going to die. How could he let me die?

Then, all at once the white heat of the fire was replaced with a feeling like ice. Though they still roared around me, the flames were no longer eating my flesh. I sobbed in as much surprise as desperate relief. Panting, I looked around me. To my eyes, a hazy darkness now shadowed the fire. With a sudden intensity, the flames billowed upwards and around me, and the crowd outside of the wall of fire was veiled entirely. They were confused. They gasped and screamed, at the sudden ferocity of the flames.

I smiled.

Slowly, I became aware that my eyes were shut. My right arm felt too heavy and strangely stiff. With a strangled gasp, I came fully awake. Attempting to push myself up with limbs that were alarmingly weak, I grasped for my spear, panic making my heart race.

"Easy! Easy girl!" The speaker took me firmly by the shoulder, pushing me back against a soft pillow.

I was on a bed, I realized then. My right arm was bound thickly in bandages, which accounted for its stiffness. The brightly lit room was the one that Aella and I shared at the inn. The person who had told me to be easy was Belinda.

"What happened?" I asked breathlessly. "We were in the sewers. There were drakes…"

"Two days ago."

"Two days?"

Belinda nodded. She grabbed a mug off the small table that was set up beside her. She passed a hand over the top of it, and steam began to curl from whatever was inside. She pressed the mug into my left hand. "Drink this."

I let the heat seep into my fingers, too stunned to do as I was told. "Aella … And Victor and Lawrence?"

"They're all fine. Drink what I've given you."

I did as I was bidden, only to blanch in disgust. "That's awful!" Now that I was paying attention to it, I realized the mug was emitting a pungent smell that matched the taste now coating my mouth.

Belinda smiled dryly. "It's my own draft. Made to build your strength up." With a groan, she pushed to her feet. "You stay here and finish that. You'll be hungry, once it kicks in, and I know a few people who will be glad to know that you're awake."

I'm Shannon McGee, avid gardener, dog and cat mom of four, amateur artist, and most importantly I'm a writer of fantasy YA.

Since I was young I've been a reader. Mostly I have been a lover of fantasy, since that is where my obsession with books began.
Still, there were some stories I wanted to read that I just couldn't find in my preferred genre, and you know what they say—if the story you love hasn't been written you must write it. I turned to making my own maps and filling those maps with people and then giving those people histories and stories to tell.

Of Gryphons and Other Monsters is my debut novel, but it's not going to sit by itself for long. *Taryn's Journey* is a quartet, and the world in which she lives has another series waiting in the wings.

You can find more information at:
www.shannontmcgee.com

Made in the USA
Monee, IL
07 July 2026

56550166R00204